About the Author

Pam Lecky hails from Dublin, Ireland, and has been an avid reader of historical fiction from an early age. Then one day she decided that reading wasn't enough and she started to write: her first published novel, **The Bowes Inheritance,** is the result.

The Bowes Inheritance

❧

Pam Lecky

ISBN-13: 978-1512331547
ISBN-10: 1512331546

The Bowes Inheritance is a work of fiction. Names,
characters, places and incidents are the products of the
author's imagination or are used fictitiously. Any
resemblance to actual events, locales or persons, living or
dead, is entirely coincidental.

www.pamlecky.com
@pamlecky

Cover Image: ©iStock.com/LiliGraphie

Dedicated to my Family

Prologue

The Safe Haven Inn, Carlisle, England, 1867

Alex Maxwell lifted his head from his hand and tried to focus on the player across the table. As his vision cleared, his whiskey-addled mind struggled to follow. The man's eyes were hard and unyielding but there was the suggestion of humour there too; but at *his* expense. Everything about the man suggested the gentleman. He was convivial and charming, spoke with a cultivated accent and was dressed with quiet elegance. But there was just something about him that Alex didn't trust. Until the last few hands he had shown no great skill at the cards, but Alex had noticed that as the stakes had gradually increased, so had the man's luck.

Fumes of alcohol and tobacco were making Alex feel nauseous and his hands were slick with sweat as he picked up his cards. His eyes momentarily rested on the piece of paper in the centre of the table, where he had placed it, minutes before. It was utter folly to pledge one of his properties as a bet, but some sort of madness was driving him tonight. He looked at his cards one last time – three queens and two aces – a great hand, but was it good enough? Slowly he revealed his cards, his stomach churning, because he knew he had bluffed once too often.

From the bar came the rumble of talk and laughter, but silence dominated the cramped and darkened backroom where the men were playing.

"I believe my hand wins, my friend," the man across the table

1

said. He placed his cigar in an ashtray before laying the cards down on the table in a leisurely and confident manner.

Four kings.

Those around the table, who had had the good fortune to fold early, drew in a collective breath of reverence; whoever this man was, he was damn good.

Alex felt the room spin as all eyes fell on him, most full of pity, one pair brimming with derision.

"Where is this godforsaken place, anyway? I hope it's a decent bit of land," the stranger said, breaking into the stunned silence. He reached for the bottle of Bushmills and poured himself a glass with surprisingly steady hands; earlier in the evening he had given the impression of being quite inebriated. With an ironic twist of his mouth, he offered to refill Alex's glass.

Alex shook his head. His tongue felt thick, dry and uncooperative. "It's down the coast from here, three miles from Newton." He felt his hands tremble; to lose such a fine farm in a game of chance was unconscionable. But he was an honourable man and he had willingly entered the game. His opponent had not cheated – as far as he knew.

"Never heard of it!" exclaimed the stranger. He eyed Alex shrewdly before leaning back in his chair. "I hope it is worth what you claim."

Alex glared back at him in horror. "Who are you, sir?"

"Jack Campbell – at your service," the man said, with a mocking nod of his head. "Perhaps we will become better acquainted now that we will be neighbours."

Alex drew a ragged breath. Had he really just lost Bowes Farm to this man? His family would never forgive him and, most importantly, he would never forgive himself.

Chapter One

Idrone Terrace, Blackrock, Dublin, September 1882

I t was late afternoon. A biting north-easterly was blowing in off the Irish Sea as Louisa Campbell descended the steps from her aunt's house. But she was impervious to both the weather and the magnificent view of Dublin Bay. It had been an incredible day. She walked briskly past the row of elegant villas as she made her way back up to Main Street to catch the No. 6 tram. She tightened her woollen scarf and checked her hat pin was in place, more from habit than awareness of the squally conditions. Still bemused, she battled her way on to the crowded tram that would take her back into Dublin. She spied the last vacant seat on the bottom deck and slid into it with a sigh of relief. The open top of the tram was not the place to be on such a day. With a jolt, the tram moved off, and as she stared out the window at the windswept streets, all thoughts of her aunt melted away. Those braving the elements were hurrying homeward, heads bent, holding on to their hats as the wind whipped about their ears. Nature was determined to rob them of their dignity, she thought, before her mind returned to the remarkable discoveries of the day.

Her reflection twinkled back at her from the window with barely suppressed mirth. A day that had promised nothing but mundane chores and worry over her sister's failing health had turned into an extraordinary succession of startling revelations. She could so easily have missed the letter that morning. Eleanor had been ill during the night, and on a whim she had decided to go to the confectioners to find a treat to tempt her poor appetite. Their lodging consisted of three small rooms on the first floor of a Georgian terrace house in Herbert Street. Down in the hallway, she had paused to sort through the morning post, piled high on a rickety table inside the door. The dusty fanlight above the door provided very little light and it was difficult to distinguish the names on the envelopes. The letter had been redirected so many times that the name was almost illegible, but the direction was Peter Campbell, Esq. – her deceased father. She inspected the envelope carefully, holding it up to catch the light. The postmark was Carlisle and it was dated six months previously. A leap of apprehension made her stomach turn over as it was most likely an English creditor looking for payment. She briefly considered returning upstairs to show it to Eleanor, but in her sister's present state it would only add to her distress. She quickly stuffed the letter into her reticule and hurried out into the weak afternoon sunshine.

She loved the hues and earthy scents of autumn, and Stephen's Green was a favourite place for her to enjoy them. The park's pathways were a quiet and tranquil oasis in the centre of the bustling Dublin streets. But today she was oblivious to autumn's display and sought only the seclusion of a bench, where she could read the letter in private. Something about it screamed officialdom and it bothered her. Clearing her father's debts had taken every ounce of ingenuity she had, including selling almost anything of value they had possessed. Now every spare penny had to be saved for Eleanor's doctor's bills. There was no cure as the damage to her heart, after rheumatic fever, was permanent. That was an insurmountable fact. Eleanor could not help feeling ill and she could not blame her for succumbing to occasional gloom, but sometimes she wished to escape it all – the responsibility, the dread and her own guilt. With both parents dead, they survived solely on a small annuity from their grandmother's estate, which barely met their day-to-day needs. They were condemned to live in genteel poverty, belonging neither to the high society world of the protestant ascendancy that should have been their birth-right, nor the honest straightforward life of working women. It was a heavy burden. If she made one wrong decision it could bring their world crashing down.

When she finally sat down, she held the envelope in her hand and stared at it, overcome with anxiety. But how bad could it be? Taking a deep breath, she broke the seal, and pulled the stiff white sheet of paper free of the envelope. She saw with a sinking heart that it was from a solicitor's office. But as she read its contents with increasing astonishment, she realised that instead of misfortune what she held in her hand was a ray of hope. Real hope. The letter stated in stilted legalese that her father had inherited an estate in England from a Mr. Jack Campbell.

It was extraordinary. Was it a mistake? She had never heard of this man. But the letter had definitely been for her father. Mesmerised, she sat pondering the startling news with a pounding heart. She would have to find out who this unheard of benefactor was, and there was only one person who could help her. This called for a visit to Aunt Milly. It was not a thing one did lightly. Her aunt, despite her soft and fluffy name, had been christened by their late father as 'The Gorgon'.

As her aunt's long-suffering butler announced her in funereal tones, Louisa vividly recalled childhood visits to the house in the company of her mother and sister. Those dreaded duty calls had always been uncomfortable at best, sitting in rigid fear of doing or saying anything out of place. Any slips in decorum were pounced on by their hostess and left their mother despondent for days afterwards. Their father had always had a pressing engagement that coincided with his wife's monthly visit to her sister, and on their return home, he would tease them endlessly about taking tea with Medusa.

The drawing room faced north with a view of Dublin Bay, but it was dark and oppressive, despite its opulence. The room paid homage to showy ornament on a grand scale. A particularly vile stuffed owl surveyed the room from beneath a glass dome. Its yellow eyes seemed to follow you about and Louisa could never feel comfortable under its gaze.

Aunt Milly, sitting ramrod straight in a chair before the fire, looked up from her book with a slightly pained expression. In spite of the tepid reception, Louisa dutifully kissed her aunt's proffered cheek and sat down; she was well used to her aunt's disdain. She knew her resemblance to her father's family, her chestnut curling hair and blue-green eyes, chafed her aunt.

Still in her early fifties, Aunt Milly was a formidable woman, always dressed in unrelenting black with her raven hair, streaked with silver, pulled back tight from her high forehead. An incongruous white lace cap did not in any way soften the effect. She was tall and gaunt and her very posture suggested a woman in a perpetual state of disgust with the world. Her strong opinions tripped off her tongue with ease, leaving most mortals utterly crushed.

Aunt Milly was the only member of her mother's family Louisa had ever known. She suspected avid curiosity had been the reason for her aunt's interest in her family over the years. Aunt Milly had sensibly secured a very eligible man, who was twenty years her senior, and dissipated to a degree that guaranteed she would not be bothered by his company for too long. There had been no children. The unfortunate Campbells' swings of fortune had been entertainment for a woman who was both bored and selfish.

"What brings you here, young lady?" Aunt Milly asked. "It must be at least a month since I saw you or Eleanor. I suppose you are both far too busy to visit your poor aunt."

She bit back the retort she would like to have made, and forced a smile. "We knew that you were planning a holiday, Aunt. How are you keeping? You look in excellent health."

"I am tolerably well, thank you," Aunt Milly said. "I spent a couple of weeks down in Bray. The sea air did me the world of good. It's such a refined place and all my friends take houses there for the summer months now."

"How lovely," she replied. Not for the first time, she marvelled at her aunt's pretensions. Her house was literally across the road from the sea and its beneficial air; what difference a few miles south could make was a mystery.

"I take it Eleanor is ill again," Aunt Milly remarked, after a few moments of awkward silence. To Louisa, it sounded more like a rebuke than genuine interest in the health of her sister.

"Yes, she was poorly during the night," she answered.

"So, no improvement?"

"Not really. She has some very good days – sometimes weeks at a time. But the weakness always returns."

"Perhaps you should try a sojourn at Bray. There is a very nice hotel on the esplanade."

"We cannot afford it," Louisa snapped, fully aware that mention of money would annoy her aunt, but unable to prevent her irritation showing at the woman's insensitivity.

Aunt Milly swiftly changed the subject. "So, I assume you have a particular reason for visiting me today?" Her tone was cold but her curiosity was obvious. Her bird-like eyes glittered with it.

Louisa removed the solicitor's letter from her bag and handed it over without a word. Aunt Milly stared at her for a moment before putting on her glasses and perusing it slowly.

"Well, well, well … Jack Campbell dead – hah! Who would have thought he would do anything worthwhile," Aunt Milly sneered. "I thought him gone to his maker long ago."

She was shocked by the vehemence of her aunt's reaction. "But who *was* he?" she asked. "I've never heard of him."

Her aunt folded the letter and stared off into the middle distance, a queer smile on her face. "I'm not surprised. He was the devil incarnate – that's who he was."

She sighed impatiently. "But what relation was he to my father? He never spoke of him. Is he a cousin?"

"No, not a cousin, Louisa. Jack was his eldest brother," Aunt Milly revealed with all the triumph of someone who loves the power of knowledge, "and a complete scoundrel with it. He was the reason that Father forbade your parents' marriage."

"Gracious! So he is my uncle! What did he do that was so terrible? Is that the reason Grandfather Dillon took so strongly against the Campbells? I always believed it was because they lost the estate."

Aunt Milly looked uneasy and took a moment before answering. "It gives me no great pleasure to tell you this," she began with a look that belied her words. "It must be over twenty years ago now. Your uncle had to leave Galway rather urgently, with various unsavoury rumours flying around." She sniffed with distaste. "There was talk of gambling … and an altercation of some description. He was just like his own father. The apple doesn't fall far from the tree and he proved it tenfold. They tried to hush it all up, but loose talk cannot be stemmed."

"But surely my father did nothing to merit such harsh treatment as well? He did nothing wrong."

"How can you be so green, Louisa? You know very well it takes very little to ruin the reputation of a family. Your uncle's actions only finished what your Grandfather Campbell had already begun. We all warned your mother, but she would not listen to reason, even after Father told her she'd be cut off. But Sophia was always a fool." Aunt Milly slapped her hand down on the arm of her chair, her face contorted in disgust at the memory. "An empty-headed, love-sick fool."

As always, she was deeply offended by her aunt's derogatory remarks about her parents, but could not afford to be distracted by her bitterness. She needed to glean as much information about Jack Campbell as possible. "This man – my uncle - did he return to Ireland?"

"No, and no one wept I can assure you," Aunt Milly replied. She held out the letter for her to take, as if it were on fire. "We all assumed he had come to grief somewhere." She smoothed down her skirts, her face set, as if in memory of something undesirable.

"But he obviously prospered. To own a farm of over a thousand acres, he must have done very well for himself indeed."

Aunt Milly laughed, a dry grating sound. "He probably married money – duped some poor female and her family. He had the charm of the devil, that one."

"But that seems unlikely, if my father was his heir," she pointed out.

Aunt Milly considered this. "I suppose not. What will you do?"

"I shall have to write back to this solicitor and inform him that my father is deceased. I don't think there is anything else I can do."

"Yes, Louisa, you must do that, but don't you realise? With your father gone, you are probably your uncle's heir. You have no brothers. There are no male descendants." Aunt Milly sat back in her chair, a half-smile lingering upon her thin lips.

"I know that is a possibility, but these matters can be very complex."

"Then you had better write your letter quickly, in case there are other heirs waiting to pounce."

She smiled to herself. It was almost as if her aunt actually cared.

The tram journey seemed endless. Louisa was anxious to get home to Eleanor to share the startling news. The elderly lady beside her snuffled into a handkerchief and coughed noisily. She inched away as inconspicuously as she could, trying not to show her distaste. She pulled the letter out of her reticule, unable to resist reading it again and thinking about her mysterious relative.

She wondered if he had resembled their father and, most importantly, what had he really done that necessitated his leaving the country. Aunt Milly's vagueness on the topic made her very curious on that point. It must have been something very shocking for him to be banished completely by his family and all of Galway society. This unknown uncle was becoming a very interesting character. Since their father's passing, their lives had been very monotonous, so she could not help but feel a surge of excitement. A genuine black sheep!

As her spirits rose, endless possibilities began to open up before her. Was this a chance to escape their hand-to-mouth existence? If she was the heir, it might be possible to sell the property and settle somewhere more beneficial to Eleanor's health. But she had no idea how much such a property would be worth or even if it would be possible to sell it as it might be entailed. She would have to trust that fate was being kind to them at last, and although it might all come to nothing, if there was any possibility that she was the heir, she had to pursue it with the solicitors.

The tram trundled past Blackrock Park, conspicuously empty of strollers, through Irishtown and into Ballsbridge. At the canal she hopped off the tram and made her way along the bank, still deep in thought. On reaching their lodgings, she felt a pang of guilt for leaving Eleanor alone so long, but hoped her good news, and the bag of macaroons she had bought earlier that afternoon, would make up for it. She gathered up her skirts and flew up the stairs, bursting into the room, unable to contain her excitement.

"Look, Eleanor, look! You will never believe it! And you will never guess where I have been this afternoon."

Eleanor shrugged, looking confused as she took the letter that was being waved in her face.

"Why didn't you light the candles?" Louisa scolded. She proceeded to do so, struggling to maintain her happy mood as tendrils of anxiety crept back into her consciousness. Even in the dimness of the room Eleanor didn't look much better than she had that morning. The shadows under her eyes stood out starkly purple and ominous against the unhealthy pallor of her skin. Her dark brown hair, limp and untidy, tumbled down over her shoulder, untamed by ribbon. She looked older than her seventeen summers.

"Good Lord!" Eleanor exclaimed when she had finished the letter. "Who on earth was Jack Campbell?"

"Indeed a very good question. I was never so shocked. He was Father's eldest brother."

"What?" Eleanor's eyes were wide in disbelief.

"Yes, I know. Isn't it incredible?"

"But I always thought it was just Father. Why did he not tell us about him?"

"It appears he wasn't terribly respectable. In fact, I suspect he did something dreadful. Well, it must have been for all the Campbells to be ostracised as a result," she said.

"Except by Mama," Eleanor said with a soft smile.

"Yes, luckily for us. Of course as soon as I read the letter I knew I would have to talk to Aunt Milly. Sure enough, she knew all about him, though I suspect she withheld the pertinent details. She looked very uncomfortable talking about him. I don't suppose we will ever find out what he did, and at this stage, it hardly matters."

"But aren't you curious?"

"Yes, of course, but who do we ask?"

Eleanor sighed. "I don't know. I have to admit, I always thought it odd that Mama and Papa hardly ever spoke about their families."

"Yes. I used to pester Mama about it, but when I realised how much it upset her, I stopped asking. I have always suspected that Grandfather Dillon was a tyrant. Wasn't it a very brutal way to treat your daughter? She couldn't help falling in love with Papa."

Eleanor frowned. "So what does all of this mean for us? If Papa was this man's heir, do we have a claim?"

"It is a possibility. I could be next in line, but I'm afraid to hope. I shall make some tea and we shall have these," she said, holding up the confectioner's bag, "and I will tell you all I know about Uncle Jack."

Louisa left for the tiny kitchen, humming softly, but her good humour unsettled Eleanor. She frowned over the letter and was overcome with a sudden fear that something outside her control was about to change their lives forever.

Chapter Two

D espite her initial doubts, Louisa eventually received confirmation that she was heir to Bowes Farm which, she discovered, was situated just outside the town of Newton in Cumberland. The correspondence with the solicitor, Mr. George Jameson, culminated in her being invited to Carlisle to prove her identity and sign all the necessary documents. With raging curiosity, she had scoured the local library for any information on Cumberland, and Newton in particular. *The Post Office Directory of the Principal Towns in Cumberland and Westmoreland,* provided a nice description of the coastal town, which lay to the west of the fells bordering the Lake District.

'Newton has stood resolute on the north-west coast of England for centuries. It is a prosperous place with some small pretensions to elegance, with tree-lined streets of stone-clad townhouses marching up the hill from the harbour. It has all the requisites of a thriving town, with a railway station, a courthouse and a town hall gracing the old centre. It has excellent rail links to Carlisle, and to the east, the pleasures of the Lake District can be enjoyed. The wealth of its citizens has been secured by centuries of investment in fishing and farming. But the discovery and exploitation of an abundance of coal deposits has raised the town's status beyond measure.'

This was all intriguing enough, but then she found an entry that listed Jack Campbell as a major landowner. It looked as though he had been a prominent citizen and very well-to-do.

On the morning of her departure for England, Eleanor became very upset at the prospect of staying with Aunt Milly in her absence. "You can't make me go! She hates me!" she sobbed.

"Don't be foolish, Eleanor, she doesn't hate you."

"Well, she certainly doesn't love me."

"Perhaps, but it's only for a few days. You are not well enough to travel to England with me. The crossing is bound to be rough at this time of year."

Eleanor dabbed her eyes with her handkerchief. "I'd rather risk it than stay with 'The Gorgon'. That house gives me the shivers. It's so dark and gloomy and her butler gives me goose bumps. Besides, aren't you suspicious that she wants to help us, after all these years?"

"Yes, I am a little, I suppose, but without her help I could not afford even the boat fare."

"I know," Eleanor said. "I just hate to be under an obligation to her, even temporarily. All these years, she has been absent from our lives, particularly when things have been difficult. If it wasn't for your skill at keeping the bailiffs at bay, I don't know where we would have ended up."

"Yes, thankfully, we have managed without her support. I share your feelings, believe me. But if there are no problems with the inheritance, we will be financially secure from now on, and can move away from Dublin and never have to see her again."

Eleanor sighed forlornly. "I hope so."

"I know it will be tiresome for you for the next few days, but you can't possibly stay here on your own. Supposing you took ill? Please, humour me in this and I promise I will come back as quickly as I can settle things in Carlisle. The cab is waiting below. We must leave now or I will miss the mailboat."

She helped Eleanor to her feet and embraced her. "You know we will be able to live wherever we wish once this farm is sold. While I'm away why don't you draw up a list of places you might like to live and we can discuss it on my return."

Eleanor immediately looked more cheerful.

George Jameson had arranged for Miss Campbell to put up at the Crown Inn just off Market Cross in Carlisle. The old coaching inn had seen better days, but it was comfortable and quiet, and he had considered it best suited to a young lady travelling alone. As pre-arranged, he waited to meet his new client in the Crown's best parlour. With some amusement, he thought back over the last six months. What had started out as a routine hunt for an heir had taxed his patience and skill to the utmost. The youngest partner in his father's firm, he was usually given the more tiresome and dull cases to look after, so he had been rather surprised that his father had handed him the file and told him to get working on it.

Although he had never had any direct dealings with him, George was well aware of Campbell's notoriety, which had spread throughout Cumberland. His father had had the dubious pleasure of representing and engaging barristers on Campbell's behalf on several occasions. When news of his death had reached them from America, his father's uppermost concern was the reduction in fee income it would mean for the firm.

All George had to work with was a name and an address in Galway. His initial enquiries met with no success at all, and he had almost given up when a letter had arrived from Campbell's niece. Frustrating as the search had been, it now looked as if the whole matter could be resolved quickly.

A few minutes past ten, a young lady was ushered into the room by the hotel concierge and announced as Miss Campbell. George immediately sprang up from his seat by the window and came forward. The pretty young woman before him in no way matched the image he had conjured up when reading her correspondence. The confidence and self-assured manner of the letters had wrong-footed him completely. He had expected to see someone much older: he guessed her to be no more than twenty-three or four. She was petite and slender, and elegantly dressed, but in clothes that even he could tell were a few years out of fashion. Her chestnut hair gleamed beneath a hat set at a slight angle. Blue-green eyes sparkled below arching brows and she shook his hand firmly when he stepped forward and introduced himself.

"Mr. Jameson, how kind of you to meet me here," she greeted him in a pleasing low-pitched voice.

"Not at all, Miss Campbell. I hope you had a pleasant journey from Ireland."

"I'm afraid the crossing from Kingstown wasn't particularly enjoyable. Some poor unfortunates had a very bad time of it."

"The sea was rough?" he asked.

"Very, but at least I wasn't ill."

"I'm glad to hear it. I'm not over fond of sea travel myself. I much prefer solid ground under my feet."

"Yes, I think I would have to agree. However, I really enjoyed the train journey up from Liverpool. The scenery was lovely. I have never been in England before, you see."

"Well, you are very welcome. I hope you found the accommodation to your liking?"

"It is very agreeable, Mr. Jameson, and so good of you to arrange everything for me."

"It is my pleasure, Miss Campbell. If you are ready, we can walk to the office. It is only a short distance to Victoria Place and it's a fine morning for this time of year."

There seemed to be an endless number of forms to be signed. George Jameson was extremely courteous, explaining everything to her in minute detail; if it was too much detail she hadn't the heart to remark on it. For the first time in her life someone was treating her with genuine respect. She supposed that having come into money was the reason, but it was a new and pleasant experience all the same. As he explained the various documents to her, she took the opportunity to study him. He had a pleasant boyish face, and a shock of black hair that fell forward whenever he became animated. Overall, she decided that she liked him.

Eventually the legal formalities were at an end and as he tidied up the papers, she decided to ask what was at the forefront of her mind. "I know this may seem odd, Mr. Jameson, but could you tell me something about my uncle? I know virtually nothing other than the fact that he left Ireland about twenty years ago." She felt self-conscious at having to admit to the family rift, but comforted herself that surely solicitors came across these situations every day.

"To be honest, Miss Campbell, I barely knew him. My father handled your uncle's affairs up to his death and knew him quite well." He appeared momentarily reluctant to continue. "I'm afraid he wasn't the most popular of men. Few people in the area knew his history or where his wealth originated, and to plain-speaking northern men, that doesn't sit well, you understand."

"I see," she said, wondering how much to read into this. "It's not that important. I wouldn't want to bother your father about it. I was just curious. It feels strange to inherit from someone I did not know or know of; almost improper, in fact."

"No, there can be no doubt, you are definitely his heir," he said. "He never married or had any … there are no children that we know of …" He stalled, obviously aware that he was straying into territory one didn't discuss with young ladies, and he blushed furiously.

"Will the farm generate much interest? Do you think it could be sold by Christmas?" she asked out of curiosity, but also to distract him from his embarrassment.

"Most certainly. It is a large property and turned a good profit since your uncle took it over. Proximity to Newton and the railway is a huge advantage. My father has already received enquiries from prospective buyers, mostly local landowners who wish to expand their own properties. Of course, we have noted these and will await your instructions. However, I think it would be wise to advertise the property. The local men tend to feel they have a divine right to property in the area and will be anxious to obtain it for the lowest possible price."

"No doubt they will all believe that a green girl from Ireland would be easy to manipulate," she said.

He nodded. "Perhaps, but don't worry. I can assure you that we will have your best interests at heart. I shall advise the property agent to put a notice of sale in the newspapers on Monday. An auction would ensure you get the best price possible."

"That's sounds like an excellent plan, Mr. Jameson."

"I will also arrange to have some funds transferred to a Dublin bank so that you may draw on the estate. The formalities of probate may take some time but there is no need for … you will have expenses and so forth that must be covered."

"Thank you," she replied, immensely grateful for such a thoughtful gesture. "Tell me, is the house near the sea? I understand that Newton is a coastal town."

"Yes, not far at all. The cliffs rise up to the west of the house and I believe you have a view of the sea from upstairs. I must say, it is a very handsome residence. It's at least sixty years old, but your uncle created a comfortable home." He paused. "As it happens, I am going out to Bowes tomorrow to consult with the steward. O'Connor is an awkward character, a bit rough and ready, but excellent at his job. The farm has been running very efficiently under his direction. I don't believe your uncle took an active interest in it of late and relied heavily on O'Connor. Your uncle travelled a great deal and was absent for long periods."

Louisa had been shocked to see the balance in her uncle's bank account. He had undoubtedly been wealthy enough to indulge a passion for travel. Her curiosity about him was growing steadily stronger.

"I must go home tomorrow evening and it is unlikely I will return … but I would like to see where my uncle lived. I won't have another opportunity. Perhaps I could go with you?" she asked.

"Of course. I would be delighted to show it to you. In fact, there may be mementos there that you would wish to take home with you."

"Thank you, I'd like that. I assume I can get a train from Newton back down to Liverpool to make the evening sailing?"

"Yes, that won't be a problem. You will have to change trains at Lancaster, but you'd have plenty of time. Let's say I collect you in the morning at nine and we can travel down to Newton on the nine-thirty?"

"Thank you, Mr. Jameson, I'm looking forward to it. It is such a pity that my sister will miss the treat."

The following day brought more unseasonably fine weather and the west coast railway proved a delightful route. Louisa was mesmerised by the scenery, and only paid scant attention to George Jameson once the sea came into view. However, after a few minutes, she was aware that he was regarding her thoughtfully.

"You look troubled, Mr. Jameson," she said.

"Well, it's just that I feel I should warn you about the steward before we arrive at Bowes."

"Warn me?"

"Yes, you see I'm not sure how he will react to you. He can be a devilishly tricky fellow. My father has always maintained that your uncle hired him for his crabby disposition. Most people do not return to Bowes if they experience his notion of hospitality."

"That doesn't sound promising."

He sighed. "No, I wish now that I had sent a telegram ahead to forewarn him."

"But he knows that I am the new owner, temporarily at least?"

"Yes, indeed, I informed him several weeks ago."

"Don't worry, Mr. Jameson, I can't imagine he'll eat me. After all, his future now lies in my hands." He didn't look convinced but he nodded and took up his newspaper. She was left to mull over all of the disquieting fragments of information she had heard so far.

They left Louisa's trunk at the station in Newton and journeyed on by hired gig. As they steadily climbed higher along the cliff road, George pointed out the various landmarks. At a fork in the road he reined in the horse. Another roadway branched off inland, which, he told her, was the way to Bowes and Thorncroft Manor. Thorncroft was owned by the Maxwell family and was the nearest estate to Bowes Farm. But she sat looking out to sea, her interest in people she didn't know and was unlikely to ever meet far outweighed by the dramatic scene before her. The headland jutted out into the sea, carved out by the relentless waves, and a small sandy cove nestled at the southern base. He explained that the headland was known locally as Bowes Head and the small beach was part of her property. He joked that it was rumoured it had been a notorious spot for smuggling at one time. With regret, she nodded when he suggested they should continue on, but she was wishing she had more time to explore.

They swung in through the old metal gates of Bowes Farm, and a red brick house came into view as the gig swept up the gravelled tree-lined carriageway. It was a sprawling farmhouse with long narrow windows that reflected the mid-morning sun. 1824 was carved into the datestone above the door and a profusion of ivy and cream roses scrambled up the walls towards the roof. Someone had landscaped the garden to the front of the house. The geometric flower beds, edged with box, were a riot of roses of every conceivable hue, throwing out the final blooms of the year. The house glowed warm and alluring, and the full reality of her inheritance struck her for the first time, taking her breath away.

George stopped the gig at the front door and stepped down to help her. A middle-aged, sandy-haired man appeared from the stable block and walked towards them. He hailed George, and then stopped in his tracks and stared at her. George hurried to perform introductions.

"Miss Campbell, may I introduce Mr. O'Connor. He was your uncle's steward and has continued to manage the farm, for the estate, for the last six months."

Much to her astonishment, O'Connor came forward, beaming at her. He took her gloved hand in both of his and gushed, "*A stór*, it's delighted I am to meet you. Good Lord, you have your uncle's eyes and as pretty as a picture! You are very welcome."

It was difficult not to respond to such warmth and there was something soothing in hearing an Irish accent after so many days, but she noticed that George was taken aback at the steward's exuberant welcome, so she merely smiled and gave her thanks.

"Would you like to see around the house, Miss?"

Without waiting for a reply, O'Connor took a bunch of keys from his pocket and unlocked the front door. She looked to George, who just shrugged, and they followed O'Connor inside. He hurried ahead of them into one of the rooms, flinging open the shutters and pulling off the holland covers. Six months' worth of dust rose up and swirled in the shafts of light. O'Connor chattered away, but she was barely listening and left George to make appropriate responses. Other than her Aunt Milly's, she had never been inside the home of any of her family. She tried to imagine her uncle living here, searching for clues to his personality from the objects he had owned.

She wandered off into the drawing room across the hall. It was a beautiful, well-proportioned room of muted green and cream, with a large chandelier, wrapped in protective linen, dangling above the centre of the room. Two large windows looked out to the rose garden and french doors led out to a small terrace at the rear. Moss-covered stone steps led down into the walled garden. She peeked under the furniture covers: comfortable sofas and chairs were grouped around the marble fireplace. Across the room, what looked like an enormous sideboard stood against the far wall. It was still draped in its dust sheet and the impulse to look underneath the covering was too much to resist.

Staring back at her was a photograph of a middle-aged man. She stood stock-still, her heart racing, for she could have been looking at her own father; a stouter bearded version for sure, but the resemblance was unmistakable. So this was the mysterious Jack Campbell. The pose was formal and unnatural, but there was something about him, perhaps in the way he held his head or the expression in his eyes, but her aunt's words came unbidden to her – 'a complete scoundrel'.

She gently pulled the rest of the sheet away. Behind his photograph, bottles of Bushmills whiskey jostled for space with various items. It was a jumble of prints and photographs, silver ornaments and some very ugly porcelain. At the back she spotted a tiny miniature in a silver heart-shaped frame. It was of a young dark-haired woman in profile. She could not shake off the impression that the face was familiar, but she could not place her and moved away.

As she explored the room she was vaguely aware of the sound of the men's voices from the hallway. Moments later, George put his head around the door.

"We are going to the estate office to look over some

paperwork. Will you be all right here on your own, Miss Campbell?"

"Of course, I'm fine. I am happy to potter about."

"That's right, Miss, take a good look around," O'Connor piped up from behind George, who raised his eyes to heaven and left.

The front door closed and she was conscious of the sudden stillness of the house. She took the photograph of her uncle over to the window seat and sat there for some time, savouring the unique feeling that she had a connection to a place. For years they had dragged themselves from one lodging to another, but nowhere had felt like a real home. The Campbell estate in the west of Ireland was long sold off to clear her grandfather's gambling debts and their mother's family had never received them. But this dusty old house – this could be a home. There was just something about Bowes Farm that was irresistible. Romanticism was not something she indulged in as a rule, but this house was having a very strange effect on her. She slipped the photograph of Uncle Jack into her reticule and made her way upstairs. Two of the bedrooms had sea views, albeit in the distance, and as she stood taking in the prospect over the walled garden, her heart was pounding. How could she walk away from this place? How could she possibly sell it?

George eventually found Louisa sitting under an arbour in the walled garden. She, undoubtedly, was oblivious to the effect, but it was a very pleasant picture. The late roses and honeysuckle were trailing untamed above her head and a shower of dark pink petals carpeted the ground around the seat. She looked miles away and barely aware of his presence. The high walls created a sheltered oasis from the westerly winds, giving the enclosed garden warmth and a heavenly scent.

But as he looked around he was aware of neglect. The flowers and shrubs badly needed pruning and were spilling over on to the gravel paths. Weeds held dominion in the flower beds, and even through the paths in some places. He had never bothered to come in here before and felt a sting of remorse that he hadn't insisted that O'Connor maintain the gardens. He had just spent the most tedious hour with him, O'Connor harrying him about Louisa's intentions regarding the farm. He had never seen the man so ingratiating. It had been unnerving and slightly nauseating.

"Come and sit down, Mr. Jameson. It is so peaceful here," she said as he approached. He dusted off some petals and sat down.

"You don't want to leave, do you?" he challenged her.

"Is it that obvious?" she replied. "I'm sorry. You must think me very sentimental."

"I think it's a natural reaction. It is a lovely property." He paused and rubbed his chin thoughtfully. "You know, you don't have to sell." His father would not be pleased, but Bowes Farm and Louisa Campbell seemed to be a perfect match and he would have the pleasure of seeing her again. "You could live here comfortably and let O'Connor continue to run things. That's certainly what's in his head."

"Yes - I guessed as much from my reception this morning. If I were to sell, would he find it difficult to find another position?"

"Locally, yes. He and your uncle managed to alienate quite a few people. None of the local landowners would keep him on."

"But he is a good manager?" she asked.

"I have found him to be so. I can only fault his manner," he replied.

"I certainly have lots to think about, but I must get back to Dublin tonight."

"I understand. Come." He stood and offered his arm. "We had better get back to Newton so you don't miss your train."

Chapter Three

N ewton station was busy when they arrived and George went to find a porter to retrieve Louisa's trunk. She waited on the platform, happy to watch people come and go, but when he didn't appear after ten minutes, her curiosity got the better of her and she followed him inside. She found him in the ticket office talking to a tall, dark-haired gentleman, who was expensively dressed in a Newmarket coat of severe black and silk top hat. He leaned slightly on a silver-topped cane. Not wishing to intrude, she hung back. However, the conversation between the two was becoming heated and she quickly realised that they were talking about her property.

"I made that offer for Bowes weeks ago. Why hasn't your father responded?" the man asked. He was a good six inches taller, and she could see that George was intimidated by both his tone and curt manner.

"I cannot discuss my client's business, sir," George replied.

"*Your* client? Your father is letting you handle this?"

"Yes," George responded sharply, an angry blush flooding his face.

The gentleman appeared to take a deep breath. "How difficult can it be to persuade some chit that it is in her best interests to sell? For goodness sake, man, this is ludicrous. From what I have heard, the family is penniless. They must need the money."

"Mr. Maxwell!" George exclaimed.

Greatly amused, she caught George's eye mischievously from behind the stranger. He made a visible effort to compose himself.

"Sir, let me introduce my client – Miss Campbell."

There was a noticeable stiffening of the man's broad shoulders before he swivelled around. He stared at her in stony silence, and then slowly raised one eyebrow in a look of disdain that marred what could have been a very handsome face. If he was embarrassed, he didn't show it. His ice-blue eyes bore into her and she had to fight the urge to step back from his intimidating stare. His animosity was unmistakeable but surely it was groundless: they had never set eyes on each other before. She judged him to be in his early thirties and obviously a man used to getting his own way, if the conversation she had just heard was any indication. She detected a subtle hint of sandalwood as he stepped forward and held out his hand. After a moment's hesitation, she slipped her gloved hand into his, half expecting it to be crushed. She held his gaze as best she could as George formally introduced him.

"Miss Campbell, this is Mr. Maxwell, one of your late uncle's neighbours."

Maxwell addressed her in a tone only slightly less glacial than his expression. "Miss Campbell."

Somehow, the thought of Bowes in this man's hands galled her. An irrational urge to annoy him overtook her usual friendly disposition. She summoned up a deceptively sweet smile.

"It is a pleasure to meet you, sir. Do forgive me for interrupting your conversation with Mr. Jameson, but my train is due any minute." She withdrew her hand and turned away without giving him an opportunity to respond. "Were you able to find my trunk, Mr. Jameson?"

She hoped it was enough of a set-down to the stranger without being blatantly rude. Most of all she wanted him to know that she had heard his unseemly remarks, even though she doubted he was the kind of man who would care. Without saying a word, Maxwell left the ticket office.

George visibly relaxed. "I do apologise. That was very awkward."

"Actually, I can see his point of view. The delay in selling the farm must be very frustrating for him. He is obviously very eager to buy it. However, I'm not sure I like being referred to as a 'chit'."

He looked uncomfortable. "He is rather forthright, I'm afraid. His land adjoins Bowes. His family used to own your property and he is very keen to buy it back. That is why he cornered me. Unfortunately, your uncle and Mr. Maxwell were not on the best of terms."

That probably accounted for the hard stare and icy hostility, she thought. It was beginning to look as though her uncle had been something of a social pariah. She chuckled softly and took his arm as they headed out to the platform where the train had just pulled in. "Now, Mr. Jameson, let's not talk about unpleasant things. I have had quite an adventure these last few days and you have been most kind."

"It has been my pleasure, and if you have any questions, just write. In the meantime, I will await your instructions regarding Bowes."

They stopped before the first class carriages and he handed her in. As Louisa settled back into her seat, she was uncertain how to put into words the plans now forming in her head.

"With regard to the farm, I would like a few days to think about things, and of course I must discuss all the possibilities with my sister. Perhaps you could hold off on those advertisements? I promise to let you know how to proceed as soon as possible."

"Very well, Miss Campbell. I wish you a safe journey."

As he watched Louisa's train depart, George caught a glimpse of Maxwell and his sister on the opposite platform. The family was one of the most influential in that part of Cumberland. They were wealthy and powerful, owning several collieries and thousands of acres. It was a matter of some concern to his father that Jamesons had never handled any business from them, but Jack Campbell being their client had precluded it. Now Campbell was gone, his father would be amenable to any request from that quarter, and he feared that might not be advantageous to Miss Campbell. He had sensed how taken she was with the property, and he was certain she would return in the near future to take up residence. With a satisfied smile, he wondered how Nicholas Maxwell would receive that little tit-bit of news.

The man in question was sitting opposite his sister on the Carlisle train, in a cold fury. Anna had refrained from conversation when he had rejoined her from the ticket office, and he was thankful for her reticence, as he had badly needed to regain control of his temper. He wasn't sure what was making him angrier: the fact that he had been caught out in a social faux pas in front of the Campbell woman or the attitude of the young solicitor.

When Campbell's death had been announced, Nicholas had been relieved to be finally free of his troublesome neighbour. It was the first opportunity that had arisen to regain Bowes Farm since that infamous card game between Campbell and his father, fifteen years before. Unfortunately, his father had passed away and he knew that he had gone to his grave still regretting his disastrous lapse of sobriety. Nicholas had been delighted to learn that two sisters, living in straitened circumstances in Dublin, were discovered to be Campbell's only family. It was unlikely that two young women would want to live in relative isolation at Bowes, and therefore they would be eager to sell the farm. He was determined that it would be back safely in Maxwell hands as quickly as possible. But it needled him that the woman had visited the property. Females were notoriously silly and mawkish about things and Bowes was an attractive property. It was difficult to judge what kind of woman she was from such a brief encounter, but something told him she was not in the usual style. There had been a hint of stubbornness in those eyes and she had dared to snub him.

"Nicholas, are you quite well? That is a fearsome frown, even for you."

He looked across at his sister. "I am fine, Anna."

"Well, something must have thrown you into a black mood?"

"I had the unexpected pleasure of meeting Jack Campbell's heir in the ticket office."

"Aha, I see," she said. "Was it that young lady in the blue coat I saw on the platform?" He nodded. "She looked agreeable."

"Well she wasn't," he said firmly. He deliberately concentrated on the passing scenery for a few minutes in the hopes she would drop the subject. When he glanced back at her, he realised that it wasn't that easy to distract his sister, who was watching him closely. Eventually she took up her book and he mulled over his encounter in the ticket office once more. Eventually, he came to the conclusion that he was worried unnecessarily. Patience would win out and justice would be done. With his equilibrium restored, he turned his attention back to Anna.

"I suppose you mean to drag me into every shop in Carlisle?"

She looked up and grinned impishly. "No, only the really expensive ones."

The Campbell ladies were back together in Herbert Street, sitting before a crackling fire, toasting muffins. Louisa's account of her trip, including the unsettling things about their uncle that she had discovered, had left her sister looking mystified. She was studying Uncle Jack's photograph on the mantelpiece.

"So, he may not be someone we should be proud of?"

Louisa followed her gaze, but how could you read a man from a moment captured in time? In the photograph he looked prosperous and benign and yet no one had spoken well of him.

"Perhaps not," she said. "Judging by the neighbour's reaction to me, I do not believe he had Papa's charm or friendly ways. He seems to have made nothing but enemies. I'm only sorry I didn't ask O'Connor about him when I had the chance, but I doubt I would have been told the truth. He was far too keen to be pleasing for his own reasons."

Eleanor continued to gaze at the photograph. "He looked very like Papa."

"I think that is the only similarity. He was definitely no spendthrift. He didn't let his money slip through his fingers at the gaming tables like Papa. However, he did create a very comfortable home. He didn't stint on that. Everything was of the first quality."

"I wish I could have seen it," Eleanor said wistfully.

"It was lovely considering it was the home of a bachelor, and the little I saw of the land, well, it is beautifully situated *and* close to the sea."

Eleanor gave her a searching look. "You liked it very much, didn't you?"

She laughed. "Oh dear, I promised myself I would be pragmatic and not try to influence you, but yes, my dear, I loved it."

Eleanor sat quietly for a few moments with a puckered brow. "Well, we must live somewhere and if it's as nice as you say, it might as well be Bowes."

"Are you sure? It would be very different to living in Dublin."

"By rights, we should have grown-up in the country. Why don't we try it? If it doesn't work out, we can always sell up and find somewhere else. There is little to keep us here, after all."

Louisa couldn't help smiling. "All right. I'll send a letter to Jamesons in the morning."

Louisa could have sent the money she owed to her aunt by messenger, but her conscience would not allow it. She decided to visit her, one last time, to repay her debt and inform her of their decision.

"So, what have you decided to do about this farm?" Aunt Milly asked as soon as she sat down.

"We are going to move to Cumberland. My visit today is to say goodbye. It is unlikely that we will return in the near future."

Aunt Milly was silent for a moment. "I see. Are you sure that this is wise? Good heavens, what do you know about farming?"

"I can learn, and if I don't wish to, there is a steward on hand to run things for me. Uncle Jack has left us comfortably off, with the luxury of choice. I do believe this is the best possible course of action. The fresh air and better food should be of great benefit to Eleanor, and what better place to settle than somewhere we have a family connection."

"What connection?" Aunt Milly scoffed. "You never met your uncle and he certainly didn't have knowledge of you. You won't know a soul there. You'll both be homesick in a month, I daresay."

"I have already met one of my neighbours," she said. She did not elaborate on the details of what she remembered as a very intriguing encounter. "I'm sure that once we are settled, we will have the opportunity to form many friendships. So why would we be homesick? For what? Dingy rooms in Herbert Street?" She could feel her temper rising.

Aunt Milly laughed dryly. "And what about me, the only living relative who has paid you any attention whatsoever?"

She sighed. "Of course we will miss you, Aunt. You'd be welcome to visit us at any time."

"I thought you were a sensible girl," Aunt Milly continued, as if she had not heard her. "You would be better to sell the farm and buy somewhere in Dublin. Plenty of superior homes to be found, if you'd only look."

"The decision has been made," she said firmly.

"You will regret it, believe me. Just don't think you can come crawling back to Dublin and expect me to put things right."

"Aunt, I assure you, I know better."

"Good."

As if on cue, the maid entered with the tea tray and Aunt Milly talked of indifferent subjects until her visit was drawing to a close.

"You will write?" she asked as she took her leave.

"Yes, Aunt, of course."

"You seem determined to carry on with this foolishness. I only hope it does not end in tears."

Louisa bent and kissed her cheek. "Goodbye, Aunt Milly, and take care."

A disdainful sniff was the only response she received.

Travelling to Cumberland had not been pleasant. Even with breaking up their journey over a couple of days, Eleanor had found it exhausting. The sea crossing had been rough, the hotel in Liverpool had been noisy and Eleanor found people's accents jarring and incomprehensible. By the time they had arrived at Bowes, Louisa was very concerned about her. They were welcomed by O'Connor, who introduced the house servants: his daughter Róisín was to be their maid and his cousin, a Mrs. Murphy, their cook. She could only smile to herself at the speedy way he had ensured his family's interests.

The following morning Louisa woke early. Pulling back her curtains in anticipation of the delightful view of the sea, she was greeted by a white wall of impenetrable fog. She'd never be able to convince Eleanor how nice it was with weather like this, she thought, and was thankful she had seen the property at its best. The room felt chilly and the temptation to go back to bed was strong, but the clock on the mantle struck eight o'clock, the time she had requested Róisín to wake her.

"Good morning, Miss," Róisín said, bursting into the room. The girl exuded energy in the most startling way, with her abundance of blonde curls trying to escape her lop-sided cap.

"Good morning," she replied with a smile and sniffing the air with delight. "Is that chocolate?"

"Indeed it is," Róisín replied, setting the cup down on the bedside table. Louisa sat on the edge of the bed, sipping the steaming chocolate, and watched Róisín light the fire and tidy the room. This was such a new experience. She could definitely get used to being waited on.

"Is my sister awake?"

"No, Miss, I looked in on her and she is sound asleep."

"Thank you. She found the travelling to be very tiring. She is a little delicate." She had decided not to inform anyone of Eleanor's illness as she wished for her to have as normal a life as possible. People tended to treat her differently when they knew of her condition.

"Aye, Miss, I can see that all right," Róisín said sympathetically. "Would you like me to help you dress, Miss?"

"No, no, I don't need you to do that for me, thank you. Perhaps for Miss Eleanor, though."

"Of course. I'd be happy to. I'll leave you to enjoy your chocolate." She closed the door softly behind her, then immediately burst back into the room. "Pardon, Miss, I almost forgot – Mrs. Murphy said she'd have breakfast ready for you in half an hour. And I have run a bath for you. Oh Lord, I almost didn't remember and he warned me. Father said he'd be here to see you at ten sharp." And just as quickly she vanished again. Louisa mused that life would never be dull with Róisín around.

That morning she spent the most frustrating hour of her life in the company of O'Connor. His manner seemed to have changed overnight from friendliness to intransigence. Her hopes of being involved in the running of the farm, or at the very least gaining an understanding of it, were severely bruised.

"Sure, what would a nice young lady like yourself be doing getting involved in the farm?" he asked with a sly look. "Master Jack was happy to leave things to me, you know. He used to say, 'Liam, where would I be without you at all?'"

She bristled, torn between the desire to assert her authority, which he appeared to almost question, and not getting off to a bad start with her steward. "As owner I should at least have a basic grasp of how the farm operates. I can understand your reservations, O'Connor, but I must insist that you explain things to me and in particular, if any major decisions need to be made, that you defer to me." He grunted and looked decidedly mutinous. "I know that my uncle travelled extensively. However, that will not be the case with us. We mean to make our home here and therefore I need to know as much as possible about country ways." Again he grunted and would not meet her eye.

"Mr. O'Connor?"

"There really is no need …"

"I am determined in this you know, so you might as well give in graciously," she interrupted him, with as winning a smile as she could manage considering her frayed temper. It was a gamble to stand her ground. She knew that she was at a disadvantage. If he threatened to leave she wouldn't have a notion of how to go on and had no idea how long it would take to find a suitable replacement.

"I suppose you'll be wantin' to see the place and meet the

tenants, so?" he mumbled, looking thoroughly miserable.

She wasn't sure if this was a concession, but decided to treat it as such. "That would be very kind of you. I assume we can use the gig?"

"I'm afraid not. It's not suitable for going over the heavy ground and some of the tracks are too narrow. Best to ride."

"I'm afraid that is a problem – I can't."

"You can't?"

"No, I never learned."

"Good Lord, why not?"

"We have lived in lodgings in Dublin all our lives. We either walked or took the tram. Our circumstances didn't allow for the stabling of horses."

"Well, I never!" O'Connor said. "How do you think you will survive out in the country if you canna ride?"

"I can learn. Perhaps you could suggest someone who could teach me? Do we have any quiet horses in the stables?"

"No, Miss, they are all hunters. Your uncle was a capital rider; no fear of fences or water. He was something to behold." He seemed lost in the memory.

"Perhaps it's in my blood too?"

He looked at her sceptically and she was sure he was on the point of making a snide comment, then thought better of it. "I will see if I can find something suitable for you. I suppose your sister will want a horse, too?"

"No, she is not comfortable around horses."

"Whatever you wish," he mumbled.

"Now, I understand from Mr. Jameson that the farm is in a very healthy financial state. Perhaps you could show me the accounts?" She could have sworn he blanched.

"I ... the ledgers are back at my house. I thought it safest, you know, with the house unoccupied. I could bring them up tomorrow ... if you wish."

"Yes, very well," she snapped. It was a small victory in an otherwise futile meeting. The best she could hope for was some kind of compromise. "Tomorrow then, at the same time."

She left the estate office in a fractious mood, determined to find books on farm management as quickly as possible. Obviously O'Connor didn't want to take orders from a woman, but she could not be content to idle away her time. If she could demonstrate some knowledge, surely the man would respect her opinions and learn to accept her involvement?

Chapter Four

"So – will you go?" Anna Maxwell asked her brother, in her best coaxing manner. "You really should welcome them. In fact, it's your duty."

It was unusual for her to have his company mid-morning, but the dense fog had prevented him from taking his usual morning ride before starting upon his duties for the day. Never one to miss an opportunity when she wanted something, she had been delighted to find him still at the breakfast table. He raised an eyebrow and continued reading his newspaper.

"Nicholas, you must." He threw her a sharp glance and she continued in a more conciliatory tone. "Besides, it's a chance to make a fresh start and be on good terms with our neighbours."

He lowered his paper and looked at her sternly. "Anna, I will pay them a call when I am ready to do so, but be under no illusion, it will not be to welcome them."

"For heaven's sake! Jack Campbell is buried in America. It's time to forget the past."

As her father and Nicholas had absolutely forbidden her to come into contact with Campbell, she had never set foot on Bowes Farm. But now, with two women residing there, it was a great opportunity for her to have friends close at hand, and she was determined that the Maxwells would hold out the olive branch, and the quicker the better.

"Bowes Farm was part of this estate for over two hundred years. I'm not about to give up the fight now," he said. He repositioned the newspaper with an impatient snap of his wrist.

"Fight. You talk as if it were a war. Only a man could be so obsessed with land."

"You'd feel differently if it was part of your dowry."

"It never was and I certainly don't want to discuss that topic. Be reasonable, Nicholas. These women had nothing to do with any of that trouble in the past. Just think how pleasant it would be to have friends close by."

He started to laugh, "You are a goose! You have plenty of friends within a reasonable distance."

"None I can walk to," she pointed out.

"Well I would rather you stayed away from them. I am convinced they have Fenian sympathies. Why else would they have come here, only to take over where Campbell left off? I don't trust them." When she started to protest, he continued, "From my one encounter I have a very clear picture of the type of women they are."

"That's nonsense and you know it. There was hardly time for you to exchange two words."

"She was rude and unladylike. I would have concerns as to what kind of upbringing they have had, even if they weren't related to Jack Campbell. I don't believe they are suitable for you to know. From what I have learnt, they grew up in poverty and of course they are Irish and Catholic."

"So are the Morrisseys and we dine with them at least once a month."

"True, but they are not Fenians."

She set down her tea-cup with a grimace. "They would be far more interesting if they were. They are uncommonly dull and uninteresting pillars of society."

"Anna, Mrs. Morrissey has been very kind to you over the years, especially since Mama died."

She sniffed. "Only because she wants to marry off her stupid daughter."

"I'm in no danger on that front."

"No, a more insipid girl than Beatrice Morrissey would be hard to find." She shuddered. "Those teeth and that laugh!"

Nicholas, making no comment, took up his paper again.

"So when will you go to see them?" she asked.

"When I have the time," he said with a frown. "What are your plans for today?"

"Oh, this and that," she replied airily, "Do you think the fog will clear?"

"It will by midday." He gave her a warning look. "You will stay away from Bowes?"

Anna finished her tea, gave him a non-committal shrug and left the room.

It had been more of a command than a question. He was used to his sister's scheming ways, having been a victim of them for the past six years since their father's demise. He sighed in exasperation. She was impetuous and head-strong but he loved her dearly. In another six months she would be twenty-five and have command of her own fortune. He would cease to have any control over her and that was a source of both alarm and relief in equal measure.

Louisa was having an exasperating week. Eleanor continued to feel unwell and kept to her bed, showing no signs of enthusiasm for Bowes. Eventually, Louisa had to send a message to Newton for the doctor to visit. Dr. Peterson gave Eleanor a thorough examination and eased her fears. It was exhaustion, he said, and with some rest she would recover soon enough. He was a kindly man and spent an hour discussing her sister's condition and treatment. He did not hold out any false hope or recommend useless concoctions as the medic in Dublin had, but advised gentle exercise if she was able for it and a light, easily digestible diet.

Then she had another unrewarding meeting with O'Connor, to look over the accounts, which left her angry and downhearted. In her frustration she turned her attention to clearing out her uncle's belongings. Róisín was ordered to find some boxes and she knelt before the large cabinet in the drawing room and flung open the doors with enthusiasm. A box was soon full and another requested.

"What am I to do with this lot, Miss?" Róisín asked, looking dubiously at the jumble of items in the box. "Your uncle loved these things, he did."

"Well I don't like any of it, Róisín. Perhaps some of the servants might like some of them."

"Very good, Miss."

"And those bottles of whiskey should be removed to the kitchen. I'm sure your father would take one."

"I'll ask Miss, for sure. He does like a dram." Róisín balanced the box on her ample hip and clumped out the door. Louisa wondered if it would make it to the kitchen intact.

She opened another door. This one revealed a wonderful Royal Doulton dinner service with a lovely blue and green delicate pattern of flowers and intricate trellis. She was taken aback – it wasn't what you would expect a bachelor to purchase; it was very dainty – something a woman would chose. It looked as if it had never been used and was covered in dust. Hearing footsteps in the hall, she called out, "Róisín, you will need to take this dinner service down to the kitchen for a thorough clean. And mind you don't drop any of it. It must have cost a fortune."

"I do beg your pardon. The maid said to come in," a soft lady's voice answered.

Louisa pulled her head out of the cupboard and looked up to see a tall and pretty dark-haired girl with twinkling blue eyes surveying her from the doorway. She wore a beautiful green riding habit of velvet and a rather dashing hat. She jumped up, embarrassed to have been caught in such a position by a visitor. She would have to reprimand Róisín for not announcing the caller, then realised that the girl probably didn't know any better.

"I'm sorry – I wasn't expecting any visitors. I have been clearing out," she explained in a rush, stating the obvious in her confusion.

"No need to stand on ceremony with me," the lady said with a smile, coming forward and holding out her hand. "I'm Anna Maxwell. I hope you don't mind my calling on you, but I just couldn't wait for an introduction." Louisa guessed she was related to the arrogant man she had encountered at Newton station.

"I do beg pardon," she said, holding up her dirty hands. "Best I don't shake your hand until I clean mine. Please sit down and make yourself comfortable. I won't be a moment."

Miss Maxwell was standing gazing out the window when Louisa returned. Shaking hands, Louisa instantly warmed to her visitor. She had an open face and a glimmer of mischief in her eye.

"You are still settling in. I should have waited, of course, but I was passing and it seemed ridiculous not to call," Miss Maxwell said.

"No, I'm very glad you did," she replied. "Please sit down. We haven't met anyone yet. You are our first official visitor and very welcome. I wasn't sure what to do, not knowing the local custom. Should I send out cards or wait for people to call? It's so confusing, this sort of thing."

"Yes and so stuffy, isn't it? Rules for this and rules for that until your head spins. Well, you need not worry. I will introduce you to anyone worth knowing. Newton is a small enough place, but there are people to avoid."

"Hopefully we aren't the people being avoided. My uncle appears to have been a bit of an oddity and not particularly popular."

"Oh yes, he was very wicked." Miss Maxwell rolled her eyes and smiled mischievously. "Of course, I wasn't allowed to know him at all."

"I see," she replied with a sudden sinking feeling.

"Don't worry. He can't have been that bad, my dear. I'm sure my father was being over-protective. He generally was. I knew your uncle to see but we never exchanged a word." Miss Maxwell looked a little self-conscious. "And, of course, I should commiserate with you on your sad loss."

"Thank you, but I feel a complete fraud about it. We didn't even know of him until a few months ago," she explained. "He was our black sheep. You probably know more about him than we do."

"My brother will give you chapter and verse. In fact, he is a dead bore on the subject so better not to bring it up at all, if I were you." Louisa recalled the look of contempt on his face and wondered if that wasn't very good advice.

"My family doesn't have any – black sheep, that is – more's the pity," Miss Maxwell continued. "We are a dull lot: lived in Cumberland for hundreds of years and so forth. How remiss of me. I should explain who we are. We live at Thorncroft – I'm not sure if you have heard of it? It's over to the east, about two miles away, and our lands adjoin along the river. But I believe you may have met Nicholas, my eldest brother?"

"Yes, yes, I think so – at Newton station?"

"That's right. I was there, but I was on the other platform so we weren't introduced. Such a pity. I have another brother, Robert. He's in the Huzzars and will be home at Christmas. He is always good fun and I think you will like him very much." Miss Maxwell sighed. "Nicholas used to be, too, but since he took over the business and the estate he has become very serious-minded and always so terribly busy. He is a Justice of the Peace as well, you see."

"There is a lot of responsibility involved, I suppose," she commented, more out of politeness than interest. The man sounded humourless and more disagreeable by the minute.

"Yes, there is of course, but it's not just that. He can be very strict with me. I have been threatened with a companion so often," she said, laughing, "but I always talk him out of it. There's just the two of us at home. Sometimes Nicholas disappears off on business for days and I'm left twiddling my thumbs. That is why it is so wonderful that you have come. Now I will have some company – if you are good enough to put up with me. And I insist you call me Anna."

She smiled and felt her spirits rise at such a friendly overture. "Thank you." But she suspected that the lady beside her was a little spoilt and probably indulged by the very brother she was casting as a villain. "I think you are lucky to have brothers. I always wished I had one. My sister Eleanor is very dear to me and we are close, but a house of females can be very sedate."

"I can imagine. Brothers are all very fine in their way, but you cannot really talk to them about some things."

Louisa's hand was squeezed and she was sure it wouldn't be long before the lady was spilling her heart out. She didn't feel it was appropriate to comment, so turned the conversation. "I'm sorry that you won't get to meet Eleanor today. She isn't a good traveller and the journey has left her feeling unwell."

"I hope she recovers quickly. There is nothing worse than feeling ill and missing out on things. I cannot wait to meet her. What age is she?"

"She turned seventeen in August."

"Has she made her come out?"

"Not as such. We have not moved in those kinds of circles, Miss Maxwell ... Anna. I'm afraid until I inherited from Uncle Jack our circumstances were modest at best."

"I am sorry to hear that, but things have changed for the better now, haven't they? You both must visit me at Thorncroft as often as you wish. I mean us to be great friends."

"Won't your brother mind us arriving without formal introduction?"

Miss Maxwell guiltily admitted that he didn't know about her visit. "Lord, we could be waiting ages for him to make you a formal visit of welcome. He will call, of course," she assured her, "but for the moment it might be best if we meet here or in Newton."

They were interrupted by Róisín wheeling in a trolley. Louisa was delighted that someone in the kitchen had realised that a guest merited some good china. She had half-feared that Róisín would arrive with chipped kitchen crockery and a few stale biscuits. Anna stayed another hour chatting about people she didn't know, but she didn't mind; it was nice to have such vivacious female company. They shared a similar sense of humour and distaste for the more pompous attitudes of society. She could not help feeling a little excitement at the prospect of being involved in the social scene that Anna described. The novelty of these things was beguiling. When her visitor had departed she resumed her housework with a lighter heart, her earlier qualms about moving to Cumberland now diminished in the light of a new friendship.

Nicholas left Newton courthouse by the back door at four o'clock sharp. His fellow Justice of the Peace had already departed but he had stayed on, making sure that the clerk wrote up and filed away the cases properly. It had been a long and tiring day, with the usual suspects before the bench for petty theft or drunkenness. Fining these men was no deterrent; it just meant their children starved and sending them to jail meant loss of income and perhaps their job. The frustration of having limited powers almost tempted him to enter politics, but with the collieries and estate to run that was just too much to take on. There were days when he would have happily dropped all his duties, mounted his horse and galloped out towards the fells. He had happy memories of climbing and fishing holidays at the lakes as a young boy, when he and Robert had run wild without a care or responsibility between them, Anna tagging along, in spite of their efforts to lose her.

He slipped down the laneway to Church Street to avoid any possible confrontation with the court spectators. They tended to congregate outside the courthouse in the hopes of abusing either the miscreants or the police. As usual, Church Street was busy and outside the bank he recognised Fr. Healy and Sergeant Cox, deep in conversation. He didn't have a high opinion of the Catholic priest. Eight years before, a group of miners had fanned the flames of discontent bubbling away in the mines and a strike had erupted when wages had to be cut. He had always suspected that Campbell had funded the strikers. The dispute had been prolonged and extremely bitter and it had taken a very inclement winter and the mysterious disappearance of some blacklegs to end the dispute. Fr. Healy had acted as an intermediary between the strikers and his father, but Nicholas knew he had been in Campbell's pocket.

Many of the workers in his own mines were either Irish or of Irish descent. Since the mid-'40s, there had been a steady stream of Irish immigrants coming to Cumberland to find employment, driven by hunger and the promise of a better life. Most were of good character and stayed out of trouble, but a handful had aspirations to be rebels, fuelled by stories of grievances and newspaper coverage of the Land War in Ireland. Recently, there had been disturbances in London and other cities. The Fenians had begun a bombing campaign which had resulted in a swell of fear and suspicion.

He bade the men a good day but continued down the street towards the livery stables, where he had left his horse that morning. Just as he was passing Newton Tea Rooms he caught sight of his sister within. She was in deep conversation with some ladies seated near the window. The temptation to continue on home was strong, but he felt honour-bound to offer to escort her if she were ready to leave. He had no doubt that she had come to Newton without a groom, despite the impropriety. It was a frequent cause of argument between them.

No matter how many times he entered a tea room, he was never really prepared for the odd combination of smells, a heady mixture of perfume mingled with beverages and confectionery. It was strange and feminine, but rather agreeable. As he made his way between the tables he was conscious of many eyes swivelling in his direction. This was a predominantly female domain which most Newton men assiduously avoided. He nodded to various women he knew, but kept moving towards the table at the window, knowing how fatal it would be to stop and speak. Any partiality shown by him would feed the rumour mill for weeks. He was wealthy and single, and therefore fair game in the eyes of the female population, and he had no desire to be ensnared.

As Anna noticed him approach, a tell-tale creeping blush affected her face and neck. His heart sank. She was obviously up to no good and he wasn't in the mood to berate her. The ride home would be tedious now and he was tired. As he drew nearer he thought there was something vaguely familiar about one of the ladies, but she had her back to him. The young girl to Anna's right was unknown to him. She was extraordinarily pale with brown hair peeping out from under her hat. Her head was bent towards Anna, who was speaking rapidly to her and the other lady.

"Nicholas! What a surprise," Anna said rather nervously when he reached the table. "You will never believe my luck today. Who do you think I should meet on Church Street but our new neighbours, the Miss Campbells. I think you have already met Miss Campbell – and this is Miss Eleanor."

"Lucky indeed, Anna," he drawled, giving her a hard look before he shook Miss Eleanor's hand and nodded to Miss Campbell.

"Do sit down, Nicholas. We can order more tea."

"No, Anna, I need to get home. I have been in court most of the day. I came in to see if you wished for company for the journey home."

"Could you not spare a few minutes?" Anna pleaded. He knew well what she was about. In spite of his protest, she had embarked on a campaign to heal the rift between the families. He frowned and shook his head. A look of defeat crossed her pretty face and she reluctantly stood. "Well, ladies, it was lovely to meet you. No doubt we will meet again soon," she said pointedly as she gathered up her belongings and, with a fleeting look of resignation towards the elder Miss Campbell, swept past him and headed for the door.

He paused at the table and waited for Miss Campbell to look up. Her cheeks flushed slightly as their eyes met. "Miss Campbell, I had hoped to call on you, as it happens. Would tomorrow morning be convenient?"

"Yes, of course, Mr. Maxwell," she said. However, he could not fail to discern the coolness of her tone or the ironic gleam in her eye. "Then I'll bid you both good day." He bowed briefly and made his way back towards Anna, who was waiting for him at the doorway.

When they had left, Louisa turned to her sister. "Anna is a rogue, don't you think?"

"Do you think he believed her?" Eleanor asked.

"Of course not! She will be scolded all the way home if his face was anything to go by."

"He looks very stern. I hope he isn't a cruel man."

"You read too many penny dreadfuls," Louisa said with a smile. Eleanor had a penchant for the dramatic. "I wouldn't worry about her. She is made of strong stuff."

"If you say so. Why do you think he wants to call on us?"

"A courtesy visit, I suppose, but I have a feeling he is not only unhappy for us to have taken up residence at Bowes Farm, but is greatly put out that his sister has befriended us."

"Why? What makes you say that?"

"I know that it is the custom for the local gentry to welcome newcomers as soon as they arrive and he hasn't called on us yet. Anna was very blasé about it, but it is a snub of sorts. She freely admitted to me that she has initiated contact without his knowledge. And, most importantly, our farm was once part of the Maxwell estate." Eleanor raised a brow, clearly surprised. "How Uncle Jack came to own it, I'm not sure. George Jameson wasn't very forthcoming on that point, but I do know that they want it back very badly. Jamesons received an extremely generous offer from Mr. Maxwell after my visit last month, in fact, an offer far in excess of its actual worth. He must have been worried when he knew that I had visited."

"Perhaps you should have accepted it, if it was that good."

"We needed a home, Eleanor, and Bowes is perfect for us. I don't want to sell it and, above all else, I don't want to sell it to him. Did you not see the way he looked at me just now – as if I were a butterfly pinned to a piece of paper? Odious man."

"It's not like you to take someone in instant dislike."

She looked out of the window, gathering her thoughts. "He barely hid his hostility the first time I met him. There is something about him – a lack of warmth, perhaps? I don't know; but I don't think he is capable of loving the place. It would just be another parcel of land to him. And as to whether I like him or not, I will reserve judgement until I hear what he has to say tomorrow."

Chapter Five

To the ladies' surprise, their first visitor the following morning was not Mr. Maxwell. At eleven o'clock, Róisín bounced into the drawing room to announce Fr. Healy, the parish priest. Louisa looked in confusion to Eleanor as an elderly silver-haired man of heavy build and ruddy complexion came into the room. He had the face of a country squire, but the dog collar and slightly shiny black suit dispelled the notion.

"Thank you, child, thank you. That will be all," he barked jovially to dismiss Róisín, who beamed back at him in delight and shut the door. "Well, well, young ladies – you are very welcome, very welcome indeed," he boomed as he advanced on them. "When O'Connor told me the young ladies had arrived it brought a tear to my eye. But 'tis awful sad to be here. The last time I was in this room it was to wish your uncle a safe trip, God rest his soul. A fine man, he was, none finer."

Louisa recovered her composure before Eleanor and performed introductions. "Thank you for calling, Father. It is very kind of you."

"Not at all, child. Sure, I must look after my flock."

Louisa glanced at Eleanor, who unfortunately looked like she might start giggling with nervous embarrassment. Why on earth did he think they were Catholic? "Please sit down, Father," she invited politely.

"Thank you, thank you," he said, before sinking with relief into an armchair that barely contained his bulk. He looked around the room. "I'm glad to see you haven't changed anything. I do miss your uncle. We were kindred spirits, you know. Many is the fine evening I spent in this very room with him. But I suppose you hardly knew him. He didn't often go to Dublin." Louisa was surprised: so Uncle Jack had not been the complete absentee from Ireland they had been led to believe.

"We never met him, Father. In fact, we didn't even know of his existence until last month," Eleanor replied.

Fr. Healy's craggy brows drew together in a frown. "I see. I know he visited family of some kind. Perhaps there was a falling out ...?" Louisa shook her head.

The priest seemed momentarily unsure how to proceed. "Well, now, I thought I'd call in to see how you are settling in. I didn't want to wait until Sunday mass, no, no that wouldn't be right at all – Jack's nieces – 'tis delighted I am to see you at last."

Louisa knew she would have to put him straight immediately, but she would have to be diplomatic. "Father, I'm sorry, we won't be attending your church ...." she started to explain, but was interrupted by the priest jumping up out of the chair.

"What nonsense is this?" he roared. "Just because you're in a heathen country you don't give up your religion."

"Father, we are Protestant – Church of Ireland," she said, feeling her colour rise.

The priest looked like he had received a physical blow. "I don't understand," he mumbled. "I was sure ... but your uncle was a good Catholic ... a fine member of my congregation."

"I can't explain it, Father. Our family is Church of Ireland – always has been. Uncle Jack must have converted at some stage after he left Ireland." Fr. Healy sank back down into the chair, clearly shaken to the core.

"Father, you look unwell. Can I offer you some refreshment – tea, or something stronger?" Louisa asked.

"The latter, child, the latter," he answered, his eyes straying to the cabinet where the bottles of Bushmills had previously resided. By the look on his face, their absence was a source of anguish.

Eleanor stood up and rang the bell for Róisín, who burst into the room almost immediately. Louisa suspected she had been listening at the door and wondered if O'Connor had put her up to it.

"Róisín, please bring some whiskey for Fr. Healy."

Róisín glanced at the priest, who nodded, and she bounced out of the room. An uncomfortable silence descended.

"Perhaps, Father, you would indulge our curiosity. As Eleanor said, we didn't know Uncle Jack, and would love to learn something about him."

Fr. Healy stared at her for a moment as if it were a strange request. "Well now, let me see: I first met Jack about fifteen years ago when he came to live here. He came to me after mass one day and introduced himself. I remember it like it was yesterday. I wondered what a fine gentleman like that would want, but he said he was anxious to help out in the parish. From that day forth, he was generous with his time and his money. A more charitable man you couldn't find in Newton."

Róisín came in with a tumbler of whiskey on a tray, which she put down on a small table beside him.

"Thank you, child," he said. He waited until she left the room before he continued. "Then about eight years' ago there was a miners' strike. It was an awful time, you understand. Alex Maxwell had cut wages to make the mines more profitable, never caring what it would do to those poor families. You know of the Maxwells?" he asked. Louisa nodded. "Aye, well, the strike was bitter and long. Maxwell used blacklegs – hired in outsiders to break the strike. There was a deal of violence and that winter was fierce cold. It was like the Lord himself was heapin' another layer of misery on those poor folks. Myself and the Rector did what we could, but there was little sympathy from the wealthy in the area. We were accused of prolonging the strike by some. Your uncle didn't stand by and let his fellow Irishmen starve. He was one of the first at my door offering to help. With the money he gave, we set up a soup kitchen, and provided meals for the little 'uns. He probably saved many lives by being a good Christian."

"I'm glad to hear it," Louisa said with some feeling. It was the first time she had heard anything positive about Uncle Jack. "I understand that he travelled a great deal and was often away for long periods."

"Aye, that's correct. He particularly liked to go to America. I understand he had many business contacts there. He would be away for months at a time but he always said it was like a home from home."

"And his last trip – he went to New York, I believe?"

"Yes, and that is where he's buried, God rest him. It was awful sudden. He was in fine fettle before he left. I couldn't believe it, but there it was in black and white in the newspapers. The shock of it … we were all reeling." The priest looked genuinely upset and drained the tumbler of its contents. "Aye, well, I thank you for your hospitality and I'm sorry about … my mistake, of course. I won't bother you again."

Louisa rang the bell for Róisín. "Please, Fr. Healy, don't worry about it. As you say, just a misunderstanding and I know I can speak for my sister in saying that we hope that you will visit us again," she said gently.

The priest beamed back at her. "I can see you have a lot of your uncle in you, child. He would be proud. I'm sure he's smiling down on you from heaven." He popped his hat back on and followed Róisín out the door without a backward glance. They could hear his booming voice fade into the distance. Róisín was obviously a favourite from his flock.

"Good Lord!" Eleanor exclaimed, picking up Uncle Jack's photograph from amongst the family photographs that now adorned the sideboard. She gazed at it as if searching for clues to a great mystery. "It's very odd the way things turn out. Fr. Healy makes him out to have been some sort of saint and yet everyone else speaks of him so badly. Who should we believe?"

Louisa took up her library book on farm management. "The truth is probably somewhere in-between. It's odd, though, that he converted. I wonder why he did. The more I hear about the man, the more baffled I become."

Eleanor walked over to the window and peered out, watching

the priest depart. "I doubt we will ever know now. No sign of our other visitor yet. Do you know, I think I will do a little piano practice while we wait."

"Yes, do. I knew you'd be pleased there was a piano."

"Wasn't it lucky I kept all that sheet music?"

Their old piano had been sold to pay off the last of their father's debts and Eleanor's medical bills. But Louisa hadn't had any choice: it was the piano or living in some disease-ridden hovel in the back streets of Dublin. Physical activity was denied Eleanor because of her illness, and she had felt the loss of the piano more keenly as a result. Some minutes later the sound of scales echoed through the house from the small parlour. She sighed over her book in contentment. Eleanor was looking a little better and the evening before she had eaten a good dinner. Surely this was proof that she had made the right decision.

The road which led down towards the sea from Thorncroft ran along the boundary of Bowes Farm. Nicholas couldn't help himself but to look over the hedgerows and stone walls as he walked along; it was a habit long ingrained. But it was November, and there wasn't much to see, except for a few flocks of sheep in the distance and several ploughed fields. In the scheme of things, Bowes had only been a small though fertile part of the Thorncroft estate, but the loss of it rankled purely because of the circumstances.

Anna had spent the entire journey home the previous afternoon telling him how lovely the Miss Campbells were, and now that he knew something of their history, a few niggling doubts were creeping in. Perhaps they were as innocent as Anna claimed? But whether they were harmless or not, he was determined to get Bowes back. The only uncertainty was the method he would have to employ.

As he rounded the bend in the road, just before Bowes, he saw Fr. Healy emerge on his nag and head down towards Bowes Head. He stopped in his tracks and his benevolent mood evaporated swiftly. They hadn't wasted much time in getting cosy with the priest, he thought sourly. His initial suspicions had been correct after all and Anna had been badly taken in. The old grievances were now fresh in his mind, and his animosity towards Jack Campbell, and by association his nieces, was rekindled. As he passed through the gates, his resolve to get the better of Miss Campbell was like a tight knot of tension in his stomach.

To add further to his growing anger, he encountered O'Connor, the steward, as he approached the front of the house. The man doffed his hat in a respectful manner but the sneer on his face was audacious, almost as if he wished to taunt him. By the time the Campbell's maid answered his knock at the door he was fuming. The girl's face froze when she recognised him and she looked terrified, her mouth gaping open. A fresh wave of irritation swept over him.

"Miss Campbell is expecting me," he said curtly, and brushed past her without waiting for a reply. The maid hesitated by the door. Whatever training the girl might have had appeared to have deserted her like a puff of smoke. He stood impatiently tapping his foot, holding out his hat and gloves for her to take.

"Well, girl, you'd better announce me or am I to be received out here?" he snapped.

"Yes, sir, I mean no, sir," the maid answered, stumbling over her words before gingerly taking his hat. "I'll see if Miss Campbell is at home."

He closed his eyes in exasperation. "If you would be so kind," he ground out.

Deep in the mysteries of the Norfolk Rotation System, Louisa was caught off-guard when Róisín burst into the room.

"Mr. Maxwell, Miss," Róisín stammered.

She looked up in surprise and quickly put down her book. Róisín was flushed and her eyes suspiciously bright. But she didn't have time to pass comment, as Mr. Maxwell was striding into the room towards her. She realised by his demeanour that he was vexed about something.

"Mr. Maxwell, it's so good of you to call. Please take a seat," she said, fixing a smile on her face. There was something about the man that unnerved her; some primitive self-preserving instinct that told her to be on her guard. She indicated the armchair opposite her own. "May I offer you some refreshment?"

"No," he answered shortly. "No, thank you." Any hopes that this was going to be a social call died quickly.

She indicated to Róisín that she could leave. With a sinking heart she turned her gaze back to her visitor. Unhappy *and* rude – this wasn't going to be pleasant. In the distance she could hear Eleanor at the piano and decided to leave her be. She had a feeling this wasn't going to be an encounter her sister would enjoy.

"I hope you left your sister well? We were most fortunate to come across her in Newton yesterday," she said. "We enjoyed her company very much."

He raised an eyebrow, obviously well aware of his sister's subterfuge. "She is always in good spirits."

"It was most kind of her to take an interest in us. Some would not do so without a formal introduction beforehand." There, you horrible man, she thought. That's a direct attack. You have had a whole week in which to visit us.

"My sister has the luxury of being able to suit herself, Miss Campbell. Whether it is always in her best interests, I am not so sure."

She had to dig her fingers into her palms. "I'm sure you are never slow to ensure that her interests are protected."

He smiled in response, and the temperature in the room dropped considerably. "I haven't come to discuss my sister, Miss Campbell. My call today is purely business," he said.

"I didn't realise that we had any business to transact, Mr. Maxwell," she replied airily, full sure now what it was he wanted. "My solicitor, Mr. Jameson, handles all of my business affairs, as I'm sure you are aware." She hoped this would put him off, but to no avail.

"Last month I wrote to Jamesons with an offer for this property – a substantial offer. Were you aware of it?"

"Yes indeed, Mr. Maxwell."

"I did not receive a formal response."

"Well, you can have it now. I am not interested," she replied.

"I am prepared to double that offer," he stated coolly.

Louisa was staggered. He was offering her a huge amount of money. They would never have to worry about finances again. She sat back in her seat and looked at him steadily, her heart pounding. "Why?" she asked softly.

"Why? Because I wish to buy it," he snapped, clearly thrown off-guard momentarily by the simple question.

"I see. That is, without doubt, a very generous offer." She paused for a few moments so that he would think she was genuinely considering it. He really believed she would accept – she could see it in his eyes. He expected greed would entice her to sell. "But we have made Bowes our home and intend to stay."

He regarded her coldly and she had the distinct impression that he was trying to control his temper. "If you accept my offer you could live anywhere you wish."

"You're starting to make me feel a little unwelcome, Mr. Maxwell."

His eyes hardened. "Nonsense. I think you are a practical woman. You can hardly have formed an attachment to the place so quickly. One farm is much like another."

"Perhaps, but we have a family connection to this place."

"Most people would be put off by that particular connection."

"I find that offensive, sir," she said.

Maxwell leant forward, both hands resting on the top of his cane, his eyes narrowed. "Do you really think that society will accept you? Your uncle had a very dubious reputation and offended everyone he came in contact with. As the local magistrate, I can assure you that his activities were less than legal. Must I spell it out? You are tainted by association, and I will ensure that fact is kept afresh in everyone's mind."

She was stunned by his ruthlessness. With a racing pulse, she tried her best to hold on to her temper and said in a gently measured voice, "I would hope that when people become acquainted with us that they will accept us for who we are and not listen to malicious gossip."

"Don't be naïve!"

She stared back at him in disbelief and could not help but let her anger show at last. "You will forgive me, sir, but as you have been so blunt, I don't feel any compunction about being so too. I am aware that Bowes Farm was part of Thorncroft years ago and for some reason you are desperate to get it back. But let me make it clear: no matter how much money you offer, you are the last person I will ever sell my home to." He flinched and drew in a sharp breath, but she continued before he could interrupt.

"And as for your accusations about my uncle, I cannot argue with you because I know next to nothing about him. However, I can only assume that you are not a very effective magistrate, if you were so sure of his guilt but never managed to convict him. The man is dead. It is hardly appropriate to speak ill of him now."

"Your sensibilities do you credit, madam," he replied mockingly, "but you don't know what you are talking about. There isn't any possibility that this farm alone could have supported his lifestyle, particularly in the last few years. With American and other imports of cheap food, farm incomes are down everywhere. Your uncle was known to be sympathetic to the Irish cause and associated with people of uncertain character. I stand over my claim: he was a criminal and a clever one. I am sure he was involved in the Salford bombings last year. It was only a matter of time before the police would have proven it. *This* is your wonderful family connection."

"That is an outrageous accusation! You really hated him, didn't you? This is some kind of personal vendetta."

"My feelings are irrelevant. I want this farm and I will do all in my power to secure it."

"I can assure you that I am not easily bullied and I find your attempts to threaten me distasteful and, I would point out, unchivalrous for someone in your position," she countered, her voice shaking with anger.

He recoiled at that and looked like he wanted to throttle her. He stood and regarded her stonily. "Very well, I can see that this is pointless. I doubt you will feel so enamoured of Bowes when you are cut by any family of standing in the district. I would add that my offer will reduce substantially the longer you wait to sell to me. I bid you good day, madam."

Louisa sat shaking with emotion for some time, staring at his vacated seat in utter disbelief. She had entirely underestimated the man. His looks were so deceiving. Behind that handsome face was a man who would stop at nothing to get his way. What was driving him to be so cruel? Uncle Jack must have done something terrible to the Maxwells to have engendered such vitriol. But why then was Anna so anxious to be on good terms? It didn't make sense.

She was still reliving the incident when Eleanor came into the room, some fifteen minutes later.

"Róisín said that Mr. Maxwell has been and gone. I'm so sorry, I was so wrapped up in the music I never heard a thing." Eleanor came across the room. "Good Lord, Louisa, whatever is the matter?"

"That man! I have never been so insulted. Who does he think he is? If he ever dares to come here again I … I will not be answerable for my actions."

"What happened? Why are you so upset? What did he say?" Eleanor asked.

Louisa jumped up from her chair and began to pace the floor in agitation. After a few minutes she had calmed down enough to describe the visit for Eleanor in detail. This helped to deflate some of her anger, but when she recounted his threat to have society cut them, she became troubled again.

Eleanor sat down, frowning. "Do you think he will do as he threatens?"

"I think it very possible. That man is capable of anything."

"But I thought he was a gentleman," Eleanor said. "He could make life very difficult for us."

She stopped before her. "Yes, I fear so. I had such hopes for a better life here. I'm sorry, Eleanor. It seems I have walked us into a worse situation than the one we left."

"No, no, it's not your fault. How could we have known any of this? Besides, one man could hardly influence the whole of local society. There will be people who will judge for themselves and accept us. We come from as good a family as those Maxwells – better even, if the truth be told. It's no matter. He cannot harm us," Eleanor said quietly, with more conviction than she had ever heard from her. She was amazed that she was taking it so well and sat down beside her to give her a hug. It was the first time Eleanor had taken on the role of comforter.

"You're right – we will not let that horrible man upset us. We have each other and that is all that matters. Let him do his worst!"

But later that evening, in the privacy of her own room, Louisa envisaged many scenarios where Mr. Maxwell came to harm. It was a balm to her bruised and battered soul and she eventually fell asleep determined to keep him at bay.

Some evenings later, O'Connor answered a knock at his cottage door.

"Is it safe to talk?" the man asked, as he shook the rain off his coat and handed it to O'Connor.

"Aye, Róisín sleeps up at the house now."

"Well, my friend, what news?"

O'Connor scowled at his visitor. "I don't like it one bit. The eldest one thinks she knows about farming and gives me orders as if I don't know how to do my job. I'm not happy. This isn't what I expected."

"Now, now, how could we know in advance what they would be like? You must be patient and keep them out of the farm business as best you can."

"Wait till you hear this: she wants to sell the hunters."

"Heavens above! Don't let her do that."

"And how do you propose I stop her? She says they are eating their heads off and no one riding them at all."

"Stall her as much as you can. Damn and blast!" the man exclaimed, very upset. He sat down at the table with a heavy sigh. "Are you sure that everything is secure?"

"Aye, they won't find anything they shouldn't, but I think we should bring our plans forward. 'Tis awful risky."

"No, that isn't possible. We aren't ready. We will bide our time and you will keep a close eye on those two. Now, where is the Bushmills? My throat is as dry as straw."

Chapter Six

F erocious storms lashed the Cumberland coast for the next week and as a result the Miss Campbells were all but confined to the house. Louisa, however, was finding the transition from factotum to being waited on somewhat challenging for her energetic disposition. To add to her frustration, there was one room that became an object of fierce curiosity. Uncle Jack's study, which was situated behind the dining room, was locked, and had been since their arrival. The shutters were closed so they could not see into the room from the outside and the keys were missing. It was only when she mentioned it in passing to O'Connor that he admitted that he had taken the keys away for safekeeping. She regarded him coldly, wondering what on earth he was up to. It was as if he was always trying to obstruct her.

The following day, he arrived with the keys and handed them over with some hesitancy. She dismissed him briskly and waited until he was gone before she opened the door. The room was north-facing and ice-cold, with a stale odour of whiskey and tobacco; a distinctly male atmosphere. In the faint light of her lamp she could see that the fire had been laid, perhaps in preparation for Uncle Jack's return from America. She found some matches on the mantle and soon the fire burst into life. Pulling back the wooden shutters revealed months' worth of dust covering the floor and her footprints standing out clearly against the dark wooden boards. It looked as though no one had been in the room since her uncle's death.

There was a large gun cabinet in one corner which housed several rifles and pistols, but the rest of the walls were lined with bookshelves containing a mesmerising and eclectic collection of books. Of more interest was a large and ornate oak desk which dominated the centre of the room. As she expected, it was locked, but a small key on the ring fitted it. Stacks of paper littered the surface of the desk when she pulled back the top. Uncle Jack had not been organised or methodical, it appeared, with pieces of paper bursting out of every cubbyhole. The drawers were similarly jam-packed with documents. With a heavy sigh, she pulled back her lace cuffs, and dove in.

She spent the entire afternoon wading through the mountain of papers, and periodically feeding the fire with those she knew to be of no value. In amongst the bills and receipts she found several invoices from Jamesons and a barrister in Carlisle, but the descriptions were not informative, bearing only the title 'Campbell vs. Maxwell' or vice versa. How she would love to have known what that was about! Clearly Uncle Jack had sought protection in the law – but why? Would the answer shed some light on the reasons for the feud which Maxwell appeared determined to prolong? She needed every weapon at her disposal if she was to keep him from destroying their peace. Sitting back in the chair, she went over the few occasions they had met and analysed his words. She came to the conclusion that something very specific had occurred to make Maxwell so bitter and vindictive – something personal between the two men. With a growl of frustration, she dismissed him from her mind, as best she could, and turned her attention back to the contents of the desk.

A small bundle of letters, tied with faded ribbon, nestled in a drawer at the bottom of the desk. They still had a very faint hint of perfume, despite being much yellowed, and the paper crackled with age as she handled it. By the state of the paper, they looked as though they had been read over and over. It felt too intrusive to look at them, so she put them back into the drawer. Uncle Jack had had a sweetheart; it was another aspect to him that she hadn't considered before. Most likely he had had several over the course of his life. But he had never married. Had his advances been rejected or was he just a confirmed bachelor?

Nothing else of interest was to be found, and with a sense of disappointment, she locked the desk and went to join Eleanor in the drawing room. Her sister was curled up on the window seat with a book in her lap. She glanced up when she came into the room.

"Did you find anything scandalous?"

"No skeletons, I'm afraid. Just lots of bills, thankfully of the paid variety, and lots of dust. Oh ... but there is a bundle of love letters in one of the drawers. Just your sort of thing," she teased.

Eleanor sat up, all interest. "May I see them?"

She frowned and shook her head.

"Why ever not?" Eleanor pleaded. "Uncle Jack is dead. What harm can it do?"

"I didn't even look at them myself – far too private. It didn't feel right."

Eleanor looked disappointed but didn't argue. "While you were busy inside, I was looking at those photographs and prints that belonged to Uncle Jack. You know, the ones you were going to dispose of? I do like this one." She held up the heart-shaped miniature. "What a sad-looking girl," she said. "Do you know, there is something familiar about her."

"Yes, I thought so, too, when I first saw it but it's unlikely that we would know her. I suppose she could be a relative – another Campbell, perhaps. Look at the style of her dress and her hair. It is quite old-fashioned. Her likeness must have been taken a long time ago. Perhaps there is an inscription inside the back plate. Did you check?"

"No, I didn't think of that."

Louisa took the miniature from her. "Let me see." But there was no name or any indication whatsoever of the lady's identity. She would remain a mystery.

"I think we should keep it," Eleanor said emphatically, taking the frame back.

"Why? We will never know who she is," she said.

"I know, but I just feel drawn to her. It's like a story in a book: a mystery lady. If you don't want to leave it here I will keep it in my room."

"Whatever you wish. I wonder if she could be the same lady whose letters are in Uncle Jack's desk?" Louisa mused.

"Yes, I hadn't thought of that. How sad – a long lost love. He must have kept her picture here and looked upon it every day. I wonder what kept them apart."

"Judging by his reputation locally, I'd say an anxious parent." Louisa smiled. Really, Eleanor was far too sentimental.

Nicholas observed the man sitting before his desk with some misgivings. He wondered if he was going too far. He looked back on that disastrous encounter with Louisa Campbell with regret. Having let his temper get the better of him, he had shown his hand far too soon. My God, she was a clever little thing and he desperately wanted to get the better of her. He knew he had overstepped the mark when he had seen the flash of temper in her eyes, but he couldn't help himself. Having had the opportunity to analyse the encounter more calmly, he could see that he should have handled it differently. What was very clear, though, was that she was no innocent; her manner was far too confident for someone her age. No doubt she had been groomed by Campbell for the very role she was playing.

"So, Jenkins, I have another job for you," he said, whilst pushing down the uncomfortable feeling of being an utter cad.

Jenkins grinned in response. "Yes, sir, and what would that be, then?"

"I need someone watched. I want to know who they meet and where they go."

"I'm your man, so – nothing easier. Who is it? Some business rival perhaps?"

"No, nothing of that nature. It's a woman."

Jenkins leered back at him. He quickly corrected the impression. "The Campbell sisters have just arrived at Bowes Farm. I believe that one of them at least, the elder, Louisa

Campbell, is a Fenian like her uncle before her. I want to know who her contacts are and what they are up to."

"That's tricky, Mr. Maxwell. Those Fenians are a tight bunch. They'll never accept an outsider like me. And they're clever, see. They run small cells and no one knows who is in the other cells; only the boss men, and heaven knows where they are."

"I am aware of all of this, but I trust that you will find a way. I will pay you appropriately, of course."

Jenkins sat staring back at him, obviously weighing up the assignment. "Sir, as it's you I'll take it on. I will get to work on it straight away."

"Good. I will expect you to report to me at least weekly, and for goodness sake, don't get caught."

"You can rely on me, sir," Jenkins said. "Would there be any chance of a payment up front? There will be some expenses involved in setting things up."

"I'll inform my clerk. Call into the colliery tomorrow. Good day, Jenkins." He dismissed him with a shudder. He really was a slimy little man.

Louisa was just finishing off a letter to George Jameson when Anna was announced. The rain had ceased the previous evening, so she wasn't too surprised to see her friend appear.

"Good Lord! Is that Eleanor playing?" Anna asked as she sank on to the sofa, a vision in lilac satin. The haunting notes of a sonata filled the house.

"Yes indeed."

"I wish I could play that proficiently. I have always struggled with it. I much prefer to sing."

"I, on the other hand, can clear a room with my singing!"

Anna laughed and patted the sofa next to her. "As I have you on your own there is something I wanted to tell you," she said, with a conspiratorial glance in the direction of the door. "I know I can trust your discretion." Louisa sat down beside her and had her hand grasped tightly. "It's about John Whitby." Louisa and Eleanor had met John Whitby, the Rector, on the previous Sunday.

She had taken an instant liking to the tall, slightly sombre gentleman, and wasn't at all surprised that his cool grey eyes and gentle manner had attracted her friend.

She was on the verge of a reply of 'I see', when Róisín burst in and announced the man himself. Anna coloured up, startled, and Louisa had to restrain the urge to laugh.

She stood up to greet him. "Mr. Whitby. Thank you for calling. Do sit down. It's most kind of you to come out all this way. We would have taken up your sister's invitation to visit, that she was so kind to proffer on Sunday, but the weather ..."

"No, not at all ... at least I felt I should come because of the misunderstanding ... most unfortunate," he trailed off in embarrassment. Whitby had been very confused on discovering them attending his church instead of Fr. Healy's. "Miss Maxwell." He greeted Anna with a nod, then sat down, looking most uncomfortable.

Louisa surveyed her two red faced-visitors with amusement. Could it really be coincidence that they both decided to visit her on the same day?

"As I said on Sunday, Mr. Whitby, it was an understandable error. I must say that we enjoyed the service very much and St. Martin's is a lovely church. How old is it?" Whitby relaxed a little, which was her intention, and explained some of the church's history.

Anna also recovered her equilibrium and joined in the conversation. "You should tell Miss Campbell about the window."

"Yes, it is very old – stained glass – 16th century, we believe."

"I shall make sure to take a look on Sunday. As it happens, I am very glad you called. I wished to speak to you on church-related business. I find myself with a good deal of spare time and hoped that you might be able to suggest some project or other that I could take up. My sister and I have known straitened circumstances, and now that we are so comfortably situated, I would like to help others less fortunate. I will consider anything you suggest, Mr. Whitby."

"That is most generous of you, Miss Campbell. There is much

poverty in Newton. I see the evils of it every day, as I'm sure your brother does in the courts, Miss Maxwell," he said, swivelling around to look at Anna properly for the first time.

"Yes, he does speak of it sometimes. He blames alcohol for a lot of the problems."

"But that is only a symptom; the real issues run much deeper. I do not wish to offend, but I do not think he has a real understanding of the working and living conditions of his own workers. Low wages, long working hours and cramped living conditions are at the heart of it all." He stopped, and coloured up, probably realising that he should not be criticising Anna's brother. He smiled apologetically. "I do beg your pardon."

"I think you are right, of course. But in defence of Nicholas, he is conflicted by being the employer."

"Granted, but he has a moral responsibility, too," he replied with some vigour.

Anna blushed. "Oh dear, now I am conflicted."

Whitby had been leaning towards Anna in his eagerness to make his point. He straightened up and looked guiltily towards Louisa, before mumbling another apology. Louisa guessed there was a strong attachment between her visitors. Both were extremely self-conscious and Anna was unusually tongue-tied. It would be very interesting to know what their history was and, in particular, Maxwell's opinion on the subject. She resolved that if these two needed her assistance to get the better of him, she would be a staunch friend to both.

Thankfully, at this point Eleanor came into the room, closely followed by Róisín with the tea tray. The Rector strictly adhered to a half-hour call. He bowed to the ladies and looked very much like a man who would like to have stayed. As the door closed behind him, Anna sighed. Eleanor excused herself and the two ladies were left alone.

Louisa could not resist teasing her guest. "So you are going to tell me that you had no idea that he was going to call here today?"

"How could I know?" Anna objected weakly.

"I don't believe you. I am in enough trouble with your brother as it is, without being accused of aiding and abetting star-crossed lovers."

Anna looked alarmed, so she relented. "You are a goose! I don't mind in the least and I like your choice. He gives the impression of being a most sensible and intelligent man. How long has this been going on?"

"Two years," Anna muttered sadly. "It was just after he arrived in the parish. I was helping to organise the rush-bearing ceremony with the Miss Kirkbrides and we spent a lot of time together and … that was that."

"Two years." She was taken aback. "That's a long time. Has he never come to the point?"

"No, it's not that. It's Nicholas. He doesn't think he's good enough for me."

"I can't say I'm surprised," she replied, but Anna immediately looked offended. "No, I mean I'm not surprised that your brother would think that way."

"Oh I see," Anna said, looking relieved. "He has been unreasonable from the outset. He insists that the connection is unsuitable. Soon enough I will be of age and will be able to take control of my own destiny."

"And how does Mr. Whitby feel about all this?"

"John does not wish to go against Nicholas's wishes, and it puts him in a very difficult position, being Rector. He does not want to be the cause of an estrangement between us."

"He may have a point. My mother married for love and was cut off from her family because of it. She hated the isolation from her parents and only one of her sisters kept up any contact. It was difficult for all of us."

"But surely she would have been equally miserable to have been separated forever from your father?"

"Yes, that is true," she conceded.

"I think Nicholas will come round when he sees we are happy."

"I hope so, because it would be very awkward if he doesn't relent." Anna's face fell. "But hopefully it will not come to that. I don't see why you should not follow your heart."

"I think being a Rector's wife would suit me very well. I love to be around people and in the thick of things. I'm glad I've told you. I knew you'd understand." Anna looked momentarily troubled. "However, I do think you have formed a wrong impression of Nicholas. He can be abrupt and he doesn't suffer fools, but he is actually a very kind brother. I know that at the root of his disapproval of my choice is his fear that I will be unhappy. And, if I am truthful, he does put up with a lot from me."

"That's as maybe, but whatever happened between him and my uncle, it doesn't excuse his threats to us. He was more than abrupt with me, Anna; he was downright rude, insulting and overbearing. I lost my temper with him."

"It's over the land, isn't it? He just can't let it go. I had suspected his visit hadn't gone well as he has been in a foul mood ever since."

How satisfying, Louisa thought. He must have expected her to be meek and gullible and couldn't believe that he had met with her intransigence. It would do him good to be thwarted. "I can't tell you how much that has cheered me up! Though I hope he hasn't been taking it out on you?"

"I just keep out of his way when he's out of sorts. What did he say that upset you so much?" Anna asked.

"He threatened to turn local society against us. He wants to make life so uncomfortable that I will sell up and leave."

Anna shook her head in disbelief. "He wouldn't do that! That is too cruel. No, he must have said it in anger or you misunderstood him."

"He was absolutely furious, but he meant what he said. Though, oddly enough, he doesn't appear to have acted on his threat yet. I half expected to be shunned by everyone at church on Sunday. Do you know why he is so obsessed with this property?"

"I'm afraid it isn't a very pleasant story."

"Please – I really need to know."

"My father lost Bowes Farm to your uncle in a game of cards."

"Good heavens!"

"Yes, and things degenerated from there. Your uncle did not behave well. Father had been very drunk when it happened and he accused Mr. Campbell of taking advantage. Your uncle taunted my father about it for years and then there were the court cases: libel and accusations of assault and trespass. It became very unpleasant indeed."

"I see. It is disappointing to learn that Uncle Jack was such a reprobate, but I don't think it justifies your brother's treatment of us."

"Your uncle's death came just as the police thought they had enough evidence to convict him. Nicholas believed that he was a Fenian."

"So he said to me, but I doubt he was. I'd more likely believe it of my steward. He is definitely capable of mischief. Still it doesn't excuse ..."

"Of course not, and I intend to sort this out. I will make him see sense, just trust me."

"What are you up to?"

"Never you mind! It will become clear in due course," Anna replied with a glint in her eye.

"Now I am worried!"

Chapter Seven

C hristmas was fast approaching and still Maxwell had stayed his hand. Louisa was baffled, and wondered if he had found people unreceptive to his nastiness. Then one morning in amongst the post was an invitation to dinner at Thorncroft, a week before Christmas. She pushed it across the table to Eleanor with an impish smile.

"Anna has been busy."

"Should we accept?" Eleanor asked, having read it twice in disbelief.

"Of course we will accept."

"But why would he include us after making all of those threats? What could have changed his mind?"

"He hasn't, I'm sure. Anna is trying to mend bridges, but I suspect he is planning something quite different."

"Oh no, I don't think I want to go if that's the case," Eleanor said with a worried frown. "It will be most uncomfortable – just waiting for him to pounce."

"Eleanor, we must go, otherwise he will think that he has won and we are cowering here like frightened rabbits. I will not give him the satisfaction."

"That's all very well for you to say, but I find him quite terrifying."

"Pooh, he is bully, that is all. When he realises that I will not change my mind, he will have no choice but to accept that we are staying, and give up this ridiculous feud."

"I wish I shared your confidence." Eleanor absently ran her fingers along the edge of the card. "Do you suppose there will be many there?"

"Anna did mention an annual dinner. I understood it to be a grand affair. Don't worry. He will hardly do anything awful in front of his guests. Now, I think a trip to Carlisle is called for. We cannot be outshone by the local ladies."

Eleanor brightened up at the prospect. "Yes – I have nothing suitable for a formal dinner. How exciting – a shopping trip!"

Louisa observed her sister's happy face with relief. Such a simple thing as buying a new gown brought her so much joy. If they had still been impoverished Dubliners what kind of festive season would they have enjoyed? It would not have included dinner parties and silk dresses, that was a certainty.

On the evening of the dinner party, the Campbell sisters were almost the last of his guests to arrive. Nicholas wondered if Miss Campbell was nervous and hoped for safety in numbers. This was immensely agreeable to him. He was playing a deep game and wanted her to be at a disadvantage when he struck. When Anna had broached the subject of inviting them, his initial impulse had been to refuse, but the more he thought about it, the more convinced he became that it would be the perfect setting for his scheme to have them ostracised. With over thirty guests to greet, he had little opportunity to do more than shake hands with them. Miss Campbell greeted him unsmiling, a definite challenge in her eye.

Anna swept them away to circulate. He took up position at the fireplace where he could observe the whole room while engaged in conversation with the Morrissey family. He watched his prey with a keen eye. The younger sister looked pleasing enough – the perfect little debutante and easily forgettable. But her sister, however, was a surprise. If he had thought about it at all, he would have said that she was unremarkable, but reluctantly had to admit that his prejudice had coloured his initial opinion. Tonight she was very striking indeed. The dark blue silk gown she wore fitted her figure perfectly; there was no surfeit of ruffles and lace as some of the other ladies indulged in, just pure simple and elegant lines. Her hair shone and was swept up in a flattering style. Her pale skin almost glowed and she wore just a modest pearl pendant around her neck. Somehow he had also missed how intense a colour her eyes were; green or blue – he couldn't be sure. As he mulled over the matter, he realised that Beatrice Morrissey was asking him a question. He would have to be careful. He needed to plant the seed of jealousy without committing himself too far. He had spent the last couple of weeks doing his groundwork.

"Are those the Campbells?" she asked.

"Yes, Miss Morrissey," he said with a heavy sigh.

She took the bait. "You would think they would have had the good grace to decline. Really, it is quite shocking how ill-mannered some people can be. Surely they are aware of all the problems their uncle caused, especially to you and your family."

"It is Christmas, Miss Morrissey. One should be charitable," he replied, with a warm smile, as if she were the only woman in the room.

"Yes, of course. You are very good to even notice them," she simpered before launching into one of her peals of laughter. Even her father flinched at the sound and Nicholas found it difficult to keep the smile fixed on his face.

On the far side of the room Louisa and Eleanor, impervious to the scrutiny they were under, were being introduced to Robert Maxwell. He was tall and his dark complexion was much like his elder brother, but there the similarity ended. He had a friendly smile and relaxed manner, and within minutes he had them laughing and feeling at ease.

"You do realise that Anna has told me all about you?" he said.

"And you still wished to meet us? How brave you are!" Louisa rejoined.

"I am a cavalry officer, you know. We're famous for bravery."

"And, I think, recklessness?"

"I can't deny it," he replied, with a boyish grin that was hard to resist.

"How long is your leave, Captain?" Eleanor asked.

"Five days is all, I'm afraid, but I intend to make the most of it. If the weather stays dry, I hope to drag my lazy brother out for a good gallop. Do you ride every day, ladies?"

"No, neither of us has ever learned. We have lived in Dublin all our lives with no need for horses, you see. Yes, I know how shocking that is," Louisa said when he looked horrified, "but I intend to rectify it as soon as I can. My steward has promised to find me a nice quiet horse."

"I understand perfectly. It's a pity I'm not home for longer or I'd teach you myself," he said with a genuine smile. Louisa knew that his brother would never countenance the idea, but she couldn't help but smile back all the same.

Dinner was served in one of the most beautiful rooms that Louisa had ever seen. The best crystal, silver and china glistened on the mahogany table and the richly decorated dining room glowed in the candlelight coming from magnificent crystal chandeliers. Much to her relief, she was seated next to John Whitby, with Eleanor only a couple of places away. But she was rather closer to Maxwell, at the head of the table, than she would have wished. He was still standing, waiting for all of the guests to be seated, and was talking to a gentlemen she did not recognise. Somewhat reluctantly, she had to admit that he looked very well in evening dress and very much at ease as the quintessential charming host. She rather envied his calm, assured manner, and if she hadn't witnessed first-hand his different behaviour at Bowes, she would have been very impressed with him.

She became aware of some unfriendly glances from a young woman across the table. When the lady was engaged in conversation with her immediate neighbour, she asked Mr. Whitby who she was.

"That is Miss Beatrice Morrissey. Her parents are Irish, as it happens. Her father, William, owns several cotton mills up in Carlisle. He is standing beside our host at the moment."

"I haven't met them yet. Are they great friends of the family?"

"I believe there are hopes of a connection," he replied. "Anna doesn't believe it will happen, but it is known that Nicholas has been paying Miss Morrissey considerable attention of late."

She had been avoiding meeting her host's eye all evening, but now stole a glance at him from under her lashes, then back to Miss Morrissey. Blonde curls and a rather determined chin were the lady's best features. No doubt she had other attractions that were less obvious, such as a large dowry, property interests or being an heiress, she thought naughtily.

Another gentleman took the vacant seat beside her and Whitby made the introductions. He looked harmless enough but, disconcertingly, his opening disclosure was that he was a widower. He proceeded to monopolise her for the entire first two courses, at the end of which it was clear he was interviewing her for the vacant post. At a convenient interval, when he had to stop to catch his breath, she turned in desperation to the Rector.

"Mr. Whitby, have you found a project for me yet?"

"I think I may have hit on just the thing, Miss Campbell. I would like to set up a night school for the young miners in Newton. Most of them started working at a very young age and cannot read or write. They are condemned to a life of scraping a living and working in dangerous conditions. These men are a rough lot, it is true, but when you get to know them they are just like you and me: good Christian souls. My sister Clara already teaches, as you know, but could not manage this particular venture on her own. Your assistance would be invaluable. The only difficulty is that you would have to teach them in the evenings after their shift. I'm not sure how you would feel about that?"

She was a little daunted at the prospect of taking on such a huge responsibility, but was glad that he wasn't fobbing her off with some meaningless scheme. "I have never undertaken anything like this, but I am willing to try."

"That is wonderful. You have no idea how grateful I am. I had a feeling you would relish the challenge. Clara will be delighted to have your assistance and the school will be the perfect location. I will talk to some of the men and hopefully you can start in the

New Year. Do you think that would suit, Miss Campbell?"

"Yes, that sounds perfect. How many do you propose we teach?"

"I thought perhaps ten or so and we will see how that works out."

"Excellent. I am looking forward to it already," she told him. She was about to ask him for more details when they were interrupted by the strident tones of Beatrice Morrissey from across the table.

"Miss Campbell, I must ask how you are settling in. You know everyone was surprised that you decided to move here from Ireland, in the circumstances." Miss Morrissey gave a sickly smile, which was more akin to a grimace, and stared with open hostility across the table.

Louisa tensed and was immediately on her guard. It was the height of bad manners for someone to speak across the table. She responded, keeping her voice low in contrast. "It is prodigiously kind of you to enquire. We are comfortably settled, thank you. "

"Indeed, most comfortably settled. What good fortune that you inherited such an estate! It must have been a relief to gain financial security. I understand your circumstances were not particularly favourable before."

"It is kind of you to take an interest," she replied. The woman was surprisingly well informed.

"Not at all. We are known to be a charitable lot here in Newton." Miss Morrissey smirked. "But you must satisfy my curiosity: just who *are* your family? What are your connections?"

By now a hush had fallen over their end of the table and she knew that everyone was listening intently and pretending not to be. She had to admit it was clever of him to use this woman to get to her. He was sitting back in his chair, glass in hand, with a look of pure delight on his face.

"Our family come from County Galway."

"Now where is that again? Do enlighten me."

"On the west coast."

"Isn't that quite a wild place? I am sure I read somewhere that the people are little more than savages." Miss Morrissey tittered and looked towards Maxwell as if for approval.

Louisa could see that Eleanor's head was bowed and that she was in some distress. Her anger bubbled up. "I would hate to disagree with someone who is so obviously well read as yourself, Miss Morrissey, but I can inform you that it is certainly a wildly beautiful country. As for the people, they no longer eat their first-born since they developed a taste for English tourists."

Miss Morrissey looked momentarily confused but recovered with aplomb. "Very witty, Miss Campbell – very diverting. But seriously, you must tell us what kind of society your family moves in. We are a very close-knit community and cautious of strangers." She lowered her voice a few tones and leaned slightly towards her. "Perhaps you are not aware of your late uncle's reputation. Indeed, it is most unfortunate for you. I do feel for you deeply. I think you very brave to enter society here when it will be so difficult for you to be accepted."

There were a few gasps around the table and she sensed John Whitby stiffen up beside her. It took incredible control not to lash out at her tormentor, but her only thought was for Eleanor.

"It is very good of you to warn me, Miss Morrissey, but we have only encountered kindness and generosity from our neighbours. I have to say I am particularly grateful to Mr. Maxwell for inviting us here tonight, a fine example of the charity you spoke of, do you not agree?" She threw him a fulminating look. "I believe your anxiety for us, which you have been so kind to divulge, may be unfounded."

Miss Morrissey flinched, and sat back in her chair quivering with rage. Gradually the uncomfortable silence was eased as the other guests made an effort to restart conversations. Louisa's appetite had vanished but she focussed on her plate, trying to control her ragged breathing. She didn't feel she had won the battle, but in the circumstances she hadn't done too badly. She had been betrayed into speaking in anger, but who could blame her under such provocation? She did wonder, however, how much damage Miss Morrissey had inflicted with her spiteful remarks.

"That was uncalled for. I'm sorry you were subjected to that," John Whitby remarked *sotto voce*. "I hope you realise she does not speak for me."

She gave him a grateful if wan smile. "Thank you. But it wasn't entirely unexpected. I just didn't know where the attack would come from."

He looked horrified. "Mr. Maxwell should have intervened. I cannot understand him allowing a guest to be abused so."

"Ah, Mr. Whitby, I'm afraid he orchestrated it. Did you not see how much he enjoyed it?"

"Good lord, I am shocked. I do not always see eye to eye with him, but I have never known him to be malicious. Surely you must be mistaken?" He cast a troubled look at their host.

"I'm afraid my late uncle is at the root of all of this."

"Indeed, it is common knowledge that they did not like each other. Anna has given me some details. Still, harbouring such dislike is not a Christian attitude. You have no father or brother to stand up for you. I have to admit that I find this very troubling." He twisted the stem of his wine glass continually as if trying to calm himself, obviously distressed to think his future brother-in-law was guilty of such conduct.

"I must put your mind at ease, sir. I have stood *in loco parentis* for the last four years and I am perfectly able to defend Eleanor and myself if needs be. Perhaps a timely sermon on the subject of forgiveness would be a good idea?"

He pondered this, not realising that she was jesting. "Yes, that is a very good idea – particularly at this festive season."

He became lost in thought, no doubt composing it then and there, and she was left in silent contemplation of her cold food. Her immediate neighbour was also uncommunicative, his pursuit of her now clearly a thing of the past. At least she had Beatrice Morrissey to thank for that.

Once the dessert course was over, a flustered-looking Anna caught her eye and stood as a signal for the ladies to withdraw. John Whitby rose and drew back her chair, giving her an encouraging smile. She kept her head held high and did not look directly at anyone as she left the room. Out in the hallway she held back and waited for Eleanor. The poor girl looked very miserable when she emerged.

"Louisa, that was so horrid," she whispered, almost in tears.

"It could have been worse. I think she has done more damage to herself. No well-bred person would behave in such a way."

"I don't know how it could have been worse. I wanted to melt into my chair. At least you tried to snub her. I don't understand why she was so horrid. She doesn't even know us."

"She did not act on her own. Our charming host put her up to it somehow, of that I'm sure," she said.

"I thought you said he wouldn't do anything in front of his guests," Eleanor complained.

"It appears I was wrong," she answered drily.

Anna rushed up to them, having shown the other ladies into the drawing room. "I am *so* sorry. I cannot tell you how embarrassed I am. I don't know what got into that awful creature."

"Don't distress yourself, Anna. We are fine. I suspected something like this might happen – but you must attend to your guests," she insisted waving her hand towards the drawing room. "We just need a few minutes to compose ourselves."

"You will stay, won't you? Though I wouldn't blame you if you left and never spoke to me again."

"Of course we will stay. I am keen to deny your brother any hint of victory."

When they entered the drawing room a few minutes later, there was a conspicuous dip in the babble of conversation, and the group of young ladies around Beatrice Morrissey closed ranks. Mrs. Lambert, an elderly lady from Newton, immediately beckoned for them to join her. Louisa gave Eleanor's arm a reassuring squeeze and manoeuvred her across the room, relieved to find an ally.

"My dears, I haven't had an opportunity to talk to you this evening," Mrs. Lambert said. "You both look very pretty. You have a natural elegance that no amount of training can give, I can tell you. Good breeding always will out." This was said in a carrying voice with a meaningful look in Miss Morrissey's direction. "Now do sit down and tell me all your news."

Half an hour later, the gentlemen joined the drawing room party, and tea and coffee were served. Louisa volunteered to fetch tea for Mrs. Lambert and joined the group around the tea table. No one spoke to her. With a sickening feeling she realised that Miss Morrissey had succeeded in her object to some extent. Maxwell was ahead of her at the table and as he turned back, cup in hand, they came face to face. She steeled herself not to react, but returned his gaze as coolly as she could manage. That damned eyebrow of his rose in a mocking gesture that required no words. He brushed past her silently, leaving her smouldering in anger.

When tea was over, Anna began to cajole the ladies to provide some music. Several of the young ladies played and others sang, all reasonably accomplished and pleasant to listen to. Soon Miss Morrissey realised that she was no longer the centre of attention, and nearly trampled several young women in her eagerness to display her talents at the pianoforte. It was not justified; her playing was mediocre at best. When she started to sing, Louisa had to exercise a deal of control not to squirm in her seat. She didn't dare look at Eleanor.

Anna soon descended on them and tried to persuade Eleanor to play next. It looked as though Beatrice was preparing to play again, impervious to the looks of dismay from several of the guests.

But Eleanor shrank back. "No, Anna, please, I'd rather not in front of all of these people."

"But you are the best player here, Eleanor. I have heard you," Anna protested.

"You should. Anna is right." Louisa joined in with an encouraging smile.

Anna nodded her head vigorously and threw an anguished glance at the source of their current misery. "If nothing else, have pity on my guests' ears!"

Eleanor looked very nervous. "Very well, but just the one piece," she said, and allowed herself to be pulled towards the piano by Anna. At the end of her piece, Beatrice stood up with a great show of reluctance and a sneer aimed at Eleanor that could have curdled milk.

Whereas there had been background chatter when the previous ladies had performed, it was soon evident that the young woman now playing was worth listening to. All conversation ceased and Louisa swelled with pride. It was hard to believe that the passionate playing came from a girl who was so ill. She closed her eyes and listened with pleasure, but was soon aware that someone had taken Eleanor's place on the sofa beside her. She opened her eyes and, much to her surprise, discovered it was Maxwell. She chose to ignore him.

"I hope you enjoyed dinner, Miss Campbell. I thought the main course particularly agreeable," he said, just above a whisper.

She kept her eyes on Eleanor at the piano, but she could sense the smug satisfaction of the man and could not resist replying, "Your guests undoubtedly found it to their taste."

"But not you?" he asked, in a mocking tone.

"I found it … a little indigestible," she replied at last, turning in his direction. "A little overdone, perhaps?"

He acknowledged the hit with a forced smile. "One cannot always control the temperature."

She listened to the music for a few moments before responding. "I have to say that I am very disappointed in you. I expected more flair, more subtlety; that display was pure childish spite. And hiding behind a woman? Is that really the best you can do?"

He leaned towards her, so close that she could feel his breath on her neck. "I will give you some advice, my dear: never underestimate me."

A chill tingled down her spine. "Do not worry, sir. I think I have your measure," she responded.

"And yet you came here tonight. Surely you must have realised how dangerous that was?"

"Suspected a trap, you mean? Actually I did, but my besetting sin is curiosity. I wanted to see what form your unpleasant campaign would take. Despite your threats, you have not acted these last few weeks. I guessed you deliberately delayed so as to maximise the effect."

"This is only the beginning. I want that land and I will get it.

"Over my dead body."

"That would definitely be a pity," he said, deliberately letting his gaze sweep slowly over her, "a great pity indeed."

She stiffened at the intimidation in his tone, but blushed uncontrollably. The last thing she wanted was for him to know he could have that kind of effect on her, so she went on the attack.

"You do appear to make a habit of threatening me, Mr. Maxwell, and it's becoming tiresome. Does the delightful Miss Morrissey welcome that kind of behaviour, perhaps? She strikes me as the kind of woman who might. In fact, I think you are a perfect match."

He sniffed derisively and looked around the room, refusing to take that particular lure. "These people are the first families in the vicinity. Did you really think you could come amongst them with impunity? Very foolish of you. Your uncle managed to upset most of the men here at one time or another. These things are not easily forgotten."

"Particularly when you and your delightful assistant take such care to remind them." He shrugged in response. If they hadn't been in company she would have taken great pleasure in slapping his face. "Well, you have done your worst and I must say that you have satisfied my curiosity to the fullest."

"I'm glad to have been of service, Miss Campbell."

She smiled sweetly up at him. "You see, I always think it best to observe a creature in its natural habitat; you will always learn something useful."

His eyes blazed momentarily, but he forced a thin smile. "And what conclusion have you reached?"

"This evening has been most illuminating. You are perfectly suited to your milieu. And above all, I suppose I should really thank you."

"Indeed?"

"Now it is clear to me that the society you keep would never do for us. We prefer to mix with people of refinement and good manners, something that appears to be sadly lacking in you and some of your guests this evening."

She was treated to a murderous look before he vacated his seat, just as Eleanor concluded her piece on a crashing chord and loud applause.

Chapter Eight

L ouisa was still mulling over the disastrous dinner party at Thorncroft the following day. Sleep had eluded her, and at four in the morning she gave up and went down to the study. She lit the fire and, wrapping herself in a woollen shawl, tried to make sense of it all. But she just stared into the flames, giving into despondency. She could not shake off the suspicion that Maxwell had been digging around in their past. It made sense that he would try hard to discredit them, but it would be a pointless search. Other than a father who could not stay away from the gaming hells in the back streets of Dublin, she could think of nothing he could use; he already knew more about Uncle Jack than they did. But the thought of him going to such lengths upset her. Blast the man: he was ruining all her plans for a quiet life! Perhaps she should leave – sell up now and just go? But why should she let him win? The idea of surrendering Bowes to him was just too awful to contemplate. Of course, she could sell to someone else, which would be an agreeable blow to administer, but no doubt he would get it back eventually. Besides, she loved the place and didn't want to leave.

She smiled as she imagined how angry Anna must be. No doubt there had been a flaming row after the guests had all left. How Anna had defended him before she did not know, but now even she must see what her brother was really like. But Whitby had found her assertions hard to believe, which niggled. How could he not see the man she saw? Or was it that Maxwell's hatred of Uncle Jack had been transferred to her and made him act out of character? Would he treat her differently if she wasn't related to Uncle Jack? But that was a dangerous line of thought.

Eventually she must have fallen asleep. When Róisín tapped at the study door the clock read ten past ten and she had a crick in her neck from sleeping against the wing of the armchair.

"I brought you some tea, Miss, and the post. This just arrived for you. It was hand-delivered," she said, handing her a cream-coloured envelope. "Oh look, Miss, the fire has died. I'll just get that going again for you so you don't catch cold."

"Thank you, Róisín. You're a good girl."

She was rewarded with a huge smile. She waited for her to leave before she moved to the desk and sorted through the post, leaving the hand-delivered item until last. It would probably be a note of apology from Anna. But when she opened the envelope there was a single sheet of paper within and it was from Maxwell. When she saw the contents she screwed up the paper into a ball and threw it with great force into the grate. How dare he? All the page had contained was his previous offer for the farm with a minus sign and the figure of two hundred pounds and a question mark. His initials were scrawled underneath.

In fury she paced the room. After a few minutes of muttering and fist-clenching, her anger subsided and she stared hard at the ball of paper so temptingly close to the flames. She contemplated ignoring it (not an option); burning it (far too easy and quick); force-feeding it down the horrible man's throat (a very pleasurable notion), but in the end settled for a curt response which she hoped would wipe the smile off his conceited face. She retrieved the paper, smoothed it out and wrote below his initials:

Dear Sir,

There is an expression about 'hell freezing over' which I am sure you are familiar with. Please regard this as my formal response to your misguided attempt to induce me to sell. My property is not for sale. Compliments of the season, LC.

Timothy, the stable boy, was dispatched with the note to Thorncroft almost immediately and told not to wait for a response, under any circumstances.

An altogether different kind of note arrived that same afternoon. It was from the Rector, inviting them to a carol concert in the town hall later that week. This kind gesture only added to her growing regard for John Whitby. Perhaps sympathy for how they had been treated at Thorncroft was behind it, but at least the Rector was making an effort to accept them. Hopefully the rest of Newton society would follow the cleric's lead. With her spirits restored, she promptly replied in the affirmative.

The night of the concert was bitterly cold. The old travelling coach, a relic of a past owner of Bowes, was resurrected from the stables and the sisters travelled in style, if not in comfort, to Newton. The town hall was illuminated like a fairy-tale, which only added to their anticipation of an evening of music. They hurried up the steps, past the enormous Christmas tree in the galleried hallway, to meet their hosts. The Whitbys greeted them affably and the Rector offered to show them to their seats. As they entered the large assembly room he explained that his sister Clara had arranged for the local orphanage children to sing the carols and the musicians, presently warming up, were from the local cotton mills. All of the proceeds were for the orphanage and Louisa dutifully put money into one of the boxes at the back of the room before they took their seats.

They sat happily watching the Newton citizens who were arriving and taking their places. The seats near the top were reserved for the local wealthy families, while the rear of the hall was standing-room only for workers and their families. A hush descended on the crowd as a large group of local dignitaries entered the room, amidst a great deal of rustling silk and superior smiles. Amongst this group were the Maxwells. Louisa caught a glimpse of them as they passed down the aisle. They took their seats right at the top on the opposite side. The doors were closed and, at a signal from Miss Whitby, the concert commenced.

From a side door a group of small children emerged, their faces scrubbed to within an inch of their lives and their hair gleaming in the gaslight. The little girls were in white smocks with red ribbons in their hair, and the boys wore little red jackets and navy trousers.

They looked adorable, but she felt sorry for them as they all appeared terrified out of their wits. A stern-looking gentleman brought up the rear and waited as the children took up their positions on the little stage. Once the children were facing him, he nodded to the musicians, who began to play, and for the next hour the children sang their hearts out.

Louisa was relieved that they were not sitting near Maxwell, but she spent the entire carol service staring at the back of his dark head willing him to turn around so that she could ignore him properly. He didn't oblige. The recital ended on tumultuous applause and the exhausted children filed out again looking bemused, and undoubtedly longing for their beds. The invited guests were shown into another room to partake of refreshments.

"There you are, my dears," Mrs. Lambert said, coming up to them, leaning heavily on her cane. "Did you enjoy the concert? Aren't the children delightful? Miss Whitby always does a wonderful job of organising these events."

"Yes, indeed; such heavenly voices," Louisa replied. "I see some seats over there. Would you care to sit down with us?"

"Very much, Miss Campbell, my arthritis is troublesome, I have to admit." Having settled herself down, she continued, "I can't tell you how glad I am to see you here tonight. I was afraid that after the dinner on Wednesday … well, I thought you might not wish …"

Eleanor tilted her head and looked kindly on the elderly lady. "You thought we might be too embarrassed to come?"

Mrs. Lambert looked uncomfortable. "Yes – though of course you have no reason to be, my dears. No, no, it is other people who should, perhaps, question their own behaviour," she said, looking towards the Maxwell party who had just entered the room, closely followed by the Morrisseys.

Louisa followed her gaze. Robert and Anna were chatting to the Rector while Maxwell had his back to them and was in deep conversation with Mr. and Mrs. Morrissey. "It is not for us to question the conduct of the higher echelons of society, now is it?"

But Mrs. Lambert failed to notice her sarcasm. "On the

contrary. They are the very ones who should be models of decorum."

Louisa flicked a glance at Maxwell, then leaned towards Mrs. Lambert and lowered her voice. "Perhaps he was just having an off day?"

Mrs. Lambert burst out laughing and patted her hand, her eyes twinkling. "You are naughty."

Remorse was a novel experience for Nicholas. After the initial thrill of achieving his goal the evening of the dinner party, he slowly realised he had let himself and his family down. Not only that, and probably more galling, he had seriously underestimated his opponent. He grudgingly had to admire how she had stood up to him, particularly on his own territory. Her note the day after the dinner was enough to convince him that she would never give in gracefully. Anna had actually cried whilst remonstrating with him that she had probably lost valuable friendships, and Robert, who was renowned for his evenness of temper, had sworn at him. His parting shot had been to the effect that if Nicholas married Beatrice Morrissey, which would be a punishment he would rightly deserve, he would never set foot in Thorncroft again. To explain to him that he had been merely using her to achieve his ends, legitimate ends in his view, would have made matters even worse, so he had endured his brother's temper outburst in resigned silence. He knew that he had erred and let his emotions dictate his actions; it had been a salutary lesson. Miss Campbell was proving singularly adept at bringing out the worst in him.

Almost from the moment he had entered the assembly room, he had been aware of Louisa's presence. On the journey into Newton he had wondered if the Campbells would attend and he had instantly lighted upon them half-way down the room. Much to his amusement, he could have sworn he heard a derogatory sniff as he had passed their row. Throughout the recital he found it difficult to concentrate and had the most uncomfortable feeling that hostile eyes were upon him – eyes that were the colour of a stormy sea and full of outrage.

On her way back from the cloakroom, Louisa was congratulating herself on having avoided any contact with Maxwell the entire evening, when she heard his deep, and now familiar voice, at her elbow.

"Miss Campbell?"

She turned slowly, her stomach doing something unhelpful to her equilibrium. As usual, he looked very well; expensively dressed and perfectly groomed. A wave of irritation washed over her. She hated the way he towered over her; all arrogance and false politeness. What resource could she call on to retaliate but her tongue? So she injected as much venom into her curt response as she could.

"Mr. Maxwell."

"Are you enjoying the evening?" he asked. The civility of the question was belied by the cynical glint in his eye.

"It has been most enjoyable – up to now," she said. Her jibe only made his mouth twitch and she plunged on. "I am rather surprised to see you here this evening, sir. Should you be neglecting your duties so wantonly?"

"I beg your pardon," he said with a puzzled look and a hard edge to his voice.

"I thought you would be out combing the area, hunting down Fenians. I had the strong impression it was an obsession of yours."

He regarded her silently for a moment, then said very quietly, "How do you know that I am not?" His eyes were glowing with malice, his meaning more than clear.

Louisa stiffened, then blinked and looked away. Did he seriously consider that she might be involved with terrorists? She scanned the room, willing herself not to retaliate at such a blatant insult. "I don't see your friend, Miss Morrissey, this evening?"

"I believe she is ill," he replied.

"Oh dear, nothing minor, I hope," she said, almost instantly regretting such a spiteful remark, but she had the most overwhelming impulse to lash out at him.

He raised a brow and said very softly, "I think that's beneath you, Miss Campbell."

"Indeed, you're right. Your ill manners must be rubbing off. Please excuse me," she said, before walking away, her cheeks flaming.

"I saw you speaking to Nicholas a little while ago. I do hope you are getting along a little better," Anna said, taking Mrs. Lambert's vacated seat between Eleanor and Louisa.

Louisa almost laughed aloud. "I think pigs will have wings before that happens, Anna." She was still mortified at how she had reacted to him. She had never felt such a strong dislike before or been so shamefully rude.

"Oh dear, I do so wish you could get along. I had hoped that he had apologised to you."

"Does he know how?" she snapped.

Anna frowned. "Of course, you have every right to be angry with him. Robert and I have remonstrated with him ever since the party, but he is incredibly stubborn." Anna reached for Louisa's hand. "I think it's time someone told you the full history between our families. It might help you understand him a little better."

She almost stopped her, suddenly fearing the words she instinctively knew would not be pleasant. The shadow of their uncle's life was hovering over them again.

"You already know how your uncle came to own Bowes Farm," Anna said, but in a lowered voice so that they had to lean towards her to hear. "Relations were very strained for some time. Then just as it looked like there might be an uneasy truce, Nicholas came home from university and met Geneviève Lambert."

"Is she related to Mrs. Lambert?" Eleanor asked.

"Yes, her eldest daughter, but I doubt she ever mentions her. Geneviève was wild and very beautiful and Nicholas fell head over heels. But Geneviève wasn't content to have just one beau. She flirted with every man she came in contact with. Then one night she was spotted by your uncle, here, in this very assembly room. He was older and charming and probably made Nicholas look gauche in comparison. He turned her silly head with his flattery and danced nearly every dance with her, despite her poor mother's attempts to put a stop to it. Of course, Mr. Campbell did it deliberately. Everyone knew that Nicholas had been sweet on her for months and was standing on the side-lines in a jealous rage. I'm sorry to say it, but your uncle was not a nice man."

Louisa groaned. "I realise that, Anna. It's just difficult to hear."

"Unfortunately, it didn't end there. Nicholas caused a scene and demanded that Mr. Campbell leave her alone, in front of the entire gathering. My poor mother nearly died of mortification. Your uncle laughed at him and bragged. You can probably guess the kind of thing. The ball ended with the two having to be restrained and the whole of Newton was buzzing with the scandal for months. Geneviève added to Nick's misery by refusing to see him. He locked himself up in his room for days, drinking. When one morning at breakfast it was discovered he had left the house at dawn, there was consternation. My father knew, without question, where he had gone. And as it turned out he was right: he had gone to Bowes to confront your uncle."

"Oh no!" Eleanor exclaimed, her hand flying to her mouth.

"It didn't end well, as I'm sure you can guess. There was a blazing row and the outcome of it was that Mr. Campbell shot Nicholas in the leg, later claiming that he had caught him trespassing and mistook him for a poacher. It was one man's word against another's. Nicholas was found by one of the grooms on the road home. Luckily for him, the wound was relatively clean as the bullet passed straight through. He was left with a very slight limp – you may have noticed he often carries a cane? Father had it put about that he had had a riding accident. I can't imagine many people swallowed that. He has the best seat in the county. It was all hushed up, of course, but after that it was like war had been declared with claim and counter-claim in the courts for years. So you see, Nicholas had good reason to dislike your uncle."

"Perhaps he had. But my uncle is dead, Anna. Why must he continue this ridiculous feud with us?"

"I believe getting Bowes back symbolises victory over your uncle and probably Geneviève, to some degree. She was ruined, of course, and ended up marrying a farmer from Maryport a year later," she said. "I don't think Mrs. Lambert ever recovered, poor soul, and my mother made a conscious effort to befriend her."

Louisa let out a slow breath. "Thank you for telling us. His animosity does make a little more sense."

Anna looked at her sympathetically. "You see, he is not used to being denied what he wants. In business he has quite a fearsome reputation, Robert tells me." Anna fidgeted with her gloves for a moment. "Nicholas doesn't know that I know. As it happened, my governess was besotted with him and passed on all the gossip from the servants' hall to me; every last gory detail."

"Your parents must have been horrified. I'm not surprised that they tried to keep it quiet. I am only amazed that Uncle Jack didn't broadcast it to the world," Louisa said.

"I think your uncle always had a reason for everything he did or didn't do. He kept people at arm's length, which didn't go down well in our small community. Father always suspected he was up to no good and Nicholas can wax eloquent on that topic, as you know. No matter how much he wanted to convict him, the police could never find enough evidence, I understand. When your uncle died, we all thought that would be the end of it."

"And we have walked blindly into all of this."

"If only someone could have warned you. Still, I hope you decide to stay at Bowes," Anna said. "I value your friendships highly." She turned to Louisa. "I think you are most brave to stand up to Nicholas."

"Brave or foolish – I'm not sure. This cannot end well."

"Give it time, Louisa. My brother will eventually accept that he cannot change the situation."

"I admire your optimism," Louisa said, shaking her head, "but I cannot share it."

Louisa sat brushing out her hair at Eleanor's dressing table. It was almost midnight. "It changes nothing," she said irritably.

"Yes, I agree, but it does explain why he hates us so much," Eleanor replied wearily. She climbed into bed with a sigh and pulled up the covers.

Louisa looked at her sister in the mirror. "You don't feel sorry for him, do you? I might have known that affecting story would resonate with you. You know whatever happened all those years ago, and no matter what Uncle Jack did or didn't do, it doesn't excuse Maxwell's treatment of us. I wish I were a man and could deal with him on an equal basis. He thinks because we are the weaker sex he can get away with anything."

"I'm too tired to think about it any more, Louisa," Eleanor said.

"Do you feel all right?" She turned and looked at her anxiously.

"Yes, just exhausted."

"I'm sorry; it's late. I'll leave you to get to sleep," she said, bestowing a kiss on her forehead.

Louisa closed over Eleanor's door and made her way down the landing to her own room. She quickly pulled off her wrap and shivered as she slid between the sheets. But her mind was racing and she knew that sleep would not come easily. She lay in the darkness staring up at the flickering shadows made by the fire on the ceiling above her. She was still bothered by the intensity of her response to Maxwell earlier in the evening. All he had done was say hello, so why had she reacted with such hostility? If she was honest, she had provoked him by mentioning the Fenians in the first place.

She squeezed her eyes shut and took a deep breath. This was silly. She had dealt with far more intimidating characters over the years. Debt collectors, in particular, had been some of the nastiest men she had ever known. There had been confrontations with landlords, haggling with pawnbrokers and pleading with shopkeepers. All these experiences had left their mark, formed part of who she was and, she liked to think, had made her resilient. But this man – he was different somehow. He was getting under her skin.

Chapter Nine

The Saturday after Christmas was a beautiful, though cold day. Anxious to take advantage of the rare dry conditions, Nicholas breakfasted early, and gave orders for his horse to be saddled. He headed out along the cliff road along the perimeter of Bowes Farm. A strong breeze was blowing in off the sea and it wasn't long before his face was stinging with the cold. The chill and salty air caught in his throat as he galloped over the frost-hardened ground but he enjoyed the exhilaration; a few hours release from the tension of the past few weeks.

By the time he was making his way home, he was feeling more at peace with the world. Just at the turn inland at Bowes Head, he chanced to look down towards the beach, and saw the solitary figure of a woman walking along the water's edge. She stooped to pick up something from the sand and then stood very still, looking out across the sea towards the west. As he watched, a sudden gust of wind caught her straw hat and sent it tumbling up the beach. She turned with an exclamation and watched the hat dance its way towards the dunes.

All of a sudden, a shaggy black dog charged down the beach and grabbed the hat. By now Nicholas had recognised Louisa, and he watched with interest as she slowly approached the dog, speaking to it in a low calming voice, trying to coax it to surrender the hat. The dog eventually obliged by dropping it from its mouth and sat panting, its tail swishing through the dry sand. She suddenly made a grab for the hat but wasn't quick enough. The dog was off again, thrilled with this new game, and the ribbon of the hat trailed behind, as it charged up the path from the beach. Nicholas dismounted, and as the dog reached the road, he commanded it to stop. The dog, recognising a voice of authority, skidded to a halt, dropped the hat and cocked its head to one side, the picture of wide-eyed innocence. He ordered the dog to sit and slowly approached it, just as Louisa gained the road. She started to laugh, much to his irritation. He would have expected her to be highly embarrassed to see him after her unladylike outburst at the carol concert.

"I was trying to help, Miss Campbell," he said. "Is this your animal?"

"No, no. We haven't been formally introduced yet," she replied, on a choke of laughter. The wind had picked up and the roar of the waves, crashing on to the beach below, was almost deafening. Without the protection of her hat, she was struggling to contain the thick coils of her hair, which were coming loose from their pins. With a gesture of impatience, she gave up. He felt a strong surge of attraction and had to swallow hard. There was something very alluring about her this morning, with her hair down and her cheeks glowing. He dragged his attention back to the dog and took a step towards it. The dog growled even louder, showing its teeth, before crouching down as if to launch an attack. He stopped in his tracks, reluctant to test just how sharp those teeth were. "This animal has no manners," he said.

"It would appear not," she responded. But he could tell she saw the irony in his comment by the quivering of her lip, as she slowly bent down and tentatively rubbed the dog's head. The dog immediately reacted by rolling over on its back. "Oh, you want to be friends, do you?" She stroked the dog's chest. Delighted with the attention, the dog made no objection to her retrieving her battered hat with her free hand. "What kind of dog is he, do you think?" she asked.

"I doubt anyone could tell you that," he answered, eyeing the dog disparagingly. "He's no breed I recognise. I wouldn't encourage him, Miss Campbell. He could be a sheep-worrier."

"Do you think so? But he looks so innocent."

"They are always the worst kind, in my experience," he drawled. He knew she would probably react to that. But to his surprise, she didn't, although she did throw him a curious glance. He wondered if it was restraint or apathy on her part. She was proving a difficult character to read. Her behaviour at the carol concert had flummoxed him. He had a notion that she had acted out of character. If he had that kind of power over her, perhaps Bowes wasn't a lost cause after all.

"No doubt he will go home now his entertainment with my hat is over," she said, straightening up.

"Is it ruined?" he asked. He knew by the look on her face that she had already lost her heart to the ball of fluff, no matter what damage he had inflicted on her hat.

"It's an old hat of my mother's and it needed new ribbon anyway," she sighed, checking it over. "Oh dear, there is a hole here," she said, poking her finger through a gap in the straw and throwing an aggrieved look at the culprit. "Go home," she commanded in a stern tone, but the dog just panted and wagged his tail, as if he doubted she meant it. She gave an exasperated sigh. "Have you seen him before? Do you know where he lives or who he belongs to?"

"No, he may have wandered up here from Newton. Do you want me to get rid of him?" he asked, reaching for the whip which was tucked under his saddle.

"No, no, please don't. I'm sure he's harmless."

"As you wish." He shrugged, but instead of mounting the horse, he retrieved the reins and fell into step with her as she turned up the road towards her home. She looked surprised but didn't comment. The canine shadow followed them at a safe distance.

The roar of the waves started to wane as they moved away from the sea, but she seemed determined not to speak. He desperately tried to think of something to say, wishing to prolong the encounter. "Do you often walk down on the beach?" he asked.

"When I can. I have just escaped the sick room to get some

fresh air. My sister is unwell at the moment," she said. Then she tilted her head and looked at him suspiciously. "Don't tell me, Mr. Maxwell, you don't approve of my wandering about the beach on my own?" There was a definite challenge in her voice.

"On the contrary, Miss Campbell, I don't see any reason why you should not." She gave him a quizzical look as if she was searching for a hidden meaning. "It's part of your property, after all."

"Yes, yes, it is," she said and looked away.

They walked in silence for a few moments before she said, "I almost forgot: I was in Jamesons on Thursday. Mr. Jameson Senior asked me to pass on his regards, if I should see you."

He stood stock-still. "Hugh Jameson?"

"Yes," she said. "The solicitor – in Carlisle."

"I am aware of who he is," he snapped, then instantly regretted letting her see how the comment had unsettled him, even though he suspected she had said it deliberately to provoke him. He couldn't help speculating as to why she would be consulting the solicitors and mulled over this all the way to the entrance of Bowes. At the gate, he nodded briefly, and offered a curt 'Good Day'. He was aware that she stayed at the gateway, and he could hear her talking to the dog as he mounted his horse.

"Well, young man, what are we going to do with you?" she asked the dog. 'Come along then. Let's see if Mrs. Murphy has anything tasty for you to eat, though why I would reward such a badly behaved dog, I do not know."

He smiled to himself as he rode away. The brief encounter had given him a glimpse of Louisa's lively sense of humour. Intimidation was never going to work on such a strong character, who was undoubtedly intelligent, as well as resilient. Perhaps a charm offensive would be the way to break down her defences. Even if it didn't succeed, it would be fun to try.

Jenkins sat squirming in his chair. He had never seen Maxwell in such a temper. He had been summoned to Thorncroft at an ungodly hour by Maxwell's groom.

"So what exactly have you been doing all these weeks?" Maxwell barked at him. "So far your meagre reports have been full of nothing but social outings and shopping trips, hardly the kind of thing I am interested in. I am paying you to report to me when she meets subversives, not who she drinks tea with of an afternoon in Newton. Were my instructions not explicit enough?" Jenkins couldn't think of a suitable response and stayed silent. Maxwell continued. "For instance, were you aware that she took a trip to Carlisle and yet," he glanced scathingly at the report in his hand and shook it at him, "there is nothing about it in here? Now why is that?"

"I couldn't say," he replied, looking at the paper in Maxwell's hand, hoping for inspiration.

"She could have been meeting anyone."

"Well, I don't understand it, Mr. Maxwell. Are you sure she was there, at all?"

Maxwell ground out, "She told me herself."

"Ah." Jenkins's stomach plummeted. He was rightly caught out.

Maxwell had come around his desk and was now looming over him, his face flushed with anger. "Is that the best you can do? Perhaps you aren't up to this job, Jenkins. I'm sure I have provided sufficient funds for you to take a train to Carlisle, when the need arises. I don't believe I am getting value for my money."

"Now, sir, I can explain," he stalled, frantically trying to come up with an excuse. "You see, that must have been the day I had to visit my sister, awful sick she was, but it won't happen again, I assure you."

"I hope not, for your sake," Maxwell said. "From now on I want to know all her movements. Do you understand?" He nodded vigorously. "God damn it, I want to know what she has for breakfast and what she dreams about at night. Is that clear?"

"Yes, sir, very clear."

"Good – now get out of my sight."

Jenkins flew out of the door, leaving it swinging in his wake.

Nicholas sat down with a muttered curse and took up the

newspaper which had triggered his wrath early that morning. The headlines could not be ignored: *'Fenians Bomb Glasgow!'* was emblazed across the front page. The article laid out the details of a night of terror, in which the Fenian dynamiters had targeted three locations in Glasgow city centre. No one had been killed, but the attacks had led to widespread panic, coming hot on the heels of similar bombings in London and Liverpool.

It was too close to home. He knew that local Fenians had to be involved, at the very least providing the nitro-glycerine. The police had recently managed to stop it being imported from America by maintaining a presence at the ports. They knew that the bombers were being trained by Professor Mezzeroff in the Dynamite School in Brooklyn, which had been set up by the Fenian Brotherhood and the United Irishmen. These men were moving with impunity between America and Britain, but they needed local intelligence and locally made bombs to carry out the attacks.

Nicholas put the paper down in disgust. He would urge Sergeant Cox to redouble his efforts and put the local militia on alert. His eyes fell on Jenkins' report, now lying crumpled on his desk. Somehow he hoped Jenkins' surveillance would vindicate, not implicate, his neighbour with the laughing blue-green eyes.

At the breakfast table at Bowes Farm, Louisa was sifting leisurely through the post. The black hat-snatcher from the beach was curled up at her feet with his chin resting on her shoe. He was snoring contentedly. He had been an instant source of comfort and amusement to Eleanor, who had pleaded his case when she would have sent him off to the care of the stable boy. He had curled up on Eleanor's bed as if by divine right, and when she was well enough to get up, he was constantly at her side. When it became obvious that he was distracting Eleanor from her illness, she knew it was a fait accompli; he was now officially a Campbell family member and she christened him Max. Eleanor had spluttered her objection to the name, saying it was a direct insult to the Maxwells but Louisa thought it very fitting and laughingly told her not to be such a coward.

She looked up with relief when Eleanor came into the room, the first time she had been up for breakfast in almost a week. Max immediately abandoned her and scampered around Eleanor until she dutifully bent down and gave him a rub.

"You're spoiling him," she teased.

Eleanor smiled. "I can't help it. Just look at those big brown eyes!"

She shook her head. "And he knows how to use them to great effect."

Eleanor sat down and asked Róisín for tea and toast.

"Of course, Miss. Sure, it's grand to see you up and about again," Róisín said, with a wide smile.

"Thank you, Róisín. By the way, I have been meaning to ask you: do you happen to know where the miniature in the silver frame is? You know, the one that was on the mantelpiece in my room? I can't find it anywhere."

"No, Miss, I don't recall seeing it this long while."

"And you didn't move it when you were cleaning?"

"No. I dusted your room yesterday and it definitely wasn't there."

"No matter, I'm sure it will turn up," Eleanor said. "Is there something of particular interest, Louisa?"

She looked up from the note she was reading. "Sorry, Eleanor – yes, there is. John Whitby has written to say that I can start teaching this week, if I wish. Twelve men have expressed an interest. Isn't it wonderful? I do hope I can do a good job."

"You will be fine. Remember when you used to help me with my reading when I was little? Mama always said you were a great teacher."

"Yes, but she was being kind, and this will be very different. What if they don't like me or I don't understand their accents?"

"Why do you doubt yourself? You will be fine, and with Miss Whitby there, what could possibly go wrong?"

"I suppose I'm just nervous now that it's all settled," she answered, taking up the neatly folded newspaper. "Are you sure you do not mind my disappearing off to do this?"

"Of course not," Eleanor replied. "I'm actually rather proud of you, and it's only one evening a week."

She smiled her thanks and unfolded the newspaper. This was her favourite part of the day. It was such a luxury to get to read a paper on the day it was printed as opposed to days later. But her comfort was soon challenged by what she saw on the front page. "Oh no!" she exclaimed as she read the article about Glasgow.

"What is it?" Eleanor asked.

"Look." She passed the paper over to her, having read the first part of the article.

"Good gracious!" Eleanor said. "You don't think anything like that could happen in Newton?"

"I honestly don't know. These men are so fanatical. They just want to create chaos everywhere. It is so misguided. The government will never give in to them. I think it will have the opposite effect and make them more determined to resist Irish independence," she said.

"Yes, but some of the grievances are just. Even I know that, Louisa."

"It's the means I object to, rather than the cause. Nothing justifies harming innocent people."

"Of course not. It's just that I can see how the seeds of discontent have been sown over time. Our own family is hardly blameless, if you think about it."

"That's all too true," she replied. Their Campbell ancestors had arrived in Ireland with Cromwell.

"Isn't it ironic? We are of a despised class of people in the eyes of the native Catholic Irish, and we come to England to find we are treated with suspicion because we are Irish born, despite our ancestry."

"I never even considered any of this before we moved here. I have been remiss. I am beginning to think that we will never be accepted," she said forlornly.

"Don't judge everyone by Nicholas Maxwell. Others have welcomed us quite readily."

"Yes," she replied, then gestured to the paper, "but this will colour everyone's perception of us – of anyone Irish – and a certain gentleman will be gratified to have his prejudice substantiated."

O'Connor was upset. His meeting with the boss had not gone well. As he walked along in the darkness towards his cottage, he mulled over the debriefing. The news from Glasgow was awful. How those idiots had managed to get caught was beyond anything. Bravado and carelessness: to leave a trail for the police was unthinkable, but that was exactly what they had done. The police had swooped down on their lodgings at the crack of dawn, and hauled them off to Maryhill Barracks.

As if it couldn't have been any worse, one of them had turned Queen's evidence and was going to put everything in jeopardy. The only thing that might save them was that the informer was based in Carlisle and didn't know anything about the Newton cell, nor could he identify the boss. Lord, he had never seen him so mad and he couldn't really blame him. Hadn't he given up so much for the cause? Everything, in fact. Still if they laid low for a while they might survive to fight another day. The boss was leaving tomorrow to return to New York to consult with the leaders of the Clan. He had to admit that he felt a little exposed. If the police started sniffing around Bowes, he would have to make a run for it. He knew that Maxwell was only waiting for an excuse to pounce. But he was jaded. The pressure of the last few weeks was starting to make him feel unwell.

He entered his cottage and wearily removed his overcoat. Lighting the oil lamp, he instantly cheered up at the sight of his dinner, waiting for him on the table. Lizzie Murphy never forgot him of an evening and Róisín would have delivered it. He was a lucky man to have both of them thinking of his needs. He lifted the cover and sniffed the air with appreciation. His favourite – lamb stew. With the fire lit, he sat down to enjoy his meal, and looked forward to his evening dram with a lightened heart.

Later, settled before the fire with a glass in his hand, his thoughts returned to more mundane matters. Tomorrow he was due to show Miss Campbell around part of the estate. He had stalled with every excuse he could come up with and the notorious Cumberland weather had obligingly given him a credible reason, but the woman was determined. The boss said he had to keep her sweet, if possible, so he would have to make the best of it.

Moodily, he kicked out his feet to the hearth as he recalled their conversation the previous day. Lord preserve him from bossy women. It was a bit much to take, even if she thought she was in charge. She might be a pretty lass, but her tongue and brain were far too sharp for his liking. He topped up his glass and held it up to admire the amber liquid in the firelight. And what was the *scéal* with the younger one? She always looked half-dead to him and he felt nervous to be near her. Róisín said she was 'delicate', whatever that was supposed to mean. Women bandied that word around so much it was almost meaningless. Her pasty face reminded him of the rookeries in London, where they had once lived, where every second family had someone with TB.

The clock struck ten, and with a sleepy sigh he headed off to bed, half hoping the morning would bring a pea-souper or heavy rain. Nothing short of that would stop Miss Louisa Campbell and her blasted plans

Chapter Ten

Louisa was standing in the middle of the Bowes stable-yard regarding the horses with profound misgivings. Just the thought of today's ride had affected her ability to sleep, and not even the sight of the lovely new riding habit hanging in her wardrobe had calmed her nerves. Eleanor and Róisín's admiring comments at breakfast had fallen on deaf ears. All she could think about was how high that saddle was and how large those teeth and hooves were.

"Come along, Miss Campbell, the horses will get cold if we don't head out now," O'Connor said.

She pushed her fear down as best she could and threw him a speculative look. "I will need your assistance. This will be my first time on a horse."

"Aye, Miss, I know, but sure, haven't you already mastered driving the gig?" he answered. She suspected he was laughing at her.

"Yes, but I think this is more challenging." She took a few steps towards the horse. The bay tossed her head, which suggested far too much spirit to Louisa's overwrought senses.

"I assume you know how to position yourself in the saddle once you're up?" he asked.

"I do, but can you help me mount?" she asked meekly, not taking her eye off the horse for one second.

He stepped up beside the bay and cupped his hands so that he could toss her up. "Now, Miss, put your feet in the stirrups like so and you must hold the reins lightly and evenly so that you don't hurt her mouth. Use your whip on the right side so she knows when you want to turn right. Don't worry, she is used to the sidesaddle."

She picked up the reins with hands that were a little unsteady, but she felt secure in the saddle, which had been one of her main worries. "What is her name?"

"Daisy," he replied disparagingly as he quickly mounted his own horse and headed towards the rear of the stable-yard without a backwards glance.

She nodded to the groom to release the horse. With a silent prayer and a displeased look directed at the steward's rapidly retreating back, she told Daisy to 'walk on'. To her amazement, the horse happily ambled after the other horse without any other encouragement.

Once she got used to the rhythm of the horse's gait, she slowly began to relax and enjoy the new experience. As they moved away from the coast, the landscape changed and became more and more agreeable, with neatly marked fields stretching out into the distance, under a winter blanket. Through a gap in the trees, she could make out the fells – dark moody shadows topped with white, against the steel grey sky to the east. The path between the stone-walled fields widened suddenly, and the steward waited for her to catch up. They continued on side by side for a while.

"You are doing very well, Miss," he said.

She beamed back at his compliment, feeling rather proud of herself. "It's not as difficult as I thought it would be."

"Well, we will keep to a walking pace today as you are not used to it, I'm thinking."

She nodded her agreement and was soon totally absorbed in the landscape: her land. They were no longer nomads wandering through the bleak terrain of Dublin lodging houses. No one could ask them to move on, though a certain person at Thorncroft might wish it.

"Which way are we heading now?" she asked, as they came towards a kind of crossroads. A large tree stood like a sentinel, its ancient crown scrambling heavenwards, its grey trunk ridged and pitted with age. It was beautiful in a strange and almost mystical way. She noted it as a useful landmark for when she would explore on her own.

"We will take this path and go east to the boundary with Thorncroft. We can then follow the river valley north and back down again along the coast road."

Scattered amongst the fields were tenant cottages. Some appeared to be well maintained while others looked deserted. She questioned O'Connor about this.

"We have lost a few of our tenants over the years. There is better money working in the mines or the mills up in Carlisle. Farming is a precarious business and some want the security of a regular wage."

"When someone leaves, do we offer the lease to our tenants or try to get new tenants in?"

"Generally our own tenants are happy to take them on and expand. With increased use of machinery it makes sense; the smaller holdings are becoming more and more unprofitable."

"I see," she replied. "I understand that is a huge problem back in Ireland, where the farms have been sublet to a ridiculous degree." The Land War in Ireland was well documented in the newspapers and was the main topic of conversation for anyone Irish. He nodded vigorously.

"But I thought that farm yields were down everywhere of late. Are we in danger of losing more of our tenants?" she asked.

O'Connor gave her a sharp look. "I hope not, Miss," he replied. He cleared his throat. "Róisín tells me that you are going a-teaching in Newton. Are you sure that's wise?"

"Why do you ask?" she inquired, amused at how quickly the news had spread.

"Those men are uneducated and are a rough lot. A single lady shouldn't really be mixing with the likes of them."

"Oh come, O'Connor, it's not as if I will be alone with them. Miss Whitby will be there as well, and the Rector will be close by. I'd like to do something meaningful with my spare time."

"Aye, well I hope you don't live to regret it," he said.

Fifteen minutes later, they had reached the Bowes River. Louisa had heard the roar of the water before it came into view, as the recent rain and snow had swelled it to a torrent. Flocks of sheep grazed on either side, and sturdy fences on both banks ensured that the animals didn't slip into the water, and get swept away.

"Do we farm the sheep for meat or wool?" she asked.

"Both, as it happens. The Herdwick's meat has a rather strong taste, but is popular around here. The wool is very coarse and is used only to make carpets. We have an agent in Carlisle who handles it for us."

"And across the river – are those ours as well?"

"No, those sheep belong to Thorncroft. The river here is the boundary. We have had problems in the past. That's why the fences had to be built."

She absorbed this without surprise.

"When will the lambs arrive?" she asked as they turned northwards.

"Not 'til April. You'll know the Herdys – the lambs are born pure black."

"Really? But I don't see any black sheep here. Do they lighten in colour as they get older?"

"Aye, they do gradually. One of nature's little mysteries that."

They rode on in silence. She began to appreciate why the Maxwell family might have felt aggrieved to lose her property. The Thorncroft land, although more extensive, led to the foothills of the fells and was probably not as fertile.

Around a bend in the path they came to a very isolated but beautiful spot. A small deserted cottage stood on a slight incline. Its once whitewashed walls were now grubby with neglect and the red paint was peeling off the door. The small garden around it was overgrown, but it was in the most magnificent location, with the river running along the bottom of the garden and the vista of the fells off in the distance. It was sheltered by a grove of ancient trees, looking quite stark without their leaves, leaning towards the little house as if to protect it with their twisted branches. The snow-laden boughs groaned slightly in the wind.

"What a shame no one lives here. It's such a scenic spot," she exclaimed, as she reined in Daisy.

"It's been deserted for years, Miss. Old Cassidy's place. No one wants it, you see. Too far out." The steward's eyes darted about anxiously. "We need to keep moving now. We still have a way to go."

He spurred on his horse with urgency and she could only follow and wonder at his sudden insistence on speed. As much as she was enjoying the tour, she was already feeling saddle-sore, and knew that sitting down for the next few days would be an uncomfortable experience at best.

A few days later, Eleanor and Louisa were in Mrs. Lambert's best parlour drinking tea. Louisa was explaining to Mrs. Lambert about her new endeavour for the Rector.

Mrs. Lambert started to laugh. "So he finally found someone to help Clara! Good for you, Miss Campbell."

"That sounds rather ominous. Is there something I should know?"

"No, dear, it's just that he has been asking the local ladies for some time to get involved in the schooling of those men." She frowned and her tone hardened. "However, I'm not so sure it's a good idea. What possible use could they have for education? It may do more harm than good and lead to trouble. It will only give them ideas, you know." She paused. "But I'm sure your intentions are worthy, my dear, and it's very Christian of you to attempt it. I am a little concerned, though, and I would like to give you one small piece of advice." Louisa nodded her encouragement. "You must keep a proper distance."

Louisa smiled. "Do you think they will try to take advantage?"

"Aye, of course," was the response. "Trust me, a woman's reputation is a precious thing and once it's gone, it's gone forever. And you are a fine-looking young lady."

Louisa cast a glance at Eleanor, thinking of Mrs. Lambert's

daughter, Geneviève, and her fall from grace. "I will be with Miss Whitby but I promise I will be careful, and I will come and tell you all about it next week. My first lesson will be next Friday evening in the schoolhouse."

A few minutes later, Mrs. Lambert's maid came into the room and announced Mr. Maxwell. The mood in the room shifted immediately for Louisa. She had been dwelling on their encounter at the beach for some days. The more she had thought on it, the more convinced she became that he had been trying to be nice to her. Could it have been an attempt at an apology? After all, he could just as easily have ridden away and left her to deal with the animal on her own. But it didn't make sense and she could only view his change of tactic with suspicion. Now his very presence made her feel self-conscious and she resented it. Why he had this effect on her, she did not know. She decided to treat him with cool detachment.

"Nicholas, how good of you to call." Mrs. Lambert greeted him with a wide smile of welcome as he came across the room towards her.

"I'm sorry, I didn't realise you had visitors," he replied, before nodding solemnly to Louisa and Eleanor and taking a seat beside his hostess. "I was passing and wanted to leave something for you."

"Nicholas, I cannot eat half of what you leave with cook. You spoil me."

"Nonsense. Besides you do me a service. Robert shot more game at Christmas than my household could possibly eat."

"Well, it is much appreciated. Do have some tea. Miss Campbell, would you do the honours? Now do tell me all of your news. How is Anna?"

Louisa did as she asked and handed the steaming tea to him in silence.

"Thank you," he said, with a sardonic look in his eye as his hand brushed against hers. He then turned his attention back to Mrs. Lambert.

"Anna is fine, as always. She is visiting some friends in Carlisle, but I expect her back tomorrow. I'm sure she will descend upon you some day later this week and tell you all."

"How lovely for her! I look forward to hearing all about it. And Robert – is he still stationed in Newcastle?"

"Yes, for the moment. They are on high alert due to the recent Fenian activity," he said. Louisa immediately tensed up.

"Yes, indeed. What happened in Glasgow was very shocking – most dreadful. Do you think there will be trouble here?" Mrs. Lambert asked anxiously.

"I think it unlikely, but I have warned the authorities to be extra vigilant. Unfortunately, this area seems to be a breeding ground for Fenians."

Louisa was concentrating on the design on her teacup, but was well aware that he had glanced in her direction. She was sure that the comment was for her benefit and smouldered. Again, he was hinting that she had some involvement; that she had stepped into her uncle's supposed Fenian shoes. He had not been able to produce any evidence against Uncle Jack, but he was obviously quite happy to believe her capable of criminal behaviour, based purely on speculation and prejudice.

Mrs. Lambert and Nicholas chatted away for a few minutes and Louisa took the opportunity to observe him closely. Despite her dislike, she had to admit that he was the kind of man that turned heads. His confident manner made him hard to ignore, and as he leaned slightly forward, listening intently to Mrs. Lambert, she was struck by the warmth of his regard for the old lady. Obviously the past was well and truly put behind them. But perhaps it spoke more for Mrs. Lambert's ability to forgive than any great effort on his part. Somehow it was easier to paint him in the role of villain than not, in her present mood.

"Miss Eleanor, I hope that you are feeling better? I understand that you were unwell over Christmas," Nicholas asked, breaking into Louisa's less than kind thoughts. She was surprised that he had remembered her sister's illness.

"Yes, thank you, Mr. Maxwell, I am much better now," Eleanor said.

"You are lucky my dear. My daughter wrote me that they have influenza in Kendal," Mrs. Lambert said. "We had it here last year. Dreadful it was and poor Dr. Peterson was run off his feet."

"But there haven't been any cases this winter, so I do not think there is any need to worry about it," Louisa piped up anxiously on seeing Eleanor's look of dismay. It would be extremely serious if either of them were to catch influenza.

Nicholas looked at her, as if surprised by her intervention, and then returned his gaze to Eleanor. Louisa was annoyed. He probably thought Eleanor was one of those silly women who succumbed to every sniffle and cough. No one knew how disastrous even a simple cold could be to her sister.

"Hopefully we will be spared this winter," he commented drily, before setting down his cup and standing up. "I'm sorry I cannot stay longer today. I have court business to attend to."

"I understand." Mrs. Lambert said. "It was good of you to find time to visit me."

"My pleasure as always, Mrs. Lambert. Ladies," he acknowledged them unsmiling, bowed stiffly and was gone.

Louisa wondered if the brevity of his visit was due to their presence. Clearly he still had only negative feelings towards them, judging by his earlier pointed remark. But it rankled somehow, as though he had won the bout today without her even knowing it was happening. All this veiled innuendo was frustrating to her. She much preferred a good straightforward verbal tussle.

Mrs. Lambert settled back into her chair with a sigh. "Such a kind man. His mother used to visit me regularly and always so gracious and generous with her time. It is such a pity that there was so much trouble between your uncle and the Maxwells. Has the situation improved?"

Louisa shook her head. "No, Mr. Maxwell appears determined to keep it alive."

"It is so hard to understand – you being such lovely young ladies. I told Nicholas off about it, you know. He should have intervened that night. In deference to their dear mother, when I see any of them err, I feel it my duty to make them aware of it. But they always take it well and continue to treat me with kindness."

"I'm glad they do, but that is hardly an onerous task. You are always so welcoming and kind."

"Thank you, my dear." Mrs. Lambert twinkled back at her. "I do love to have visitors, you see. I cannot get about much, so I rely on my guests to be my eyes and ears and to bring me all the news. When the weather turns bad I do not even go to church and the poor Rector has to come here instead."

"Have you no family living locally?"

"No. Unfortunately my daughters are living some distance away. Sally lives in Kendal and visits me a couple of times a year, but it's hard for her. She has a young family to take care of. There is a family photograph on the cabinet over there – see?"

"What pretty children she has," Eleanor remarked. "Is your other daughter in Kendal, too?"

"No, Geneviève lives in Maryport. You pass through it on the way to Carlisle. Poor Geneviève. Her husband died two years ago and she has no children. I keep asking her to come and live here, but she does not like Newton and rarely comes back," she said, her tone subdued.

"I'm sorry. That must be hard for you," Eleanor said.

Mrs. Lambert mouthed 'yes', and appeared momentarily troubled before reaching across and clasping Louisa's hand. "Remember what I said about reputation, my dear young lady. Nothing is more important than that."

The following afternoon Nicholas received an unknown caller at Thorncroft. A tall and rather lanky young gentleman with glasses was shown in by his butler, and announced as Detective Inspector Fletcher of the Metropolitan Police. Nicholas thought he looked more like a university professor than a policeman, but knew from experience that looks could be deceptive. He was put in mind of a stick insect he had seen in a book; it had been all legs and sharp angles. The men shook hands and the Inspector sat down, refusing the offer of refreshment.

"I'm sure you are not all that surprised by my visit, sir," the

Inspector said with a wry smile. "My superior thought it would be a good idea for us to meet."

"Well I am glad to have the opportunity to speak to you. Recent events have caused great alarm locally. We have been aware of possible Fenian activity in the area for some years. I send reports to London whenever we come across any information in the courtroom or from local police sources."

"Yes, and we are very grateful. I'm sure you understand that our resources are stretched to the limit. We are taking all reports very seriously and I have read your correspondence with great interest. Your last letter was most informative."

"I cannot prove any of it as yet, I'm afraid. It has been very frustrating over the years. The late Mr. Campbell was a clever and devious man and his steward has proven equally slippery. It has been a game of chasing shadows."

"I don't doubt it. Time and again these men have proven to be highly organised, very clever and with exceptionally deep pockets. The American Irish are funding and training them, and we have only limited resources in comparison to the vast network they have here. But I am glad to be able to tell you that we have evidence to suggest that there was some connection between Glasgow and Newton."

"Indeed!" Nicholas exclaimed with delight. At last there was a ray of hope of catching these lunatics and breaking up their organisation, at least locally. He suspected that O'Connor was now running things since Campbell's death, but a niggling doubt about Louisa's role continued to exasperate him. Was she an active participant or an innocent dupe? She had certainly looked uncomfortable when they had touched on the topic in Mrs. Lambert's. Was that guilt? He hoped that Jenkins' investigations would bring clarity.

"A cache of dynamite was discovered in a barn just outside Carlisle. We had information from one of our informants that this was the source of the dynamite used in the Glasgow bombs. We had men watching the place for a few days and one of the men they arrested at the scene lives in Newton. A fisherman by the name of Cusack. A tenuous link perhaps, but promising. Unfortunately, the man won't talk."

"He is not known to me," Nicholas replied with disappointment.

"But you do appear to be on the right track," the Inspector said, pursing his lips against his steepled fingertips.

Nicholas nodded with satisfaction. "That is comforting to know, Inspector. I have employed a private agent to look into some matters for me here. There are some things that the local constabulary are incapable of doing without falling over their own feet. Forgive the criticism, but I do not have much faith in them."

The Inspector smiled. "No offence taken, I assure you. I have had many dealings with country policemen in my time. You need specialists for this kind of work. Shortly, we are hoping to set up a dedicated unit in London to look into Fenian activities."

"That is an excellent idea."

"It will succeed if we get the proper funding and manpower. It was mooted before but shot down by the politicians; but my superior informed me that it is to go ahead now, particularly after what happened in Glasgow. But this man of yours – is he up to the job?"

"I do have some concerns about him. He tends to be lazy, but he usually gets the results in the end. After the recent incident I have re-ignited the fire under him, so to speak."

"Well, if you hear anything of interest you can contact me in Carlisle. I am basing myself there for a few weeks to see if we can get to the bottom of things. Unfortunately, our friend who has turned Queen's evidence doesn't know much about the local networks, but the little weasel is very anxious to sell out his Carlisle co-conspirators."

"They do appear to attract a rather repellent lot," Nicholas remarked dryly.

"It will be a pleasure to put the lot of 'em behind bars for sure, sir. I'll bid you good day and hope to hear from you shortly."

Chapter Eleven

Twelve men. Twelve hefty-looking miners sitting at the children's desks. They looked so out of place and uncomfortable, their knees barely fitting under the table tops. There was evidence of faces and hands scrubbed clean, but still the tell-tale black under their fingernails. How different a world the schoolhouse must be to them, so used to the dark damp underworld of flickering shadows and perpetual coal dust.

Reverend Whitby had spoken first, of course, and had urged the men to take full advantage of the opportunity now being offered to them. Louisa stood nervously, waiting to be introduced. The men's faces were blank and with a coincidental twist of memory, she thought of all those 'empty vessels' Mr. Dickens had described in *Hard Times*. The blackboard behind her loomed ridiculously large. The thought of writing on that board made her hand shake and she tightened her grip on the sheaf of notes to disguise it. The enormity of what she was undertaking made her mouth go dry and her confidence ebb away. The Rector invited her to speak and she swallowed hard. Her voice echoed around the schoolroom, like an accusation of how unfit she was for her role.

John Whitby took his leave and suddenly she and Clara faced them alone. Thankfully, Clara was bristling with energy and soon she was handing out the small slates and pieces of chalk to the men. There were smiles and thank-yous in broad Cumberland accents and the apprehension that had been hanging in the air started to dissipate.

There were few times that Stephen Jenkins regretted his choice of career, but this was one of them. He was sitting on a damp wall in the field opposite the Newton Schoolhouse. He was fed-up. The cold was seeping slowly through the thin fabric of his trousers and his hands were numb. But the problem was that the life suited him – he had never been able to stick at anything else for long. He'd had a brief flirtation with mining and even Morrissey's mill up in Carlisle, but he always ran afoul of someone. Stupid rules and endless shifts did not suit a man of his talents and ambition. No, better to be your own boss. Sure, wasn't it grand: his office was in the Duck and Drake with all the advantages that provided. No questions asked and certainly none answered, and over the years he had set up a network of sources which provided all the information he needed, with little effort required on his part. Sometimes it was too easy and clients like Maxwell usually paid well and happily ignored his methods.

After months of tailing Miss Campbell, he had come to the conclusion that she was not involved in anything other than a rather pathetic and dull social life. He soon lost interest in the case, even though his client appeared convinced that she was up to no good. Jenkins put this down to some kind of warped obsession. You only had to look at the woman to realise she was far too open and friendly to be mixed up in that daft nonsense. Most days he didn't even bother keeping watch. But then his luck had changed last Friday, when he had spotted her by chance in Newton after dark as he had been en route to the Duck. His antennae had twitched and he could not believe his luck when he saw where she went.

The wall was a good vantage point as he could see the main door into the schoolhouse. In the shadow of the trees and dressed in dark clothes with his hat pulled down over his eyes, he would be visible only to the keenest observer. At least now he would have something worthwhile to report to Maxwell. He was afraid of him – and not just because he was a magistrate. That temper of his made him shiver.

Maxwell would be delighted when he got to hear about all of

this. Two weeks in a row, Miss Campbell had taken the gig to Newton, stabled the horse at the Rectory and gone into the schoolhouse. With fascination he had watched the men arrive, not quite believing his luck at discovering this. They appeared terribly eager to go inside. There was no standing around to chat. Of course, he recognised them. Most were his neighbours; young, strong and passionate men. Most of them worked in Maxwell's mines. Surely Maxwell would be more than grateful for this kind of information? So what were the Irish miners doing late in the evening at the schoolhouse? In spite of his own educational inadequacies, he could add up two plus two, if needed. Did these Fenians think they could hoodwink the likes of Stephen Jenkins? No, sir, they could not. It looked very much as if Maxwell's suspicions were well founded after all.

Newton Tea Rooms were alive with the hum of female chatter. They were happily ensconced at a small table and Louisa had been telling Anna about Nicholas's veiled accusations during the visit to Mrs. Lambert's.

"Oh no! I cannot believe for one minute that he actually believes you are involved in anything of that nature."

"Then why did he say what he did and in such a pointed way?"

"I don't know, my dear. Mind you, he has always had a mischievous streak and he is frightfully pig-headed." Anna shifted in her chair. "I can't believe he is still behaving so badly though."

"Don't worry about it, Anna. I do not hold you responsible for his behaviour. Now let's talk of pleasanter things: tell me about your trip to Carlisle."

Anna accepted the change of topic and spent some time recounting details of her visit to an old school friend. A trip to the theatre, a concert in the Assembly Rooms and a dinner party at her aunt's house were all examined with precision and humour.

Louisa had her back to the door, but noticed a sudden flash of distaste on her friend's face.

"Lord! You'll never guess who has just come in. Don't look around, whatever you do – it's Beatrice Morrissey," Anna hissed under her breath. Louisa had seen Miss Morrissey on previous visits to Newton since Christmas. She had been studiously ignored and was happy for it. But Beatrice was bound to want to acknowledge Anna.

"Is she coming over?" she asked.

"No. She has joined the Miss Kirkbrides. We are safe," Anna informed her. "She is such an awful bore, besides being so conceited. I really have no time for her any more."

"But are you not about to become a sister to her?" she said, and had to smile at the expression of pure horror that came into Anna's eyes.

"Good heavens! Is that what people are saying? I don't believe he has been near her since ... well, not to my knowledge at least. What have you heard? He has never declared himself while I was away? Surely he would have told me?"

Louisa was amused by the panic in her friend's voice. "I have heard nothing. I'm only teasing."

"That's downright cruel, Louisa! I've a good mind to ask her over now just to spite you."

She laughed and shook her head. "I beseech your forgiveness."

Anna pursed her lips. "I suppose you do have more reason to dislike her than I."

"Most definitely. Her attempt to discredit Eleanor and I did do some damage," she said. "I do wonder how your brother persuaded her to go on the attack."

"Oh it wouldn't have been difficult. Beatrice and her mother had been trying to ensnare Nicholas for years. She would do anything to please him. But I believe you are wrong to think she succeeded, and judging by his foul mood, he thinks the same. I have never seen him so moody. I have my head bitten off at least once a day," Anna said.

"I'm sorry to hear that, but hopefully he will accept the situation and we can put all this nonsense behind us. He must realise by now that I will not sell up."

"I'm not so sure. I have never seen him like this. Be on your guard. I will tell you something; I have had enough of his moods and the sooner I am married and out of Thorncroft the better."

"So you are going ahead with the wedding? That's wonderful. Have you set a date?"

"My birthday is in late May and we plan to marry in June. My Aunt Gwen – Lady Ashbury – has offered to host the wedding at Ashbury Lodge in the Lake District. Well, to be truthful, I dropped so many hints that she had to. I have always dreamed of having my wedding there. Wait until you see Buttermere. It is a magical place. Thorncroft cannot compare to it. Even Nicholas had to admit to that when I told him. I think he has finally accepted that we are going to marry and has been remarkably civil to John of late. I am so excited, Louisa. My head is full of plans and I have something very particular to ask of you. I was hoping that you would agree to be one of my bridesmaids."

She was surprised but delighted. "Thank you. I would be honoured."

Anna reached across and squeezed her hand in gratitude. "That is wonderful and John will be so pleased. He admires you greatly and when I told him that I was going to ask you, he said that I must persuade you at all costs."

"Has he told you about the classes?"

"No."

"Your betrothed has agreed to let me teach."

"To help Clara with the children?"

"Not quite. We are teaching some of the miners to read and write in the evenings after their shift. You may recall I asked him to find me something to do? It would appear that he has been looking for someone to help Clara to teach basic reading and writing to the working men for some time, without any success."

"Yes, I know. He cannot understand the general reluctance of the local ladies to get involved. In fairness, most of them are too nervous or their husbands or fathers object to them being 'imperilled' in such a way, or some such nonsense. Nicholas would not give his permission when I mooted it some time ago, though, if I recall, he just thought I was far too flighty, if you please."

"Mrs. Lambert wasn't very encouraging. She seemed to think I was endangering my reputation and inciting revolution. Do you think I should have refused? Will it be considered inappropriate because I am a single woman?"

"By some it will, particularly the older generation, but on balance I think the majority will laud your efforts."

Louisa sighed. "Perhaps it might be best if this is kept quiet."

"I will certainly not say anything if you do not wish it to be known, though I do believe that word will get out eventually. It is impossible to have any secrets in Newton. How has it been so far? I don't wish to discourage you, but I imagine it is rather challenging."

"That's why I am enjoying it so much. The men were initially reluctant to speak up, but by the end of last week's lesson that had all changed. They have an astonishing desire for learning. Your fiancée chose the pupils well. They are all young enough not to have been ground down by their jobs and can see the benefits of education. They are all much younger than I originally thought. I think working in the mines from a young age has that effect. Some of them look quite comical, sitting hunched over their slate, barely fitting behind the desks."

"Were you nervous?"

"Lord, yes. I was terrified the first night. I was sure I would make some terrible mistake or say the wrong thing. But Clara is wonderful and totally at her ease. I am learning so much from her."

"She has been teaching for years," Anna said. "She can be quite formidable, though. I have to admit she makes me quake sometimes. I'm not really sure she approves of me."

"I don't think you need worry that she won't accept you. After all, John chose you and she sets great store by his judgement. If you were a flibbertigibbet, she would dislike that for sure, but you are a sensible young woman."

"Why, Miss Campbell, I do believe you just gave me a compliment!"

From across the room came the jarring sound of Beatrice Morrissey's unique laugh, followed immediately by uncontrollable coughing. Louisa twisted around in her seat to see Beatrice doubled over, clutching at her throat. Her companions had jumped up, confused, and looking at each other in alarm but doing nothing to help their choking friend. Beatrice was turning a strange colour and desperately trying to catch her breath. In an instant, Louisa was at their table. She gave Beatrice a few good thumps on the back. The crumbs which had been lodged in Beatrice's throat popped out and she no longer had to fight for breath. One of the waitresses ran up with a glass of water, which Louisa, kneeling beside the heaving Beatrice, gently encouraged her to sip slowly.

"Well done, Louisa!" Anna exclaimed.

"Yes, Miss Campbell. How clever you are!" echoed the elder Miss Kirkbride, sitting back down, embarrassed.

"Are you all right?" Louisa asked Beatrice, who was still looking distraught, with a very high colour and tears streaming down her cheeks. She could only nod in response.

"Perhaps when Miss Morrissey has recovered a little, you could accompany her home, Miss Kirkbride?" she suggested, as she stood. With a meaningful look at Anna, she went back to her seat. Calm was now restored and the background hum of conversation gradually resumed. Even with her back to the room, Louisa was well aware that the topic was her good self, and wished she was miles away.

"That was dramatic," Anna remarked as soon as she sat down.

Louisa smiled ruefully. "I've just realised: I have neglected to take advantage of the proverbial gift-horse."

"You have?"

"Yes, indeed. I could have allowed your future sister-in-law meet her maker and secured my revenge in one fell swoop."

Anna bubbled with laughter. "I'm sure you will have my brother's undying gratitude that you spared her."

"That is a huge consolation, of course," she remarked, as she speared the last crumb of chocolate gateau with her fork.

An all-consuming gloom had settled over Nicholas as he sat immobile at his desk in the semi-darkness. He could still smell the faint unpleasant odour of Jenkins, who had just left the house. He had arrived just as dinner was over, saying he needed to speak to him urgently. With a feeling of foreboding, he had told his butler to show Jenkins to his study while he made his excuses to Anna.

Damnation! Yet he should have been prepared for this. Wasn't this the inevitable conclusion of hiring Jenkins in the first place? He stared down at the blotter, his mind idly tracing patterns from the ink drops, as if something so mundane could douse the burning rage that was fighting to be unleashed. If only it had been evidence against someone else – anyone – just not her. He sank his head in his hands and closed his eyes but that just made her image even stronger. In frustration, he cursed the fates that had dropped such a fascinating woman into his life; a woman he might have to send to the gallows. Could Jenkins have misconstrued what he saw? So much of this did not make any sense. What possible excuse could she have used for the Rector to let her use the schoolhouse for her clandestine gatherings?

A log settled in the fire with a crack. He got up and poured himself a drink, then stood motionless before the fire. A voice in his head was screaming, 'No, she is not guilty!', but Jenkins' report lay on his desk, its condemning words impossible to ignore. He wanted to burn it, to deny its existence, but that would negate everything he stood for, everything he was.

What was he to do? He knew what he should do, but a small part of him wanted to warn her – to give her a chance to escape. The thought of her standing in the dock before him was horrifying. She could face the noose if implicated in treason and murder. Slowly, he made his way back to the desk, glass in hand, and sat down to read the report again. Jenkins had carried out his duties well, for once. The report was clear, concise and very damning. Perhaps if he read it again he would find an anomaly – some glimmer of hope. But his eyes swam at the cold hard facts, and with the pit of his stomach cold and heavy with dread, he drank the brandy in one long swallow. The alcohol burned his throat but brought little relief. Feeling like an executioner, he took up his pen and began his letter to Detective Inspector Fletcher.

The police station in Newton had never been designed to hold so many men at one time. The resident police officers, all of whom were crammed behind the public desk, grumbled amongst themselves and Sergeant Cox was barely holding on to his temper. He didn't welcome interference in what he considered his town. But what could he do? The JP and that odd-looking Detective Inspector from London had demanded his co-operation. And then there was the matter of Fletcher's men, who seemed to be lounging in every vacant inch of his precious station, not to mention those that were sitting around out back in the stable-yard, smoking and drinking tea all afternoon. They were all carrying ugly-looking pistols as well and some were cleaning them in full view. Really, it was all too much. The greatest indignity, of course, was that young London fella taking over his office, without a by-your-leave. Now he and Maxwell were in there making plans.

When Maxwell had come to him two days earlier, he had been shocked to learn that nice Miss Campbell was involved in something illegal. He knew well the rumours that had surrounded her uncle, but she was such a pleasant young lady, always polite, besides being a treat for the eyes. These modern women – they would be the death of him. What was she thinking, getting involved in that Fenian malarkey, when her time would be better spent finding a husband?

How he longed for a cup of tea, not to mention the restorative drop of the hard stuff that he normally added to it. But he couldn't get near the kitchen without stepping over those good-for-nothing London boys, and he couldn't very well interrupt the council of war in his office to retrieve the whiskey from his desk. He suspected his blood pressure was rising steadily as the minutes dragged by.

"Sergeant." It was Maxwell calling him, and about bloody time, too. He made his way slowly through the public area towards the back of the station, where his office was situated.

"Take a seat, Sergeant," Fletcher said, waving to a rickety chair against the wall, the one Cox kept for interviewing the criminal classes. It was purposely low and very uncomfortable, part of his arsenal for intimidating those scoundrels he had to deal with on a daily basis.

Maxwell was leaning against the desk looking like he wanted to strangle someone. Cox felt sorry for whoever had displeased him. He knew only too well what that blistering tongue was like; he had heard Maxwell lambast many a defendant in court, and it was not something one would wish to bring down on oneself a second time.

"Now, Cox, we have come up with a plan for this evening and wanted to know what you think," Fletcher revealed, with an unflinching stare made more intense by the thickness of his glasses. Cox stiffened at his tone and wondered if he was he supposed to feel appeased by the sudden inclusion. But he didn't have the nerve to say what was on the tip of his tongue because Fletcher was a senior officer, even if he was from a different jurisdiction.

"Yes, sir, thank you," he replied miserably.

"From our information it would appear these meetings usually start around eight in the evening. As soon as they are all inside and their meeting underway, I will bring my men down and surround the place. At a signal from me, I want you to enter with your men and stop the meeting. Bring them all outside and we will escort the lot of them back here to the station for interrogation." He paused. "Any questions?"

Cox could feel his temper rising again. "No, sir."

Fletcher flicked a glance at Maxwell. "Right: you had better brief your men and have them ready." It was a dismissal. Cox left his office with his shoulders hunched.

"Was I clear enough?" Fletcher asked Nicholas, with a twist to his mouth that might have been a smirk.

"I think so, but I get the distinct impression he is not too happy about you being in charge."

"Of course not, but we cannot leave it to him. There is no room for error. These people normally live in the shadows. I can't quite believe our luck. For them to meet in such a public place is fortuitous, to say the least."

Nicholas straightened up and walked over to the window. He

stared out into the gathering dusk, troubled. Something didn't add up, but he could not be sure it wasn't just wishful thinking on his part. He hadn't slept much the night before and had spent an unproductive morning at his desk, staring blankly at letters and reports that his secretary put under his nose. Sleep deprivation did strange things to the mind.

"You are concerned?" Fletcher asked, as he cleaned his glasses slowly and methodically.

"Yes," Nicholas said with a grimace. "Very."

Fletcher gave him a long and penetrating look. "It is certainly unfortunate that this woman is your neighbour and your sister's friend, but you cannot allow any emotion to cloud your judgement. The reality is that there are many women in the Fenian ranks. My colleagues in Dublin could tell you hair-raising tales. The most innocent-looking women from well-to-do families as well. Look, sir, it's not as if we are acting without good reason. Jenkins' report was pretty damning."

A wave of fatigue swept over Nicholas. "I know and I suspected her from the very beginning, but I had begun to hope that I was mistaken." He rubbed at his tired eyes. "Can you assure me that she will be treated with respect? After all, she is innocent until proven guilty at a trial."

"I always follow the letter of the law," Fletcher replied stiffly.

Maxwell stared at him for a moment. "I don't doubt it."

Fletcher shifted in his seat and cleared his throat. "Well then, we will meet up again here at half-past seven, if that suits you?"

Maxwell nodded as he picked up his hat and coat. "I wish this day was over."

Fletcher just shrugged. "It will be soon enough and I cannot foresee any difficulties – unless they are armed of course, which could make things interesting."

"Good God, you don't think they could be, do you? We cannot have a shoot-out in the middle of Newton."

"We have to be prepared for anything. Desperate men are capable of drastic actions, especially if they feel cornered."

Nicholas felt ill. "You must assure me that there will be no unnecessary violence. I will not condone this operation without it, Fletcher."

"Sir, you misunderstand me. My men are well trained and will only use force if it is absolutely necessary," Fletcher said. "We have the advantage of surprise. They are hardly expecting us."

Nicholas was uneasy but could not find sufficient reason to withhold his support. "All right, do as you think best, Inspector, but please remember that there are civilians about."

"Of course, sir, but I think you will find that the public will give their support for any action that guarantees their safety. Everyone is worried about where these people will strike next."

"Be that as it may, I don't want bodies on the street."

"I have absolute confidence in my men, Mr. Maxwell." There was a hard edge to Fletcher's voice.

Nicholas had to be satisfied with that, and with a troubled mind, he made his way out to the stables. He had to pass Fletcher's men, but was reluctant to look at any of them. The sight of their guns made him very uncomfortable, to the point that he began to regret instigating any of what was to transpire. He left the station yard in a solemn mood, welcoming the cold blast of winter air that greeted him as he came out on to the street; it suited his mood perfectly.

Chapter Twelve

N ewton high society, like most others, tended to be populated
with ladies obsessed with the appearance of always doing or
saying the right thing, whilst in private they maligned many of their
acquaintances. Louisa knew this was the way of the world and
could laugh at it, so she was delighted to discover, as she became
further acquainted with Clara Whitby, a refreshing honesty and
integrity when dealing with people of any rank. At first she had
found her cool reserve a little intimidating. If someone were to
paint a portrait of how a typical spinster or stern governess would
look, then surely Miss Whitby was the living embodiment of such a
woman. Her angular features and cool grey eyes presented a severe
facade to the world, but Louisa had discovered that those same
eyes could exude great warmth in an instant when something
pleased her, and her deep affection for her brother was expressed
in subtle ways that the unobservant might miss.

Their teaching sessions together had been very enjoyable so far
and she had been fascinated to watch Clara's instinctive teaching
style. The men appeared to like the no-nonsense approach. Plain
speaking and clear instruction suited them. It was what they were
used to in the mines. Clara's years of experience with young
children had given her confidence and method, something she
could only dream of, so she gladly watched and learned as best she
could.

Clara had sent her a note inviting her to dine with them that
Friday evening before the lesson, so she had set out early from

Bowes. She dispensed with the services of the groom, who would only be hanging around bored at the Rectory, and drove herself to Newton in the gig. During the journey, she wondered how Clara felt about John's relationship with Anna Maxwell. Clara never mentioned it to her, but if they were to marry she could hardly stay in the Rectory playing second fiddle, where once she had had sole charge. Louisa could not imagine two more different women. It just could not work. There would be fireworks within days. She felt sorry for her. To be displaced at her age would be testing and she hoped that John and Anna would be sympathetic to her needs.

As she drove into the Rectory stables, the sky above was a steely grey and a few flurries of a snow began to swirl in the air. Disconcertingly, the Rectory groom gloomily predicted a blizzard before the night was out. She fervently hoped he was mistaken and hurried inside.

When she was shown in to the dining room, she discovered that it was to be just herself and Clara, as John had been called out to an elderly parishioner who was about to breathe his last. The two of them sat down to a simple meal.

"John was most anxious that I apologise for his absence but it could not be helped. Poor Mr. Knox has been wasting away for the last six months and it has been most distressing for his wife and family. It is a comfort to them that John can visit so he would not deny them. We received a note an hour ago to say that the end was very near. Unfortunately, he will have to administer The Last Rites this evening."

"Of course, I understand, and parish business must always come before anything else."

"I knew you would appreciate how important duty is to John, though he does not see it as a tiresome chore, you must understand. It is something he wishes to do wholeheartedly. He feels there is great value in bringing the comfort of the Lord to those who are going through such difficult times in their lives. When the time comes he will be there for Eleanor, too," Clara said with a sympathetic smile.

"Eleanor?"

"Yes. I believe she is most unwell."

She was dumbfounded. She had told no one of Eleanor's condition. "She is delicate certainly but ..."

Clara put down her knife and fork. "I am certain it is more than that. Come, Miss Campbell, let us be frank with each other. I know you are a woman of sense and hate prevarication as much as I do. It is obvious to me that your sister is seriously ill."

She exhaled slowly. It would be good to share the burden. "I must ask that what I tell you is treated as the strictest of confidences. I want her to have a normal life and not be regarded as an invalid." Clara nodded. "Eleanor *is* ill. I do not know how long she will live, but her heart is growing steadily weaker." The words came out in a rush, each one more painful than the last. "The deterioration is slow. A distance she could have walked a year ago with ease now brings on breathlessness and even piano practice sometimes has to be curtailed." Clara nodded and gestured for her to continue. "Now that our circumstances are more comfortable it highlights the more upsetting aspect of her illness, in that it is robbing the joy from her life. Most seventeen-year-olds live their lives in a whirl of activity. All of this is denied to her. The simple pleasure of riding a horse or dancing the night away at a ball could be fatal."

"Has it always been thus?" Clara asked.

"No. She contracted rheumatic fever a few years ago. An unlucky and fatal complication is that the disease can attack the heart. There is no cure."

"I am sorry, but I did wonder," Clara said. "Every time I see her it's as if something of her has faded away – some intrinsic essence of who she is. We lost a brother to consumption. It was a long, protracted illness that ate away at us all, and left us reeling when he finally passed. There were moments of hope that raised our spirits, but always it proved false. But John and I had each other. You are alone and very young to carry this all by yourself."

Louisa felt a lump in her throat and swallowed hard a few times to ease it. "I'm sorry to hear about your brother." She had to pause to compose herself. "I believe coping with this has made me stronger *and* we are close – far closer than I think we would be otherwise, because we are essentially very different people."

"But when the time comes – have you thought about that? If looking after her is the source of your strength, how will you cope? I don't mean to be cruel, but I believe the greatest trial you will face will be when you are alone."

"I try not to think about that. I could not function at all if I were to dwell on … I need to focus on each day as it comes," she said quietly. Clara was poking around in the darkest recesses of her mind; a place she was scared of; a place she avoided. To think of Eleanor's death was taboo, almost as if it would be tempting fate.

"But you must consider what you will do, my dear. You will need friends to lean on so that you can take comfort and gain your strength once more. You do not have family here to support you, so I hope you will consider me one of those you can rely on, when the time comes."

"That is very kind, Miss Whitby." She was overwhelmed and tears were not far away. She had vastly underestimated the woman who was sitting across from her; she was obviously a keen observer. Most people had accepted Eleanor's frailty at face value and thought no more about it.

Clara straightened in her seat, looking emotional herself. "You must call me Clara, please. I intend to call you Louisa from now on, whether you like it or not." Louisa knew it was the closest to humour that Clara could get and smiled in response. "Come now, eat up. The chicken is going cold and we have a class to prepare for."

Louisa and Clara made their way to the schoolhouse through driving snow. None of the men had arrived and, after lighting the lamps and setting a match to the fire, Clara set Louisa the task of writing up the first few letters of the alphabet on the blackboard, while she put the slates and chalks on the desks. Tonight they planned to test their students' vocabulary.

In spite of the bad weather, the men appeared on time, shaking off the snow from their coats and hats, and greeting each other cheerfully. Louisa watched as they took their places and wondered at their determination. The weather would have been the perfect excuse to stay at home by the fire, but every single one of them had made the effort, and was seated looking expectantly to the ladies to start.

"Welcome, gentlemen. Thank you for coming out on such a night. We are going to test your vocabulary again this evening. You will see that Miss Campbell has written up the letters you have learnt so far on the blackboard," Clara explained. "Starting with 'A', I am going to ask each of you to give me a word that you think begins with that letter. Now, I will start with you, Cormac. Can you give me a word that starts with 'A'?"

"'Anthracite', Miss Whitby." This was followed by guffaws of laughter.

"Very good, Mr. McGuinness – very apt." Clara responded with a repressive frown. "Perhaps you could write that up on the board, please, Miss Campbell?"

Louisa did so, trying not to smile.

"And Mr. Murphy, do you have anything to match the splendid answer of your colleague?" The sarcasm wasn't lost on Murphy who made a great show of scratching his head before shouting out, "Eh, 'ablutions', Miss Whitby."

"Well, we are all in high form tonight, it seems. Very good, Mr. Murphy. That will do, gentlemen, thank you." The quelling tone made the chuckles subside.

The lesson continued in a similar vein for a quarter of an hour with the men trying to outdo each other in verbal prowess. Louisa was surprised at how good their vocabulary actually was. The answers the previous week had been apple, boat and cat. She had a sneaking suspicion that they had anticipated the exercise and deliberately sought out the biggest words they could find. To quieten things down a little, Clara suggested that the men practise writing down the words from the blackboard and the two ladies withdrew to the top of the room.

"That was enlightening," Clara whispered with a twinkle in her eyes. She tapped her pocket and her face fell. "Oh dear, I appear to have forgotten my glasses. Will you excuse me momentarily, Louisa, I think I left them in the drawing room."

"Of course, Clara, take your time."

Clara wrapped her cloak tightly around her thin body and slipped out through the side door. This brought a blast of cold air and a flurry of snowflakes into the classroom. Louisa shivered. The drive home would not be pleasant and she was sorely tempted to ask Clara if she could stay overnight, but of course she could not. Eleanor would be very worried if she did not come home at the usual time. She threw a few logs on the fire and then began to stroll up and down between the desks, in the hope that if she kept moving, she would warm up. The only sound to be heard was the tapping of chalk on slate and the crackle of the fresh logs on the fire. The clock struck the half hour and she heard the door open behind her. She did not turn around as she assumed it was Clara returning, but she quickly realised something was amiss by the look of astonishment on the faces of the men before her. When she turned, she discovered the police sergeant and four of his men standing just inside the door.

Cox pulled himself up to his full height. "This political gathering is illegal and must cease immediately." A snigger of disbelief was heard from the back of the room.

Cox grew very red in the face and stepped further into the room. "You must all leave this building immediately and accompany us to the station."

She was torn between the desire to laugh and outrage at the ridiculousness of what he had just said. The men were looking at each other in bewilderment.

"Sergeant, there must be some kind of misunderstanding. This is a night school and these men are learning to read and write," she explained as calmly as she could. "We do not discuss politics here."

But Cox was having none of it. "You will cease what you are doing immediately and come outside," he almost yelled. "There are reinforcements outside and they are armed," he warned. Her pupils leapt up out of their seats protesting, but the policemen drew out their batons and spread out around the perimeter of the room.

"Sergeant, this is ridiculous," she said crossly. "We are doing nothing wrong here. This is an outrageous and an uncalled for intrusion."

Cox looked agitated, obviously not best pleased to have a woman question his authority in front of his men. "I have my orders. Out with the lot of ye!" he shouted, signalling to his men to round them up.

In exasperation, she turned to her pupils. "I am sorry, but it might be best if we do as he says, until I have a chance to sort this out." The men muttered and looked mutinous but began to edge towards the door.

"No time for that," Cox spat out, when a few of the men started to pull on their coats. "Outside now."

The snow had eased, but it was bitterly cold, and Louisa and her pupils were soon shivering as they stood outside the school. Cox ordered a few of his men back inside to search through the classroom for anything incriminating. She looked at him in disgust. She was beginning to suspect who was responsible for this farce. Dark shadows lurked in the gloom beyond the street lights, anonymous and threatening. There were disembodied voices all around them – Cox's reinforcements, she surmised. He stood before them, barring the way to the gate, a look of snug superiority on his face. Her students stood in a huddle around her as if to protect her. They looked baffled and she could only shrug in response to their whispered questions. Within a few minutes the policemen came back outside.

"Nothing, Sergeant," one of them said.

"You're sure?"

"Yes, sir."

"You see, Sergeant, you are mistaken. Now, can we go back inside please? It is rather cold out here," she said.

"I have my orders, Miss. You're all to come down to the station," Cox ordered.

She stepped forward and touched his arm to get his attention, to try and reason with him. Cox reacted abruptly and shoved her away. "Keep back, do you hear!"

Louisa stumbled but was prevented from falling by one of the miners reaching out to steady her. A deadly silence descended and she saw knowing looks being exchanged between the men. Then one of them pulled her gently back out of the way and before she knew what was happening a brawl had broken out. After that it became a blur, as the miners, took out their indignation on the outnumbered policemen. She soon realised that there was little point in trying to reason with anyone. Her best tactic was retreat. And she nearly succeeded.

From their vantage point across the road, Nicholas and Fletcher had been watching the proceedings with avid interest. Nicholas had been dismayed to see the way the suspects were herded out and had watched with growing horror as Louisa had tried to engage with the harassed-looking sergeant. When he saw her stumble back when Cox shoved her, he felt a restraining hand on his arm. He looked at Fletcher in a blaze of anger. "Let go of my arm."

"We cannot interfere, sir. Let Cox do his job." But as he uttered the words, the fight broke out in the schoolhouse garden. Nicholas angrily shook off Fletcher's hand and stepped forward towards the wall, anxious to see what was happening. The policemen were coming off the worst in the fistfight and Fletcher's men, who were still outside the wall, were drawing their pistols and looking to their commander for instruction. Fletcher drew out his own gun and fired into the air.

The sound of the gunshot reverberated around the school and the fight came to an abrupt halt. Then there was a shout of alarm from one of the miners. Louisa was lying immobile against the boundary wall. Without further thought, Nicholas vaulted over the wall and ran over to where she lay in the snow. His blood turned to ice when he saw the trickle of blood from her mouth.

Chapter Thirteen

L ouisa had not been seriously hurt. As she had tried to remove herself from the fray she had been tripped up, slipped on the icy ground and slammed against the boundary wall. The impact stunned her and she slithered down into the snow that had drifted against the wall. She heard the gunshot and braced herself with her eyes squeezed tightly shut.

After a few moments, she tentatively opened her eyes. Nicholas Maxwell swam into focus, mere inches from her, and the intensity of his concerned gaze made her catch her breath.

"Are you all right?" he asked. She blinked, trying to ward off the dark shadows at the edge of her vision. She was still too dazed to answer him. "Are you injured, Miss Campbell?"

To cover her confusion, she slowly shook her head. A streak of pain shot across her brow, making her grit her teeth and draw in a sharp breath. It felt as if someone was driving a nail through her skull, without any compassion whatsoever. He momentarily placed his hand on her shoulder and she found his touch extremely disconcerting. Realising that panic wasn't far away, she tried to calm her breathing.

Slowly the details of what had happened earlier came back to her. She could see, over his shoulder, that her pupils were being herded into the centre of the garden, surrounded by police who appeared to be brandishing pistols. She frowned and looked back at him. "What is going on and where is Clara?" she asked a little groggily, and tried to pull herself up into a better position. "Is she all right?" He took her arm as if to help her but she shook him off impatiently.

"She is outside on the road with the Rector. Please let me help you up," he said softly. She hesitated for a moment, but cold and the embarrassment of her position decided her and she grasped his outstretched hands. Slowly, he pulled her into a standing position, but no sooner was she upright than the world was not. A jab of pain shot through her head, making her wince and she passed out.

As she slipped down again, Nicholas grabbed hold of her and took her up in his arms.

Fletcher appeared at his side. "Is she injured?" he asked, frowning.

"I'm not sure. She just fainted. I found her against the wall."

"Did you check if she's armed?"

Nicholas looked at him in disgust. "No, I did not."

Fletcher grunted. "None of the others appear to be either – just as well. Right, she can't answer any questions in that state. We will take the rest of them to the station. Perhaps you could follow when she's well enough?"

Nicholas nodded impatiently and watched Fletcher and his men leave, the suspected Fenians marching down the road between them. A few bystanders had gathered at the school wall and were looking at him with curiosity. He pointedly turned his back and started towards the school building. At least he could get her out of the cold.

"Mr. Maxwell." It was Clara Whitby calling to him. She had just come around the corner from the side of the schoolhouse. She urged him to follow her into the Rectory. He followed as briskly as he could with the semiconscious Louisa in his arms.

"This way. You can put her down on the sofa in the drawing room," Clara said. "Lay her down there, Mr. Maxwell," she directed him brusquely, as he entered the room.

He followed her instruction and laid Louisa down as gently as he could, trying not to jolt her. She was deathly white. Clara slipped a cushion under her head and pushed back her hair which had come loose and was half covering her face.

"I don't believe she is seriously injured – she probably bit her lip when she hit the wall," Clara said, as she wiped the blood away with her handkerchief. Louisa muttered and twisted her head away.

"But she will be all right?"

"I hope so, but she is very chilled," Clara declared and started to rub Louisa's hands.

Nicholas stood by feeling helpless. "Is there anything I can do?"

Clara looked at him dubiously. "Yes, take over from me. I must fetch a blanket," she said, then hurried out of the room. He was left gazing down at Louisa, baffled by a strange mixture of emotions. He sat on the edge of the sofa and took her ice-cold hands in his and rubbed them gently. Her eyes fluttered open momentarily, but were unfocussed and soon closed again.

During the skirmish outside his overriding emotion had been fear. Fear that she had been hurt and that he was ultimately responsible. It didn't matter that she had been caught in what appeared to be a compromising situation. He did not want to believe her guilty, and he could delay her interrogation by Fletcher, but he could not protect her from the consequences of her foolish actions.

Clara came back into the room with a woollen blanket. He stood and Clara tucked it around Louisa. Then she went to build up the fire, using the poker with great enthusiasm. He began to feel slightly nervous.

"What is all this about, Mr. Maxwell?" Clara asked when she had straightened up. She was staring at him hard. He hadn't felt that wrong-footed since he was a little boy caught out in the stables by his father, when he should have been at his lessons.

"I was just about to ask the same," John Whitby declared as he strode into the room, looking extremely angry. His face fell when he saw Louisa unconscious on the sofa and turned to him with a look of outrage. "How has Miss Campbell been injured and why were all those armed policemen outside the school?"

"And I would like to know how you came to let a group of Fenians hold meetings in your schoolhouse," he answered, immediately on the defensive. "Did you not ascertain what they wanted it for? Surely you know that political gatherings are banned?"

The Rector stared at him, his colour rising. "You cannot be serious, Mr. Maxwell. That is the most preposterous thing I have ever heard. Miss Campbell and Clara are teaching the men to read and write and, let me add, it was I who organised it."

He felt the blood drain from his face. "*You* organised it?"

"Yes, Miss Campbell offered her services. She wanted to help me with some parish work and I accepted gladly."

"John, I think you should fetch the brandy. More than one of our guests is in need of it. Sit down, Mr. Maxwell," Clara said. He sat down feeling dazed.

Louisa began to stir again and opened her eyes. She pushed back the blanket and sat up, looking a little muddled.

"Welcome back to us, Louisa," Clara declared bracingly, sitting down beside her.

"What happened?" Louisa asked, rubbing at her temples.

"You fainted."

"I never faint," Louisa protested, but Clara just patted her hand.

John came back into the room, followed by the maid carrying a tray with a decanter and glasses. "Ah, Miss Campbell, I am very glad to see you are recovered. I don't normally approve," he held up the decanter, "but in the circumstances ..." He poured out several measures and handed them around. Louisa took a sip and grimaced.

Nicholas downed his in one swallow. To say his mind was in turmoil would be to underestimate the shock of John's revelation. One part of his brain was relieved to learn that Louisa was innocent; the other was stunned by the realisation of what he had done. Most of all he wanted to throttle a certain gentleman by the name of Jenkins. The unravelling of all of this with Fletcher, not to mention trying to explain himself to the woman sitting across from him, would take some resourcefulness on his part. He was relieved to see that she looked a little better. She was dishevelled, certainly, with her hair loose and her clothes marked, but she had some colour back in her cheeks and her eyes looked clear.

Whitby remained standing before Louisa, encouraging her to drink the brandy. She struggled with a few more mouthfuls and then put the glass down with a shake of her head. An awkward silence descended on the room. Whitby moved over to stand before the fireplace, rocking back and forth slightly on his heels, his brow deeply furrowed. He could tell that he was upset and angry and deep down he couldn't blame him.

Clara broke the silence. "Come along, Louisa. If you feel strong enough, let's go upstairs so you can tidy up."

Louisa was only too glad to escape the tension of the room and was content to let Clara lead the way. Clara linked her arm as they made their way up the stairs and when they reached the bedroom, she closed the door.

"I'm sorry Louisa. You should not have had to face that alone." Clara motioned for her to sit at the dressing-table. "Use what you need. There is water in the jug, over there, if you want it."

"Thank you, Clara," she replied, looking at the ghost in the mirror, a ghost with dirty smudges on its nose.

"You must have been frightened," Clara said.

"Not so much frightened as bewildered. I couldn't believe it. That stupid police sergeant would not listen to me and then when we were outside things went from bad to worse. I tried to reason with him."

"I can imagine how it was. Sergeant Cox is not renowned for his intelligence, and I believe he is considered a bit of a bully. When I tried to get back to the school I was blocked by those other men. They would not let me pass and one of them waved a gun in my face. I was so alarmed that I went to find John immediately. By the time we came back things had degenerated into a fracas. I was in time to see you slip and fall against the wall. How do you feel now?"

"I am sure I will be fine, but my head aches terribly." She felt her scalp with unsteady fingers. It was tender to the touch but she was able to brush out her hair and tie it back with a ribbon.

"I'm not surprised, my dear. You hit that wall with some force."

The maid knocked and came in with some fresh towels. The sound of raised voices drifted into the room from below through the open door. Clara rolled her eyes. "I don't know what good will come of arguing. What's done is done. That will be all, Agnes, thank you."

Louisa turned in the chair to regard her companion. "But I want an explanation. Somehow the police thought that we were holding political meetings."

"Mr. Maxwell said as much before you came to."

"So someone must have said something to the police. Someone was spying on us."

"That would appear to be the logical and rather distasteful conclusion."

"And of course *he* was predisposed to see anything about me in a prejudicial light. I am certain he is to blame for tonight's proceedings."

Clara pursed her lips. "I am not condoning what was done, but as a magistrate he has a duty to protect the interests of the people if he believes there is danger."

She frowned at her. This wasn't the time to be objective. Her legitimate anger needed feeding. "But a few simple enquiries would have avoided all of this. Whoever was doing the snooping wasn't particularly good at it. They appear to have jumped to conclusions about what we were doing in the schoolhouse without verifying the facts. Why did the police not ask the Rector about it?"

"Only the Lord knows, Louisa." Clara shook her head sadly.

"This is going to ruin everything. I was so enjoying the classes. I hope the men don't turn their backs on us after this."

"My dear girl, I imagine, if anything, it will make them more determined than ever. Wait till you see – we will have twice the number at next week's class!"

She laughed but winced and clutched her head as daggers of

pain danced behind her eyes and down her neck. "Mr. Maxwell must be very pleased with himself; he said he would ruin me in the eyes of Newton, and when this becomes common knowledge, he will have succeeded. There will be many only too happy to believe there was some substance to his stupid assertions."

"Nonsense! John will make sure that the correct version of events is told. Do not worry about it. If anything, people will see the funny side of it." Louisa sighed not quite convinced that there was any humour in the situation, but too tired to argue the point. Clara continued, "My concern is our pupils. The police have taken them all down to the station."

"Oh no!" she groaned. The night was a complete disaster. All of a sudden, she felt very weary and wished she was at home. "Clara, I'm going to leave now. I don't think I can take much more."

"You cannot drive yourself in this weather. You are not well enough. You should stay here tonight or at least let Dr. Peterson see you before you leave."

"No, Eleanor would be sick with worry. I'm late as it is. Thank you, but I will be fine. Please don't be concerned. I promise to take my time."

"The road may be impassable," Clara warned.

"If it is, I will come back."

Her hostess accepted this with a nod and they made their way downstairs. When they got to the bottom step Louisa hesitated, looking at the drawing room door with a frown.

"I do not trust myself to speak to that man. But please give my regards to your brother. I will slip out to the schoolhouse to fetch my things and I'll be on my way."

"Very well, as you wish," Clara replied, leading her down the hallway to the door. "I will send orders to the stable to ready the gig. Please be careful, my dear. The paths are slippery."

She made her way to the schoolhouse as quickly as her pounding head would allow. Thankfully, the police were gone. The grounds were eerily silent, all signs of recent activity obliterated by a fresh fall of snow. Inside the schoolhouse a small fire was still clinging to life in the grate but the oil lamps were out. A faint glow from the streetlight was sufficient for her to find her coat and bag. There was something soothing in the silent darkness, so she sat down at one of the desks to mentally prepare herself for the journey ahead. The confounded drum tattoo in her head would not ease, but she would have to pull herself together if she was to make it home. She rested her sore head in her hands.

After a few minutes she got wearily to her feet, but something caught her eye on the floor near the blackboard. It was a broken slate. Clara would be annoyed. School supplies were expensive. She retrieved it with a sigh and put it on the teacher's desk. She stood looking at the blackboard. The letters of the alphabet, which she had written up earlier in the evening, were still there, caught in the light from the streetlight. She smiled as she remembered the fun during the lesson. Perhaps they would be able to recapture that next week; if there *was* a next week. She picked up the cloth and rubbed out the words that had been the cause of so much laughter earlier in the evening.

As she dwelt on the evening's events, she became steadily angrier. How far would Maxwell go to get rid of them to acquire the farm? What if he planted evidence against her to make her look guilty? She suddenly felt very vulnerable and wondered if that was why her uncle had sought refuge in the law. Hopefully, morning would bring clarity and perhaps a plan to deal with whatever the outcome from tonight would be.

But just as she prepared to leave she heard footsteps in the passageway outside and a tall dark shape formed in the doorway. It was the last person she wanted to see: it was Maxwell.

"Miss Whitby says you intend going home. I have come to offer my assistance," Nicholas said quietly from the doorway.

"I do not require any help from you," she responded.

"I think it might be best. The road will be treacherous and you are not used to driving a gig in these weather conditions."

"You are the last ...."

"Yes, Miss Campbell, I fully appreciate that you are angry with me. I apologise for what happened earlier, but I would qualify it by saying that the evidence against you and those men was very strong." He stepped further into the room. "Political meetings of any kind have been banned for some time. A group of men meeting late at night suggested mal intent."

"And yet no one tried to verify that evidence? No one asked the Rector what was going on?" she asked. "Even Anna knew of the night school."

"She never spoke of it to me. I admit we erred, but there was no malicious intent on my part."

"I don't believe you. I think the truth of the matter, Mr. Maxwell, was that you were only too glad to have incriminating evidence against me and you couldn't wait to use it."

He gave a helpless gesture, and then asked her what she was doing back in the schoolhouse.

A humourless smile tugged at her lips. "Why, I am preparing next week's lesson." She went up to the board and picked up the chalk. "We master criminals believe our men must have the right vocabulary. It is vitally important. One cannot forge a proper campaign without good communication and intelligence gathering." She looked at him pityingly. "You know, you might learn something yourself – your own failures in that regard must be embarrassing." She turned back to the blackboard. "Now where was I? Oh yes – the letter 'A'. Any ideas Mr. Maxwell? No? I think perhaps 'army' – a nice short word and no ambiguity to it." Louisa wrote it down next to the 'A' on the board. "Now 'B' – always a difficult one … but you know I am feeling inspired tonight – how about 'bomb'?" She turned to look at him but could not read his expression in the semi-darkness as his back was to the window. "I will take your silence as approval. Hmmm, 'C' – a little ingenuity is required here, but I do believe we will allow ourselves some licence. After all, coming up with a Fenian-related vocabulary is not easy. 'Clan' as in 'Clan na Gael'? I know it's technically Gaelic, but who will quibble with that? And last of course, but by no means least, we have 'D'. Oh, there is a whole plethora of lovely words for 'D': devil, deception, devious …," she looked at him pointedly, "but none is quite right, is it?" She stood in mock contemplation for a few moments. "Of course – it will have to be this one. It wins hands down." She turned back to the board and began to write 'dynamite'. "There, I think that should do it. In fact, we may rename the school *Dynamite School* like our American compatriots – or would we need special permission for that from the local magistrate?"

Much to her annoyance, his mouth twitched suspiciously as if he was trying not to laugh. Just when she thought he would remain silent, he said, "If you have that out of your system I think we should attempt our journey, before the weather closes in."

She was stunned. He was mocking her. To her mind he was being deliberately provoking and she trembled with rage. "Do you really think I am going to ignore what happened tonight? This time your actions have put me and others in danger. My pupils have been forced down to the station and I can only imagine what is going on down there. This senseless feud that you insist on perpetrating has gone on long enough. You have no foundation for anything you have said or done to us. When will you be happy? What will it take for you to leave us alone?"

"I have already apologised," he answered stiffly.

"You amaze me! You really are, without doubt, the most arrogant, ruthless and prejudiced man I have ever had the misfortune to encounter. I no longer wonder that my uncle shot you. If I had a gun to hand I would gladly do the same."

He froze. "How do you know about that? No one knows about that. Who told you?"

Too late she remembered that she had been told in confidence, but she wasn't sorry. She was far too angry and had an insatiable urge to hurt him. "It hardly matters," she scoffed. "And I'm sure you more than deserved it."

He took a step towards her and she grew alarmed. She stepped back. "Keep your distance!" she cried out and, before she could stop herself, she had picked up the broken slate from the desk beside her and flung it at his head. His reflexes were good and he ducked in time for the slate to sail past his ear and smash into the desk behind him where it shattered into pieces. She stood transfixed, appalled at what she had done. Her temper drained away and along with it all of her energy. She covered her face with her hands, close to tears. Had she walked herself neatly into a trap? She had threatened and assaulted a magistrate. Surely he would have her arrested now?

Even in the dimness of the room Nicholas had seen her horrified expression before she hid her face. She started to sway slightly and before he even thought about it, he was holding her tightly. She stiffened momentarily and then the floodgates opened.

He held her while her body was wracked by silent sobbing. Her distress touched some long buried part of his heart. But he didn't want to trust the feeling that was swelling up inside of him. Bitter experience had taught him that no good could come of it. That path led to pain and crushing self-doubt. He didn't need the complications of a woman in his life and yet he wanted to protect her, this Irish vixen who had dominated his thoughts for months now. The irony of that was all too plain. Should he say comforting words or would that antagonise her further? He was floundering in uncertainty, and fighting an uncontrollable urge to kiss her senseless.

After several minutes she seemed to be struggling to regain control, and he reluctantly loosened his hold. She lifted her head from his shoulder, her breathing still uneven, but she would not look at him directly. He fished out a handkerchief from his pocket and handed it to her, denying the urge to dry her tears himself. His instinct told him that would not be welcome.

"Come," he said, picking up her coat from the chair and helping her put it on. "The gig is ready. We must leave now before the weather closes in."

She was shivering from cold and shock. He had never seen her look so vulnerable and he felt a complete blackguard. But there was nothing he could do but try to get her home. He led her out into the night and was relieved to see that the sky was clear. Hopefully they would make it to Bowes without snow driving into their faces. He was concerned, however, about the state of the roads. They would have to get home before the snow froze and became lethal and that wouldn't be long under a clear Cumberland sky. He knew from experience how treacherous the Bowes Road could be in winter. Most of the locals avoided it, taking the longer inland route. He was reluctant to do so, for it would take two hours using those back laneways. She was far too quiet for his liking, so he did not voice his fears, but led her gently towards the Rectory stables. Clara and John appeared from the house as he helped her up into the gig. Neither needed to voice their concern. It was all too evident on their faces.

"Put this around her," Clara said, handing him a blanket. "It will help to keep the cold out a little." He wrapped it around his silent companion and thanked Clara.

"Safe journey," Clara said anxiously.

"Be careful. If it's very bad, return here," John said.

"I will," he said as he urged the horse to move on. "Good night."

"Do you think they will make it?" Clara asked her brother as they made their way back into the warmth of the Rectory.

"If anyone can, it's Maxwell – through sheer bloody-mindedness."

"John!"

"Sorry, my dear, I apologise for swearing, but you know how stubborn the man is. If he has to carry Miss Campbell and the horse to get there, he will."

Clara laughed. "I do believe you are right."

Chapter Fourteen

There was only a crescent moon, but the carpet of snow gave off enough light for Nicholas to distinguish the Bowes Road easily enough. But that was where the pretty picture of a winter scene ended. The road was already slippery and in some places the drifts of snow were deep and treacherous. Added to this, the horse was stiff-legged from waiting in the Rectory stable-yard when he had gone to fetch Louisa. The gig had not been designed for winter travelling conditions and it took all of his skill to keep it from slipping into the ditch on either side of the road. The cold was starting to creep into his very bones but he was determined to get her home.

Much to his surprise, he was grappling with the realisation that what he had taken as mere physical attraction, and easily set aside, was something much deeper. He was convinced that his ill-fated blunder this evening, and his previous appalling behaviour, had destroyed any hope of her ever returning his feelings. But perhaps getting her safely to Bowes would be a small gesture that would go some way towards improving the situation. However, she sat huddled beside him, silent and barely moving, the living embodiment of outraged sensibility.

When they reached the bottom of the incline that led up to the headland, he reined in the horse. This was always the most treacherous stretch of road when conditions were bad. The steep drop on one side, coupled with the gradient of the slope, gave him pause for thought. Added to the problem was the fact that the horse was now exhausted. There was only one possible solution. Louisa shifted in her seat beside him and from within the folds of the blanket two dark questioning eyes peered out at him.

"It is too slippery and too steep for the horse to pull the gig," he explained. "I'm sorry, we will have to walk this last stretch."

"Very well. I understand." She pulled herself free of the blanket and climbed down from the gig before he could assist her.

They each took hold of one side of the bridle and began their slow ascent. They reached the top without incident and continued to walk the short distance to the entrance of Bowes Farm. He kept a firm grip on the bridle and continued down the carriageway. He wasn't going to abandon her at the gate.

A few minutes later, they stood outside the dark and deserted-looking farmhouse.

"It looks as though they assumed you were staying in Newton," he said, taking in the closed shutters.

"Yes," she replied. "They must all be in bed by now."

"I'll look after the horse. See if you can rouse someone to let you in," he said, leading the horse and gig off towards the stables without waiting for a reply.

Louisa noticed that he was limping slightly and felt horribly guilty. She already deeply regretted her insistence on going home now that she realised that her friends' warnings about the road conditions were all too true. She stood momentarily unsure at the front door, reluctant to bang on it and scare the women needlessly. But she did not want to remain outside in the plummeting temperatures either, so she made her way around the back of the house towards the kitchens. As luck had it, the back door had been left unlocked for her and she was greeted by the warm fragrant air of Mrs. Murphy's domain. She lit the lamp that stood on the scrubbed table in the centre of the kitchen. As the range was still hot she put a kettle of water on to boil and searched out the tea caddy.

While she waited, she stood with her hands outstretched to the range. Sensation slowly began to return to her icy fingers. Her thumping headache had lifted a little during the drive home; the cold air had acted like a balm. Her embarrassment, however, was very much still there. What must he think of her? She was still a little fearful that an unpleasant fate awaited her at his hands. After all, she had assaulted him. Shaken, she could not believe how her self-control had deserted her. She closed her eyes, feeling unsure of herself. She should still be very angry with him but instead she desperately wanted his understanding. She would have to assess how he behaved towards her when he came back in from the stables and consider how best to respond. But her wretched mind wasn't going to give her any peace. She found herself dwelling on how it had felt in his embrace and her face burned.

Ten minutes crawled by and there was no sign of him, so she put on her coat and went back outside to the stables, to see if he needed help. The gig was out in the yard where he had unhooked it. From the stables, she could hear him talking gently to the horse, trying to persuade the exhausted animal to go into a stall. She followed the sound of his voice and stood in the doorway watching him as he threw a blanket over the horse's back.

"He should be all right. I've given him a quick rub down but get your groom to check him over in the morning," he said when he saw her.

"I will, thank you. Come inside. I have made tea." He raised a quizzical brow, but whether it was surprise that she had invited him into the house, or the fact that she could make tea, she wasn't quite sure and didn't wait to ask.

Once back inside, she went about her task, while Nicholas removed his overcoat and sat down with a sigh. "I'm sorry. I should have asked if you would prefer coffee or something stronger." She stood uncertain with the teapot in her hand. "I think there is whiskey down here somewhere."

"Tea will be fine. I need to keep a clear head for the journey home."

"You cannot mean to continue on to Thorncroft?" she responded, horrified, thinking of him limping home through the snow. "It will take you hours and could be dangerous. No, you must stay here. It would only take me a few minutes to make up a bed." She couldn't believe that she had just asked the enemy to sleep under her roof. She put it down to tiredness. Tomorrow would be time enough for regrets.

He smiled, as if reading her thoughts. "Thank you, but I think it would be best if I continue home."

"I do not want it said that I was responsible for your death," she said as she poured his tea.

"You were quite happy to despatch me to heaven earlier this evening."

She blushed furiously. "That was different. I spoke and acted in anger, as well you know." She sat down with an angry little motion of her slim shoulders. "I was provoked beyond what was possible to endure."

"You were indeed. I'm sorry: the urge to tease is far too strong." He didn't look very contrite. "In fact, now that I think of it, I happen to know that the local cricket team is in need of a fast bowler. Do you think you might be interested?"

She glared at him over the rim of her cup. He returned her gaze steadily and there was a warmth to it that she had never seen before. It made her a little uneasy. His manner towards her this evening was most unsettling and uncharacteristic. Was he trying to catch her off-guard? Playing games with her again?

"More tea?" she asked coolly, hoping to distract him from his bantering mood.

"No, thank you. I must be going." He drained his cup and stood. He reached for his coat.

"I won't hear of it!" she exclaimed. He swivelled around, a look of surprise on his face. "Wait here. If you won't use one of the bedrooms, I will fetch a pillow and some blankets and you can sleep on the sofa in the drawing room. At least it will be warm."

He regarded her for a moment then eventually shrugged, clearly too exhausted to argue with her. "As you wish Miss Campbell – if you insist on it. The sofa will be fine."

"Go on up. You know where the drawing room is. I won't be long," she said over her shoulder as she slipped from the room.

When he entered the drawing room it was in darkness, but he

found and lit a lamp and sat down to await his hostess. He shook his head, perplexed by her reaction. Really, she was a most unpredictable woman. He knew very well she wanted rid of him, but was afraid that something untoward might happen to him on his way home. Perhaps there was a tiny spark of hope after all? If she really hated him she would have pushed him out the door without a second thought.

It was the same dream again. He was trapped down a mine shaft, with the water rising inexorably towards him, and he could not move his arms. He was going to drown and panic was rising in his throat. But what was that growling sound? Was the shaft caving in on top of him? His eyes flew open. Two large brown eyes and a black shiny nose were inches from his face. He froze; there was something familiar about that canine. The dog growled again, a deep rumble in its throat. A figure sailed into view, apron crooked and cap askew. It was Louisa's maid, that young Irish girl, and she was in a flap, with two spots of high colour in her cheeks and wringing her hands in distress.

"Oh dear, I'm so sorry, Mr. Maxwell, but he won't come away. Max, Max. Oh dear, I'll fetch Miss Eleanor." She disappeared.

Nicholas's arm was trapped beneath him and it was numb. He slowly tried to ease himself upright but this brought on another low growl from the dog. He decided it would be prudent to wait for rescue.

"You cannot be serious, Róisín," he heard a female voice exclaim in the distance. Seconds later he heard footsteps approach and Eleanor Campbell was soon before him, the maid hovering behind her, eyeing him suspiciously. He could have sworn Eleanor was trying not to laugh.

"Oh, you bad dog! Come away at once." The dog's tail dropped and he slunk away to the fireplace before positioning himself so that he could stare menacingly at him.

Nicolas sat upright, rubbing his arm back to life. Eleanor was gazing at him as if he were mad. Clearly Louisa was still asleep and Eleanor knew nothing of the previous evening's adventures.

"I suppose you are wondering what I am doing sleeping on your sofa?" he asked.

Eleanor came further into the room. "I am sure there is a good reason. I assume the weather prevented you ..."

"I escorted your sister home and she insisted I stay. I hope I didn't startle you."

"No, no, it was a surprise that is all. I do apologise for Max. He is rather protective, you see."

"Not at all," he replied, looking at the dog with new-found respect. The mutt had inveigled his way into the household and was king pin; short work indeed.

"Can I offer you some refreshment? Róisín can set another place if you wish to join me for breakfast. Louisa is still abed. It is most unlike her."

"She had rather a trying evening. I'd let her sleep, if I were you."

Eleanor gave him a curious look but was too polite to comment in front of the maid. "Róisín can show you upstairs if you wish to freshen up?"

"Thank you, that would be very welcome," he said. Eleanor left the room and Max trotted after her, nose in the air, now quite bored with guard duty. Róisín hovered in the doorway, still eyeing him nervously.

He caught a glimpse of himself in the mirror above the fireplace as he stood up. It was not a pretty sight. He ran his fingers through his hair and straightened his collar in a futile effort to look respectable. No wonder the women had been disconcerted by him. He shrugged on his jacket and followed the maid upstairs.

When he came back down, the tantalising smell of food drew him across the hallway. He hadn't eaten since luncheon the previous day. Eleanor greeted him unsmiling, bade him sit down opposite her and dismissed the maid once she had served the coffee. He sensed he was about to be interrogated.

She did not look particularly well. Her pallor was emphasised by the cream blouse she wore and her eyes looked heavy, as if she had not slept. However, there was nothing feeble about her tone when she broached what was obviously at the forefront of her mind.

"Perhaps you could enlighten me, Mr. Maxwell, as to what occurred last night. I do not wish to be rude, but ..."

"Why would I, of all people, be sleeping on your sofa?"

Eleanor smiled. "Yes, indeed. Is my sister all right?"

He took a fortifying sip of coffee, then told her what had happened, as succinctly as he could. Some details he omitted, feeling it would be best to let Louisa divulge what she wished. A range of emotions flitted across her face and when he had concluded with Louisa's insistence that he stay rather than risk the walk home to Thorncroft, she looked baffled. He had the strangest feeling that if she had been in Louisa's shoes he would have been traipsing home through the snow, instead of having nightmares on the Campbell sofa.

"She must have been very angry with you," she said at last, getting to the nub of it in her disquieting way.

"Yes."

"With good reason, I think."

"I have apologised to her and the Whitbys, but we did act based on information we believed to be correct."

She put down her cup with forced gentleness. He could see that she was angry on her sister's behalf. "If the evidence had been against anyone else, would you have acted so precipitately?"

"Miss Eleanor, you must understand the seriousness of the Fenian threat. Although I could not prove it, I am sure that your uncle was heavily involved..."

"... Yes, yes, I have heard this before, but based solely on that, you assume that we are too?"

"The police have strong evidence that links the Glasgow bombings with Newton."

"Be that as it may, sir, you cannot seriously believe my sister is involved in such things. It is utterly preposterous."

"I no longer believe it. She is innocent of any wrongdoing."

"I am greatly relieved to hear it." Louisa had entered the room behind him, unseen and unheard.

He stood, as courtesy dictated, and drew out a chair for her. He searched her face anxiously for any sign of distress. She was pale with a hint of shadow under her eyes but otherwise appeared to be composed. She nodded to him, unsmiling, before sitting down and reaching for the tea-pot.

An uneasy silence descended and he was aware of Eleanor's curious gaze flickering between him and Louisa.

"Were you able to sleep, Mr. Maxwell?" Louisa asked.

"Yes, thank you," he answered politely.

"Max found Mr. Maxwell in the drawing room – sleeping in his spot," Eleanor said trying to keep a straight face. "He wasn't best pleased."

"Oh my! Max is worth his weight in gold. He is a great guard dog, you know, Mr. Maxwell," Louisa said.

"Yes, he was a lucky find, wasn't he?" he said, amused that she had named the dog after him, no doubt in the hopes that he would be annoyed by the slur.

Eleanor stood. "If you will excuse me, I'm sure you have much to discuss. Good day, Mr. Maxwell. Please give my regards to Anna."

"I will, and thank you for your hospitality," he said, holding the door open for her.

Louisa rose up from the table. "Perhaps you would join me in the study, Mr. Maxwell. I wish to speak to you in private."

She had lain awake half the night, swinging between anger, frustration and mortification. Eventually she had fallen into a deep and dreamless sleep and had woken feeling as though she had been dragged through a battlefield. But she had managed to reach a decision. For her own sake, as well as Eleanor's, she had to put a stop to the feud.

She led the way to the study, feeling extraordinarily nervous.

"Please take a seat," she said, sitting down in her uncle's chair behind the desk. She had deliberately chosen the study for this conversation to give herself more gravitas, but now realised that she would never feel she had the upper hand with this man. He took the seat beside the fire, appearing totally at his ease, despite having spent the night on a sofa. His hair was standing up in little spikes at the back and a dark shadow covered his cheeks and chin. It was most bizarre how he managed to look more handsome than ever. How tiresome he was, she thought crossly.

"You are well?" he asked. "You had a very unpleasant experience."

"I am perfectly well, thank you," she said, thrown a little by his concerned look. Her back hurt slightly. She suspected it was bruised, but otherwise she was physically well. It was just her mind in utter turmoil.

"Perhaps you should have Peterson out?"

"No, there is no need, I assure you." She took a deep breath. "Mr. Maxwell, I wish to ask something of you." He raised a brow, a mannerism which she was really beginning to hate. "I'd like this infernal wrangle over Bowes to end. All of this stress is detrimental to my sister's fragile health. Perhaps we could agree to some kind of truce, at least until such time as she is better." She paused, trying to judge his reaction but she could not read his thoughts. Anxious that he would not construe her words as defeatist, she said, "Do not think that I am intimidated by you, for I am not, but all of this unpleasantness upsets her greatly."

He looked taken aback, then frowned deeply. "Is it consumption?"

She started, surprised by his perception. He knew it was no temporary affliction. "No; her heart is weak."

He sat back in his chair regarding her thoughtfully. "I'm sorry," he said simply. "Is that why you came here? I could not understand why two young women would leave Dublin and bury themselves in the country."

She nodded, finding a lump in her throat.

"Look, Miss Campbell, as I said earlier, I know that you are innocent, and I apologise again for what occurred last night, but the fact remains that Fenians are active here and I have a duty to root them out and bring them to justice."

"I am well aware of your responsibilities, but I would be

grateful if you directed your attentions away from us," she said feeling her temper rise.

"Unfortunately Bowes keeps cropping up in relation to these men." He held up his hand when she started to protest. "I'm just stating a fact. You may not be involved, but I am convinced that some of your servants and tenants are. An unfortunate legacy of your uncle's ownership, if you will."

She was dismayed, but she wasn't a fool. Most of her servants were Irish and their loyalties would be questionable. The present state of affairs back in Ireland was constantly reported on in the newspapers, and the recent bombings meant that the Irish question was discussed everywhere you went. It had to colour the views of any Irish living and working in England, and inevitably made it easier for the Fenians to recruit. Most of the tenants were still unknown to her, but she suspected that most had been loyal in some way or other to her uncle. But did that make them Fenians? She was fairly certain now that Uncle Jack had been one, having gone through some of his papers and reading some of the well-worn books in the study. And then there was O'Connor, her steward. He was a decidedly complex character and if she was honest, she didn't trust or like him, but she had seen nothing to confirm Maxwell's assertions. She didn't trust him enough to reveal her doubts.

"What do you advise? Am I to spy on my own servants; interrogate my tenants?" She could not keep the sarcasm from her voice.

"Miss Campbell, please! You must take me seriously. I think you underestimate how dangerous these men are. If you suspect anything at all, let me know and I will deal with it. Do not attempt to investigate yourself. I don't doubt you have courage, and I know that you are strong-willed, but please leave this to the authorities. If this is the only piece of advice you ever heed from me, I will be a happy man." She smarted at his words but didn't trust herself to speak. It was obvious he was trying to unnerve her in the hopes she would give in and leave.

His eyes strayed to the corner of the room. "I see you have a gun cabinet. I don't suppose you know how to use a gun?"

"I certainly don't and have no wish to." She was stunned by the implication of his question. "You are deliberately trying to scare me."

"No, I am trying to make you see the reality of the position you are in. Learn to defend yourself, take that lunatic hound with you when you go out on the estate and don't take foolish risks."

"Oho, I see what you are about! You think if you frighten me enough I will sell up and flee. This is still about the land."

"No," he replied angrily. "Don't be foolish, Louisa. I am trying to protect you." He stood abruptly and went over to the window, seemingly struggling to control his temper.

"I don't need your protection. We have managed perfectly well up to now. How do you think we survived in Dublin? We lived by our wits, faced the challenges day by day and we will continue to do so. I will do whatever it takes to protect my sister."

In her agitation, she had been twisting a paper knife over and over in her hands. He came across the room in a couple of strides and grasped one of her hands. "I did not mean to alarm you, but you must promise me that you will keep me informed of anything untoward; even something small that appears irrelevant. Be vigilant, Miss Campbell, and be careful who you trust. In particular, keep an eye on O'Connor. Please remember that silence on your part could be construed as cooperation by a court of law. Do you understand that?"

She stared right back at him, defiant, but eventually she nodded her agreement. He appeared satisfied and released her hand. "I have overstayed my welcome. I'll bid you good day."

He was gone. She stared down at her hand, which still bore the imprint of his long fingers, and wondered if she was going mad. Was he threatening her or warning her? He said he wanted to protect her, but surely it was protection from him she needed.

Chapter Fifteen

L ouisa was only too aware that the incident at the schoolhouse was the main topic of conversation in Newton and the surrounding areas for several weeks. The disappointed parishioners of John Whitby were deprived of the company of the Thorncroft and Bowes Farm residents for two Sundays in succession due to the continued inclement weather. In the absence of the chief protagonists, the topic slowly withered and died. Louisa took advantage of this imposed seclusion to lick her wounds, and no one was the wiser.

By early March, there were tiny hints of spring in the air, and with it came anticipation of an event, that had been postponed by the weather: Mrs. Kirkbride's annual benefit ball. A new date was set for Easter. Louisa had mixed feelings about attending but Anna persuaded her that the Campbells' absence would give rise to more comment and conjecture than it was worth. Louisa could only shudder at the thought. Her instinct was to keep a low profile and let the storm of gossip blow over, but when Eleanor expressed a strong wish to attend she gave in and accepted the invitation.

One morning, Louisa was busy writing letters in the study, when she received a visit from Fr. Healy. She had seen him in Newton on several occasions, but he had not come to the house since he had visited shortly after their arrival and she had not been particularly troubled by his inattention.

"Father, this is a pleasant surprise!" she said, rising up to greet him. "Do take a seat."

"Thank you, my dear, thank you," he said, taking the seat close to the fire. He began to cough.

"Are you unwell, Father?"

"A trifling cold, that is all."

"Perhaps you might like something to warm you up?" she asked. His eyes twinkled back at her. She nodded to Róisín who still stood inside the door.

They spoke of local news for several minutes and Louisa wondered why he had come. "Is there something in particular that I can do for you, Father?"

"Well, next week is the 17th," he stated, as if she should know what the significance of that was. She looked back at him blankly but her mind was racing. "The 17th," she repeated slowly; then it dawned on her. "Yes, of course, St. Patrick's Day."

There was a knock on the door, and Róisín returned with the whiskey before the priest could enlighten Louisa any further. "Will the ball go ahead, Father?" Róisín asked in an excited voice, as she held out the tray towards him. "I do hope so. It's always such fun."

"That's why I'm here, child," he said impatiently. This seemed to convey a great deal to Róisín who clasped her hands together and beamed at Louisa in her childlike way. For one horrified moment, she thought that she was going to be asked to organise or host this ball.

"Now, Miss Campbell, you're an Irishwoman through and through so I won't beat about the bush. We hold this ball every St. Patrick's Day in the Imperial Hotel, to raise money for the impoverished of our congregation. All Irishmen and woman have a duty to their own – those poor souls who are so far away from home. There is a great tradition of the local landowners making contributions and your uncle was always very generous, very generous indeed." He sighed and took a sip from his glass, his watchful eyes never leaving her face.

She was relieved he only wanted money. "Well, who am I to argue with a family tradition? Perhaps you could give me some indication of how much my uncle used to give and I will do my best to match it." He indicated a modest enough sum.

Róisín looked like she was going to burst with excitement and skipped happily out of the room.

"Is this usually a grand affair?" she asked.

"Indeed yes, but we limit the numbers by making it ticket-only. It is always a most respectable and highly anticipated event, you understand; everything above board and well organised. It would be wonderful if you and your sister would come along; grace us with your presence, as it were."

"Unfortunately, that won't be possible, Father, but thank you for the invitation," she said, as she opened a drawer and pulled out her cheque book. "I hope this will go some way towards meeting your costs." She signed the cheque with a flourish.

"My child, that will do very nicely indeed," Fr. Healy said, taking it from her outstretched hand and noting the sum with a satisfied smile. "You are a credit to your uncle's memory."

The six o'clock evening train from Southampton to London was always quiet and that was the principal reason that Jack Campbell had chosen it. Every time he entered the country he used a different route and a different passport, courtesy of his kind American friends. Even when you're dead, you have to be careful in case some eagle-eyed peeler might be suspicious, and start asking awkward questions.

"Thank you, sir," the ticket inspector said, handing him back his ticket, doffing his cap and leaving the first-class compartment. Jack grinned at his travelling companion who had met him from the steamer.

"It's good to be back," he said, stretching and settling back into the cushions with a sigh.

"I assume O'Connor has been keeping you informed of events?"

"Oh yes."

"What do you make of it all then?"

"Naturally he is worried and he should be. After that fiasco in Glasgow and the arrests in Carlisle, we had to regroup. The last thing we needed was activity on our own doorstep."

"Word is the peelers had definite information linking Glasgow to Carlisle and Newton," the man said, rubbing his hands together vigorously. The compartment was cold and draughty. "They are a wee bit close for comfort."

"They can't have anything definite. It's Maxwell, of course – firing over the bows to see what happens."

"I don't know, Jack. Those were London boys outside the school and they were fully armed. Those boyos were expecting trouble."

"Hmm, well, whatever they expected they were chasing the wrong scent. I wish I could have seen Maxwell's face. Ha – a night school of all things! I'm sure that niece of mine had something to say to him afterwards. O'Connor tells me she has a sharp tongue in her pretty head."

"So what now, Jack?"

He leaned forward and lowered his voice. "Dublin is screaming for guns. Our job is to source them and ship them over."

"I see. From Bowes?"

"Aye. It's the perfect place with shore access and quiet as you please. We can easily run guns into Dublin or Wicklow, or even Louth if needs be. If we time it well, when the peelers are chasing their tails somewhere else, we shouldn't have any difficulty at all. We will organise a nice little diversion for them somewhere: say a 'fortuitous' find of a few guns or dynamite."

His companion nodded. "Sure that would be no problem at all."

"Excellent. You know we already have some guns hidden on the estate, but not nearly enough. That's where I was hoping you could help out, my dear old friend."

His companion sat back and smirked. "I think I know where we might relieve the government of some of their weapons. There is a certain armoury in Newcastle that is poorly guarded. We've been keeping an eye on it, as it happens."

"Good man. I knew I could rely on you, and you can be sure you won't go unrewarded."

Nicholas was no stranger to the quirkiness of life, but the very last thing he expected was a visit from Louisa. The fact that he had been sitting at his desk thinking about the self-same lady for most of the morning, instead of the papers in front of him, lent an almost surreal quality to the experience. But in she walked, announced by the butler, and she looked real enough, in fact very pretty indeed. At first he assumed that she had come to visit Anna, but when he saw how nervous she was, he realised it was him she had come to see. Had she found out something in relation to the Fenians and come to tell him about it?

"I hope I'm not disturbing you?" she asked quietly as she sat down. He couldn't think of a nicer intrusion to his day but could hardly say so. Her scent wafted across the room, making him feel slightly intoxicated.

"No, no, not at all," he answered, trying to appear calmer than he felt. What could she have found out? Did this mean that she trusted him?

"It's a rather delicate matter and I need some advice," she said rather hesitantly, her eyes sliding away from his gaze after a few moments. The objects lying on his desk seemed to hold a deep fascination for her all of a sudden.

"What appears to be the problem?" he asked, in what he hoped was an encouraging tone.

"It's regarding Róisín O'Connor. You have met her – the young housemaid?" He nodded, wondering where this was leading and feeling a twinge of disappointment. A housemaid was hardly a master criminal, even if she was the daughter of O'Connor. "Something very worrying took place at the St. Patrick's Day ball in Newton."

He leaned forward with a frown, deeply curious. "What exactly?"

"She was assaulted and badly frightened. It occurred in the gardens of the Imperial. The poor girl is still in a state. She didn't come back to Bowes that night. I found her, quite by accident, on the beach the next morning."

"Good Lord! This sounds very serious. Is she badly injured?"

She hesitated and looked embarrassed. "No, but she is very upset. She is a very simple soul and has a propensity for listening to uninformed gossip from her friends. The whole incident was blown out of proportion in her mind." She sighed. "She eventually admitted to me that she thought she might be with child; that her father would kill her; and the priest denounce her from the altar. You can imagine her distress."

He nodded. "Were her concerns well-founded?"

"Not at all. From what she described to me it was an opportunist kiss, that's all, but she knew no better."

"But you said she had been assaulted. A stolen kiss hardly constitutes that. If it did, half the male population would be behind bars."

That earned him a withering look before she continued. "It seems her father had taught her what to do in such an encounter. She managed to disable him, but he retaliated by hitting her. She has the most impressive black eye."

"So the silly widgeon thought it was the end of the world. Do you know who her attacker was?"

"No; that is the problem. I have told her to report it but she says that she is too frightened of the man to do so. She refuses to give me his name. I have urged her father to go to the police about it but he refuses, saying he will deal with it himself. So what can I do?" she pleaded.

"Nothing at all, I'm afraid," he answered. "I assume you are coming to me in my capacity as magistrate?" She nodded. "How old is she?"

"Seventeen."

"So she is a minor. If neither she nor her father reports it, then there is nothing you can do."

"But that's outrageous. Surely ..."

"I can't intervene in something like this, if that is why you have come to me. You must understand: if this did progress to court I would have to be seen as impartial, or I could not hear it."

She looked down at her hands which were tightly clasped in her lap. She did not look happy. "I understand," she replied.

"Does O'Connor know who the man is?"

She looked up with a worried expression. "Róisín won't tell him either, but he probably would not find it difficult to discover his identity. What do you think he will do?"

Nicholas knew exactly what he would do. "He doesn't strike me as a man to take something like this well. I imagine he will dole out his own version of justice."

"That's what I'm afraid of. Róisín has been terrified enough. What if there is some kind of retaliation for O'Connor's actions and the whole thing spirals out of control?"

"Unlikely. In my experience these things sort themselves out and the Irish community look after their own. I imagine the perpetrator is quaking in his boots waiting for O'Connor to strike. These young lads tend to drink too much on these occasions and lose their self-control. There were a few instances of brawling and drunkenness that night, as there are every year after that confounded ball. The police sergeant has already lined these up for my next sitting. It's not that unusual, Miss Campbell. I have to deal with the consequences of stupidity and excess every month in court."

"So I can do nothing," she said.

He shook his head. She turned her gaze towards the window, which afforded a lovely view of the park, but he was sure she was oblivious to it. He felt sorry for her. "I can understand your concerns and that you feel a level of responsibility for the girl, but as the law stands, you have no role to play in this. My advice, for what it's worth, is to encourage her to speak up, but you will have to accept her decision, whatever it is. Keep an eye out for any … unfortunate consequences."

Louisa pulled her gaze back to him and dismissed the suggestion with a wave of her hand. "I have no fears on that front, Mr. Maxwell. I believe her version of the story."

He nodded. "I'm sorry I cannot be of any further help," he said, sitting back in his chair. "Problems like this crop up all the time when managing staff on an estate."

"I never thought it would be easy, Mr. Maxwell."

"It isn't. You have done what is right in the circumstances, but you have to learn when to distance yourself. If you get caught up in their lives, you will pay a heavy price for it. You have enough worries of your own, I think."

She suddenly looked flustered and then her chin went up. "Thank you for your counsel. I will intrude upon your time no longer," she said abruptly, before rising from her seat. He knew that he had unsettled her and she wished to escape his presence. But it wasn't anger that was driving her any more, he was sure of that. His confidence grew, even though he knew that their relationship was on a knife-edge. It was like trying to handle a trapped bird – all flapping wings and terror.

He accompanied her into the hallway and out on to the front steps.

"You walked here from Bowes?" he asked, when he realised there was no horse waiting.

"Yes. It is a very pleasant walk."

"But alone? You have no servant with you?"

"I'm well beyond the need for a chaperone, Mr. Maxwell."

"On the contrary, Miss Campbell, I think you are in very great need of one."

She cast him a flustered glance, bade him a hasty farewell and walked briskly away. He watched her until she was lost amongst the trees that swept along the curve of the carriage-way. He knew he had disconcerted her; it was turning out to be rather a good day.

Chapter Sixteen

Easter Monday, The Imperial Hotel, Newton

When Louisa entered the Imperial ballroom she was struck by its magnificence. It was a large rotunda with a high vaulted ceiling which was decorated with elaborate plasterwork. Gas lights flickered along the walls and from the ceiling. The furthest end of the room had full-length windows, and she could just make out a balcony along the outside.

Mrs. Kirkbride and her daughters were greeting their guests at the main door. "Miss Campbell, Miss Eleanor – how lovely. You have both come." Mrs. Kirkbride greeted them with a cold smile. "I do hope you enjoy the evening," she said silkily, before her eyes lighted on the gentlemen who were behind them. Suddenly she was all animation and they had become invisible. Louisa linked Eleanor's arm and steered her away, smiling at the absurdity of it.

"How rude," Eleanor remarked, *sotto voce*, as they walked away.

"Pay no attention to her, Eleanor. Let's join the Whitbys. We can be sure of a genuine welcome there."

"Ladies," exclaimed John when he saw them approach. "How nice to see you both."

"Thank you, Mr. Whitby, you are very kind. Hello, Clara, how are you?" Louisa asked. "What a beautiful gown you are wearing," she said, as she took the seat next to her. Clara was wearing a lovely grey silk dress.

"Nonsense, this old thing?" Clara actually blushed. "I have no intention of competing with you young ladies."

John was standing beside them and chuckled at his sister. "Don't believe a word. I have it on good authority, that in her day there were very few who could compete."

Clara sniffed. "And how would you know? You were still in leading strings when I had my season." John smiled back at her and shook his head.

"Was it in London?" Eleanor asked.

"Yes, my dear, a very long time ago. Those were the days when my family was quite well-to-do. Unfortunately, Papa wasn't a particularly frugal man, and shortly after my season we had to retrench to the country. The suitors didn't follow," she concluded a little wistfully. She looked over to her brother. "John, I'm sure she will be here soon. Do come and talk to us."

"I ... I think I'll take a turn around the room. Excuse me, ladies," John said distractedly, before heading off towards the main door. His progress was hindered, however, as he had to stop and talk to parishioners every couple of yards.

Clara smiled. "He is at sixes and sevens waiting for Anna. Is it not foolish at his age?" she declared, but she had a twinkle in her eye. Louisa had come to realise that Clara was fond of Anna and happy for her brother in his choice.

"I thought she would be here before us," Louisa said.

"They have gone to fetch Mrs. Lambert and her daughter in the carriage; so typical of them to think of the less fortunate."

"I didn't know her daughter was visiting. She must be delighted," she said.

"Yes, it was unexpected. She arrived yesterday. Poor Mrs. Lambert sees her so little. Look, they have just arrived."

Louisa looked over and sure enough the Maxwells had arrived with Mrs. Lambert and the most striking woman she had ever seen. It didn't look like the girl in the photograph in Mrs. Lambert's sitting room. Could it possibly be the other daughter, the infamous Geneviève?

Whilst introductions were being made, she had the opportunity to observe the newcomer closely. It was indeed the eldest daughter of Mrs. Lambert, who had caused so much trouble in her youth.

She was willowy and slender, dark in the Italian style, with eyes of a melting blue. Her raven hair was elaborately dressed, held in place with beautiful silver and pearl clips, and her gown was of the finest quality pale yellow silk. Louisa did not consider herself particularly vain, but suddenly felt very ordinary in her apple green silk poplin.

There was idle conversation for several minutes and then the party broke up. Mrs. Lambert and Geneviève were hailed by old friends and wandered off to join them. Louisa did not fail to notice the long, lingering look the woman cast at Nicholas before she joined her mother. Her curiosity was now raging.

"Come, take a turn about the room with me," Anna said, as soon as the Lamberts were out of earshot. Louisa could tell she was bursting to tell her something, so she made her excuses to Clara and Eleanor, and linked her friend. Once they were safely out of earshot, Anna dragged her into one of the window embrasures.

"Can you believe it?" she almost shrieked.

She shook her head in puzzlement. "What?"

"She's back."

"I assume you are referring to the very glamorous Mrs. Rathbone."

"Yes. As bold as brass. You would think she would be ashamed to show her face even after all this time. How delicious it all is!"

"Anna!" she exclaimed, half laughing at her friend's enjoyment of the situation.

"Poor Nicholas. I've never seen him look so shocked. When she walked out of the house to the carriage, I swear the colour drained from his face. And I can tell you that her reputation is justified. She was simpering at him all the way here. She is an outrageous flirt."

"How awkward it must have been for everyone."

"Not at all. I enjoyed seeing him squirm."

"That I can believe – but poor Mrs. Lambert must have been very embarrassed," she said, looking across the room to where Geneviève was chatting animatedly to a group of admiring gentlemen. "There is no doubt she is very beautiful. Do you think your brother will fall under her spell again?" she asked in a playful tone, but she half feared the answer.

"Lord knows. Men are such fools for women like that. I am so glad she has come. It's going to make this evening very interesting." Anna looked at her shrewdly. "What is the matter? You don't look happy to be here."

"I didn't want to come, you know that. Our reception from our hostess was enough to convince me that we are viewed by many as social outcasts, either because of recent events or my uncle's notoriety. I feel as if everyone is watching, waiting for another disaster to befall us."

Anna could not contain her mirth. "You are such an innocent. Yes, of course they are watching everything you do, say and wear, but it's because you have standing in the neighbourhood. You are a landowner and well-off now. Being unmarried makes you a *very* interesting person. Fathers are sizing you up for their sons, and mothers are wishing you would disappear and give their poor daughters a chance at the few remaining bachelors of any standing."

She groaned. "This is attention I'd rather not have."

Anna just grinned at her. "Now – who is here? I have already promised John the first two, but one cannot dance the whole evening with ones fiancé." She popped her head out further from where they were and looked around the crowd. "Well, we won't find partners hiding behind the flowers. We had better go back to the others," she said. Her enthusiasm was infectious and Louisa's earlier lack of spirits was soon forgotten.

As they made their way through the crush, she heard her name. She turned around to find George Jameson looking very dapper in his evening clothes. He had recently taken up position as manager of the new branch office of Jamesons in Newton. He stepped up to her with a shy smile. "I was hoping to meet you, Miss Campbell. Perhaps, you would do me the honour of dancing the first with me?"

She was delighted to accept, as she had feared that recent events and the consequent notoriety would mean an evening of sitting with the chaperones. She introduced him to Anna, who she could tell was assessing him with keen interest.

"I must find John or he will be fretting. It was nice to meet you, Mr. Jameson," Anna said. She turned, but not before raising a brow at Louisa, very much in the manner of her brother. George led her out on to the floor where other couples were now lining up.

Sometime later Eleanor was sitting by herself when Nicholas approached. "Would you care to dance, Miss Eleanor?"

Eleanor smiled at the chivalrous offer. "You are very kind, Mr. Maxwell, but I will not dance tonight. I am very happy to sit and listen to the professional musicians. That is the reason I wanted to come." Nicholas sat down beside her. "We used to attend concerts in Dublin and I do miss that. You may find it hard to believe, but this is a real treat for me. I only wish we had more opportunities to hear professional musicians," she said rather wistfully.

"So do I take it you are finding Newton dull after Dublin?" he asked.

"Yes, a little, I have to admit but it has its compensations. We are comfortably situated and no longer have to worry about ... anything." It would be indelicate to mention finances but he looked as if he understood. "To be settled in one place at last is a great relief, Mr. Maxwell. Louisa loves it here. She has taken to country life."

Just then, Louisa waltzed past in the arms of George Jameson. Nicholas turned to her with a sharp look. "Why is she dancing with that pup of a solicitor again?"

"I would imagine because he asked her, Mr. Maxwell."

"He needs watching," he said. She was delighted to see signs of jealousy, confirming her suspicions of a tendresse for her sister.

"I do not think she regards him in any light other than a legal one."

"I hope that she is cognisant of how appearances can be misconstrued, particularly at events like this. ... But I'm sure you need not worry about her."

She was amused. "I don't. She always acts with propriety." He nodded, but still looked disgruntled. They both looked out to the dancers again. Whatever George had said, had her laughing. They looked very well dancing together. Eleanor could almost feel the tension in her companion.

Since the unfortunate episode at the schoolhouse Louisa had become preoccupied. Eleanor guessed the cause. She had seen for herself how Maxwell had looked at her sister that morning at the breakfast table. If her sister had lost her heart she was keeping the knowledge of it well hidden, perhaps even from herself. Of late, if Mr. Maxwell came up in conversation, it prompted a tirade of abuse, but was there any real heat in it any more? Ever since, if they all met in public, both parties were studiously polite and stiff. Louisa appeared unusually tongue-tied; surely that was proof of something.

"I must admit that I am anxious about her for a different reason, Mr. Maxwell. She has built her life around looking after my needs. I do not know how she will cope when I am gone."

His eyes widened. "Surely your family will be a support to her?" he asked in a tight voice, obviously shocked to hear her talk about death so candidly.

"There is no one. Our parents married against the wishes of my mother's family and were cut off. We have never even met any of our cousins. We do have one aunt in Dublin, who received us, but she is an embittered and selfish woman. She is the last person Louisa would turn to."

"I'm sorry. That is difficult but not uncommon in these situations." He paused. "You know she will have friends here to help and support her if ... when the time comes."

She gave him a long probing look. This was the kind of response she had been eager to hear. "I hope so, Mr. Maxwell, because I fear she may take my passing very hard. I'm glad I am able to say these things to you. It comforts me to know that she will not be alone. I do not know how long I have," she continued, having made up her mind to accomplish the task she had set herself for this evening. "It may only be months, but I do not believe I will see another year. For that reason I am going to be very direct with you and I hope I do not give you offence."

"Please say whatever you wish," he said in a strangled voice.

"What are your intentions towards my sister?"

He stared at her incredulously. "That is direct indeed, Miss Eleanor," he said. "I'm not sure how to answer you."

"It is a simple enough question."

"Ah, but it holds the world within it."

She chuckled. "I think you have just given me your answer."

He shrugged and smiled sadly. "Is there any hope for me, do you think, or have I ruined my chances with my stupid and boorish behaviour?"

She did not answer immediately but turned her lace brisé fan over in her hands several times. Eventually she said, "You upset her greatly. I imagine you will have to work hard to gain her trust, but I believe she is not beyond your reach." She was nervous. Should she be so honest with him? She still could not be sure how Louisa felt about this man, but time wasn't on her side. "However, before you do or say anything, you should know that currently any reference to you tends to include boiling oil, thumb screws, and if I recall correctly, on one occasion there was mention of a firing squad."

"At least I feature in her thoughts, albeit in a negative way," he said forlornly.

"I am doing my best to help you, as it happens. It was I who persuaded her to seek your advice over Róisín. And if it weren't for me, she would not be here tonight. The rest is up to you."

"And I thought it was she who was resourceful. I have sadly misjudged you."

She breathed out slowly. "I hope that I am not misjudging you. If you hurt her ..."

"I'll have you to answer to?"

"Exactly – and I will show no mercy."

As George escorted her off the floor for the second time that evening, Louisa saw Mrs. Lambert beckoning to her to join her and her daughter. Deeply curious about the newcomer, she asked George to walk her over. He greeted the ladies, bowed over her hand and walked away.

"Miss Campbell, you appear to have made quite a conquest there," Geneviève exclaimed in a silky tone as she watched George depart.

Mrs. Lambert looked appalled at her daughter's pert comment and quickly stepped in. "You do look very well tonight, Louisa. That shade of green is lovely on you."

"Thank you, Mrs. Lambert," she answered, sitting down beside her. "How are you enjoying the evening?"

Geneviève jumped in, cutting her mother off before she had an opportunity to reply. "It's wonderful to see all our old friends. I have missed Newton so much, you know. I just couldn't resist a visit. Nothing changes here. It's as if time stands still – so quaint."

Irritated by her rudeness, Louisa could only simmer as she had no wish to upset Mrs. Lambert, who was looking miserable after her daughter's outburst. She was starting to dislike the woman very much and couldn't resist alluding to her neglect of her mother. "I'm sure your mother is delighted to have some company for a while."

Geneviève raised a brow, but it was Mrs. Lambert who replied. "Yes, Miss Campbell, it's lovely to have visitors, especially family, and it was so lucky tonight. I had not intended to come at all, but Mr. Maxwell was adamant that I should and offered to fetch me. I am so glad that Geneviève isn't missing out. It would have been such a shame."

"He is always very attentive," Louisa said drily.

"Imagine his astonishment when he saw me, Miss Campbell. What a surprise it was. I did enjoy the joke. He is a particular favourite with us, of course. There is a *long* history between our families, you know." Geneviève's beautiful face bore a smug expression. "Such old friendships stand the test of time."

She was amused by the woman's transparent territory marking, and wondered if he felt the same way about rekindling their previous association. Geneviève obviously felt sure of her charms, but Nicholas was no longer a young and impressionable man.

"He begged me to save at least one waltz for him," Geneviève went on, "but I told him that he would have to wait his turn – though I did put his name down on my card." She flashed her dance card at her. "As if I would leave him out," she trilled. "I know he has some duty dances, so he will appreciate my company so much more by the time he dances with me."

Louisa was amazed by her unseemly remarks, but in deference to the girl's poor mother, she merely nodded and smiled.

"Look, here he comes now. No doubt he cannot wait any longer." Geneviève said, clasping her hands together in an exaggeratedly excited gesture. As Nicholas approached, she jumped up. "I'm sure Miss Campbell will keep you company, Mother, as she appears to be without a partner," she said, before stepping forward to intercept him.

"Nicholas, I suppose you could not wait, you naughty man! For old time's sake, I will forgive you and agree to dance now."

A hint of irritation crossed his features, but he politely nodded to Louisa and Mrs. Lambert and offered his arm to Geneviève. She had the distinct impression that asking Mrs. Rathbone to dance had been the last thing on his mind.

"I'm sorry, Miss Campbell. My daughter forgets herself sometimes. All the excitement of a ball and seeing everyone again," Mrs. Lambert said.

"There is no need to apologise. I understand," she answered. "She is very beautiful."

"Yes – the image of my dear mother, but highly strung. Unfortunately, it has been her downfall in some respects. I thought marriage to Mr. Rathbone would calm her down and it did for a while, but since his death she has been very restless." Mrs. Lambert shook her head. "I do hope she doesn't cause any trouble."

Louisa patted her hand sympathetically. "How long will she stay with you?"

"She hasn't said. Of course I would be delighted if she decided to settle with me permanently. It must be very lonely for her on her own in Maryport. They had no children, you see, and I suspect the marriage wasn't particularly happy. I do not believe his family are kind to her. Yes, perhaps she will stay."

Feeling displeased at the prospect, she watched as Geneviève and Nicholas swept past. Her visits to Mrs. Lambert would not be as enjoyable if that woman was present. It was astonishing that someone like Mrs. Lambert could have a daughter who was so vain and empty-headed, but she supposed the girl had enjoyed male attention all her life, the idea that any man would not fall under her spell, impossible to believe. She did not wish to dwell too closely on the possibility of her relationship with Nicholas springing back to life. If she was honest, it was making her feel hollow inside.

Chapter Seventeen

L ouisa yearned for home and her bed. She had not been
without a partner the entire evening and she was exhausted.
Wishing to escape the heat of the ballroom, she grabbed her shawl
and made her way along the perimeter of the room before slipping
outside on to the balcony. It was a breach of decorum to indulge in
a solitary interlude, but she could not resist.

A refreshing gust of cool salty air greeted her. It was a fine
night with a crescent moon and she was relieved to find the
balcony deserted. It ran along the outside of the ballroom in a
sweeping curve, hugging the building and overhanging the sea.
From below, she could hear the waves breaking against the rocks.
It was the most extraordinary sensation. She leaned over the
balustrade, curious to see what was below.

"You should be careful. It's a long way down and I don't
particularly wish for a swim," a familiar male voice remarked. At
the far end of the balcony, almost out of sight, was Nicholas,
leaning back against a pillar smoking a cigar. In his black evening
clothes he was practically invisible.

"This is incredible," she said, leaning over again to watch the
foamy waters below. She was fascinated by the sensation of almost
floating above the sea. The drop must have been at least forty feet.

"Yes – a marvel of British engineering," he drawled. She
looked up, surprised by his tone and wondered what was putting
him in such humour. Why would he wish to escape the ballroom?
It wasn't to smoke his cigar. There was a room specially put aside

for that. And like her, he had not suffered from a wont of partners all evening; she had found herself taking note. Was he trying to avoid someone? Her curiosity got the better of her.

"Why are you out here?"

"I might ask the same."

"But I asked first," she countered, moving towards him.

He shrugged. "Very well, if you must know I detest these grand affairs. I usually avoid 'em."

"So why did you come tonight?"

"Anna insisted. She thought I should try to make amends for my recent misdeeds."

"I don't follow," she said.

"Make amends to you, Miss Campbell," he said. "One dance together should scotch all rumours of a falling-out."

Amused, she could not resist saying, "I see, but you are hiding out here. You are running out of time, you know. They will be calling for the carriages soon. You may miss your chance."

"Time enough. I wanted to speak to you in private first, as it happens," he said, straightening up. "I have some news regarding your steward."

"Really? What has he been up to now?" she asked with a sigh. She'd had her fill of O'Connor the last few days.

"As I suspected, he has dealt with his daughter's problem rather efficiently. A young Irish lad was found in a laneway down near the harbour a few days ago. He had been badly beaten but would not talk to the police. Cox brought him to Dr. Peterson who patched him up and escorted him home. I suspect he was your maid's assailant."

"Most likely. I just hope it ends there."

"It will, but I would emphasise to you again just how dangerous a man O'Connor is. I think you underestimate his power and influence."

"As much as I hate to admit it, I am coming round to your view on things," she replied glumly. If O'Connor was capable of doing that to a young lad who gave his foolish daughter a fright, what would he do if really crossed? A shiver ran down her back at the thought and she pulled her shawl tighter. "He has threatened to send Róisín back to Ireland to live with his sister. I had to put up quite a fight. I'm rather fond of her and she has lived here all her life. She would be miserable amongst strangers."

"You are far too sentimental," he teased her.

She could not help defending herself. "On the contrary, I am being practical. I have invested a lot of time and energy training her up, and besides, Eleanor is very fond of her, too. Róisín often sits with her when she is unwell. She finds her a great comfort."

"I can't imagine that O'Connor was best pleased that you interfered in his plans."

"He wasn't," she smiled in memory, "but when Róisín started howling like a banshee he couldn't leave the room fast enough. There has been no mention of it since."

He shook his head and laughed. "I almost feel sorry for him. Between the two of you he most likely ended up a quivering wreck."

"I doubt it. He is nothing but a bully. I'm glad I stood my ground. He won't get the better of me."

"Don't I know it. Just be careful. For some reason it suits him to have you in situ. If that state of affairs changes, you could be in danger," he said. "Did you have an opportunity to look at those pistols yet?"

"No," she said, greatly put out. "No, I am not comfortable with the idea of using one, as I told you before."

"That is foolish. The next time you come to Thorncroft I will give you a lesson. Humour me in this: it will put my mind at rest."

Amid her protestations, the door nearest them opened and William Morrissey stepped out on to the balcony.

"Maxwell – there you are. I've been looking for you this half hour. There is something of importance I would like to discuss with you." He gave her a disparaging glance. "Servant, Miss Campbell." She could tell that he was displeased to see her alone in Nicholas's company and was on the point of excusing herself.

"It will have to wait, William, I am promised to Miss Campbell for the next waltz," Nicholas replied irritably.

He chucked his cigar over the balcony with a flick of his wrist and took her by the arm, practically marching her down the balcony to the other door. When they reached the dance floor the strains of a waltz were just starting up. She was surprised to see how angry he was and wondered what Mr. Morrissey had said that had annoyed him so much. He seemed to read her thoughts.

"Ridiculous man!" he exclaimed. "He knows a ballroom is not the place to discuss business."

She could not resist teasing him. "But we were not exactly making polite conversation outside either. If I recall, we were discussing firearms."

He glowered at her. "That is different and you know it." She suddenly realised that he took the social niceties very much to heart. "Can we please get on with this?" he grumbled.

Slightly miffed at his tone and attitude, she stepped closer and they took their positions, Mrs. Rathbone's comment about 'duty' dances popping into her head. If she could have walked away, without causing a scene, she would have. They danced in silence. She was uncomfortably aware that they were under surveillance; surreptitiously by some, but quite openly by the majority. She caught one particularly nasty look from Mrs. Rathbone and decided to ignore their observers altogether. It was too unsettling being the centre of attention. Was it her imagination or was this a particularly long waltz? She wished it would end.

"I know it's a rather fine shirt, Miss Campbell, but I don't think it merits quite that much attention." His lips almost brushed against her ear and she knew that he was being deliberately provocative. She gave him a fierce look.

"I would never have believed that someone could commit murder with just a glance but I think you may have mastered it," he said. She did her best to stare him down, which was difficult when the object was taller and looking at one in quite that way.

"You are determined to remain silent and unsmiling, I see. This rather defeats the purpose. I thought we were to put pay to any rumours of a falling-out, not fuel them. Anna was quite clear on that point, to me at least. Were you not given instructions as well?"

he asked, in an innocent tone that didn't deceive her for one minute.

"I am happy to go through the motions but I draw the line at feeding your ego," she said through gritted teeth.

"Ouch! I don't think I'm going to survive this evening intact." His reward was a brittle smile. "That's a little better – a smile at last. Anna is watching, you know, and your sister. Quite a scheming pair, don't you think?"

"What do you mean?"

"Between the two of them they have manipulated us rather skilfully."

"I don't know what you are talking about."

"Oh come, Miss Campbell, you must realise by now that my delightful sister is never happy unless she is scheming. She lives for intrigue. I'm impressed that she managed to involve your sister, though; she usually works alone."

"Eleanor is not like that, I'm sure of it," she said with more certainty than she felt. Her sister had been saying some odd things lately.

"Really? Well then, tell me who convinced you to come to me for advice last week over that housemaid, and who persuaded you to come to this ball tonight?"

Goodness, she thought, he might be right. But how did he know? "But she … she's never done anything like this before. No, you must be mistaken."

"I am sorry to contradict you but I had a very interesting tête-à-tête with her earlier. She is most unnerving. She seems to look into your very soul and read what is written there. Don't be alarmed on my account, Miss Campbell: I have survived the experience and am the wiser for it. But I digress – I'm sure she is motivated by the best of intentions. It would appear she does not want you to be isolated from your nearest neighbours."

She frowned, shaken by what he had revealed. If Eleanor had voiced fears to Nicholas, of all people, she must have had a good reason – but what could it be? Had Eleanor had some kind of premonition that her time was running out? A tight knot of anxiety formed in her stomach. "Oh dear, you may be right."

"It's rather sweet really, so you shouldn't be cross with her," he said gently. "But I dread to think what my sister's motives might be."

She smiled, remembering her conversation with her earlier. "Anna is mischievous certainly, but she is not vicious or cruel. Are you not used to her ways by now? Surely you have been a victim before?"

"Frequently, and Robert also, though I pride myself on having got the better of her quite spectacularly, and, to add to my glory, she hasn't the faintest idea that I orchestrated the whole thing. I'm looking forward to revealing it to her some day very soon," he said.

"What have you done?"

"How do I know that I can trust you with my secret?" he asked airily, but she could see that he was dying to tell.

She thought for a moment. "… because I am a fellow victim?"

"I suppose so, but you must promise not to breathe a word."

"I promise. Now, what have you done?" she demanded.

"Married her off."

"Married her off? I don't understand."

"When John Whitby arrived in Newton I thought he would make her an ideal husband. When they met they got along very well and I could see that he was enamoured. But John was shy and far too conscious of social status to make a declaration. Anna was flitting about between suitors, most of whom were highly unsuitable, and I feared she would never settle down. It was only when I voiced my strong opposition to such a match, saying I had heard rumours pairing them off, that she became really interested. After that her wilfulness and my continued protestations sealed the deal."

"Oh my, you're good!"

"Why, thank you."

"… and conceited with it."

"Don't ruin my moment of glory! I was basking in your admiration for a moment." He pulled a very sad face which she could not hold out against and burst out laughing.

"That's better," he said. "You are lovely when you smile, you know."

Her heart skipped a beat and she nearly missed her step. He deftly made a correction and they continued to waltz in silence for several more minutes.

"Do you think the weather has changed for the better?" she asked, deliberately changing the subject and avoiding his gaze.

"It's hard to know Miss Campbell, but I have a feeling there could be a few storms ahead yet."

Jack was late and in a bad mood. It was a rainy dank evening in Manchester and his only thought was trying to find a particular house in a back street of Angel Meadow; a notorious slum district inhabited almost entirely by impoverished Irish. Added to his misery was the belief that he was being followed through the grimy streets since he had alighted from the tram. He kept moving, dipping through the shadowy thoroughfares formed by the rows of identical terrace houses. The squalidness of the area was well reported, but Jack was shocked to see the state of his fellow countrymen. An air of gloom hung about the dirty streets and, despite the rain, unfortunate wretches were prostituting themselves on every corner or sitting in huddled misery begging under the dim and flickering gas lamps.

He passed St. Michael's church and graveyard and turned on to Ludgate Street, pulling up his coat collar in a vain effort to stay dry. He found the house he wanted and knocked once. The seconds ticked by and just as he raised his hand to knock once more, the door opened a crack and a husky voice enquired what his business was.

"Beware *Dearg Due*." He uttered the password impatiently. There was a stream of water now coming off the brim of his hat and trickling down the back of his neck. His greatcoat could not keep out the chill dampness and he could not help but shiver.

"Enter," the man said, opening the door enough to let him in.

There was now enough light for Jack to see him, a young lanky lad with a jagged scar running down his left cheek. The door was slammed and bolted immediately after him, plunging them both into near darkness. "Can't be too careful. Straight ahead and down the stairs," the lad instructed.

He strained his eyes in the dimness. He would have felt his way along the wall but for the overpowering smell that assailed him. The thought of touching anything in this house made him nauseous. As his eyes adjusted he could make out a faint light ahead and he made his way towards it warily.

"Mind the steps," the voice behind him admonished. He gingerly felt for them with his foot before descending into the nether regions. He had to stoop his head in the low-ceilinged basement. The small room was lit by a pathetic fire in the grate and a few tallow candles giving off their pungent odour. A pile of rags and straw lay in the corner beside the fireplace upon which a young child was fast asleep. He could not tell whether it was a boy or girl. Two thin dirty legs were visible, the feet bare and covered in grime. The child's hair was long and matted, and, he suspected, extremely dirty if the clothes were anything to go by. He was fastidious in matters of hygiene and felt his stomach turn over in disgust.

Seated at a small table, near the grimy window high up in the wall, were two men he knew well: Tomás and Peadar – the O'Griofa twins. They were second generation Irish and ran the Manchester Fenians with a rod of iron. This was the first time he had met them on their home turf and he swore to himself it would be the last. He was almost gagging on the smell in the room. Cassidy's old place was cleaner than this.

"*Fáilte romhat isteach*," Tomás, the elder man, reputedly by several minutes, greeted him, his sharp blue eyes sizing him up in an instant. His grizzled beard and greying hair made him look much older than his forty years. The younger man was beardless but had the same piercing eyes. His violent reputation was legendary in Manchester; he was not a man to cross.

"*Cáisc Shona dhaoibh*," he replied before taking off his sodden hat and putting it down on the table. He removed his damp coat and sat down on a hard wooden stool, suppressing a weary sigh.

"Murphy – get that bottle out. Our friend is chilled to the bone," Peadar snapped. Murphy, who had followed him into the room, scurried off back up the stairs and returned minutes later with a half bottle of Jameson and some glasses. Jack would have loved to take out his handkerchief to clean his glass but could not risk offending his companions; he was outnumbered after all. Even with a pistol in his coat pocket he wasn't going to take any risks.

"Watch the door!" was the final order barked out to Murphy, who disappeared up the stairs again. Peadar proceeded to pour the whiskey.

"*Slainte mhaith*." The men saluted each other, raising their glasses before taking a healthy swallow.

"What news for us, Jack?" Tomás asked, shifting in his seat but never breaking eye contact.

"I was hoping you had news for me," he replied, swirling the whiskey in his glass. "I need to know what stage your plans are at."

Tomás and Peadar exchanged glances. "Sure, they are grand, Jack – some minor problems but nothing to worry about," Peadar drawled at last.

"What minor problems?" he asked. He could smell prevarication a mile away.

"Well now, Jack, you see, Murphy – the lad who let you in tonight – he is having problems sourcing some materials."

"The money didn't come through?"

"No, the money came through all right, and very grateful we are. It's just that we had to change supplier. We had reason to believe the man was in the pay of the peelers."

Jack slammed his fist down on the table, making the brothers jump. "I've warned ye before about this kind of thing. We cannot afford carelessness."

"Relax, Jack. We are not taking any chances. Murphy says he has found someone reliable and the previous supplier has had his cards marked. There's devil a need to worry."

He let out a heavy sigh of frustration. "So the bottom line is that you are not ready to carry out the operation yet?"

"No. We must delay a few weeks at least."

"That's too vague. I need to know exactly when you will be ready."

"Now, Jack, calm down," Tomás said as he topped up his glass. "Sure, a few weeks here or there won't matter."

"That's where you are out. Other matters afoot rely on accurate timing at your end."

"Now just what are you planning?" Tomás asked.

"Nothing that need concern you," he replied. Success depended on each cell being completely independent and he didn't particularly trust this pair. "Mind you organise yourselves well. I don't want to hear of any more delays. I will contact you in a month. You'd better have firm information for me then." Jack emptied his glass then stood as best he could and surveyed the room with distaste. The sleeping child began to cough in its sleep. "God almighty. How do you live in these conditions?"

Tomás grinned, showing blackened teeth. "Ah sure now, Jack, 'tis the perfect place for the likes of us. Peelers are too scared to come anywhere near Angel Meadow. The gangs hold sway here. Sure, who do you think shielded you from the moment you entered the district? You were watched, followed and protected."

He could not help his distaste showing. "It's a hell hole."

"Aye," Peadar laughed, "but it's our hell hole."

Chapter Eighteen

William Morrissey was a contented man: twenty-five years of marriage was an unparalleled opportunity to show those who mattered how far he had risen in the world. He looked down the length of his dining-table with smug satisfaction. The most important and influential people from Carlisle and Newton were enjoying his famous hospitality. He hoped that his continuing rise would result in a good marriage for his daughter Beatrice. She had done him proud tonight and he felt sure that she was soon to wed well; a very satisfactory outcome even if Maxwell had no title, but he did come from an old landed family, not to mention being a magistrate and a shrewd businessman. To add to his growing sense of satisfaction, he had finally pinned him down before dinner long enough to make his business proposal. Maxwell had been disappointingly non-committal. His hints that the deal might include Beatrice's future happiness didn't seem to go down well, but he hoped the lad would come round. Wasn't he sitting beside her tonight and looked like he was enjoying her company. He was unsure how that young widow had managed to be seated the other side of him, though. He would have to question his wife as to what she was thinking. How did she think Beatrice would succeed if Maxwell was distracted by that rather vivacious woman? And worse still, that Campbell girl was sitting opposite him, no doubt throwing out lures. He recalled seeing Maxwell in her company during the Kirkbride ball a few weeks ago and grew agitated. He would have to watch that situation very closely indeed.

Further down the table, Nicholas was having the very same thought, but for a very different reason. Robert, having turned up unexpectedly at Thorncroft the previous day, had enthusiastically accepted a belated invitation from Mrs. Morrissey. He was now seated opposite him and engaging Louisa in animated conversation. They appeared to be getting on very well indeed. He could not hear what they were talking of, owing to the fact that he was trapped between Scylla and Charybdis, both of whom seemed determined to monopolise his attention to the detriment of the other. The result was a growing headache and a sense of impending doom.

"Mr. Maxwell, it must be so exciting in your house at the moment with all the wedding plans," Beatrice said in her penetrating voice.

For a moment, still taken aback by Morrissey's earlier proposition, he feared she was referring to him, but quickly realised that she was alluding to Anna. "I stay well away from the affair, I assure you, Miss Morrissey," he answered. "Besides, my sister would not welcome any interference on my part."

Mrs. Rathbone piped up. "Well said, Mr. Maxwell. Besides, these events are so tiresome really. So much fuss and bother for one day. When you are more experienced in the ways of the world, Miss Morrissey, you'll understand what I mean." She gave her rival a pitying smile, with her hand resting on his arm, in a manner that could only be described as possessive. It sent a shiver of horror down his spine.

"If you mean that cynicism comes with age, then I am glad that I am only one and twenty," Beatrice countered with a sneer. "I, for one, consider weddings delightful occasions."

He could have sworn he heard his brother snort and shot him a look promising violence. Louisa's eyes were downcast but her shoulders were shaking rather suspiciously. That pair were enjoying his discomfort thoroughly, he thought grimly.

"Are congratulations in order, Miss Morrissey? Are we to understand that your own happy day is imminent?" Geneviève asked.

Beatrice regarded her sourly. "No – I speak generally."

"I see," Geneviève responded. "My mistake. I do apologise I had no wish to embarrass you."

He swallowed hard. She really was vicious. Thank goodness his eyes had been opened to her true nature all those years ago. Beatrice coloured up with embarrassment and he actually felt sorry for her.

"I believe you are thinking of travelling to Europe this summer?" he asked her in the hopes of diffusing the situation. She smiled at him gratefully and launched into the details of the proposed trip.

Across the table Louisa was pleasantly surprised at how Nicholas had handled the tension between his tormenters. When he next glanced over at her she gave him a tiny sympathetic smile.

"I am thoroughly enjoying myself, but do you think we should launch some sort of rescue?" Robert said beside her.

"I think your brother is quite capable of extracting himself, don't you?"

"Hmm, I'm not sure. Of course it's entirely his own fault, but I don't envy him his choice." He shook his head sadly, but then belied it by grinning wickedly at her.

She regarded him seriously. "So you know all about Mrs. Rathbone ..." His smirk answered the question. Anna had been hard at work, it seemed, filling in her brother on the family history. "Do you think he will choose between them?"

He merely smiled and shrugged. "Nicholas never confides in me ... but if he were to consult me, my advice would be to run for the hills, and as fast as his legs could carry him."

She choked. "I'm sure both ladies have their good points."

"You cannot be serious." He leaned in close and lowered his voice. "One could raise the dead with her voice alone, and the other is an ambitious fortune hunter. Could you really see either of them as mistress at Thorncroft?" He gave an exaggerated shudder. "Neither is right for him. In fact, if I could influence his selection, I would choose someone refined but with a lively mind; someone who will stand up to him. … Of course, it is such a shame that you two don't get along. Though Anna seems to think that things have improved lately?"

She felt herself blush. "We have managed to meet and not argue, if that is what you mean."

"Indeed? That would appear to be amazing progress. At Christmas things appeared at an impasse."

"They were, and continued to decline, as I'm sure your sister informed you. But lately we have achieved a truce of sorts," she explained. "You left rather hurriedly if I recall," she continued swiftly, anxious to change the subject.

"Yes. Nicholas and I had a flaming row over that cursed dinner party, but we never fall out for long. I returned to the fold yesterday like the prodigal son."

"I'm relieved to hear it. How long can you stay this time?"

"Unfortunately, not long at all. I return to the regiment tomorrow evening. I must keep my leave for the wedding in June. Tell me, did you ever learn to ride?"

"I did and furthermore, I can manage to stay in the saddle and look like I know what I'm doing."

"Always a good thing. Well done."

She smiled. "In all probability my poor horse Daisy is what you might term a slug, but I am happy with her passive nature. I know you will find it hard to believe, but I still prefer to walk."

"I'm shocked," he said, clutching his chest in mock horror. "That is the most distressing thing you could say to a cavalry man." Her gurgle of laughter seemed to catch Nicholas's attention, and both she and the Captain were subjected to a curious glance laced with annoyance.

"And how about Miss Eleanor? Has she overcome her fear of horses?"

"No, she is happy for me to be the one to make a fool of myself in that regard. Her talents lie in another direction."

"Yes, indeed they do. I hope she plays this evening. She only played one piece at Christmas, but it was exceptional. I shall certainly encourage her to play if I get the opportunity."

"Thank you, that would be a huge boost to her confidence. She tends to be shy in company."

The reluctant performer did play several pieces, much to the delight of those present who had an appreciation for music. Each time Eleanor finished a piece she was cajoled to play again. Captain Maxwell remained at her side throughout, and performed the office of page-turner for her, and when she would finally play no more, he escorted her back to Louisa.

But as soon as Eleanor returned to her seat she confided that she felt very fatigued and wished to leave. Louisa was disappointed as she was enjoying the evening, but Eleanor did look tired. Amidst the bustle of the large crowd it was not difficult for the two women to make their adieu to their hostess, who didn't seem particularly concerned at their early departure. They slipped out, hoping no one noticed, and went down the stairs to await their carriage. Eleanor sat down on a sofa while Louisa wandered down the hall examining the eclectic collection of artwork that graced the walls. A young maid had promised to fetch their coats, so on hearing someone coming down the stairs, Louisa did not turn until she heard Nicholas enquiring if Eleanor was feeling well.

"I'm afraid I have overtired myself, Mr. Maxwell. We are waiting for the carriage. It should be here shortly," Eleanor replied. "Louisa is watching out for it."

"I'm sorry to hear you are poorly. Is there anything I can do for you?"

Louisa came back down the hallway and looked at Eleanor with concern. A few minutes earlier she had been sitting up straight and alert; now she was slightly slumped and had two patches of high colour in otherwise pale cheeks. Her heart began to race with anxiety.

"Are you feeling worse, my dear?" she asked, sitting down beside her and putting her hand to her forehead. She didn't feel as if she had a fever but it wasn't always easy to tell.

"Oh no, I'm sure I'll be fine – just very tired," Eleanor said so quietly it was almost a whisper.

"Should I have Peterson fetched?" Nicholas asked turning to Louisa with a look of concern.

"Please, no – I just need to go home," Eleanor jumped in. "Please, Louisa. Dr. Peterson always pulls me about so. I do hate fuss." She was becoming quite agitated, which was usually a sign that she was frightened by her own symptoms.

"It's all right, Eleanor, we will go home. Just rest quietly. I will go and see if the carriage is at the door," she said, trying her best to placate her.

But as she began to rise Nicholas forestalled her. "I'll look. Stay with her," he said as he headed off to the door where Morrissey's elderly butler was standing to attention. She sank back down next to Eleanor and tried to give her an encouraging smile, but deep down she was starting to feel sick with worry. She watched anxiously for his return, her arm around Eleanor's frail shoulders.

"It's here," he informed her a few minutes later, as he came back up the hallway. "If you give me a few minutes to say my farewells, I will assist you."

Astonished, she watched him disappear up the stairs before she could even object. The maid appeared at that moment and helped her put Eleanor's coat on, but worryingly, Eleanor had to lean heavily on her for support as they waited. When Nicholas appeared back in the hallway, he took one look at Eleanor's condition, picked her up and headed out to the carriage. She trailed behind, suddenly grateful for his decisiveness. This was the kind of incident that she had feared for months.

Nicholas settled Eleanor down in the corner of the carriage and wrapped the blanket around her, then alighted to hand Louisa up. Once she was seated, he took the seat opposite.

"There really is no need to put yourself out," she told him hurriedly. "I can manage from here. You shouldn't miss the party on our account. You should go back."

He gave her a kindly look. "Don't concern yourself. I'm only too happy to have an excuse to leave," he replied. "This evening has been rather tiresome."

"But what about Anna? Didn't she mind?"

"Why should she? I explained what had happened. Her only concern was Eleanor's welfare. Besides, Robert is quite capable of getting her home."

"Well, if you're sure, thank you. I do appreciate your help," she replied quietly. Eleanor was half asleep, leaning back into the squabs. She took hold of her wrist and felt for her pulse; it was reassuringly normal. She was very grateful that he had come with them, as Eleanor's rapid deterioration in the hallway had been unusual and frightening.

"Will she be all right?" he asked gently.

"I hope so. A good night's sleep should help."

As they left Newton and its street lights behind, the interior of the carriage dimmed and only a faint flicker from the exterior lanterns gave any illumination. Eleanor muttered in her sleep and leant her head on her shoulder. Within minutes she appeared to have dropped off into a deep sleep, lulled by the rhythm of the carriage. Louisa desperately tried to think of something to say. The silence was unbearable.

"Do the Morrisseys always entertain on such a large scale? I think half of Carlisle was there tonight. I hardly recognised anyone."

"William always likes to make a statement with his hospitality. He never misses an opportunity to show the world how important he is."

"Do I detect disapproval?"

He sighed. "Rampant ambition is not an endearing quality in anyone."

"But surely the power and wealth of the nation is built on just that? It is regrettable that he conducts his social life along those lines, but he is hardly unique. I know enough of the world to realise that moral hypocrisy goes hand in hand with social climbing."

"I take it you are a keen observer of the human condition."

"I speak as I find, Mr. Maxwell. But I do admit to having an aunt who would surpass even Mr. Morrissey's social aspirations."

"She sounds delightful. Do let me know if she plans to visit."

She could not keep the scorn from her voice. "It is unlikely that you will have the pleasure of meeting her. She is not particularly fond of us and unlikely to darken our door. She was put out that we left Dublin. I think she liked having us to look down on. She loved to boast to her cronies about how charitable she was, even though it was pure fiction."

"You really must invite her. She sounds like a family treasure. I don't believe for a minute that she has ever bested you."

"No, she hasn't and that's why she dislikes me so very much. I can't imagine that she has ever liked anyone, not even her poor husband. But I never knew him. He died a few years after they married."

"Better and better! A widow so young – how convenient!"

"You are jumping to conclusions. He was much older than her, I believe, and in ill health."

He burst out laughing. "You couldn't make this up. You have a fascinating family."

"I don't know about that as I never met any of them, bar my aunt. If the rest are anything like her I'm happy to remain in ignorance."

"They can't be any worse than most families, I think you'll find."

"Perhaps," she conceded. "Unfortunately, Uncle Jack caused quite a rift which resulted in us being cut off from my mother's family. I do not know what he did to merit being ostracised, but we bore the brunt of it, while he seems to have led a very prosperous life here in England."

"I imagine it was somewhat distressing for you to discover that."

She was surprised by the sympathetic tone to his voice. "More astounded than distressed. Until the letter from Jamesons arrived, we were unaware that our father even had a brother."

"I see." He frowned. "I wonder what he did to warrant exile."

"Yes, it is intriguing but I don't believe I will ever know."

"I cannot enlighten you. His past was a mystery and sparked a lot of speculation. Obviously we didn't mix socially, so we were unaware of his family situation. He was an odd character though. He deliberately antagonised local society and never associated with anyone unless it was to cause mischief. In fact, he cultivated an aura of secrecy, deliberately I believe. He liked the notoriety – he certainly courted it."

"I wish he had not," she complained, thinking of all the trouble it had caused for her and Eleanor. "It sounds as though he had quite a high opinion of himself."

"He did. But I have to admit that I had some degree of appreciation for your uncle's 'talents'. He outwitted my father and me continually."

"You're just being kind. I know very well you loathed him," she protested, which caused Eleanor to stir. She continued in a softer tone, "I think I owe you an apology, firstly for defending him – though that was before I realised that you might be right – and secondly for his making your life so … complicated."

"There is no need for you to apologise on that man's behalf," he said with a frown.

"All the same, I wish I could undo all the trouble he has caused," she said.

He reached across and took her hand. "My dear Miss Campbell, don't be foolish. Forget about him as best you can. You must concentrate on the future." His voice was full of concern, causing her heart to lurch. He blinked rapidly, looking startled himself. He released her hand and she could breathe again. Her physical awareness of him had just soared and she found that her mouth was dry. She found it best to concentrate on a point just above his left shoulder. She could not bring herself to meet his penetrating gaze.

He cleared his throat, sounding uncharacteristically tense. "I do have one reason to be thankful to him. He did save me from a most unfortunate alliance, though not intentionally."

"Mrs. Rathbone?"

"Yes," he exclaimed. "How do you know about that?"

"Anna."

"Ah, yes, my dear sister is never slow to lay me open to

ridicule," he grumbled. "She can never leave well enough alone."

"No, no, that wasn't her intention. She wanted me to understand the nature of your relationship with my uncle."

"I must remember to thank her," he said, clearly exasperated. "That particular episode has now come back to haunt me, of course, but I'm so glad it offered you and Robert some amusement this evening."

"But our host provided so little entertainment – we needed some light relief," she said flippantly, hoping to diffuse the tension that had suddenly crept into the conversation.

"So much for my standing in the community. I might as well take to the stage."

"Now you're just feeling sorry for yourself. Anyway you looked like you were well able to deal with the situation."

"Indeed. So well in fact, that I have decided to go into hiding until both women lose interest. I can't think how else to escape their clutches."

"Where will you go?" she asked, playing along.

"I'm not telling you! You'd give them my direction just for the fun of it."

"That is harsh … but probably true. However, I don't believe you are that cowardly that you would run away."

"Well, you are wrong: I am a coward when it comes to those two harpies. And I am going away, as it happens."

"Oh, I see," she said, feeling surprisingly deflated at the thought of him leaving.

"I leave for Devon in two days. Some friends have been urging me to visit them for some time."

"A holiday then? Not a strategic retreat."

"Correct. Though I have to admit that I was wavering slightly as to when to go, but tonight's impositions by various parties have decided me," he replied. "However, I do have one difficulty which I was hoping you might be able to help me with."

"Certainly; if I am able."

"I'm not happy leaving Anna alone for so long. All kinds of mischief is possible, so I was hoping you might call on her now and again. Now, of course, if Miss Eleanor is unwell I would not expect you to leave her ..."

"Not at all. She is rarely ill for long. It would be no trouble at all. In fact, Anna may like to visit us for a few days."

"She would, of course, but I must warn you, she can be very overpowering. You will have no quiet moments for contemplation with her in the house."

"That might be a good thing, Mr. Maxwell," she replied with feeling. "But tell me, how will you cope when she gets married and leaves for good? You will have a whole house to rattle around in by yourself."

"Oh, I intend to enjoy the peace and quiet, Miss Campbell. I shall grow old disgracefully and turn into an irascible hermit who delights in tormenting his unfortunate relations and neighbours whenever they darken my door."

"No doubt *I* will be on the receiving end of this delightful behaviour."

"But of course – I'll be particularly nasty to you."

"You appear to have given this some thought. Thank you for the warning," she laughingly replied.

Chapter Nineteen

"**M**iss Campbell." Róisín was trying to catch her attention. It was breakfast time and she was sitting staring off into the middle distance, her tea untouched and cold. "Miss – your post."

"Sorry, Róisín, I was miles away. Is Miss Eleanor awake yet?"

"Awake and getting dressed, Miss. Don't you be worrying about her. As fresh as a daisy she is, thank the Lord."

"Oh, that is marvellous; I didn't expect to hear that!"

"Yes, Miss. She seems fine this morning, after giving us all such a fright last night." Róisín left the post down on the table beside her, beamed at her in her friendly way, and left the room.

She sat back in her chair. Eleanor's speedy recovery was a surprise; she had appeared so unwell the previous night. Usually it took days for her spirits and her energy to be restored. She picked up the letters and absentmindedly looked through them. When she saw the cream hand-delivered envelope her heart skipped a beat. She recognised the writing immediately and knew it had come from Nicholas. The memory of the previous missive such an envelope had contained rushed back to her and she hesitated with the letter opener in her hand. She couldn't bear the thought that it might contain something unpleasant, but equally she hoped it didn't contain something else entirely.

His manner the evening before had left her in no doubt that her growing suspicion regarding his feelings had been correct. When they had arrived at Bowes, he had carried Eleanor into the house, and up the stairs to her room. While waiting for Anna and Robert to collect him, he had sat chatting to her in the drawing room in an easy manner that had left her feeling well disposed towards him. On taking his leave, he held her hand far longer than necessary and kissed it. She had retired for the night in a bit of a daze.

She propped the envelope up against the milk jug and stared at it. I have too much to deal with as it is, she thought. Between Eleanor's health and deep distrust of her steward, she felt as if she was always on the edge of a precipice. Deep down there was the uncomfortable notion that Nicholas was up to something. It just didn't make sense that he should be trying to drive her out of her home one minute, and then making amorous advances the next. She scolded herself for cowardice, and was on the point of reaching for the letter when Eleanor entered the room. She hopped up from her seat and embraced her.

"I'm delighted to see you. I thought you would be in bed for the day. I hope you are well enough to be up?" she asked.

Eleanor appeared a little flustered. "Yes, I feel fine – a little tired perhaps, but I could not stay in bed." She gestured out the window. "It's such a beautiful morning." Louisa thought there was something a little forced about her brightness and began to wonder. While Eleanor helped herself to some breakfast at the sideboard, she tucked Nicholas's letter away in her pocket. She would deal with it later, away from curious eyes.

"Are you sure you are all right?" she asked with concern, as she watched Eleanor sit down and proceed to smother her toast in marmalade. Nothing was wrong with her appetite, that was for sure.

"Yes, I overdid it last night, that is all. My vanity got the better of me. I should have stopped playing sooner but when everyone was so kind I couldn't refuse. Such a lovely grand piano, too. It must have cost a fortune."

"So nothing to do with Captain Maxwell being so attentive, I suppose?" she teased.

"No. But he is such a pleasant man," she remarked. "Such a

pity Mr. Maxwell isn't more like him in manner."

"They have different personalities, that is all," she replied.

Eleanor gave her a quizzical look. "But even if Mr. Maxwell's manner is not as easy-going, he is terribly kind, isn't he? To have accompanied us home was so thoughtful. How would we have managed without him?"

"The groom would have managed perfectly well."

Eleanor cocked her head to the side. "Was there any awkwardness? I understand he had to wait to be brought home."

"No, it was fine."

"You didn't argue?"

"No."

"Really? So what did you talk about?"

"Eleanor," she answered impatiently, "we talked of nothing – polite conversation. I could hardly pick a quarrel with him after his kindness." She picked up the newspaper in an effort to still the uncomfortable line of questioning from her sister. But she couldn't resist adding, dipping the stiff white wall of paper enough to look directly at her, "Besides, he wanted an excuse to leave. He was being plagued by Miss Morrissey and Mrs. Rathbone. Surely you noticed?" The newspaper snapped back up into position, forming a barrier.

"I see. Any post?"

"Nothing of interest."

"Not even from Aunt Milly? She has been very quiet of late."

"We are out of sight and therefore out of mind."

"Have we any plans for today?"

She put the paper down again. Eleanor was in an irritating and peculiar mood, she thought. "Nothing specific, but I do have some news as it happens. Anna may be coming to stay with us for a couple of days."

"Really? How lovely," Eleanor replied. "Is there any particular reason?"

"Mr. Maxwell is going on holiday and was anxious about leaving her alone at Thorncroft. He asked us to visit, which I was happy to agree to, and I suggested it would very nice to have her to stay with us as well. It seemed to ease his mind about her."

"I see," Eleanor said with a smile. "I'm glad. It will be fun to have her here with us for a while. She is always so amusing."

"He leaves tomorrow, I understand. If you feel up to it, we could pay her a call in the afternoon."

"Of course. I must say, I do envy him going to Devon. I've read it's a really beautiful place." Eleanor blushed suddenly and bit her lip. "Oh dear!"

"Eleanor!"

Louisa stared at her sister, astonished. She had not told her where he was going, which meant that Eleanor had not been asleep in the carriage after all, and had heard their entire conversation. Suddenly the swift recovery was making more sense. Had the whole episode been orchestrated to throw her and Nicholas together? It would explain the odd circumstance of her falling ill so quickly in the hallway. This Machiavellian streak in Eleanor was unexpected and would be amusing if it wasn't directed at her. But how could she be angry with her when she obviously had only the best of intentions? It was just unfortunate that her feelings towards the man were hard to define.

Nicholas's note had been brief. He expressed his hope that Eleanor was better and thanked her for offering her hospitality to Anna. There was nothing intimate about it whatsoever, other than a casual closing salutation of 'Nicholas'. A small part of her was slightly disappointed.

The days that followed were a flurry of activity, including an exhausting expedition to Carlisle for wedding and bridesmaid dress fittings. She could only wonder how Nicholas kept up with his dynamo of a sister, and concluded that his manipulation of Anna's love life was purely a self-preserving attempt to get some much needed peace and quiet.

The weeks leading up to Anna's wedding flew by with alarming speed and although she spent many hours with Anna, supporting her friend through all the tiny 'disasters' that threatened the wedding of the season, she saw next to nothing of Nicholas, who seemed determined to stay well out of the way of his sister's frenetic last-minute arrangements.

One afternoon at Thorncroft he came across them in the middle of an argument over some tiny detail. He looked as though he was going to beat a hasty retreat, but then with a look of mischief, he leaned against the door frame and cleared his throat.

"My dear Anna, I think I was mistaken in letting Robert join the army. It should have been you. You have undoubtedly missed your calling."

"Whatever do you mean, Nicholas?" Anna demanded crossly.

"Well, it seems to me that there have been military campaigns with less organisation put into them."

Louisa fought hard to smother a laugh.

Anna looked at him askance. "Do you have any idea how much planning has to go into a wedding? Do you?"

Nicholas bit his lip, trying not to laugh. "My apologies. I bow to your superior knowledge on the subject."

"You're being tiresome."

"And you, dear sister, are overwrought. Poor John – my heart goes out to him." He shook his head sadly.

Anna looked as if she might explode. "Out!"

"I'm going, I'm going," he said. Then he paused and winked at Louisa before escaping out the door.

Louisa could feel Anna's eyes on her and could not help but redden self-consciously.

"Well, well! Is there something I should know?" Anna enquired with wide-eyed curiosity.

"I really think you should choose the white lace handkerchiefs for the bridesmaids," she said in a futile attempt to forestall interrogation.

Louisa was looking over the account books in the study one wet afternoon. It was a job that she disliked, but she was determined not to let O'Connor have an opportunity of patronising her about the estate finances. The problem was that she was bored and her mind soon wandered off. Every time she sat in the study she had a strong sense of her late uncle's presence. The smell of books and a faint lingering hint of cigar probably accounted for it.

After all the months they had lived here, she still didn't quite know what to make of Uncle Jack. Had he been as bad as Nicholas believed? It was odd that no one ever mentioned him, as if society had agreed tacitly that he was a taboo subject. Even O'Connor never spoke of him to her. As she sat pondering his possible misdeeds, she remembered the love letters she had found the day she had first tackled the desk. The temptation to read them at that moment was very strong and soon she was sliding open the bottom drawer where they had lain undisturbed for months. She lifted out the folders at the top and paused in bewilderment. The letters were gone. At first she thought she had left them in the drawer on the other side, but that was revealed as completely empty. She was disconcerted: she was the only one who had a key to the desk and she always locked it when she was finished. Where on earth could the letters be?

Later that evening she brought the subject up at dinner, and asked Eleanor if she had taken them.

"No, you said I shouldn't read them," Eleanor replied, looking aggrieved. "I wouldn't take them without asking."

"I know."

"You must have mislaid them. You have been a little distracted lately," Eleanor remarked pointedly.

"No, I had almost forgotten about them," she replied. The absence of the letters bothered her. Had someone been snooping around in the study and the desk? Why would they take a dead man's old love letters? It didn't make sense.

"You don't think one of the servants took them, do you?" Eleanor asked, her eyes wide with concern. "It would be horrible to think that someone was going through our things."

She didn't want to distress her and casually replied, "No, you are right, my dear. I must have moved them. They are probably caught up with other papers somewhere in the desk. I'll look for them again."

The incident was to bother her for days afterwards, so much so that she searched all the drawers in the hopes of finding the missing billets-doux, but they had vanished without a trace.

It was early June, and after weeks of overcast skies, the sun had finally peeped out from behind the clouds, and deigned to shine. Even though they had left for the Maxwell wedding early in the morning, it was soon uncomfortably warm in the confined space of the carriage and Eleanor was complaining of feeling travel-sick. When they turned off the main road and headed inland towards the Lake District, they were painfully aware of every rut and hole the carriage found on the twisting country lanes. Róisín was soon turning an alarming colour as well, and Louisa had to swap places with her and complete the journey in the dreaded position of her back to the horses.

As the carriage trundled through tiny villages, the fells began to loom large and slightly ominous to the east and south. Their first glimpse of a shimmering distant lake gave Eleanor false hope that they had reached their destination, but Louisa had to point out from the guidebook that it was Ennerdale, and they still had some distance to travel to Buttermere, where Anna's wedding was to take place. She almost laughed at the dismayed expressions of the two girls opposite her.

As they journeyed further, the scenery evoked an unexpected homesickness in her. She recalled a journey her family had undertaken when she was about five years old and Eleanor was just a baby, fast asleep in her mother's arms. They had travelled through the wild Connemara landscape, past brooding mountains and still dark lakes. The names of those places still resonated with her; it was her one and only memory of Galway, for they had never returned. For some time, her thoughts remained on her parents and she wondered had their love for each other been enough to compensate for all they had lost. She had never seen regret in her mother's eyes, but there had been sadness. No doubt her dreams of married life and what it would hold had evaporated quickly when the reality of a life of poverty, exiled from her family, was fully felt.

From brooding on her parent's marriage, it was a short leap to matters of her own heart. For weeks now she had been mulling over the twisty dilemma of Nicholas. When they did meet there was no mistaking the look of ardour in his eyes. She was grateful that he was not forcing the issue and was pleased that he realised her priority would always be Eleanor. It was a significant mark in his favour. But now they would be thrown together for several days, staying under the same roof and socialising with the same people. Her heart beat faster at the thought. She wasn't a fool. Despite everything that had happened, and the fact that she didn't trust him completely, she had fallen in love with him. Where that would lead, she did not know. For now, it was enough to acknowledge her feelings. There was comfort in it, being her secret from the rest of the world, and she hugged it to herself like a warm blanket.

After the three-hour journey the ladies were more than eager to reach their destination. It was with great relief that they finally entered the gates of Ashbury Lodge. They were shown to their room and Eleanor immediately lay down on the bed with a sigh. She had been an alarming shade of green for most of the journey. "This is lovely, but I just need to rest a while, Louisa," she said closing her eyes.

Louisa had barely sat down when a very agitated Anna burst into the room.

"Thank heaven you are here, ladies. Oh Louisa, there is so much still to be done."

"Hello, Anna," she said, smiling. "What is the matter?" Eleanor remained on the bed but raised her hand in salute without even opening her eyes.

"The stupid gardener has picked the wrong colour flowers and Aunt Gwen is in a foul mood and has retreated to her room. We argued about the canapés ... again."

"Oh dear," she said, trying to sound sympathetic.

Anna sat down on the bed with a helpless shrug of her shoulders. "Nicholas and Robert disappeared off into the fells at the first sign of trouble this morning."

Louisa could not help but think they were wise to have made an escape. "Why don't we take a walk in the garden and think about it all calmly."

"Yes, all right," Anna said looking relieved. "Just so you know, Mrs. Lambert and Geneviève arrived this morning. They are staying here – in the next room to you, in fact."

"Mrs. Rathbone? Wonderful!" she exclaimed, with a sinking heart.

"I'm sorry. I don't particularly like her either, but Nicholas insisted that they were both invited." Anna shrugged. "There was nothing I could do. We could not ask Mrs. Lambert and ignore Mrs. Rathbone when she is living with her at the moment."

"Of course not," she assured her friend, but she had an uneasy feeling about it. Was Nicholas insisting on her inclusion for politeness sake, or was there another, more personal reason? "Now; Eleanor needs to rest. Let's take that walk," she suggested, as much to distract herself as her harassed friend.

Chapter Twenty

A far from calm John Whitby watched his bride walk up the aisle of St. James' church on her eldest brother's arm. All the fuss of the previous weeks was soon forgotten and by the time Mr. and Mrs. Whitby left the church in Buttermere, more than one guest was wiping their eyes. Everyone then travelled back to Ashbury Lodge, by carriage, for the wedding breakfast.

As the weather was so fine, tables and chairs had been set up on the front lawn of the house and the guests were able to wander about, admire the views and mingle at their leisure. Relieved of her bridesmaid duties, Louisa was able to relax at last. She spotted a nice shady table under an oak tree where they could avoid the strong afternoon sun, and manoeuvred Eleanor towards it. They settled down in the shadow of the trees.

"Doesn't she look lovely – and so happy?" Eleanor observed. The bride was holding court in the centre of the lawn surrounded by guests. John stood at her side, looking slightly bewildered. The mingled sounds of chatter and laughter floated over the lawn towards them.

"Indeed, she is blessed in all her choices," Mrs. Lambert said, as she came up to them. "May I join you, ladies?"

"Of course. I insist on it!" Louisa said, pulling out a chair for her friend.

"This is a lovely spot you have found," Mrs. Lambert said as she sat down with a grateful sigh, resting her walking stick against the table.

"You are not too fatigued by the heat, I hope?" Louisa asked.

"No, my dear, every comfort has been offered me."

They sat in companionable silence for a few minutes. A continuous stream of footmen came past offering food and drink.

"I think I could happily sit here forever," Eleanor said with a contented sigh.

"Ladies, is there any room for a poor soldier ready to collapse?" Captain Maxwell had suddenly appeared before them, looking very hot and woebegone.

"Captain, sit by me, please," Mrs. Lambert said, patting the seat beside her. "You poor boy. Louisa will pour out a glass of lemonade for you." She did so, knowing full well it wasn't lemonade he wanted but something far stronger. She handed him the glass with a sympathetic smile.

"Thank you." He downed the drink in two gulps. "I think I am in great danger of expiring. Hot sun and this uniform are an unfortunate combination," he said. "I wish Anna would let me change. It's too cruel to expect a man to melt for the sake of a few photographs," he complained.

"Oh no, I had forgotten about that. Does that mean I have to go too?" Louisa asked.

"Yes, Miss Campbell. I believe the torture in the name of posterity is imminent. Look: John is rounding everyone up as we speak." Mr. Whitby was beckoning to them to hurry over. "Come, Miss Campbell. Let us go into battle together."

She took his offered arm, but not before she warned the ladies to mind her seat.

The photographs were to be taken on the front steps of the house. Just as they passed the corner of the house, Geneviève emerged from the rose garden and headed off down the path, completely ignoring them, her face contorted in fury.

"I wonder what that's about." Robert gave her a quizzical glance. She shrugged, equally curious.

The wedding party was slowly gathering at the bottom of the steps, so they joined the group and waited as the photographer and his assistant set up the equipment.

"Where is Nicholas?" Anna hissed at her brother as soon as she spotted him. "This is no time for him to disappear."

"He'll turn up, sis, calm down," Robert replied, with a roll of his eyes. "Look, here he is now." Nicholas had just appeared around the very same corner as Geneviève and came striding up to the group. He didn't look in a particularly good mood. Robert raised his brows conspiratorially at Louisa. He was obviously thinking the same as she: there had been some kind of confrontation in the rose garden.

For the next twenty minutes they underwent the tedium of being pulled in and out of different groups for photographs. Nicholas remained silent throughout, fuelling her curiosity. By the end of it all everyone looked out of sorts, and Robert made a swift escape back into the house, muttering about demanding sisters and stupid uniforms. Wilting a little herself, she beat a hasty retreat back to the ladies sitting in the shade. As she took her seat, Eleanor gave her a warning look.

Mrs. Lambert appeared to be distracted and sat peering into the distance with a frown. "Did you see Geneviève anywhere, my dear? I'm getting anxious about her. I haven't seen her since we got back from church. Where can she have got to?"

Louisa could not help hoping that the woman would not intrude into their little haven of tranquillity. At the celebratory dinner the previous evening she had been tedious, constantly needing to be the centre of attention and flirting outrageously. She had quickly perceived that even Nicholas was exasperated by the woman's behaviour.

"Yes, I did see her, a little while ago up at the house. I'm sure she is mingling with the guests and will seek you out shortly." She tried to sound reassuring but Mrs. Lambert still looked troubled. She felt sorry for her. She had to put up with a great deal from her highly-strung daughter. "Why don't I take a walk around and see if I can find her for you?" she offered.

"That would be wonderful," Mrs. Lambert replied. Eleanor gave her an encouraging smile as she passed, and she patted her shoulder, resigned to her fate; at least Eleanor was enjoying herself.

She headed back up the path towards the house. With over a hundred and sixty guests present, it wasn't going to be easy to find the elusive Geneviève, especially if she didn't wish to be found. 'That will teach me for being so helpful,' she muttered to herself, lamenting her own impetuous nature.

"I believe it is considered a sign of madness to talk to oneself." It was Robert Maxwell, coming along the path to meet her.

"There may be truth in that, Captain, for I cannot have been thinking clearly to have taken on such an impossible task," she replied.

"That sounds intriguing, I have to say. Can I be of assistance, perhaps?"

She let out a slow breath. "Mrs. Lambert is concerned about her daughter. She hasn't seen her for some time. I foolishly offered to find her. You don't happen to know where she is, by any chance?"

Robert shook his head. "No, I haven't seen her since we saw her leave the rose garden earlier."

She sighed in exasperation. "She could be anywhere."

Robert smiled in understanding. "Why don't I help you? I'll check the house if you look amongst the guests in the gardens. She must be here somewhere, no doubt keeping an assignation of some sort." She nodded in agreement, equally sure that Geneviève was up to no good.

Robert turned around and disappeared up the steps of the house. For Louisa, the temptation to make just a cursory search was strong. Geneviève's disappearance was most likely deliberate, just to draw attention. She did not wish to pander to such manipulative behaviour, but neither could she bear to sit with Mrs. Lambert and do nothing when the elderly lady was so concerned. The dear lady had so often been their ally that it seemed churlish not to help. She slowly and methodically worked her way down the garden, searching for Geneviève's blue dress and bonnet amongst the scattered clusters of guests. But there was no trace of her.

As she stood undecided, she spotted the little chapel down at the water's edge. It would be the perfect spot for anyone in a solitary mood or keeping a clandestine rendezvous. She stalled before the chapel door. What if Geneviève didn't want to be found or was indeed meeting someone? She didn't relish any manner of confrontation with her but she remembered Mrs. Lambert's anxious face and relented. She took a calming breath, ready to do battle and pushed open the oak door. Half expecting to find her waiting inside, she stepped into the cool interior. But the little chapel was empty. She stood transfixed just inside the doorway. The walls were pristine white with small murals depicting biblical scenes down each side. Interspersed with these were memorial family plaques. High-set windows of stained glass filtered the sunlight, creating a rainbow of colour on the opposite wall. She slowly made her way down one of the side aisles, examining the art work.

As she stood admiring the skill of the painter, she heard voices from outside and looked up. The window above her was open. Some of the guests must have decided to stroll along the lake shore, she thought, and moved away to the next mural.

"Mrs. Rathbone." That was Nicholas's voice she heard – she was sure of it. She quickly retraced her steps and stood beneath the window, straining to hear, unable to help herself.

"Geneviève, I implore you …" His voice drifted away.

Louisa looked about her in frustration. If she was closer to the window she might hear better. She hopped up on to the nearest pew and leaned towards the window, her heart beating faster. If someone came in and discovered her in this position she would have great difficulty explaining herself, but her curiosity was raging.

"But Nicholas, I don't understand how you could be so cruel," came Geneviève's plaintive voice. "There is nothing to keep us apart now."

"Madam, I cannot make it any clearer to you. I do not wish to have any manner of relationship with you."

"No! You don't mean it. I've seen the way you look at me. I have seen the desire in your eyes. Why else did you dance with me at the Kirkbride Ball? I know you feel the same way. Why have you not married all these years? Explain that to me."

"You believe that I have been wearing the willow for you?" Nicholas asked. "You are delusional."

Geneviève laughed. "You don't fool me. Nothing has changed. It is just like all those years ago before we were torn apart."

"Your memory is very selective, Geneviève. I will remind you that it was you that tore us apart. For my part, it was blind infatuation. It could not have stood the test of time or your fickle nature." Louisa could hear the revulsion in his voice.

"Last night, you were all attention," Geneviève complained.

"I tolerated your behaviour only because your poor mother has had enough to bear from you. I did not wish to make a scene in front of so many of my friends and family. But let me make it clear to you now: your behaviour since you have returned to Newton has been inappropriate, and quite frankly disgusts me. Whatever we once had, is long gone. I'm sorry to be so blunt, but you must understand that this situation cannot continue."

There was silence for a moment. "I'll make you sorry. Who do you think you are that you can speak to me like that? You want to humiliate me in front of all these people? Well, we will see who is in charge, won't we?"

"Geneviève …"

There was the sound of ripping fabric.

"Well, Mr. High and Mighty, let's see what people think of you when they see me like this. Who do you think they will believe? You will have no choice but to marry me, unless you want a scandal." There was a pause before she continued. "You have half an hour. I'm going back to my room. You can let me know your decision, or should I say your agreement? It's no idle threat, Nicholas. If you don't agree, I will create such a scene, just as the happy couple are departing for their honeymoon."

Louisa's feet almost got entangled in her skirt as she dropped from the pew to the floor in haste, staggered at what she had just overheard. Geneviève was quite capable of carrying out her threat. It was incredibly ruthless of her – to pretend that he had compromised her to trap him into marriage. It was hard not to feel sympathy for Nicholas; to be ensnared like this was appalling. She would have to help him. Her sense of justice, if not her own feelings for him, demanded it.

Just as she was gathering her things, the chapel door opened and she spun round. Nicholas came through the door, white-faced and grim. He stopped when he saw her.

"Miss Campbell," he said, his voice hollow.

She took a step towards him but didn't know what to say. He stood staring at her, his hands clutching the back of a pew

"I heard it all," she blurted out. "What she said; all of it." She glanced up towards the window. "I could not help but overhear."

Embarrassment flickered in his eyes. He sat down heavily.

"You cannot give in to her," she said, taking a few steps closer.

"It would be her word against mine," he said, running his hand through his hair.

"No, Mr. Maxwell," she said firmly. "I am your witness. If she tries to make good her threat I will back you, even publically, if necessary. I know you did not touch her or compromise her in any way."

He looked up sharply. "You would do that for me?"

"I would do that for anyone in such a position," she said. "Go and tell her that her horrible scheme will not succeed. When she knows what I am prepared to do, she will back down." He looked at her in disbelief. "However, I strongly advise you bring someone with you as a witness; ideally, her mother. She may try a different tactic. You really must avoid being alone with her again."

Nicholas closed his eyes momentarily and nodded slowly. "Yes, I know. Thank you, I will do as you suggest." He regarded her with an expression that made her knees feel suddenly unsupportive. "You are a marvel, Miss Campbell. I am indebted to you."

Slowly, he got to his feet and gave her a bleak smile. When he reached the door, he hesitated with his hand on the wrought-iron handle, and turned to her with a look so full of emotion that she caught her breath. She gestured for him to go. When the door clicked shut she sat down and contemplated the vagaries of fate for quite some time.

Chapter Twenty-One

T he next morning, with a pine tree to her back and the wonderful Buttermere scenery before her, Louisa had settled down to a cosy read down by the lake. She did not wish to see Geneviève and felt it best to stay out of the way until the Lamberts had left for home. But she was soon lost in a daydream, her book forgotten. Her peace was broken, however, when Nicholas appeared around the corner of the chapel. They had not spoken since they had parted the previous day. She had retired to her room once Anna and John had departed for their honeymoon and had spent the rest of the evening pacing her room, dying to know the outcome of Nicholas's predicament.

His face broke into a smile when he saw her. "There you are. I've been looking everywhere for you," he said.

He walked along the shore to where she was sitting, and she shaded her eyes to look up at him. He was dressed informally in a Norfolk jacket and tweed trousers and was carrying a backpack on his shoulder, every inch the country gentleman. She wondered where he was off to.

"I'm not hiding, if that is what you are implying," she answered. "I just thought it best to absent myself."

"I was ordered to by my aunt. I had to inform her of yesterday's debacle and she wasn't best pleased that Anna's day was nearly spoiled," he said. To her surprise, he dropped down on the grass beside her, depositing his bag at his feet. "I am in your debt, Miss Campbell. If you hadn't been in the chapel ..."

"Yes, well, I'm glad I was able to help." She could not meet his eye but watched a bird as it swooped down into the water. It rose up again seconds later with a wriggling fish in its talons.

"I understand they are leaving this morning," he said after a few minutes.

"Good," she replied, before turning to him. "I can't help thinking I have a made an enemy, though."

"I didn't name you," he said. "I just said that a guest had overheard our conversation, was upset by it, and was willing to give evidence that would vindicate me."

"I see. And she believed it?"

"She had calmed down enough to know that trying to cross me would bring her nothing but trouble. Her mother's presence and angry words dealt the final blow to her plan."

"So it is over?"

"Yes." They both sat silently, looking out across the smooth surface of the water.

"Can you swim, Miss Campbell?" he asked after a while.

"Rather gracelessly I'm afraid – I have had very little practice. Most sensible people keep well away from me in the water, no doubt fearing I will drag them down with me."

He chuckled. "I can, but I have nightmares about drowning. I'm always in a mine shaft filling with water and it's pitch dark."

"That's awful!" she said. "But have you ever actually been in a mine shaft?"

He looked at her reproachfully. "Of course I have. I own enough of 'em."

"It doesn't necessarily follow..."

"You think I'm too grand to get my hands dirty?"

"I can't quite see you shovelling coal, I do admit."

"Hmmm," he said. He picked up her book, flicked through a few pages, then put in down again.

Seeing his distracted state of mind, she sought a safe topic. "It is really beautiful here. The park is wonderful. You must find it difficult to leave whenever you visit."

He turned to her with enthusiasm. "Yes, it is one of my

favourite places. We spent a lot of time here as children. It's almost a second home to us. Many summers were spent up in the fells or larking about on the lake."

"You're very lucky. It sounds like an ideal childhood." And a huge contrast to her own, she couldn't help thinking.

"It was. Unfortunately, I must leave tomorrow. I have petty sessions on Wednesday. What are your plans?"

"I think it best we leave tomorrow, too, but I'm not looking forward to it. Eleanor and our maid were travel-sick the entire journey here. I don't suppose you want to swap carriages?" she asked.

He raised a brow. "No thanks. I had enough of that with Anna over the years."

"Coward."

"Sanity-preserving coward, if you must."

She tossed her head and tried to look wounded. "Well, no doubt we will survive."

He smiled. "Break the journey and it may not be too bad. I can recommend a few inns on the route," he said, standing up and brushing off the sand and grass from his trousers. "I'll leave you in peace with your book." He looked at her intently, clearly wishing to linger.

"Where are you going now?" she asked.

"I usually try to climb at least two peaks when I'm here. I already did High Stile the other day with Robert," he said, pointing up to the left. "It's a tough climb, but the views are worth it. I am going to climb Haystacks today."

"Which one is Haystacks?"

"You can't see it from here. It's behind the house. It's not as high, but has equally lovely views."

"What an unusual name for a mountain."

He indicated the outline of it with his hand. "It's because of its shape. It's steep in places, but not the most difficult of climbs in this valley."

He looked thoughtful for a moment. "You walk a lot, don't you? Haystacks is a hard enough climb – it takes a few hours – but you would be well able for it. Why don't you come up with me?"

She could think of a million excuses, but somehow they all seemed trifling and she actually wanted to go with him. "I have never climbed before. Would I not need the proper boots and clothes? I don't have anything suitable with me."

"Stout boots and a warm jacket is all you need. My aunt keeps a supply of hiking gear for visitors up in the house. If you run up and get what you need, I'll meet you at the gate leading up into the woods behind the house." He seemed to be holding his breath, waiting for her answer.

"Yes, I'd like to go," she said at last.

He held out his hand to pull her up, looking every inch as if he had just won a prize.

Half an hour later, Louisa was walking quickly along the path towards the woods, full sure that Nicholas would have given up on her and left. But when she arrived at the designated spot he was sitting on a log with a resigned expression.

"Aunt Gwen?" he asked with a wry smile.

She nodded. "I'm sorry, but she insisted that I change," she explained, looking down at the wool skirt and thick boots she had borrowed from his aunt. He gestured for her to precede him through the gate.

"Aunt Gwen is an experienced climber. She knows what she's about. Even when its warm down here, it can be chilly on the mountain," he informed her as he followed her through, before shutting the gate firmly.

"Now, a couple of things before we go any further: if you get tired or feel unwell, tell me immediately. A tired climber is more likely to have an accident. Do you give me your word?" Louisa looked at him suspiciously. "Seriously, Louisa; a mountain is a dangerous place if you don't know what you're doing. We are not moving another inch until you promise me."

"I promise," she answered meekly.

"Good. Let's go."

A few minutes later they came out of the cool greenness of the woods. Ahead of them the sun shone on the slopes of Haystacks. From this vantage point, she started to doubt her ability to climb the mountain. It looked very high to her novice's eye, but there was no way that she would admit her doubts to the man beside her.

"Did you see anything of the Lamberts?" he asked casually.

She wasn't deceived by his tone: he was as rampantly curious as she. "No, but your aunt said they were almost ready to leave."

"That is a relief."

She stopped. "Nicholas, I think you should tell me what happened yesterday. I know only too well how brutal you can be when you're angry."

He winced. "Do you have to throw that back at me? I have relived every conversation we have ever had, and if I could take them back, I would. I regret every harsh word, Louisa, you must believe me." He stepped towards her as he spoke, looking contrite.

She could sense his sincerity and dismissed his words with a gentle smile. "I know – but what about Geneviève? What drove her to do such an idiotic thing?"

He gave a helpless gesture. "She has been pestering me since she returned to Newton. Once she was invited to the wedding she became nothing short of tenacious. I have been doing my best to avoid her for weeks. Well, you saw her behaviour the other night. When we returned to the house after church yesterday she kept following me. I had no option but to take her aside and tell her bluntly that I wasn't interested in her."

"Was that in the rose garden?" He nodded. "You must have known she would not take that very well, considering your previous history."

He groaned. "Of course – I forgot you knew about all of that." He closed his eyes in dismay.

"Oh yes," she said.

"Well, she did *not* take it well. She became almost hysterical and when that didn't get her anywhere, she let rip. Lord, what a vocabulary she has. I heard words I'd be shocked to hear from miners, never mind a well-brought-up lady. I thought that was the end of it, but she turned up again as I tried to mingle with the other guests and she was more determined than ever. Of course, I never imagined for one moment that she would try something so underhand, or I would never have been alone with her at the lake. Thank God you were close by. Thank you again for coming to my rescue."

"I could not let her get away with it. Hopefully she returns to Maryport. After all of this trouble I would hope she would be too embarrassed to stay with her poor mother."

He raised a brow. "Do you really believe that? I'm not so sure. Mrs. Lambert has no control over her – never did."

"Poor Mrs. Lambert. She doesn't deserve any of this."

"No, but it's not the first time Geneviève has caused uproar. I'm sorry you had to get caught up in it," he said with a frown. "Let's not talk of it any more. I'm heartily tired of the subject."

She nodded her agreement and they continued along the path for a time in silence. Then he pointed ahead. "That's the easy bit over. We will be starting to climb once we cross the beck." Before her, she could see the path dip, before crossing a little stream, then upwards on a rough stony path that zig-zagged its way towards the crags.

"Are you all right to continue?" She inclined her head and gestured impatiently for him to go ahead. As the path had narrowed, they would have to continue in single-file.

As they climbed, the terrain became rockier and the scree was difficult to negotiate, moving unexpectedly underfoot. She had to concentrate hard. Eventually he stopped ahead of her and waited for her to catch up. He was hardly out of breath, while she was hot and breathing hard. He smiled at her but said nothing. When she caught up to him, he gently turned her round. Laid out below were the dales of Buttermere and Crummock Water. It was truly breathtaking. Mesmerised, she could only stand and look, the difficult climb and her aching legs forgotten.

"Worth it?" he asked.

"Yes."

"Better views await. Come on," he encouraged her. The

ground flattened out a little and the going was slightly easier for a while. The path wound its way between boulders and heather, slowly rising towards the top of the crags. They clambered over a rise and before them was a tarn. "We can rest here for a while. It's sheltered." He led her down to the water then skirted around to a sandy stretch of shoreline on the far side.

From his backpack, he took out a hip flask, followed by wrapped sandwiches and fruit. As they ate he told her about his childhood trips into the fells with his brother, father and uncle. "We even camped here one night. Anna was disgusted because she wasn't allowed to come with us. Uncle Arthur told some hair-raising stories around the campfire and I was terrified. It was pitch dark, and I was convinced I'd be dragged into the water by some creature that my ten-year-old mind had conjured up. I couldn't say a word. I lay there rigid with fear and there was Robert, my younger brother, totally unconcerned and sleeping soundly. It was years before I would come up here again. Now it's my favourite fell walk."

"I can see why. The views are amazing."

"Don't thank me yet – we still have a way to go," he teased. "I'm glad you came. I didn't think you would."

"You should know by now that I can't resist a challenge. That's why I keep getting into unfortunate scrapes."

He smiled at her wickedly. "And what kind of scrape do you think you'll get into with me?" She caught her breath and blushed furiously. He roared laughing. "Come on, we'd better keep moving or I *will* end up in the water."

He jumped up and held out his hand to help her up. He tidied up their lunch, still chuckling, while she stood looking at him, suddenly tongue-tied. It was ridiculous that he could reduce her to this state as if she were a mere schoolgirl. She wanted to be angry with him, but what was the point? He seemed to be able to read her so well. She looked around her as she struggled for composure and saw a steep path led up and away from the tarn towards the summit.

"This section will be difficult. It's best you take your time. Go up in front of me," he said, looking serious again as he swung the backpack on to his shoulder. It crossed her mind that he thought she might slip, which made her more determined to prove him wrong. At this height the warmth of the sun was negligible, but the ascent was hard work. With a concealed sigh of relief, she reached the top and stopped to catch her breath. The path ahead continued on towards another tarn, smaller than the one below, but above it was the actual summit.

"Nearly there," he said. "You've almost earned your dinner." There was a light-heartedness about him that she had not seen before. Surely accompanying him had been the right decision? Above all else, it felt right, and for the first time in months she felt at peace with herself, and him, despite his constant teasing.

The final scramble brought them up to the flattened plateau at the top of the mountain. Everywhere she looked, the views were stunning. He pointed out the various mountains to her, but she was barely taking it in. She was overcome by the sensation of weightlessness as if she were soaring above the land, like the birds she had watched that morning at the lake. She had often wondered what it would feel like to stand in such a place.

"Louisa," he broke into her thoughts, "you have to stand on the top." She gave him a puzzled look – she thought she was at the top. He was pointing to where a small cairn marked the summit. It looked precarious to her. There was nothing holding the stones together. He grabbed her hand and brought her over.

"Up you go," he said, and lifted her up before she had time to object. "Now you can say you are a mountaineer," he said.

For a moment she felt almost giddy, but could not help grinning back at him. "So I am," she replied with delight, drunk with her achievement. She savoured the moment, taking in the impossibly awe-inspiring landscape below, and the panorama of mountain ranges stretching out in all directions in the afternoon haze.

He caught her as she came back down and held her tightly in the circle of his arms. There was a definite challenge in his eyes, but she felt equal to it.

"Your guide demands payment," he said very softly as he lowered his head.

It was a kiss she would never forget.

Jack Campbell stood on the bank of the Bowes River enjoying the warmth of the sun on his face, but deep down he was a troubled man. Timing was crucial, and the delays caused by the O'Griofas in planning the Newcastle attack had already meant pushing their plans out several times. The boys in Dublin were becoming increasingly vociferous and abusive. He couldn't really blame them. He was equally unhappy having to constantly reschedule. This operation would be his grand finale. When completed, he would have to go to the continent and lie low, perhaps never return to the British Isles at all.

Since his 'death', Jack had made only a handful of visits back to Bowes, and all of those had been at night. The estate held a special place in his heart and he wished that he could have continued to base himself there, but it was too risky. He frequently wondered how it was that an English property could hold any interest for him at all. When he had won it in that game of cards, he had planned to sell it immediately, but when he laid eyes on it his only thought had been that it would be the perfect home for him and his dear heart. Over the years he had done everything in his power to persuade her to live there, but nothing would sway her. He had spent a fortune on the house and gardens, but she would not give up her comfortable existence or status in society and had stayed stubbornly away. Yes, he would miss Bowes – even the continuous bleating of the Herdys.

He took a deep breath, trying to shake off his gloomy thoughts and remembered that O'Connor had mentioned that his nieces were returning from the Maxwell wedding the next day. The temptation to take a look at them was strong and it had been playing on his mind for some time. Just a little peep. He was curious to know if there was any family resemblance. Surely they would not recognise him if he was careful? He was rather proud of his disguises. He had fooled O'Connor the first time he had appeared back, and O'Connor knew him so well. Involving them in his plans was putting them in danger and he should have felt a twinge of guilt about that, but his hatred for their father had not diminished over the decades.

'Were my crimes *that* terrible?' he often asked himself. He would never forget that awful night. Peter had found him in the back room of the tavern and, standing over him with a sneer on his handsome face, he had given him the message from their father: he must leave Ireland and never return. Jack saw the undisguised pleasure in his brother's face as he had uttered those harsh words and he knew why: his exile would guarantee that Peter inherited everything that should have been his. Desperately, Jack had tried to speak to his father, but all appeals had fallen on deaf ears. Two days later, deeply embittered and very drunk, he was on the boat to England. Standing on the swaying deck, he had sworn to himself that if fate offered him a chance for vengeance he would take it.

Ironically, when their father died, Peter had inherited nothing but debts. Their father's love of gambling had led to the re-mortgaging of the property and the creditors closed in before the deceased was barely cold. Peter was compelled to sell large tracts of land at a time when land prices were rock bottom. Newly married, Peter and his bride had to live in a small rented house in the nearby village. The main house was rented out, but lack of investment over decades and little land meant that the income it generated was negligible. It wasn't long before the doors were finally locked and Peter and Sophia left for Dublin. He had seen the auction notice in *The Times* and had gone on a drinking binge for a week.

Peter had succumbed to the family evil and followed in their father's footsteps to the gaming hells in Dublin in the vain hope of turning the tide; a slow slide into poverty was the inevitable outcome. The irony of that pleased Jack greatly whenever he thought about it. He had followed the family's fortunes from afar, but had never intervened. Any pity he had for his sister-in-law or the children was suppressed by his hatred for his brother.

He exhaled slowly and flicked the butt of his cigar into the water, where it bobbed on the surface and was swiftly taken downstream on the current. It was time to head back to the barn and see what progress had been made in his absence.

"Jack," O'Connor greeted him as he appeared in the doorway, "that's the last load out. We're making fierce good time. Nearly done for today." Two young lads were standing panting in the heat of the old barn, both drenched in sweat. Jack was expecting the consignment of guns at the end of the week. The chamber they had excavated under the barn years before wasn't big enough to hold the extra cases, so they had to dig it out by hand, barrow the soil out to the river bank, and tip it in to the fast-flowing river. The old Cassidy place was the most deserted part of the estate, so they could afford to work in daylight, but it was still risky. Three days of hard slog were now finally over and all trace of their activities would have to be removed.

"Good work, boys," Jack said. At least something was going to plan. "Let's get those timbers back down. O'Connor will fix up with you. We'll let you know when you're needed again. It should be soon, though."

The men nodded and set to work hauling the heavy timbers back across the joists and nailing them down, except for the last couple of feet, as they would need to access the chamber quickly when the cases of guns and ammunition arrived from Newcastle. O'Connor then spread some straw across the barn floor and dragged out some of the old machinery over the loose boards. Hopefully, they had done enough to conceal the chamber in the unlikely event that someone came snooping around.

O'Connor followed him outside.

"Have you decided? Will you stay until the guns come next week? You could use the cottage again," he said, tilting his head towards it. "Sure, it's grand for a few days anyway."

"Yes, best I'm here. Surely nothing can go wrong now," Jack said with a scowl.

Chapter Twenty-Two

"She's asleep, Miss," Róisín informed Louisa, who was sitting in the private parlour of the Bridge Inn.

At his insistence, they had travelled with Nicholas from Buttermere in the Maxwell carriage, but its better suspension had failed to ease Eleanor's travel-sickness and after three-quarters of an hour they had had no alternative but to interrupt their journey to give her some relief.

"Thank you, Róisín. Would you keep an eye on her, please?"

"Of course, Miss," Róisín replied. "I'll stay with her."

Nicholas was standing by the fireplace. He walked over to her at the table, where she was pouring out tea. "Thank you," he said, taking the cup she held out. "Will she be well enough to finish the journey today?"

"I should think so. An hour's rest should be sufficient. Thank you for organising the room for her. I don't believe the landlord would have been quite so accommodating for me."

He dismissed her thanks with an impatient shake of his head. "I have been stopping here for years and he knows me well. I'm glad to be of help," he said, sitting down opposite her. "You carry a heavy burden, Louisa. One which, I am ashamed to say, I would crumble under."

"You may think that, but life is strange: you find the strength when you need it."

"Perhaps, but it cannot be easy for either of you." He gave her a searching look. "She is incredibly brave for someone so young."

"Yes, she is. She rarely complains, and we go along quite nicely. Undoubtedly she hides things from me. I sometimes try to imagine what it is like for her, but I cannot dwell on it too much. I don't think I could stay sane if I did."

"That is perfectly understandable. I only wish I could take some of your worries away."

She took a sharp intake of breath. "I ... that is very kind ..."

"You don't know what to make of me, do you?" he asked putting down his cup. "I can't blame you after all that has happened. I'm not proud of myself. I had every intention of driving you away from Bowes, and I was totally blind to your innocence. I would have seen it quite clearly if I had actually thought about it properly. But instead I wanted you to be like your uncle, to legitimise my own need for revenge. Can you understand that?" She nodded and he got up abruptly and began to pace the room.

"I suppose it was anger, too, that was driving me. He was always one step ahead, always goading me and then he died just before I could close the trap." He stopped and looked at her. "When I think of the way I tried to bully you ... setting that dog Jenkins on you, well, I would not blame you if you hated me."

"Nicholas, I don't and never did, even when you were at your worst. I have to admit that I have enjoyed battling with you. You challenge me and treat me as a worthy adversary."

He looked incredulous. "Louisa, I must have made your life extremely difficult and unpleasant those first few months."

"Yes a little, I have to confess. But our lives in Dublin had been so stultifying and grey. You can have no idea what a relief it was to come here; to have standing in the community and finally have a purpose in my life ... even if sometimes it was purely to annoy you."

He smiled. "And you did. But your defiance certainly made me sit up and notice. I soon realised I wasn't dealing with a timid mouse and had met my match."

"I have never been accused of being a mouse, I can assure you." She couldn't help thinking of her Aunt Milly, who had always hinted darkly that her forward manners would one day get her into trouble. Thankfully, the man standing before her appeared to rejoice in her independent streak.

"Yes, I imagine you have always been a handful."

"I was a model child, I'll have you know."

"So what changed?"

"I met you."

He laughed and acknowledged the hit.

"You know, it almost seems a shame that we have nothing to fight about any more," she said, struggling to keep a straight face.

"I think if we worked very hard at it we might just come up with something to argue about. Life would be very dull if you agreed with me all of the time," he replied.

"I don't believe there is any danger of that happening, do you?"

After a few minutes of companionable silence, he said, "I wish you didn't have all this uncertainty about Eleanor's health."

"Thank you, but I'm used to it. I believed that country living would ease her symptoms, but unfortunately I was mistaken. Her decline is slow but it is irreversible. All I can do is watch and hope for a miracle."

"Have you considered consulting a London doctor, perhaps?"

She shook her head. "I don't think there would be much point. Dr. Peterson is excellent and both he and our Dublin doctor were very clear about the prognosis. Besides, it would upset her. She hates being fussed over and has a particular dislike for doctors. She barely tolerates poor Dr. Peterson."

"I could make enquiries, if you change your mind," he offered.

She nodded and felt her eyes prickle. On previous occasions his sympathy had felt like an intrusion, now she suddenly wanted to take comfort in it. But despite the intimate interlude on Haystacks the previous day, she still felt unsure of herself in his company. When they had returned to Ashbury Lodge, there had been no further opportunities to talk privately, as Nicholas's social duties to his family took precedence. So although he had kissed her and left her in no doubt as to his feelings, she was still wary of committing herself. She was strongly attracted to him, but was afraid to give in to it. Something of her confusion must have shown in her face because he crossed the room and sat down beside her, reaching for her hand.

"We have not had the best of starts, Miss Louisa Campbell, but I think if you are magnanimous enough to forgive my previous behaviour, we could be great friends," he said, an unmistakable glint in his eye.

"I think I would like that," she answered softly. When she met his gaze, she was taken aback at the intensity of it and her heart began to pound ridiculously fast.

"Excellent. Though I wasn't really prepared to accept any other answer, you know," he responded, then gently caressed her cheek. "I have been a great dunderhead, and made many mistakes in my life, but I believe the greatest mistake of all would be to let you slip through my fingers."

She blushed. "Despite my connections?"

"I thought we had put all of that behind us," he said.

"I hope so, but I just want to be sure that you don't have regrets. I am probably not everyone's idea of a great catch, even without Uncle Jack lurking in my family tree. I'm on the shelf," he rolled his eyes, "can be stubborn to the point of idiocy and as for my temper – you just ask Eleanor."

He raised an eyebrow. "I am no paragon, Louisa. You are already painfully aware of that."

"Oh, you're not so bad now that I know you better," she teased. "But you should realise I may drive you so demented that your family have to commit you to the asylum in Carlisle."

"You can try, certainly. I would deny you nothing."

She gave him a reproving look. "Foolish man. You'd be far better off with Beatrice Morrissey or Mrs. Rathbone."

"Now that's just cruel." He laughed and kissed the tips of her fingers. "No, it's only you I want. I think you're perfect, sweetheart."

Louisa was still laughing at his sheepish expression when Róisín came into the room to announce that the patient was anxious to get going again, and would be joining them in a few minutes. With a look laced with regret, Nicholas left the parlour to settle with the landlord and call for the carriage.

Louisa's state of happiness didn't last very long. Eleanor had immediately taken to her bed when they had reached home. The following morning she complained of feeling worse and Dr. Peterson was called. Louisa waited anxiously for him outside Eleanor's room, the old fears crowding into her mind as she paced the landing. When he emerged her heart dropped when she saw his serious expression. He closed the door gently behind him, and motioned for her to go downstairs, leaving Róisín to watch over the patient.

"How bad is it?" she asked him, as soon as they were in the drawing room.

He frowned. "It could just be fatigue after the long journey, but there is evidence of swelling in her feet and hands."

She groped for a chair and sat down, her stomach churning. "Oh no." She knew what this meant. "Is there anything we can do?"

"Rest." He paused, his own frustration evident. "Bed-rest may help if you can keep her quiet with her feet up. A light diet – but you know all of this, Miss Campbell. Her heart is struggling to pump properly. The dropsy is a direct result. We can try a diuretic. I will make up some squill and vinegar. It should give some relief in a few days."

"Thank you," she answered, her fears slightly alleviated. At least there was something he could try.

Dr. Peterson sat down opposite her. "It may relieve the symptoms, but it cannot fix the underlying problem. I have always been honest with you, young lady, but you know I can only make her comfortable. I cannot prevent …"

"I know," she whispered, close to tears, "but is it so wrong to hope?"

He smiled. "Of course not. I am a man of science, but I have seen the power of prayer on the mind. Not that I would admit that to the Rector, of course." A wan smile was the only answer she could manage. "I shall return this evening, but I will send that medicine up as soon as I can," he said as he stood to leave. "My advice is to keep busy and cheerful. We don't want you or our patient succumbing to melancholia."

Three days later, Eleanor was well enough to leave her room and join her sister for a light lunch. Dr. Peterson called in the afternoon and pronounced her on the mend, much to Louisa's relief. She accompanied him out to the front door.

"That medicine appears to have worked very well," she commented cheerfully.

"Yes, I am pleased with her progress. Keep her quiet for now – no agitation of any kind. It could set her back," he warned.

"I understand. Thank you for calling again. You are so good to us," she said with a slight tremble in her voice.

He took both her hands in his. "You are a very brave young woman. There's many would fall ill themselves under this kind of pressure. Make sure you look after yourself." She nodded, and he released her hands just as Nicholas rode up the carriage-way.

The groom appeared with the doctor's horse and helped the elderly man to mount. With a courteous nod to both her and Nicholas, he set off back to Newton.

Nicholas dismounted and handed the reins to the groom, who headed off to the stables. "Do I have competition? I hate to mention it, but I doubt he'd have the stamina to keep up with you."

She tried to disguise her pleasure at seeing him. "If you haven't anything sensible to say, I suggest you get straight back on that horse."

"Sweetheart, if I thought you meant that, my life would lie in ruins," he exclaimed in mock horror. She gave him an impatient look. "How goes the patient today?" he asked in a more serious tone.

"Much improved, thankfully. Dr. Peterson's medicine appears to have worked. She's up out of bed, managed some lunch and is now reading in the drawing room."

He tucked her arm through his as they passed through the archway and into the garden. "That's a relief. Your note yesterday had me worried. I'm sorry I have been so busy. With court on Wednesday and problems at the colliery yesterday, it was impossible to come and see you. But I am at your service today, I promise. How are you? You look a trifle pulled, if you don't mind me saying."

"I haven't been sleeping well."

"I'm not surprised," he said. "You must look after yourself,"

"Dr. Peterson says the same."

"And he is correct. You'll be of little use to her if you fall ill yourself." They strolled along the gravel path towards the arbour. When they reached it he stopped and pulled her down on to his lap. "Perhaps I can take your mind off things for a little while," he said, his eyes alight with mischief.

"Behave yourself! Eleanor or the servants might see," she protested lamely.

"I really don't care," he replied kissing her cheek and then her ear. "I haven't seen you in four whole days."

It was several minutes before he let her pull away and slide on to the seat. She found it difficult to ignore the happiness bubbling up inside. He grinned at her wolfishly, and she had some difficulty in keeping her voice steady when she tried to distract him. "Have you heard from Anna yet?"

"I received a telegram yesterday. They were about to board the boat for France. Her main concern was that John might be sea-sick. He usually is, it seems."

"Poor John. I hope for his sake the crossing is calm. I do envy them. Paris will be lovely," she sighed. "But I expect it is very hot this time of year."

"... and full of tourists. Well, if you are a good girl and resist running off with the good doctor, I might just take you there myself."

From the vantage point of the window-seat in the drawing room, Eleanor saw Dr. Peterson leave and Nicholas arrive. It was her favourite spot, looking out on to the front rose beds, which were bursting with the new blooms of the season. Some minutes later she heard voices coming from the garden. She closed her book with a contented sigh, absentmindedly rubbing Max's silky ears. Dr. Peterson's medicine had reduced the swelling in her feet, but had upset her stomach. It had tasted revolting, even though she had washed it down with copious glasses of milk, on the best advice from Mrs. Murphy who knew about these things, being a martyr to various unspeakable conditions. She changed her position on the seat and gradually drifted off to sleep.

It was the strangest dream. She was on the beach looking out west towards home. It was cold, with a salty spray coming off the foaming waves before her, and black-tinged rain clouds scuttling across an angry sky. She felt threatened and panicky. They were going to bury her here on the beach, not with Mother and Father. Why would they do such a thing? There was a gaping hole in the sand. Looking into it, she saw rose petals of every hue, but they were turning brown and curling up as she watched, and a stale smell of rotting vegetation wafted up. Calm again ... she was in a lovely lavender-scented garden. The Ryan children were playing with a ball. She hadn't seen them since they had lived in that ramshackle house in Macken Lane. How they had grown! Little Maria threw the ball to her and she bent to pick it up, but found she couldn't move. Neither could she breathe. Deep crushing pain seared through her body with every breath.

She woke up with a jolt, drenched in perspiration and straining to catch her breath. Inhaling was painful, as dragging spasms wracked her body. Slumped against the window pane with her cheek pressed up against the glass, she slowly realised that she was conscious. The house was quiet and Max was asleep on the floor. It was the worst attack she could remember. Slowly, she righted herself, shaking uncontrollably, with fragments of her dream still flitting about in her head, like startled birds disturbed at dusk.

It was the following afternoon and Eleanor was sitting contentedly in the walled garden, Max at her feet as usual, when the steward came in. He approached Louisa, who was kneeling a few feet away, hard at work rooting out the weeds.

"Miss Campbell, would it be convenient for you to come to the office? I have those accounts ready for you to look at," he asked, sounding rather subdued.

With a sigh, Louisa looked up. "All right. I'll be along in a minute." He nodded and headed off towards the estate office.

Louisa smiled over at her. "Sorry, I shouldn't be too long. Will you be all right there? I'd better go or he will be pestering me about it."

She nodded. "Yes, I'm fine. It's lovely here in the shade. I'm quite content."

Louisa removed her gloves and apron, patted Max on the head, and followed O'Connor out of the garden.

Eleanor was feeling considerably better. The attack of the previous afternoon had scared her, but there had been no repetition of chest pain. She did not tell anyone about it, almost petrified that speaking of it might bring it on again. For now, though, she was happy, her fears tucked away once more. It was warm and sheltered in the garden. In the distance she could hear the sea and perched up in the cherry tree a blackbird was singing; a small private recital, just for her.

There was a slight movement to her left, just out of her field of vision. She turned her head. There was a large man standing in the archway that led to the stables. A stranger. She felt a moment's anxiety, not liking the way he was staring at her. He removed his hat and slowly walked down the path. As he brushed past the lavender that overflowed from the beds, the distinctive scent wafted towards her, bringing back the strange dream she had the previous day. Max sat up and sniffed the air, watching the stranger approach. His growl didn't appear to bother the man, who paused only slightly. Eleanor could feel her heart racing. There was something familiar about him; something about his eyes.

"Hello," the man said in a choking voice. There were tears coursing down his face as he reached out to stroke her cheek. She pulled back in absolute terror.

As usual, any dealings with O'Connor left Louisa feeling horribly frustrated. She closed the office door with as much restraint as her failing temper would allow. Leaning back against it, she took a few deep calming breaths. It was too nice a day to let that man ruin it. It was still early afternoon, so she would go back to her weeding, follow that by hard-earned afternoon tea, and a pleasant chat with Eleanor.

Clara was joining them for dinner tonight, and she was looking forward to hearing all of the Newton news from her. Clara had moved into rooms near the school, anxious to be settled in her new home before the newlyweds returned from Europe. She was particularly keen to have news of the Lamberts; to know if Geneviève had retreated to Maryport, her pursuit of Nicholas abandoned for good. By tacit agreement, they had not discussed the woman at all since they climbed Haystacks. She knew she had no grounds to be jealous. In fact, she could only feel sorry for the woman.

Humming softly to herself, she made her way slowly back towards the garden. Since their return from Buttermere she found herself daydreaming, something she had rarely indulged in before. Nicholas was to blame, of course, and yesterday he had hinted strongly of their future together. Just thinking about him, which she found herself doing almost constantly, left her awash with feelings that were novel and, she had to admit, very nice indeed. He was still a bit of an enigma. His past behaviour was so at odds with the man she was coming to know and love. She smiled to herself as she remembered their less than pleasant first meeting at Newton Station. She could never have imagined that cold and hostile man would become so important to her.

She paused before the roses to pick off some blown blooms, and stood lost in thought, the velvety petals fragrant and soft, held loosely in her hand. In a fortnight's time Anna would be back from honeymoon and any chance of keeping their relationship secret would be well and truly over. Anna would be delighted about it, but she feared she would try to pressurise her into marrying without thought for Eleanor's welfare or feelings on the subject.

She felt guilty for not confiding in Eleanor as it was. She had hugged the knowledge of Nicholas's regard to herself, especially while Eleanor had been so unwell earlier in the week. She gave so much of herself to her sister. Was it really selfish to keep one thing private? Of course, it was possible that Eleanor had already guessed. After all, it was she who had thrown them together so often. Perhaps she would say something this afternoon before Clara arrived.

Sudden frantic barking interrupted her thoughts. She snapped out of her reverie. Why was Max barking? He never barked. A wave of fear swept over her and she was momentarily frozen to the spot – she had left him at Eleanor's feet. Now he was starting to whine. The petals fell from her hands, crushed and forgotten, as she started to run.

When she reached the entrance to the garden she frantically scanned the various paths, a tight knot of cold terror sucking away the hope that had sustained her all these months. Max was still barking and whining over by the arbour. As she rushed towards him, she saw Eleanor lying prostrate on the ground, the dog desperately licking her face. Seconds later, she was kneeling beside Eleanor, cradling her head in her lap. She had to push the dog away.

Eleanor was deathly white, but the tell-tale blue tinge was creeping into her face around her mouth. Her eyes were unfocussed and her chest was heaving, desperately seeking the now elusive oxygen she craved. Louisa could only whisper her name over and over. A spasm of pain shot through Eleanor's body, but it seemed to bring lucidity with it. She looked up, her mouth working frantically. Louisa couldn't understand or hear her properly and leant down closer.

"Jack," Eleanor wheezed. Louisa recoiled and shook her head, confused. Had she misheard? Clearly Eleanor was delirious.

"Don't try to talk, Eleanor, please – just breathe," she sobbed. "Please try. Don't give in. I'm not ready to let you go."

But Eleanor's need to communicate was still strong. "You ... must ... leave," she finally managed to whisper, her eyes wild with urgent warning. Louisa stared at her in horror and disbelief. Then Eleanor's eyelids fluttered, and Louisa could only watch in agony as her fragile life-force slipped away, on one last gentle breath.

Chapter Twenty-Three

"Sir." His butler coughed to get his attention. "This just arrived from Bowes."

Nicholas had been sitting in his study reading through some court papers, and looked up in surprise at the interruption. He had left explicit instructions that he wasn't to be disturbed.

"I believe it's urgent," the butler explained as he handed him a folded piece of paper. "The stable boy must have run most of the way."

When he unfolded the note, *"Please come"*, was all it contained, but he knew it was from Louisa and could guess the reason for it: Eleanor must have taken a turn.

"Have my horse brought around as quickly as possible," he ordered, jumping up out of his chair and racing from the room to change into riding clothes.

His worst fears were confirmed when he arrived at Bowes. A distraught Róisín eventually answered the door to him, clutching a handkerchief to her mouth. He didn't wait to be announced but headed straight for the drawing room. Standing before the fireplace was Clara Whitby, looking pale and upset. She was alone.

"Clara, what has happened? Has Eleanor taken ill again?" he asked.

Clara swallowed hard. "No, Nicholas, the Lord has taken her. They have just brought her up to her room. Louisa asked to be left alone with her for a few minutes. I'm afraid the house is in turmoil."

Dumbfounded, he went up to her and took her trembling hand in his. "I can't believe it. What happened? I thought her condition had improved? Peterson said he was pleased with her progress."

"I arrived about half an hour ago. I had been invited to dinner," she explained. "From what I can glean from the servants, Louisa found her barely conscious near the arbour in the walled garden. She had collapsed. She died shortly afterwards. The steward found them."

He was horrified that Eleanor had died that way and that Louisa had witnessed it. "How is Louisa coping?"

"Far too well for my liking. She hasn't shed a tear. I suspect she is in deep shock. It might be a good idea to call for Peterson."

He released her hand and nodded, relieved to have something to do. "I will organise that."

Clara continued. "The cook has offered to help me lay Eleanor out. As soon as Louisa is ready, we will make a start."

"That is very good of you, Clara," he said gently, impressed as always by how kind she was.

She dismissed his words with a wave of her hand. "Laying out is an honour. I do it for many parishioners," she said shakily. "Louisa could not be expected to do it."

"Of course not. Is there anything else I can do?"

"Comfort her if she needs it. For now that is the most valuable assistance you can give," she advised.

He raised a brow at her words, but knew it would be pointless to prevaricate. She obviously suspected how things stood between him and Louisa. He walked over to the french doors and looked out towards the arbour. "I just can't believe that it has happened so quickly. Eleanor never looked well, but the suddenness of this is ... shocking."

"Her heart must have been weaker than anyone knew," she said as she sat down. "It is unfortunate timing with John away. I have been thinking: should we summon them back from France?"

He came back across the room and stood with his back to the fireplace. He knew Anna and John would never forgive him if they weren't informed, but it felt almost cruel to cut short their honeymoon. "Yes, that would be best. They would wish to be here, and John will want to officiate at the service. I'll have a telegram sent to the hotel in Paris immediately." He took a deep breath to calm himself.

"Are you all right, Nicholas?" Clara asked.

"Yes, I'm sorry it is all so sudden. The poor girl. I admired her, you know. She handled her illness and unfortunate prognosis with such maturity."

"They have both been very brave," she said. "Don't be too surprised by Louisa's outward calm just now. It's deceptive. When grief eventually hits her, she may fall apart. I've seen this before. Without family she will be relying on us to organise things, but there will be decisions only she can make and they will be difficult. Your advice will be crucial."

"Is there something specific that worries you?"

"She may wish to take her home to Dublin."

"Lord!" he exclaimed. "I hadn't thought of that. It would be impractical, surely?"

"I believe so. Far better that she is laid to rest here, where Louisa will have a focus for her grief. There is something cathartic about tending a grave."

He nodded in agreement, but his fear was that she would not come back if she went to Dublin, where he knew she still had many friends and some family. With a groan he remembered the aunt. "Someone needs to write to the aunt in Dublin," he said. It was not a task he would relish taking on. How do you find the right words to inform a stranger of such news?

"Louisa has already written her a brief note. She was doing it when I arrived."

"I see," he said, surprised.

"I will go up to her now," she said rising slowly. "I will send her down to you. Don't worry; we will get her through this."

Louisa stood at the window, Eleanor's prayer book tightly clasped in her hands, painfully aware that her sister was lying on the bed behind her, for all the world as if she were asleep. Except that she was waxen white and so very still. She had always known that she would have to face Eleanor's death, but whenever she had let herself think about it, she had envisaged her sister slipping away peacefully in her sleep. The reality had been more horrible than she could have imagined.

There was a gentle knock on the door and she turned. Clara entered and her eyes welled up when she looked down at Eleanor. She took a step further into the room.

"My dear," she said gently, "Mrs. Murphy and I are ready to lay her out. Why don't you go and get changed. Do you have any mourning clothes?"

"I ... I do."

"Come, I will help you," she said. "I'm afraid your maid is very upset, so I sent her to her room. She will be of little use today."

Louisa gently placed the prayer book under Eleanor's hands and, with a final lingering look, she followed Clara out of the room. Mrs. Murphy stood out on the landing, her eyes suspiciously red-rimmed. Her lip trembled and she clutched at her hand as she went past.

She stopped and smiled wanly at the cook. "Thank you, Lizzie," she said, deeply touched by the woman's offer to help. "God bless you for doing this."

"It's only right, Miss Campbell. She was an angel," the cook responded with a quivering lip. "Not a bad bone in her body."

She had no response to that and turned slowly to follow her friend. By the time she entered her bedroom, Clara had pulled the black dress from the back of the wardrobe, and was shaking out its dull folds. Louisa stood and looked at it, remembering the last time she had worn mourning. Due to their impoverished circumstances at the time, she had kept her old mourning clothes instead of discarding them, as most did.

"It will do for now, my dear, but I think we must get you something a little better," Clara said. "Mortimer's on Church Street will have something suitable. We can go there on Monday. You will need several dresses and gloves and ... well, a whole new wardrobe for your mourning."

"It may not fit, Clara. It's four years since I wore it last."

"Let's try it on anyway."

As she stepped into the dress Louisa felt almost like a machine. No emotion seemed able to break through the numbness that enveloped her. Thankfully, Clara was being her usual pragmatic self. She did up the buttons at the back of the dress with deft fingers.

"You have grown a little since you wore this last," Clara remarked. "I hope it's not too tight. Oh dear, it is a trifle short."

Louisa looked at her reflection in the mirror and felt as though a stranger was looking back at her. "It will do."

"My dear, Nicholas is downstairs waiting to see you. We will call you when we are finished. The vicar from Wadsworth will be here later, to say a few prayers. I'm so sorry that John is not here for you, but I know this man. He will do what is necessary. John and Anna will be home in a few days. I know that you would want John here for the service."

Louisa turned slowly and tried to smile her thanks. No words would come. Clara hugged her a little awkwardly, but it didn't help. Everything felt wrong. Eleanor was gone.

As she descended the stairs, she could hear Nicholas giving curt instructions to O'Connor in the hallway. He looked up and gave her a look so full of sympathy that she almost stumbled. He dismissed O'Connor and came forward to greet her. She stalled on the bottom step and stood looking at him, feeling lost and empty. He stepped forward and gently guided her down, keeping a firm hold of her hands.

"You came," she whispered.

"Of course," he replied, his voice breaking on emotion. But even his distress could not touch her yet. As she leaned her head against his shoulder, in the safety of his comforting embrace, all she could think of were those last words that Eleanor had uttered: *You must leave.*

O'Connor had no intention of carrying out Maxwell's instructions. Instead he passed them on to the groom and saddled his horse as quickly as he could. He was panicking; he had to find Jack and tell him what had happened. Everything was in jeopardy now – all their plans, all their hard work.

He found him in Cassidy's cottage where he had been hiding out all week. He was nursing a bottle of Bushmills, or, to be precise, what was left of it. He had never seen him in such a state in all the years he had known him. He guessed that Jack knew his niece was dead, but wondered how. He sat down on the rickety stool opposite and waited nervously.

Jack eventually became aware of his presence. "Liam, what have I done?" he exclaimed. "I killed her – my own niece."

He sat rigid with shock. "Jack, you're scaring me. What do you mean you killed her? What has this to do with you?"

Jack was crying now, great heaving sobs wracking his large frame. He fought for control. "I was there – I scared her – there was nothing ... I couldn't help her."

"Jesus!" He grabbed Jack's glass and swallowed its contents in one gulp. "What possessed you to go near her? Bloody hell, Jack! What are we going to do? The place will be crawling with visitors and the funeral at the end of the week. Have you forgotten? We have those guns coming in on Friday."

Jack glared at him angrily. "I don't give a damn!" he shouted. "Do you hear? I as good as killed her – my own niece. Are you not listening to me?"

O'Connor jumped up and started to pace the tiny room, frantic. Jack wasn't in a fit state to think things through; *he* would have to act. He stopped and stared at his friend's heaving shoulders. He was a lost cause for now. There would be no reasoning with him and he couldn't afford to wait until he had sobered up. Without a backwards glance, he left the cottage for Newton. He would have to work quickly to stop the Newcastle plan from going ahead; failure would see them all swinging from the gallows.

The Whitbys arrived back from France the day before the funeral. When they reached Bowes, Clara immediately took Anna away on the pretext of seeing Eleanor where she was laid out in the parlour, so that John would have time alone with Louisa. They retired to the study where they would not be disturbed.

A growing pile of letters of condolence were on the desk, letters she could not bear to open. She turned her back on them and gestured for John to sit. No matter which room in the house she went into, she felt on edge. She put the odd atmosphere in the room down to the covered mirror and the silent clock on the mantle. Clara was being thorough, even down to the black crepe that covered the front door brassware. The morbid rituals seemed pointless to Louisa. It was difficult to reconcile the gloomy atmosphere in the house with her own love of life or with Eleanor's gallant but doomed struggle.

"Is there anything I can do for you?" John enquired as they sat down. "You know you need only ask." His sombre condolences were like a balm to her troubled mind.

"Thank you, but Nicholas and Clara have thought of everything."

"It is excellent that the practicalities are taken care of, but I am more concerned with your spiritual welfare," he replied, with a look of empathy that almost undid her.

Her eyes prickled with unshed tears. She instinctively trusted this man and the need to unburden herself was strong. It was a huge relief to be able to finally admit her own weakness. "I am struggling, John. I've known this time would come, but I had not anticipated how difficult … I'm afraid to grieve."

John raised a brow, but smiled kindly. "That is a very common affliction for the bereaved, believe me. Death always leaves a trail of self-doubt, anger and guilt for those left behind. You will grieve when you are ready. There are no rules."

She nodded eagerly. He did understand. "Perhaps, and you are right - I do feel guilty. I am glad that her suffering is over. I did not want her to die, but watching her life deteriorate was torture. We did everything to keep her alive, but sometimes I thought the struggle wasn't worth it, that it was almost cruel to prolong it. She never complained; she rarely wallowed in self-pity." John nodded in understanding. "Her stoic acceptance of her fate makes me wonder how she really felt. Did she just accept her approaching death or was she trying to protect me? You see, we never discussed her illness. It was this awful black cloud that overshadowed everything. It coloured every decision, even coming here to live. I never even asked her where she wanted to be laid to rest." Her voice broke with pent-up emotion. "We just never spoke of it, and we should have."

"You were both in a very difficult situation and coped as best you could. Of course we must preserve life, that is God's will, but you fear that in cherishing her you prolonged her suffering?" he asked. She looked down at her clenched hands before nodding.

"You have nothing to berate yourself with. From the little I saw, she was as happy as her circumstances would allow. She was a very lucky girl to have a sister who looked after her needs in somewhat trying circumstances at times; it cannot have been easy."

She shrugged helplessly. "You are being kind, but you see I wish I had been more understanding. I deliberately avoided thinking about how scared she must have been because acknowledging it would have destroyed me. I could not cope with the reality of her illness – no, the reality of her death." She had to pause to control herself. "I'm no saint, John," she murmured sadly.

"No, just human," he replied, with a reassuring twinkle in his eye. He pulled his chair closer to hers. "Now, would it help to talk about what happened on Saturday?"

This was the moment; an opportunity to confide in someone about the strange and unsettling circumstances of Eleanor's passing. For some reason she had not been able to confide in Nicholas or Clara and she knew she had to disclose her fear to someone before it destroyed her sanity. With a churning stomach, she told him what had happened and Eleanor's last words. He frowned and took some time before making any comment.

"In my experience it is common for a dying person to think they see relatives that have gone before them. I believe it is the Lord's way of comforting them and easing their distress as they pass. I do not see any reason to read any more into it than that,

Louisa. The Lord would have been with her in those final moments."

"But she was in *torment* – as if she was trying to warn me of some danger. Why would she think she saw Uncle Jack and not our parents? We never even met him. It doesn't make sense."

"But think, Louisa. What possible danger could there be to you here? No, I think you must accept that her passing was difficult. She knew her time had come. Living here at Bowes, where your uncle lived, is probably the reason that he was at the forefront of her mind."

She realised that he could not solve the conundrum for her. She would have to accept his explanation for now. Perhaps in time she would find a more satisfactory and rational one herself.

There was a gentle knock on the door and a woebegone Róisín came in.

"If you please, Miss, I've left the tea trolley in the drawing room."

"Thank you, Róisín. We will be in directly."

When Louisa entered the drawing room, she discovered that Nicholas had returned from Newton, where he had been making the final arrangements with the undertakers. He was trying to comfort Anna, who was very distressed. Anna rose on seeing her and rushed to embrace her. She held her stiffly and after a few moments John gently drew Anna away and back to the sofa. Louisa sat down in the chair beside the fireplace, feeling weary and bone-shatteringly sad. She could feel Nicholas's concerned gaze on her but could not speak or meet his eye. Her throat felt tight and sore and her eyes gritty.

Clara stepped into the breach immediately and began to pour out tea, all the while keeping up a soft chatter which was most uncharacteristic. John responded quietly and peppered his sister with questions about local news.

She knew they were trying to ease her distress, but a horrible guilty frustration with her friends was starting to simmer beneath the surface. Suddenly, above all else, she wanted to be alone to nurse her grief in her own way. This pretence that everything was normal – sitting down to afternoon tea, for heaven's sake – when her sister lay dead only a few feet away in the parlour was agonising to her. She contemplated excusing herself, but was wavering between her own needs and what she knew was her duty. Finding consolation in the thought that Eleanor would want her to behave well in the circumstances helped stiffen her resolve. Surely they would leave soon and she could escape to her room? Tomorrow would be awful and she needed to prepare herself. Lost in her thoughts, she failed to hear the commotion out in the hallway. It was only when the door opened that she realised that everyone was silent and looking towards it expectantly. Róisín stood in the doorway with a worried frown. She stepped forward.

"You have a visitor, Miss. She says she's your aunt."

"Good gracious, girl, is that how you announce a visitor?" came an outraged voice from the hallway.

Recognising Aunt Milly's strident tones, Louisa slowly rose from her seat. Her aunt appeared from behind the bewildered maid, a vision in black bombazine.

"Well, child, are you going to welcome me or not?" she demanded in a voice that crackled with indignation.

Louisa found that her throat was constricted. She did not like the woman but she was her only link to her family now. Emotions that had been held in check all week, now rose to the surface. She stumbled towards her aunt, tears coursing down her face.

"Well," Aunt Milly sniffed, holding her sobbing niece awkwardly, "it appears I have arrived just in time."

Chapter Twenty-Four

L ouisa woke early the morning of the funeral. She lay very still listening to the soft creaking of the house and the now familiar Cumberland westerly wind. The day had finally come: Eleanor would leave the house for the last time. She closed her eyes and said a little prayer that she would find the strength from somewhere. She had to say goodbye with dignity, or she would regret it for the rest of her life.

She sighed and turned over. There was Aunt Milly to deal with today. Why on earth had she come? When she had written to her it had been a matter of courtesy only; she had never expected her to make the journey from Dublin. Dealing with her was going to be tedious and they would probably fall out, repeatedly. Seeing her had been a tremendous shock which had prompted her to fall apart in front of everyone, despite her best efforts to maintain control. But now at least the awful numbness was gone. As John had so succinctly put it – she was only human.

They buried Eleanor in the little cemetery behind the church of St. Martin in Newton. As if in sympathy, the good weather had disappeared and the day was cool and overcast with a sharp breeze that nipped at her veil. Thankfully, most understood her need to attend the funeral. Only ten years before it would have been frowned upon for her to do so. John's familiar voice helped her through the worst of it, and she knew, without having to look, that Nicholas kept close at all times. Aunt Milly stood beside her at the graveside, sombre and unapproachable behind a thick net veil. If she shed tears, she wasn't aware of it.

She had taken great comfort in the generous turnout of Newton society. The day was a blur of faces, some familiar and some not. Amongst the former were the Morrisseys, the Kirkbrides, George Jameson and his father and poor Mrs. Lambert, who had looked so upset. Some had muttered their condolences in that embarrassed way of mourners who didn't really know the bereaved or perhaps the deceased that well. But it was the large numbers of Bowes servants and tenants, along with a group of miners waiting for her outside the church, that almost caused her to lose her fragile self-control. It only struck her afterwards that many of them, from Bowes at least, would have attended as a mark of respect to her late uncle. It all helped, but it could not fill the void. Eleanor was gone forever.

It wasn't until the day after the funeral that aunt and niece were finally alone and could speak in private.

"They are a strange lot in this part of the world," was Aunt Milly's opening comment at breakfast, "but I expect they did their best for a provincial backwater. I don't suppose you considered bringing her home to Dublin? It would have been far more convenient. She could have had a beautiful service at St. Stephens and we could have buried her in Mount Jerome with your parents."

"Convenient for whom?" Louisa asked contemptuously. Her aunt's insensitivity was mind-boggling, but not surprising.

Aunt Milly sniffed. "Well, nothing can be done about it now."

Silence reigned for several minutes before Aunt Milly spoke again. "I suppose the house is just about tolerable. These old places are so pokey, don't you think? It's no better than a farmhouse really. Such a shame that it isn't more substantial."

Louisa made no comment.

Aunt Milly looked about the room as if it were hovel. "The décor is interesting but hardly the height of fashion. A bachelor's taste, perhaps. Men know nothing of these things. Did your uncle leave you *anything* of value or interest? I assume his effects and such had been dealt with by the solicitors before you came?"

Louisa wondered what her aunt was getting at. "No, most of his belongings were as he left them."

"I see," Aunt Milly said. "A thousand acres, I believe you told me. Is the land any good?"

"Bowes is perfect," she replied quietly and firmly. She wasn't in the mood for a fight. Another long silence followed.

"I hope you can see now what a foolish decision it was to come here. It's hardly the most civilised of places, if what I saw yesterday passes for society."

Louisa let out a slow breath. "We have been happy here and made some very good friends. It may be too rural for you, Aunt, but I happen to like it here very much and intend to stay." She clenched her hands in her lap to control the urge to let fly.

"On your own? Well, I suppose you were always a little odd. It's not surprising, considering your upbringing."

Was the woman deliberately baiting her? She really had to fight for control.

"And this fellow that's sniffing around. Who are his family? What are his prospects?"

"I can't imagine who you mean," she replied icily.

"That Maxwell fellow, who was following you around yesterday. I'll give you he is a fine-looking man but you really ought to have discouraged him from being so … attentive. It was most unbecoming."

"Aunt, it is really none of your business, but if you must know, the Maxwell family have been an emotional and practical support to me this week in the absence of family of any shape or form."

Aunt Milly shook her head in a condescending way as she buttered her toast. "I suppose you expected me to drop everything; to come here to hold your hand when I received that letter of yours. What ridiculous notions you entertain. I have recognised you and Eleanor all these years purely for your poor mother's sake. The rest of the family would have nothing to do with you, and for good reason. Your father's family were the talk of Galway. I can only guess that your father beguiled poor Sophia with honeyed words and false promises. I warned her but she was determined to ruin herself. She threw herself away."

"So why *did* you come Aunt?" Louisa demanded angrily.

"I had nothing better to do."

The atmosphere in the house did not improve much over the next few days and Aunt Milly showed no sign of decamping. Louisa spent as much time as she could out of the house. She walked for miles, finding it therapeutic. Her aunt seemed to be deliberately trying to sour what was left of their tenuous relationship. But she could not fathom why she stayed. She never missed an opportunity to criticise and what she said about the servants, invariably in front of them, was so awful, that Louisa feared she would have mass resignations.

A return to sunny weather tempted Louisa to head for the beach one afternoon. One of her favourite spots was a rocky outcrop with a flattish top in the shelter of the headland. It was the ideal spot to sit and contemplate the world, or read a book without being disturbed. It was hidden from the road above, but this was where Nicholas found her.

"The elusive Miss Campbell, I declare," he said, as he approached along the sand. "I was beginning to think you were just a figment of my imagination."

She turned and gave him a puzzled smile. "What can you mean?"

"All attempts in the last few days to storm the gates of Bowes have been thwarted, my lady. I assumed you didn't want to see me."

"You have been refused at the door?" she asked incredulously.

"They are not at home." He mimicked Róisín's accent very poorly. "I'm feeling unloved."

She could feel her anger rise. "I'm sorry, but that is not my doing. I assumed you were busy having spent so much of your time with me last week. I don't expect you to be at my beck and call all the time."

"Louisa, I would be happy to see you as often as you could

possibly stomach it. Don't look so concerned. I suspected it wasn't your doing. I have been prowling the laneways and beach every day in the hopes of finding you. From my thankfully brief encounter with your delicious aunt at the funeral, I had guessed that you would seek refuge away from the house. Am I correct?"

She nodded sadly. "Yes, she is slowly driving me mad. She loves nothing better than to meddle." She closed her eyes briefly in frustration. "She is constantly picking fights, criticising everything and everyone and generally being a complete ... nuisance."

"I could remove her for you if you wish," he said. "I could always trump up some charge and have her arrested."

"It could be me you will have to arrest. If things get any worse I may dispatch her myself and with violence. I am at my wits' end, Nicholas."

He smiled sympathetically as he clambered up to join her. "Move over." He put his arm around her waist and kissed her.

When she could pull away, she said, "I desperately need advice."

Nicholas held her close. "Do you want me to speak to her?" he asked seriously. "I could ask her to leave. She doesn't scare me ... too much."

"No, that would be cowardly of me. Normally I would be well able to deal with her but at the moment I ..." She raised and dropped her hand in a gesture of frustration.

"I understand. Perhaps you should just be blunt. Ask her outright what she wants, and let her know that you won't put up with her insensitive behaviour in your own home. Just tell her to leave."

"That's easy for you to say," she complained. "She knows my weak points: how to really hurt me. Every argument becomes extremely personal. By the way, you should know, she doesn't think you're good enough for me."

He laughed heartily. "That will teach me! I'd heard the Irish aristocracy held themselves very high." She frowned at him and he became serious. "Enough of your horrible aunt. How are you feeling otherwise? You look tired and pale," he said. He tucked a wayward curl behind her ear but the breeze kept pulling it loose.

"Sometimes I'm fine, and at other times I just feel empty. It's hard to explain. I walk into a room and half expect to see Eleanor there or hear her voice somewhere in the house. Isn't that strange? When my parents died, I had little time to think or grieve as I had Eleanor to look after. This is different. There are countless jobs to be done, but I can't find the energy to do them. I'm floundering in indecision – I am not myself."

Nicholas said nothing for a few moments and she could sense that he was struggling with something. "We could just disappear," he said softly, looking into her eyes intently, then kissing her gently. "Louisa, you know how I feel about you. I had been working up the courage to ask you to marry me but Eleanor's death came far too soon ..."

"Nicholas, I'm in mourning. I can't marry you ... even if you had actually asked me," she trailed off with a half-teasing smile.

He pulled a face. "You always home in on the details, don't you? Look, Gretna is two hours north. We could be back in a day. Or a special licence. There are several magistrates who owe me favours. I want you with me at Thorncroft, not moping about down here either alone or with that dragon of an aunt."

"Nicholas, no. I don't want a havey-cavey marriage and neither do you. If you ever ask me, and *if* I say yes," she poked him in the ribs, "we will do it properly," she stated firmly. "We're not underage or desperate."

"Speak for yourself," he muttered, kissing the top of her head. "So you won't elope ... I suppose there is always kidnapping."

"And you a magistrate."

"Shocking, isn't it! What you have reduced me to. If you're not careful I'll go into a decline and fade away. Then it will be too late, and you'll be sorry."

She couldn't help but laugh. "You are an idiot." But her hand crept into his and held on tight.

Milly waited until she was sure everyone was in bed. She crept down the stairs without making too much noise, not completely happy in having to resort to such measures, but secrecy was paramount. She had received several frantic notes from Jack since her arrival, each of which had ended up in the fire, but the last one, which had been left in her room that afternoon, had threatened to expose all to Louisa if she didn't meet with him. Her own curiosity had landed her in this situation. She really should have stayed safely in Dublin.

She crossed the stable-yard and entered the dark stable block. Holding up her skirts in distaste, she walked the length of the stalls; most appeared to be empty. Even so, the smell of horse was all-pervading and she disliked anything to do with animals. Like children, they always seemed to be smelly or hungry, and often both.

"Hello, Milly," Jack said, stepping forward out of the shadows and lighting his lamp. "I knew you'd come." His voice trembled with emotion.

She turned slowly and scrutinised him. It was over a year since she had laid eyes on him. There was something not quite right; he seemed a shadow of the man she remembered. He was beardless and wearing what appeared to be old tattered clothing. The fastidious well-dressed gentleman was no more. She shuddered in distaste. He continued to look at her, and much to her disgust, there were tears in his eyes.

She sighed impatiently. How pathetic he was. "What's this all about? You know how dangerous it is for us to meet, here of all places."

"I needed to see you," he said, moving forward and trying to take her hand.

She shoved him away with force. "Stay away from me!" she hissed.

"You cannot mean that – after all we have been to each other," he pleaded.

"I told you the last time we met in Dublin, this cannot continue. This whole situation is ludicrous, pretending you're dead and dragging the girls into it. Worst of all, you have put me in danger as well. Have you gone completely mad?"

"It was necessary. The police were too close," he snapped. "Peter's children never mattered to me. Only you."

"You live in the past, Jack. Whatever we had all those years ago," she paused and made a frustrated gesture with her hand, "it's gone now."

"I don't believe you," he replied forcefully. "You are the love of my life, Milly."

"You destroyed me, Jack. I was quite happy in my marriage until you came along with your promises and soft words," she sneered. "Nothing was the same after that. You took away my peace."

"That's unfair, Milly. You were miserable with Nathan. I offered you everything. When he died you could have joined me here. Look at the house," he said with a sweeping gesture out towards the grounds. "I built this place up for you. Everything – even down to the best linen and plate. I bought the best to please you."

"You should have saved your money, Jack. Why on earth would I come to live here, in the middle of nowhere, when I have a very satisfactory life in Dublin?" she asked scathingly. "You know Nathan left me comfortably situated."

His face fell. "But he never gave you love, Milly. You could have had anything you wished for here with me."

"No, Jack, not everything," she informed him with a scowl. "We are finished, do you hear? I never want to see you again."

Dinner had passed off relatively calmly that evening, much to Louisa's relief. Her conversation with Nicholas earlier in the day had bolstered her confidence and she was ready to lock horns with her aunt. But instead, Aunt Milly appeared distracted and ate sparingly, and in almost total silence. Louisa excused herself early and sought the tranquillity of her room. For some time she sat at the open window listening to the outside world and watching the shadows fall. She thought about Eleanor, and about Nicholas, and wondered what the future might hold. When they had first decided to come to Bowes, she had known that Eleanor's death would eventually prompt her to reassess her life. Would she stay in Newton or sell up and move away? She was wealthy enough to travel or move anywhere, even abroad. That was, of course, before her relationship with Nicholas had developed in such an unexpected direction. Their conversation that afternoon had left her in no doubt about what he wanted. She knew she loved him, but she needed time to grieve. Her heart was in tune with his wishes, except in the matter of haste. She hoped he understood.

As dusk fell, she lit her lamp and picked a book at random, before settling down on her bed to read. She soon nodded off and woke to find it was dark outside and the room chilly. She got up to close the window. Crack. She could have sworn she heard someone out on the landing. The clock said one-thirty. She stood very still, straining her ears, her heart starting to pound. Yes, that was definitely someone going downstairs. It could only be Aunt Milly. What could she be up to?

Louisa turned down her lamp and opened her door as noiselessly as she could. The landing and stairway were in darkness. Maybe her aunt was peckish and heading for the kitchen. How incongruous that would be, her stiff–necked aunt raiding the kitchen like a grubby schoolboy. This she had to see. She followed as quietly as she could, feeling her way down the stairs in the darkness, but when she entered the kitchen there was no sign of Aunt Milly – where could she have gone? She stood in the centre of the room. Was her mind playing tricks? After all, she was over-tired. But just as she decided to go back to bed, she caught something out of the corner of her eye. A lamp flared out in the stables, glowed momentarily, then moved slowly down the block. There *was* someone out there. Was it her aunt or someone else? Suddenly she didn't feel brave any more. With a sinking feeling, it occurred to her that it might be those blasted Fenians. What should she do? She couldn't tackle them on her own. She stepped back into the shadows and waited to see what would happen. The light flickered now and again as someone walked to and fro, but she could not tell who it was or how many people were there.

After about ten minutes the light was suddenly extinguished

and her aunt came striding across the stable-yard. Another dark figure appeared behind her and scurried off in the direction of the orchard. Just as Aunt Milly opened the back door Louisa managed to hide herself in the pantry, pinning herself to the wall. The door was slightly ajar and she saw her aunt pass by. By the set of her shoulders and the agitation of her movements she could tell that she was very angry. Aunt Milly disappeared out of sight and she realised that she had been holding her breath. She exhaled slowly. What was going on?

Aunt Milly was packed and gone before breakfast the next morning, leaving no note of explanation. Louisa was left baffled and relieved in equal measure.

Chapter Twenty-Five

S omething was very wrong. Jack was pacing up and down in the barn but it was his face that warned O'Connor to be careful. He could see that he was absolutely livid and wondered why.

"Any news?" Jack snapped as soon as he saw him.

"I've heard nothing, but I assume the attack went ahead this morning."

"Excellent."

"There should be some word by this evening. I'll go into Newton for the newspaper," he said.

Jack kicked at the straw on the floor. "Today will go down in history, Liam. We will shake them up so badly. You know, by rights we should have organised more mayhem."

"We had enough trouble co-ordinating the O'Griofas," he muttered under his breath.

But Jack was oblivious, caught up in his own fervour. "We should have struck in London again for good measure." An ugly smirk spread across his face. "You know they'll write songs about us, boyo, and will be singing them in the pubs of Ireland for years to come."

"Aye, but how soon will the guns arrive? I need to organise things and have the men ready."

"My friend assured me they would be here by the end of the week. He has never let me down so stop your worrying. He will send a telegram when they get to Brampton."

O'Connor was worried. Jack had been in a queer mood ever since the young girl had died, and there was an edge to him now that he hadn't seen before. It was pure anger and it was dangerous. His greatest fear was that Jack would become reckless and endanger them all. He was not as keen to die for the cause.

Nicholas was in his study the next morning, when he read with growing anger of the Fenian attack in Newcastle. The target had been the armoury which was part of the barracks where Robert was stationed. They had blown a hole in the wall which had resulted in several casualties. He had a tense two-hour wait before he heard any news: a telegram arrived informing him that Robert had been injured and was now in the Royal Victoria Infirmary. He left immediately for Newcastle.

The ward was on the top floor of the hospital with magnificent views out across the city, but the men who occupied the beds were unable to appreciate it. As he walked down the long narrow room, his own footsteps sounded overloud. He was struck by the near total silence, which now and then was punctuated by a low moan from some poor soul. A young nurse approached him and brought him over to Robert when he explained who he was. Although he had tried to prepare himself for what he might see, he was still shocked to find his brother in such a condition. Robert's face and arms was covered in abrasions and the coverings on the bed were raised up by some kind of cage, he assumed to keep the weight off his injured legs. One arm was encased in a splint. Robert was fast asleep.

"He has been sedated with laudanum, sir, but he had a reasonable night. The surgeon has removed the shrapnel from his leg and believes he will make a full recovery."

"Thank you, nurse. Is it all right for me to stay?"

"Yes sir, of course, but it is unlikely he will be conscious much today."

"I would just like to sit with him for a while just in case he should wake up." The nurse smiled sympathetically and went about her duties.

Each morning Nicholas went to the hospital to sit with his brother. Robert was still under sedation and was drifting in and out of consciousness. He utilised his time writing letters of business and notes to Anna and Louisa, keeping them informed of the patient's condition.

Dear Louisa,

Robert continues to make slow but steady progress. It is my hope that I will be able to take him home to Thorncroft very soon, and have organised for a nurse to be employed during his convalescence.

It is dreary here, but not just because of the inclement weather. There is fear also. The Fenians have openly admitted to the attack on the barracks and my blood boils at their audacity. The police here are convinced that the perpetrators came from Manchester and further afield. I understand that they have managed to plant spies deep within the organisation. But my deepest concern, as I am sure you can guess, is that they had some connection to Cumberland. The link has not been made yet, but I suspect that Newton is the centre of their operations for the whole of northern England. Somewhere there is a head man, like a spider sitting in the centre of a web. I believe it is O'Connor. I urge you to take extra care in my absence. I do not like to think of you alone at Bowes. If you are uneasy, please go to Anna and stay with her until my return. You are constantly in my thoughts,

Yours, Nicholas

Aunt Milly's abrupt departure had left Louisa bewildered. Bowes was plunged into gloomy seclusion and, with Nicholas away, she began to grieve in a more profound way. She could not put her mind to anything. Her usual channels of relief had dried up. She could not bear to go into the small parlour where the piano now lay silent. She wandered about the house, going from room to room, restless and listless in turn, in an endless search for something, without knowing what it was. She paced the garden paths, too, but they held unpleasant memories and gave her no comfort. Max followed her about, equally lost. At night he slept on the floor beside her bed.

Nicholas's absence, and the reason for it, added to her anxiety. She had been upset to hear of Robert's injuries, but thankful that he was alive. She missed Nicholas very much and longed for his return, but his notes to her were too brief and full of anger. She put it down to concern for his brother's condition, but at the back of her mind she began to fear that his old prejudices were resurfacing, particularly since his own family had now been directly affected. If she was honest she could not blame him. After witnessing her aunt's strange behaviour that last night she herself began to wonder what was really going on at Bowes. Who had her aunt met in the stables that night? She could not fathom it out at all. Any explanation she could think of just seemed too preposterous to be true. Did her aunt have Fenian connections? Surely not. The woman was far too selfish to put herself out for anyone, let alone a cause that would be so alien to her upbringing and beliefs.

After several days of self-inflicted seclusion, she finally realised that she would have to make an effort to get back to normality. Indulging her grief was unforgiveable when others were in distress. Anna must be in need of comfort. Her own vague worries were nothing compared to what the Maxwells must be going through. She ordered the gig and set off to the Rectory to visit her. She was received with kindness, but she detected a slight reserve in Anna that had not been there before.

The Fenians' actions, coming hot on the heels of bombings earlier in the year, had horrified everyone and it wasn't surprising that there was a public backlash against anyone Irish. Speculation was rife in the press and the more sensational papers were whipping up public outrage even further. Still, it upset her to think that her friends had doubts about her. She was not pressed to stay at the Rectory and her journey home was glum.

By prior agreement there was no communication between the O'Griofas and Jack just in case the authorities had them under surveillance. The reports coming from Newcastle were that the police were rounding up possible suspects. Soon news of early morning raids in Angel Meadow in Manchester came through, but the O'Griofa twins were long gone, having prearranged an escape north of the border to Scotland. As they were the only ones he thought could identify him, Jack was confident that the loop was closed and he was safe.

The months of meticulous planning had paid off, and the long-awaited consignment arrived from Newcastle, over several moonless nights. The covered wagons with their precious cargo, disguised as tradesmen's supply wagons, had been split up into small convoys. Each travelled via a different route in order to look less suspicious and evade detection. Some came through Carlisle, others through Penrith, Kendal and Barrow-in-Furness. Jack was on tenterhooks during this time, sure that at least one consignment would be discovered and the game would be up, but their luck held.

The arrival of the wagons was scheduled for the early hours of the morning, but it was too risky to take them in through Bowes Farm, so a waiting guide directed them along the coast road to the northern end of the estate. Teams of men silently unloaded the cases of guns and stored them in the chamber under Cassidy's barn. Once they were finished, the floor was put back down and the barn left looking disused and abandoned. Only a very close examination of the floor would have revealed anything unusual.

The wagon drivers were paid off and slipped away again. Jack was satisfied that the first part of their plan had been successful and turned his mind to making the final arrangements to convey the guns to Ireland. A ship had been chartered out of Glasgow, and lay offshore up the coast, awaiting communication from him. By agreement the guns were to be landed north of Dublin city along the coast at Loughshinny, a tiny fishing village with a pier large enough to facilitate the ship but without an RIC or British army presence. Once the guns were unloaded, they would become the problem of the Dublin men and Jack's task would be completed.

A vicious storm came in off the Irish Sea and their plans had to be stalled. Jack and O'Connor were anxious. The longer they had the guns on site and that ship was anchored off-shore, the higher the risk of discovery. They knew Maxwell was away, but didn't doubt that he would have spies on the ground. Jack was worried that his niece would be warned by her beau; any hope of her being sympathetic to the cause was long gone. He had her activities watched closely.

Detective Inspector Fletcher walked into the foyer of the Queen Anne Hotel in Newcastle and was directed to a small room where Maxwell was waiting to receive him in private.

"Inspector! It's good to see you again, though I wish it were under different circumstances," Maxwell said, rising to meet him.

"Sir," Fletcher responded, shaking his hand. "Indeed. I suspected something was in the offing. They were so quiet since London in March." They sat down opposite each other. "I was sorry to hear about your brother; I hope he will make a full recovery."

"So far the signs are good. He is conscious now, though in some pain. He was lucky but will carry the scars for the rest of his life," Maxwell said, his bitterness clear.

"Do you have any intelligence on this that might help me?" Fletcher asked bluntly. His superiors were pressing him for results.

Maxwell shook his head and Fletcher felt his optimism slide away; another dead end. "My gut feeling is that the Newton men are involved, but in what capacity, I cannot tell you. I hope to travel home with my brother in a few days but, in the meantime, I have instructed the local police to watch carefully for anything unusual. I suppose it's unlikely they'll find anything. This was well planned and the ringleaders are long gone."

"That is possible, certainly. They have managed to take a considerable amount of munitions, much more than we are admitting to in the press. If the public knew the full extent, there would be uproar and widespread panic."

"The question is, what are they going to do with it all? It can't be easy to transport or hide such a large amount of weaponry. They must have a hiding place somewhere."

"I suspect they could be on their way to Ireland already," he said despondently, "but how do we watch the entire coast? It's an impossible task without deploying vast resources."

"You will have to pressurise every informer."

"Trust me, that is being done as we speak. It is our best chance. So far, no one is willing to talk. The navy have been alerted to patrol the Irish Sea but if the Fenians split up the cargo it will be impossible to find, unless we are lucky. The Dublin police are also investigating, but so far there is no information coming through from that end."

Maxwell leaned forward. "You know my suspicions regarding my neighbour's property. Do you think we should search it?"

He looked at him over the rim of his glasses. "It would certainly be the perfect hiding place for them. The coastline is deserted. They could easily get the guns away without being spotted. But my resources are very limited outside of Newcastle at the moment. I could get a warrant, but we would have to have some positive information pointing in that direction."

"I will see what I can find out. I cannot stand by and do nothing," Maxwell said.

Louisa had had very few visitors since the funeral and was delighted when Róisín announced Mrs. Lambert. Unfortunately, she was not alone and was followed into the room by Mrs. Rathbone. Louisa greeted them as cheerfully as she could.

"My dear child, how are you?" Mrs. Lambert asked, squeezing her hands before taking the seat beside the fire. "I'm sorry to have taken so long to make my call of condolence, but I have been unwell. Geneviève has been kind enough to stay and take care of me."

"I am sorry to hear you have been ill. If I had known, I would have called on you, but I have not been venturing out much."

"That is perfectly understandable, you poor thing. Oh dear, it was all so sudden. She was such a sweet girl. You must miss her terribly."

"Yes I do, but I am managing, Mrs. Lambert. You are very kind to come out all this way to see me – both of you – I do appreciate it."

"Not at all, my dear. Anna Maxwell – oh no, Whitby now, of course – insisted on lending me her carriage. We were talking of you only yesterday and I was explaining to her how badly I felt about neglecting you, and she insisted and so here we are."

Mrs. Lambert could not have known what a relief it was to her to hear of her friend's kindness. Perhaps their relationship was not as damaged as she had feared.

"Anna is very kind-hearted," she said.

"Yes; a very noble family, the Maxwells," Geneviève piped up. Mrs. Lambert blushed and rapidly changed the subject, and they spoke of various safe topics for some time.

Geneviève remained quietly observing. It puzzled Louisa as to why she had come at all, when she suddenly spoke up. "Miss Campbell, I wonder if you would be so kind to indulge me – a quiet word perhaps?" Her ingenuousness instantly aroused her suspicions. Mrs. Lambert frowned but made no comment.

It was rather rude to leave Mrs. Lambert alone but Geneviève had put her on the spot. "Perhaps you would like to take a turn around the garden while we wait for tea?" Louisa suggested, even though she had no desire to be alone with her. She rang the bell for Róisín.

"Perfect. You will excuse us, mother?" Geneviève said, jumping up and linking Louisa's arm. "We won't be long."

They went out on to the terrace and down the steps into the garden. Louisa was determined not to give the woman any encouragement and remained silent. After one turn of the perimeter path Geneviève spoke. "I suppose you are curious to know what it is I have to say?"

She stopped and gave what she hoped was a discouraging look in response; unfortunately it did not have the desired effect.

"I feel we could be great friends, you and I," Geneviève said with a coy look. "Friends look out for each other and I cannot remain silent on the subject any longer. Oh, look at the lovely arbour! Let us sit there for our tête-à-tête. Now isn't this cosy?" she said as she settled herself before turning and giving Louisa a sharp look. "You know it is most unfortunate, black really doesn't become you. How pale you are." Louisa swallowed a biting retort and commenced a slow mental count to ten.

Geneviève took a deep breath. "Now how can I put this? You see, I could not fail to notice that a certain gentleman is showing a marked interest in you. But you must resist, Louisa. You do not know him as I do. I have had the misfortune to have been tricked by him, too. I once believed that he loved me and that he would offer for me. I was a young and innocent girl." She paused and looked at Louisa from under her eyelashes. Louisa doubted the woman had ever been innocent, even as a babe in arms.

"You are being duped. Don't be disheartened," she said. "I have heard how things were when you first arrived. He tried to bully you into selling the farm, didn't he?" Louisa's heart sank; she didn't like the direction this was taking.

"He is relentless when he wants something. When that plan failed he had only one other course of action open to him and that was to pursue you romantically. If you marry him, he will get the land without having to pay for it."

This thought had traitorously crossed Louisa's mind before, but hearing someone else voice it was devastating. She knew the woman was driven by jealousy, but what if it were true? She had always mistrusted Nicholas's sudden change of attitude towards her. Could his professions of love be false?

"You are most kind in warning me, Mrs. Rathbone, but I have no reason to doubt Mr. Maxwell's integrity," she responded, even as she doubted the very words coming from her own lips. But she would not give this creature any satisfaction.

Geneviève looked at her pityingly. "It looks as though I am too late. Well, I hope you do not rue the day. I have done my best by you." With that she stood and walked stiffly away.

Chapter Twenty-Six

L ouisa looked at the warrant she had just been handed in utter disbelief. Inspector Fletcher and Nicholas had arrived just after breakfast, both unsmiling – forbidding almost. Her initial joy at seeing Nicholas had soon disappeared to be replaced by alarm. Geneviève's awful assertion days before had resulted in her dwelling almost continuously on the possibility that he was being less than honest with her. Now he was standing before her in his capacity of magistrate, supporting the police in their barely veiled accusation that she was harbouring criminals – possibly even being one herself. Her mind was racing with all the implications of what the search could mean. If they found anything of an incriminating nature, how could she prove that she had no knowledge of it? What if evidence had been planted by someone who wanted her out of the way? She knew O'Connor was capable of anything.

"It would be best if we had your permission, Miss Campbell," the Inspector said. She looked from him to Nicholas, who at least at the decency to look uncomfortable. But she was in no doubt that she was being tested; by both of them.

"Certainly you have it," she snapped, her anger now showing through her fragile self-control. "Get on with it." She let the warrant fall from her hand on to the table in disgust and walked to the window, shaking like a leaf. She did not want them to see how furious she was.

Fletcher left to organise his men, who were waiting outside.

"Louisa, I am sorry," Nicholas said.

She turned around and held up her hand to ward him off. "Don't say a word. I can't believe that you would be a party to this."

"You have to understand that this is necessary. Time is against us. We have to find those stolen munitions before they are used on more innocent people."

"And you believe I have them hidden under the beds?"

"Don't be foolish. You know I do not suspect you. Others on the estate are not so innocent, Louisa. You cannot hide from that fact any longer," he answered angrily. "You have seen the reports in the papers. You know what happened to Robert. These people are ruthless. They do not care who they hurt. How can you doubt how serious this is? Someone from here is involved, I am sure of it."

"Don't tell me: you have such definite information this time," she replied angrily.

"Yes," he said quietly, "we do. One of the Manchester Fenians has turned informer."

She sat down because her legs were trembling so. Should she tell him about Aunt Milly's strange behaviour? But she stayed quiet, her trust in him shattered like shards of glass, sharp and infinitely painful.

"Louisa, please try to understand the position I'm in."

She bit her lip to stop herself from letting fly. If she said what was in her mind she knew there would be no turning back.

"You should probably get Jameson here as quickly as possible," he said.

Her head snapped up and she glared at him. "So much for my innocence! I think it best you leave, Mr. Maxwell."

He flinched at her words and turned away. She knew he hesitated at the door, no doubt willing her to look up at him, but she kept her eyes downcast, her body rigid. She heard the door shut gently after him, and let the tears she had held in check fall freely.

For two days Fletcher's men scoured the Bowes estate; houses, barns, and outhouses were all searched. They found nothing. Frustrated, Fletcher reported to Nicholas at Thorncroft when the search was called off.

"You are absolutely sure?" Nicholas asked.

Fletcher nodded. "Short of digging up every field. If the guns are there, they are very well hidden."

He dropped his head in his hands. "Hellfire, Fletcher, this is a disaster."

"Yes, we have wasted precious time," he complained. "That young ruffian, Murphy, seemed so sure, but it could have been a deliberate red herring to steer us away from Manchester." Nicholas nodded. "Anyway, I have to return to Newcastle immediately. Look sir, the guns may well be here, and I have taken the precaution of alerting the navy in case they try to ship them across the Irish Sea. That is all we can do. The bastards may sit on them for months, of course, but if they do attempt to move them we will have some chance of catching them in the act."

"Have you informed Miss Campbell of the result of your search?"

"Yes."

"What did she say?"

"Absolutely nothing. She just looked at me as if I were something unpleasant she had stepped in. I fully appreciate the difficult position she is in, and the timing is most unfortunate with her being recently bereaved, but I only hope she understands that I have to do my job."

"She will when she calms down. I cannot stress strongly enough that she is innocent of any wrongdoing. She has merely had the misfortune to inherit the situation from her uncle."

Fletcher didn't look entirely convinced. "By the way, her solicitor was there."

"Had he anything of value to say?" he asked bitterly.

"Only what I would expect: demanded an apology; hinted at abuse of power, etcetera. You can imagine the kind of thing."

"Yes indeed. I half expect to be sued for defamation of

character. Well, I'd better go and see her," he said with a heavy heart. He anticipated a frosty reception at best.

Later that afternoon, after much soul-searching, which was of absolutely no benefit, Nicholas went to Bowes hoping the right words would come to him when he faced her. He did feel guilty that she had been subjected to yet another slight on her good name, but they could not have ignored the possibility of the guns being hidden on her property. However, he wasn't entirely surprised to be told at the door that Miss Campbell was not receiving visitors. Though he pleaded with Róisín, the young maid was fiercely loyal and would not relent. He rode home in a despondent mood. He didn't want to leave to fetch Robert home without resolving matters, but she had left him no choice. He had gambled that their love for each other would be enough, but with dismay he realised that his own inconsistent behaviour would ultimately be his downfall.

"So, do we go ahead as planned?" O'Connor asked Jack. It was past midnight and the men had been discussing the search of the estate for some time.

"Yes. I don't want to risk the police coming back again. I want the guns out of here once and for all," Jack replied impatiently. He had spent the last few days on one of the outlying farms, masquerading as a labourer. He had found it immensely satisfying to watch the police in their futile search, and he was in great good humour as a result.

"Aye, but their spies will be on the look-out."

"They have never been an issue," Jack sneered. "The London boys are good, but their resources are stretched and the public outcry has them under time and political pressure to get results. Just look at all the furore in the papers. No, I believe they will have gone back to Newcastle with their tails between their legs. My friend, you know that Maxwell has considerable influence. No doubt he used the opportunity for his own ends. They can't have had any definite information." Jack beamed. "I'm sure he's as mad as fire that they found nothing. And all the time our spoils were right under their noses."

"You seem very sure about informants, but someone must have said something. They can't get search warrants that easily."

"In the present panic, I'd say it's easier than ever." Jack laughed.

"I don't like it, Jack."

"Hold fast, my friend, and stop worrying. The O'Griofas would not squeal and they are the only ones who know me. They are safely north of the border by now. You forget I'm officially dead, Liam."

"I suppose you are. So what now?"

Jack leant towards him. "Friday night will be moonless – our best opportunity to move everything down to the caves in readiness. On Saturday night the ship will anchor off-shore and we will have to run the stuff out in the smaller boats. It will take a couple of hours, but we daren't do it during the day. Tomorrow get a crew ready – and mind, only the lads we are really sure of. Don't take any chances. I think it best that we hide the row boats in the caves. It will look suspicious if they are left on the beach. I will send Sean Óg up to signal the ship tomorrow evening after he sends the telegram to Dublin."

"What about your niece? She often walks down on the beach. What if she notices something odd?"

"Well, we will just have to make sure that she doesn't. I suggest you get Lizzie to ensure she is unwell for the weekend."

"Good idea. I'll talk to her tomorrow, so. She'll know what to do."

Thursday morning was overcast and heavy, with the promise of rain. Louisa was suffering the effects of another night of tossing and turning. After breakfast she curled up with a book in the drawing room and tried to relax. But she found she could not concentrate. She gazed out to the garden which was coming into its full summer glory, but it left her unmoved. The joy that came from the little things was gone. The Bowes estate felt like it was mocking her with its vile secrets. She didn't know who to trust any more. Cumberland had made her soft, she thought with disgust. In Dublin she had lived by her wits, but she had fallen into the trap of letting people get close to her here. Why hadn't she sold the cursed estate and stayed in Dublin? How ironic, she thought, she should have heeded Aunt Milly's warnings.

She closed her eyes. She was fooling herself: fate alone had made the move a disaster. Her uncle's legacy was much more than she could ever have envisaged. She was embroiled in his machinations without knowing what it was he had orchestrated. But she guessed those guns were on her land. They just hadn't looked in the right places. Her suspicions were based on how edgy O'Connor had been of late. He was never around when she called into the office and when she did track him down, he was evasive and nervy. It was a dilemma she was ill-equipped to deal with, and approaching Nicholas for advice was now out of the question. Perhaps she should discuss it with George, or even his father. She would take a trip into Newton to seek George's advice the next day. Having reached a decision, she felt more at peace and sat back again, curled her feet up beneath her and tackled her book once more. Within five minutes she was fast asleep.

Some time later she awoke to her face being licked enthusiastically. Her eyes flew open and she shoved the dog away in fright. He fell back to the floor and whimpered.

"I'm sorry, Max, you gave me such a fright," she said, as she lovingly rubbed his silky head. He looked up at her with those huge brown eyes and she realised just how much she had neglected him recently. "Sorry, boy, I'm not a very good mistress, am I? Why don't we go for a little walk?" Whether he understood or not, his tail began to thump out a steady beat on the floor. She smiled down at him. "It will do me good as well."

Having been cooped up for so long, Max was straining on his leash as soon as he sniffed fresh air. She had intended going towards Newton, but Max had other ideas. His preferred destination was the estate land and he wasted no time in pulling her in that direction. She had no choice but to push down her qualms, let him off the leash and follow. Max bounded through the deserted stable-yard, through the gateway and out on to the track. Following at a more leisurely pace, Louisa soon found herself relaxing and starting to enjoy being outside again.

Lost in thought, she wandered after him as he took the path at the oak tree that led to the river. But it wasn't long before she was struck by something odd. Not one person was to be seen in the fields or outside any of the cottages she passed. This was one of the busiest times of year on the estate. Where was everyone? By the time they had reached the river she was concerned and wanted to turn back, but Max disappeared off towards the water and ignored her calls to heel. Grumbling under her breath, she walked on, following him northwards towards the far end of the estate.

As she rounded a corner, she caught sight of Max going through the gate into Cassidy's cottage. She stood still, reluctant to follow. When he didn't appear after a few minutes she moved a little closer. To her surprise, the front door of the cottage was open. A tingle of apprehension went down her spine as she passed through the gate. She gently pushed open the door and called out, 'hello'. No one responded. Max was out of sight, but she could hear faint scratching noises from somewhere inside.

When her eyes adjusted to the gloom she could make out that she was in an extremely untidy kitchen. On the table a half loaf of bread was rapidly succumbing to the stifling heat of the house; blue mould covered the cut surface. An unpleasant smell of sour milk wafted up from a jug. She had to hold her handkerchief to her face as the smell was making her gag. The signs were that someone had been living here very recently. Puzzled, she moved forward. There was a door to another room to the side of the chimneybreast. Maybe that was where the dog had gone.

It was a tiny bedroom with a straw mattress on the floor covered in some old blankets. A ragged red piece of fabric was nailed up across the small window, giving the room a strange pink hue. Max was nosing frantically through the straw on the hunt for something. As she looked around she recognised items that had come from her house, including the little silver heart-shaped picture frame that had disappeared from Eleanor's room. Panic started to build.

"Max, come away, you bad dog." He looked up at her, but whatever he was after had a stronger pull than obedience to her. She watched, both fascinated and horrified, as he continued to paw and nose the straw until at last he met with success. He pulled away with what looked like a wad of paper in his mouth, wagging his tail furiously.

"What have you got there, Max?" she asked, kneeling down beside him. She gently tugged at the paper and he released it, but a faint hint of perfume triggered an elusive half-formed memory and she decided to hasten her departure.

"Come along. We are trespassing, you know," she told him, her voice unsteady.

As they passed out through the kitchen she stowed Max's booty in her pocket. Something wasn't right. O'Connor had told her no one lived here, yet there was evidence to the contrary, and why were items from her house scattered about? She was suddenly anxious to put as much distance as possible between herself and the cottage.

When she reached the house, she rushed up to her room and closed the door. Sitting on the bed, she gingerly pulled out the bundle of paper from her pocket. At first she didn't recognise them; the old yellowed pages were torn in places and crushed, as if they had been rolled up in a ball and then straightened out again. But the random pages were not random at all; they resolved themselves into letters, Uncle Jack's letters that had gone missing weeks before. Jumping up, she dropped them in her agitation, and stared at them as they lay scattered on the floor. Swallowing hard, she sat down again on the bed, trembling uncontrollably. She tried to come up with a reasonable explanation as to why they had turned up in a supposedly deserted house. Who had taken them and why? What did any of this mean?

She picked the letters up off the floor, selected one and began to read; it was dated ten year's previously.

My dearest Jack," it began, but it was the closing salutation that left her stunned; *Yours always, Milly.*

She froze. The perfume which had triggered her unease in the cottage was her aunt's. She still wore it. The love letters were between her uncle and her aunt! Which meant the person her aunt met that night could have been *Uncle Jack* ... No – that was impossible! But the more she let that thought settle in her mind, the more feasible it became; an explanation for all of the odd things that had happened, including the missing objects, probably of a personal and sentimental nature to her uncle, turning up in a supposedly deserted cottage. It would also explain Aunt Milly showing up for the funeral, and, most importantly of all, it confirmed Eleanor's dying words of warning. Surely to even think it she must be going mad. If Uncle Jack were alive, then Eleanor's last words had definitely not been delirium. He must have had a hand in her death. The sight of him alone would have been enough to trigger a heart attack, or even worse – could he have done it deliberately? It was a horrifying thought.

The more she considered it, the more convinced she became that her suspicion was correct. If his activities had been drawing too much attention from Nicholas and others, faking his death abroad was the perfect escape from prying eyes. He would have known her father was dead from Aunt Milly and that she, Louisa, would be his heir. He had been prepared to gamble that they would come to live here, giving the estate an air of respectability, which would allow him to operate unseen and unimpeded. If it was true, she had to hand it to him: it was an astute plan. It also meant he was extremely dangerous and incredibly clever. Worst of all, the evidence pointed to him hiding out at Cassidy's cottage.

Now genuinely alarmed, she sat there trying to decide what she should do. She had no proof, so who could she tell without looking utterly ridiculous? If things had been different, she would have gone straight to Thorncroft, but that was impossible now that her relationship with Nicholas was in tatters. He and everyone else would put it down to her grief and shake their heads sadly.

But she could not ignore the situation either. Her instincts were telling her to run, but where was safe and who could she trust? Perhaps it was time to return to Dublin for a while. That would give her some space and time to think a little more coherently. Yes, the more she thought about it, the better she felt. She would catch the first train south in the morning. It was possibly the cowardly option, but she would make sure that a letter explaining her reasons and laying out all of the evidence she had found was delivered to George. If he believed her, he could take the information to the authorities; that way, at least, she would be doing the right thing. Decision made, she sat down at her dressing-table and composed her letter to George.

Then she packed a bag in preparation for her trip. By the time she was finished, it was time for dinner. In the hallway she handed her letter to Róisín with instructions for it to be hand-delivered as soon as possible. Her last order of the day was for the gig to be ready first thing in the morning to bring her to the station.

"I tell you, someone was in the cottage. My letters are gone."

"What?" O'Connor spun around in shock, his mind reeling. "Who could have known they were there?"

Jack had burst into his house moments earlier. "Someone was snooping around. I found this on the kitchen floor," Jack said, pulling out a white lace handkerchief with the initials 'LC' embroidered neatly in one corner. O'Connor recoiled in disbelief.

"I've checked with Lizzie Murphy. Louisa went out for a long walk this afternoon and returned about three o'clock. She stayed in her room most of the afternoon, but appeared for dinner, then retired early. She has ordered the gig for first thing – and you'll never guess where she's going."

He shook his head.

"The station," Jack announced grimly.

"We can't let her leave if she suspects something," he said.

"Of course not! I think it's time my niece and I had a little chat. She is proving far too nosy for my liking."

Chapter Twenty-Seven

F riday morning was to be busy for George. His client was in Maryport and he had to catch the early train. However, as usual he was running late, and as he rushed out the door of the office, his clerk handed him the post. He shoved it into his case with the intention of perusing it on the train. Two hours later he was back on the train in a bad mood. His client had changed his mind – again. Some poor devil of a relative had said the wrong thing and was now to be cut from the will. George considered using the journey to work on the new version of the will, but his heart wasn't in it. Soon more cheerful thoughts took over; he was heading north to Carlisle to spend the weekend at home. It would be bliss to forget about the mundane business of being a country solicitor for a short time. With a happy sigh, he shoved his client's papers back into the case, pushing his post down to the bottom of the bag. Relaxing back into his seat, he entertained pleasant thoughts of the weekend ahead all the way to Carlisle.

It was Saturday morning during breakfast that George suddenly remembered his post. With a groan, which elicited a stern look from his father, he hoped that he hadn't missed anything important. The last thing he wanted was a lecture on diligence. When he got back to his room, he pulled out the post and started going through it half-heartedly. The hand-delivered letter caught his attention. He quickly tore the envelope open and read Louisa's astonishing letter.

It had been some time since the Maxwell family were all together at Thorncroft. Nicholas and Robert had arrived home from Newcastle amid much fuss. It was a jovial evening and it didn't take too much persuasion for Anna and John to stay the night. On Saturday morning, Dr. Peterson called and reassured the family that Robert was doing well, considering his injuries. He would have to rest his injured leg for a few weeks and would have to walk with a stick until it was fully healed. This did not please Robert until Anna suggested it would make him a very sympathetic figure in the eyes of every female in the vicinity. But the hardest thing for him to hear was that he would not be able to ride for at least three months and a return to his regiment was very much in the future.

They were just sitting down to lunch, when George Jameson was announced.

"Sir, something has happened to Miss Campbell!" he declared in a rush, looking wildly about the table. "I have just come from Bowes. I cannot access the house."

"Jameson, calm down," Nicholas said, indicating he should sit down. "She isn't receiving visitors. I was refused at the door a few days ago."

"No," Jameson exclaimed forcefully, "you don't understand! I received this letter from her." He handed it to him. "I was so concerned that I came back from Carlisle immediately. Bowes is deserted."

"That does seem odd, Nicholas," Anna said.

"This is dated Thursday," Nicholas said, looking over at the young man. He thought he saw a slight flush stain his face and wondered why he would not meet his eye.

"Yes, unfortunately I did not receive it until this morning," Jameson stammered.

Nicholas stared at him for a moment before he read on. "It says here," he held up the letter, "that she planned to leave for Ireland yesterday morning."

"Yes, but I checked with the station master when I got in at noon today. She did not catch a train yesterday or today. He was very sure of that. That is why I am so concerned, Mr. Maxwell.

You must read on, sir. Her claims are quite extraordinary."

"Nicholas, what does it say?" John asked.

Nicholas continued to read, her words swimming before his eyes. Why hadn't she come to him with all of this? She was clearly overwrought when she wrote the letter. Some of the suspicions she had were ridiculous and could be put down to grief, perhaps. But echoes of his warnings to her about her servants and tenants were called to mind. He could not just put the letter down to grief and anxiety. They would have to investigate further. He looked up to find all eyes in the room upon him.

"Well?" Anna asked anxiously. "What does it say?"

Nicholas handed the letter over to John. "Don't be concerned, Anna. We will go down to Bowes and see what we can find out. I'm convinced she *has* gone to Ireland and closed up the house."

John quickly read through the letter before tucking it into his pocket. Nicholas was relieved; he didn't want Anna to read it.

"I'm coming too," piped up Robert.

"No, you most certainly are not," Nicholas said, ringing the bell and giving him a warning look.

He ordered the butler to have George's horse brought back around and two horses saddled up and ready, as quickly as possible. He then beckoned the men to follow him out. He led them straight to the gun room. Both men looked at him in surprise. "It's just a precaution," he explained.

"So you *do* think there is something wrong?" Jameson asked. "I was right to come to you?"

"Yes, of course, but I don't want to alarm my sister or get Robert over-excited. Now, can you use one of these?" he asked, as he loaded a pistol. Jameson nodded, looking nervous. Nicholas loaded another two and handed one to John. "Right, gentlemen, I suggest we don't waste any more time."

Before they left Thorncroft, he sent an urgent message to Sergeant Cox and Fletcher. He hoped he would not need them.

Bowes was just as George had described. It was eerily quiet. They dismounted at the front of the house, but no groom appeared.

Nicholas tried not to read too much into it, but his concern was deepening. Having no success at the front door, they peered in the windows. Everything looked normal enough, but there was no sign of Louisa or any of the servants.

They stood uncertain at the entrance to the stables. "It's odd that there is no one around," Nicholas commented. "Jameson, did you try the estate office when you were here earlier?"

"No, I'll do that now." He hastened away to check.

"Let's look around the back," Nicholas said to John.

The kitchen door was locked. Nicholas stared at it for a moment. "Stand back, John," he said. He took the gun from his pocket and used the butt to break the glass panel in the door. He reached in and turned the lock from the inside. Half expecting to be met by an irate cook or servant, they entered the house, but the kitchen was empty. They made their way up to the hallway and began to search the rooms. The first sign of mischief was the study door: someone had forced the lock. Both men drew their guns and gingerly Nicholas pushed the door open. The desk had been ransacked and the gun cabinet was empty, the glass door hanging precariously from its hinges. Broken glass crunched under their feet.

Hearing a noise out in the hall, Nicholas came out of the study with his gun raised, but it was Jameson. "Nothing, sir," he gulped, his eye firmly on Nicholas's gun.

"Damn!" Nicholas said under his breath. "All right, let's search the rest."

A few minutes later their search of the downstairs was complete and they met up again in the hall.

"We had better look upstairs, don't you think?" John said.

Nicholas nodded, but he dreaded what they might find. Every instinct was telling him that something was very wrong. Guns drawn, they slowly and quietly climbed the stairs. Nicholas pushed open the door of the first room. The room was empty. Some of Eleanor's things were still there on the bedside table, but the bed was stripped and the curtains open. Just as he turned to leave he heard the other two exclaim in horror.

"Nicholas, come quickly!" John shouted.

Heart thumping in his chest, he found them in the next bedroom, staring at a pile of shaggy black fur lying there in a pool of congealed blood. Louisa's dog had been shot in the head. Nicholas skirted around the dead animal to the window and pulled back the curtains with trembling hands. The bed had been slept in, but the blankets and sheet had been pulled down to the floor on the door side. Clothes had been laid out for the morning and were untouched.

It looked very much as though Louisa had been dragged from her bed in the middle of the night, her only ally shot in cold blood. He wondered if she had put up a struggle, but it was impossible to tell. If she had been abducted, at least there was a good chance she was still alive. If they had intended to kill her they would be looking upon two corpses in the room, not just the unfortunate dog.

"Now what do we do?" Jameson asked in a trembling voice.

"I have absolutely no idea," John said, grim-faced.

Nicholas snapped out of his trance-like state. "Come on, there is nothing we can do here. This is tantamount to a declaration of war."

She found it difficult to sleep. She did try, but the cave floor was hard and the cold seeped through the sacking she had been laid upon. A flickering storm lantern in the far corner was the only light, and in the semi-darkness of the cave she had lost track of time. She still could not believe she had been abducted. It was like something out of one of Eleanor's stupid novels which she had teased her about. Now she wished she had read them. Perhaps they might have suggested a way to escape. The heroines in those books reputedly always did, seemingly, and without a hair out of place.

When the men had burst into her room in the early hours, she had been absolutely terrified. Max had exploded into action, barking and growling furiously which seemed to stall the intruders momentarily. But a voice shouted out, "Kill it, for Jasus' sake!"

There was a shot and the barking ceased abruptly. She froze, petrified that she would be next. But she was dragged from the bed, bundled into her dressing gown, and hustled down the stairs and out of the house before she had time to react. They brought her down to the beach and she feared that they were going to drown her, but instead she was dragged through the water and around the headland before ending up in the cave. She hadn't recognised any of the men, but she was very sure who was behind it.

That was hours ago, but she comforted herself with the thought that they didn't appear to want to harm her. Lying down made her feel vulnerable, so she spent some time wiggling around until eventually she was sitting up with her back to the cave wall. Not that it helped much; she was still stuck. She vaguely recalled George telling her about smuggling that day they had first visited Bowes, and caves and smugglers went together rather well. Would anyone local remember their existence? Blast it. She recalled with a sinking heart that she had indicated in her letter that she was going to Ireland. No one would even be looking for her. That thought nearly undid her. Maybe Róisín or Mrs. Murphy would raise the alarm. They could not have slept through the commotion of the night before. That was unless they were complicit – and of course they had to be. It was lowering to realise just how stupid she had been.

She heard footsteps approach and her heart started to race. Three figures appeared out of the gloom carrying lamps. The sudden brightness hurt her eyes, and she had to turn away. One of the men came forward and a bag was dropped beside her. He knelt down and roughly turned her face towards him.

Louisa gasped. She was face to face with her uncle and he was very much alive.

She recoiled instinctively but he held her chin tightly and stared at her, a deep furrow in his brow. She stared right back. She should have been afraid, but the resemblance to her father was even more marked in the flesh: the same blue-green eyes and straight nose. Enveloped in a long black coat with straggly grey hair, he looked older than his photograph. His face was grubby with several days' growth and he looked as though he hadn't slept for some time. He reached behind her head and, to her relief, undid the gag. It had tasted disgusting.

"It's a pity there is no one to formally introduce us, Louisa, but I see you recognise me." His voice was surprisingly cultivated, which was at odds with his appearance.

Louisa's mouth was desperately dry. "You know, I guessed you were alive when I found those letters yesterday. Who else would possibly want them?" she croaked, with a bravado she was far from feeling.

He grunted and opened up the bag. "Clever girl. But it's that shrewdness that has undone you. If only you hadn't gone snooping around you might still be safely in your own bed."

"You know you will be caught. They know the guns are here. They just couldn't find them. They will come back."

He laughed. "No, niece, I think that very unlikely," he said. "Now, I've brought you some food. Can't have you starving to death." His words were somewhat belied by the look in his eyes. He pulled out some bread and a flask.

She glared back and shook her tied hands at him. "Is this really necessary?"

He gave her a humourless smile and took out a knife. "A precaution during our absence. We couldn't have you straying and getting lost. These caves are extensive. There – that should be better now."

Louisa rubbed her sore wrists but never took her eyes off him. He opened the flask and offered it to her. "It's water, you goose," he said, when she looked at it doubtfully. "You will be here for some time. You had better eat and drink while you can."

"What is going on?" she asked, finally taking the flask from him and taking a sip.

"Don't you worry your pretty head about it – though you seem to indulge in far too much thinking, young lady. No doubt you'll figure it out. Now, as much I'd love to chat, I'm afraid we are rather busy this evening. You just sit tight and you won't come to any harm," he said as he stood up. "I almost forgot – I brought something for you. It may be cold later."

So saying, he took out a blanket from the bag and draped it over her shoulders in an almost fatherly fashion which made her blood run cold. Everything about him was strangely familiar, but there was something in his tone and the way he looked at her that made her deeply distrustful of him. He might look like her father, but the only thing she sensed from this man was detached hostility. Though what else could she expect from the man who had killed her sister – whether it had been intentional or not? She must keep this to the forefront of her mind; she could not afford to be beguiled by any overtures of friendliness.

"Try to get some sleep," he said. "The night is young yet." She watched him and the others disappear into the darkness of the tunnel, curious as to what he was up to and what her own fate might be.

Jack made his way back to the cave entrance. Meeting his niece for the first time had been disturbing; she was so like her father. Such a pity, he thought. She was definitely going to be a problem. He had expected to find her cowering and terrified, but instead she seemed to have remarkable composure for someone who had been abducted in the middle of the night. She unnerved him, but he had to admit a grudging respect for her. Milly had always described her as unusual and he was beginning to see why. But he was wrong, he realised; that self-assured manner reminded him of his father. And that probably wasn't a good thing for her chances of survival.

A soft thud in the sand interrupted his thoughts. The guns had started to arrive. Each box had to be lowered down on a rope to the front of the cave. Jack watched as the young men untied the boxes and put them into wheelbarrows. All had to be done in total silence and one storm lantern at the entrance of the cave was the only light they could risk. He had left O'Connor to direct operations up on the road and hoped he wasn't expecting too much of him; he had been very jumpy lately. After Louisa had been abducted, O'Connor had escorted Róisín and Lizzie to

Carlisle to keep them out of the way. Both women had objected strongly and there had been a standoff, but Jack had sorted it out very quickly indeed. He could not understand why they were more loyal to Louisa after all he had done for them. Women were so damn fickle.

The first barrowloads disappeared past him into the darkness of the cave system. It would take hours at this rate, but they should have everything moved and ready for the next evening. With a sigh, he lit up a cigar; it was going to be a long and tedious night.

"Good morning, niece." She woke up with a jolt.

Uncle Jack was kneeling down beside her, offering food again. "Best eat, girl," he said, tossing the bread at her.

He looked wretched, she thought with little sympathy for his troubles. She was more concerned about what this day would bring for her. She had watched them stack the crates of guns for hours the previous night. Surely they could not keep her or the guns here indefinitely. She fervently hoped that someone would remember the caves' existence and think to search them before it was too late.

Jack stood up and walked over to the other side of the cave. He ran his hand along the top of the crates, humming to himself. She could sense that he was vastly pleased with himself; his plans must be progressing well.

"What are you going to do with them?" she asked. "Kill more innocent people?"

He turned around with a snarl. "These," he gestured dramatically, "will be the means of freeing Ireland from the yoke of British rule. You should be proud to be a witness to all of this."

She nearly choked on the bread. "You cannot be serious. Every action you have taken in the name of Ireland makes me sick and ashamed. Your actions have destroyed any public support you might have had."

"You're wrong!" he shouted back at her. "The people are just waiting for the right time to strike back. Look at the tenants in the West: they are asserting themselves at long last. Landlords and their filthy agents are being shown the wrath of those who have been trodden on for centuries. The time for talking is over. The only thing they understand is firepower. When these arrive in Ireland you will see the results before long. Tonight these leave for Dublin and there is nothing you or anyone else can do about it."

It struck her forcibly that her uncle was fanatical, but at least she now knew the destination of his precious cargo, which meant they had to transport them by water, and that would be incredibly risky. Whatever happened to her, there was some small comfort in the high probability that they would be caught at some stage of such a risky operation.

"Where do I fit into all of this madness? If I get out of here, I'll go straight to the authorities. You cannot hide behind me any longer," she replied angrily, throwing caution to the wind. She was a dead woman already – she knew too much now.

He came across the cave and stood above her, his face red with anger. "You free? Don't count on that happening. My men are armed. They will not hesitate. Don't think your relationship to me will save you," he said. "You are nothing to me."

"Just like Eleanor?"

He flinched and took a step backwards, his eyes wild. "It was an accident. I did not mean ..."

"You killed her!" she shouted, all her pent-up anger and fear spilling over. "Her dying words were to warn me. How could you – your own flesh and blood?" She could not hide her disgust.

He ran his hand through his hair and glared at her. "I didn't think she'd recognise me. There was nothing I could do. I just wanted to see her. I regret it," he paused, struggling with his emotions, "but it's done. I can't bring her back." His eyes went dead again.

His words burned into her soul. "You're a monster! You'll rot in hell and you deserve it."

He rushed at her so fast that she didn't have time to defend herself. The impact of his fist sent her flying to the floor.

Chapter Twenty-Eight

Early Saturday afternoon at Thorncroft, the men were in conference. Although outwardly calm, Nicholas's mind was in turmoil. Why had he not insisted that she leave Bowes? With hindsight he could see that there had been enough warning signs to warrant it. Guiltily, he recalled that the search had been his idea; perhaps that had triggered her kidnapping. All of this could not have happened at a worse time, when she was grief-stricken and already in a distressed state. Her letter was evidence enough of that. He had to stay calm and think. Reckless action now could cost her dearly, and she was too precious to him to gamble with her safety.

Reluctantly, he had asked Robert to sit in on their council of war, hoping that his local knowledge and military training might aid them. They only numbered a disappointing fifteen men, including some of the estate workers and the local policemen.

"It must be O'Connor behind this," he said. "Louisa's idea of Campbell being alive is just too preposterous." He was standing at the window looking in the direction of Bowes, thinking up all the things he would like to do to that fellow when he was found.

"So where would they take her?" Jameson asked. "Should we not be searching?"

"There are a thousand acres – tell me where to start?" Nicholas asked grimly. "It would be a pointless waste of our energy and time. If Fletcher couldn't find the guns, what hope have we of finding one woman?"

"And they may have taken her away from Bowes altogether," John added.

"No, I don't believe they would. It makes more sense that she's still here close by," Nicholas said. "They didn't kill her. They would have left her body at Bowes for us to find like the unfortunate dog. They must need her alive for some reason. Perhaps as an insurance policy of some kind?"

John frowned. "You mean as in a ransom?"

Robert jumped in. "Maybe. Perhaps they want to bargain her life for safe passage which means that the guns *are* here and they are about to move them. Could they possibly have known that she was about to inform on them – that she had sent a letter to Jameson?"

Nicholas sighed in frustration. "Unfortunately, knowing why they took her doesn't help us find her."

Robert gave him a sympathetic look. "No, but surely they would have to hold her where the guns are, in readiness to depart?"

"That is possible," Nicholas said.

"Well, think about it: how many places could hold that quantity of guns and ammunition?"

"Go on."

Robert stroked his chin. "I think you need to find a vacant farm or building. The guns and ammunition would have to be kept dry, probably hidden under a floor." Robert frowned, "Did Miss Campbell mention such a place in her letter, by any chance?"

John pulled the letter from his pocket and quickly read down through it. "Yes, she did: Cassidy's. Do you know it? She says it was supposed to be a derelict house, but there was clear evidence of habitation and she found items missing from her house there."

"There you are, Nicholas. Remember we used to hide out up there when we were in trouble?"

"Yes, I do," Nicholas answered, "though I'm sure Fletcher would have searched there and he didn't find anything untoward."

They all lapsed into downcast silence.

"Nicholas! I've just remembered. The caves at Bowes Head:

they would be the perfect place to hide the guns – dry and on the shore," Robert said.

"Of course. How could I have forgotten?" Nicholas said.

"What caves?" John asked, looking perplexed.

"Only locals would know of them, John. You can access them at low tide. They are on the far side of Bowes Head and cannot be seen from the road. We found them useful as children," Robert said.

"So do we search this Cassidy place and the caves?" George asked.

"We'll send a scout up to Cassidy's to see if there is anything going on up there and mount a watch on the coast road. I hope we are right," Nicholas said. His whole world was at stake and they were gambling on hunches.

The captain of the *Pride of Arran* was confused. When he had met Tomás O'Griofa in a Clydeside public house in Glasgow, they had discussed the plan in some detail. His understanding had been that he was to wait offshore up the coast from Newton until he received the signal to go to the rendezvous point out in Bowes Bay. They were to anchor there just before sunset.

The previous evening a signal from shore had finally come, but when the young sailor converted the morse code from the signaller with the lamp on shore, it had indicated seven in the evening, when it would still be daylight. He questioned the young lad rigorously, but he was adamant that he had taken it down correctly. The signaller was gone, so they could not double-check. Captain Flynn could only assume that there had been a change of plan. That made him nervous; he didn't like surprises. This operation was high risk as it was without running afoul of the British navy half way across the Irish Sea. Darkness at least would have given them some protection. Gun-running was a serious crime and he already had a somewhat chequered history with the law. Disgruntled, he dismissed the young lad and ordered his crew to weigh anchor and head south.

The night ahead would be physically demanding. Speed would be essential to ensure that the guns were loaded into the row boats and taken out to the waiting vessel as quickly as possible. Jack and his men had taken the opportunity to rest up for the afternoon. Jack slept fitfully and when he woke his mind was dwelling on all the little details of the plan. He looked across at O'Connor, who was sleeping sitting up, with his back to the wall, mouth open, snoring sporadically. It irritated him and he didn't know why.

He sprang up, impatient to be doing something, and walked down towards the water. He looked out towards the horizon. Such a vast nothingness. The sea always made him nervous: all that water, dark with secrets. Even as a child he had hated it. It became a challenge, though. He would make himself go down to the shore, strip off and dive in, swimming until he was exhausted. That triggered an old memory: an eight-year-old Peter sitting on the beach watching him. All this time later, he could still be taken unawares by recalling those days. Such simple, stupid memories they were, too: Peter following him around the estate like a shadow, always wanting to know what he was doing or where he was going. Jack knew his younger brother held him up to be some kind of hero, but he had been irked by his obsessive adulation, and shooed him away with disparaging comments. It then became a habit, until it dawned on him one day that Peter's hero-worship had transformed into something darker. Not only that, but Peter had become their father's favourite. As the years had passed, the gulf between them had grown.

Jack had known that his rebellious nature irritated his father and he happily indulged his own self-destructive urges never believing his father would even consider going against the rule of primogeniture. But his father had fumed and waited for an opportunity to strike, until Jack had handed him his chance far too easily. He had engaged in a drink-fuelled brawl in public, his adversary slipping into a coma and the man's family demanding a public apology and substantial compensation. The resulting scandal had been hushed up as quickly as possible, but his punishment had been exile.

And now Peter's daughter was at his mercy. He would decide today if she lived or died. It should have felt good: here was an opportunity to get revenge not only on his brother but on Maxwell, too. Maxwell was everything he should have been had the fates not been so cruel and his inheritance wasted away by fools. Well, they would all pay the price, and they would remember his name for hundreds of years to come.

Constable Paul Monk was hiding in the little coppice of trees on the coast road. His colleagues were positioned at various points along the road, but he could not see them. His instructions were to look out for anything unusual and, in particular, activity down below on the rocky shore near the caves. Above all else, he was not to be seen. Two hours had passed and it was a typical sleepy Saturday afternoon. Nothing had passed behind him on the road and, other than a few squawking seagulls, nothing was happening out to the west either. He was very bored. His stomach rumbled and his thoughts turned to what his mother might be doing for dinner. He hoped it was lamb chops – he was very partial to lamb chops. Some nice fresh green peas from the allotment, flowery potatoes with the butter sliding down – his mouth began to water.

He snapped to attention: there was movement below. A large grey-haired man in a long black coat appeared from directly below him and walked down the shingle beach. He stopped at the water's edge and stood looking out to sea. The constable's heart began to race. Slowly, and as noiselessly as he could, he backed out through the undergrowth to the road. Keeping low, he crossed over to the boundary of Bowes and jumped the wall. He ran to where he had stored his bicycle and cycled as fast as he could to Thorncroft, all thoughts of his dinner forgotten in his excitement.

Louisa opened her eyes. She was alone. Her face was very tender where Uncle Jack had hit her. Perhaps she needed to be a little more careful in what she said to her uncle, she thought glumly. The urge to cry was very strong. She was hungry, sore and fed-up, but most of all she was scared. She would have given anything just to see Nicholas appear and she had to dig deep to find the strength to stay calm.

Convinced that she was dealing with a lunatic, she tried to figure out her best chance for escape. The cases of guns were still there, but she knew that they would be moving them soon. Her best opportunity would be while they were busy doing that. There was, unfortunately, the small problem of her feet being tied, which she needed to rectify, but her efforts to undo the knots were fruitless. Spotting a rough piece of rock, she shuffled over to it and began to run the cord against it, ears straining in case someone should come.

A couple of hours later Nicholas had joined Constable Monk in his hiding place. They didn't dare go out on the headland in case they were spotted. Nicholas crept out as far as he could on his stomach to look over the cliff, but it was impossible to see the entrance to the caves due to the angle of the overhang. Disgruntled, he had to back away. All any of them could do was wait for the Fenians to make the first move. There was only one entrance to the cave system and they did not want to risk storming it in case it put Louisa in danger. It was a gamble, of course. She could be elsewhere, for all they knew. The minutes ticked by very slowly; too slowly for Nicholas. He wasn't a particularly religious man, but he started to pray. He promised himself that if they all got out of this alive he was going to drag that woman to the altar, kicking and screaming if necessary, and to hell with mourning. He also found solace in thinking up suitable punishments for her abductors, none of which were entirely legal.

Monk interrupted his thoughts by poking him in the ribs and gesturing out to sea. His eyes were wide with surprise. Nicholas could not believe his eyes either. A large fishing boat was coming into view.

"Monk," he whispered, "go back to Thorncroft and get the rest of the men down here as quickly as possible."

At about the same moment, Jack happened to look up from where he was sitting at the cave entrance. "Oh no," he groaned, the *Pride of Arran* was slowly coming into view from the north.

O'Connor heard him and came out of the cave, then stood transfixed looking at the fishing vessel that was going to take the guns to Dublin. "Aren't they early?" he asked.

Jack turned to him in fury. "Yes they bloody well are! They shouldn't be here for another two hours." His plans were unravelling. The fools must have misread the signal.

"What do we do, Jack? It's still daylight - we could still be seen."

Jack turned on him. "I know, I know; I need to think." He began to pace. "The boat will look suspicious just sitting there for hours. No one fishes this bay. We'll have to chance moving the guns. Now wake the boys up and get those row boats down to the water as quickly as possible."

Her ankles now free of their binding, Louisa was sitting back against the wall. It was all ominously quiet. Just as she was plucking up the courage to take a peek, she heard hollering from the tunnel. Then she heard them dragging something heavy, but the noise moved away and then silence fell again. Mystified, she strained her ears. After a few minutes she could discern the sounds of approach again. She braced herself, but when the men entered the cave they went straight to the cases and started to load them into the barrows. They worked feverishly, ignoring her. They appeared to be in a panic, cursing each other in their haste. Soon the two barrows were full and they headed out down the tunnel without even looking at her. She stood. This might be her chance. She crept across the cave to the tunnel entrance. Feeling her way along the wall, she started down the tunnel after the men. She had to risk it because she didn't know if there was more than one entrance. If the caves were extensive, as her uncle had claimed, she really didn't want to get lost in them. It was almost pitch black as she advanced, but after a few minutes she could detect faint traces of daylight. She stopped, uncertain what to do. She could hear distant voices coming from somewhere ahead. She moved forward tentatively; the light increased, and soon the cave entrance came into view a few feet away.

To her relief, she could see that the tide was out, but the scene that greeted her was discouraging. By the position of the sun she guessed it was early evening and she could make out eight figures down at the water's edge loading the cases into two large row boats. Beyond them, out in the bay, she could see a boat. It looked like a fishing trawler, which must be their means of transporting the guns. Uncle Jack was shouting and cursing at them to hurry up. They all had their backs to her, but they were very close to the headland and she could not get around it without being seen.

Nervously, she put her head out and looked rapidly left and right. Up to the left was the sheer wall of the headland; to the right there were outcrops of rock further along. If she could just make it that far they would give her cover until such time as the men went back into the caves. She waited undecided, breathing fast. The boats were finally loaded with their cargo and two men were getting into each of them. This was her chance. She came out into the open and edged her way along the cliff wall as quickly and silently as she could, the shingle biting into her bare feet. Her luck was holding; the men on the shore were busy watching their colleagues' progress in the row boats and did not look back. She reached the outcrop and ducked down just in time. Minutes later Uncle Jack, O'Connor and two others went past back into the caves. She knew it would not be long before they would discover her absence.

Chapter Twenty-Nine

S he took off at a run down the shingle beach, and gritted her teeth as she plunged into the icy water. It was vital that she make it around the headland before they came back outside. In the distance she could see the row boats edging ever closer to the ship. Her feet kept sinking and she had to slow down and keep one hand against the headland cliff face for support. Just as she reached the furthest point out into the water, she heard a roar of rage from behind her. She chanced a quick look back. Uncle Jack was running down the beach towards her, yelling at the top of his voice. A rush of adrenaline and she rounded the headland and as quickly as she could, waded through the water to shore.

Lack of sleep and food over two days had weakened her. The soft sand impeded her progress as she tried to run up the beach. She only made it halfway before she was tackled to the ground by her uncle. She lashed out with her hands and kicked out with her feet, frantically trying to free herself from his grasp, but it was futile. She was too drained and he was too heavy and too strong for her. He had her pinned down, but suddenly he froze. She became aware of voices echoing around her. Jack was looking up towards the road with a horrified expression. He released her arms but quickly pulled a gun out of the pocket of his coat. Pulling her upright, he twisted her around and pointed the gun at her head. Still breathless from her escape, it took a few moments for her to be able to focus properly, but if she wasn't mistaken there were people up on the roadway. It must be the police. She could have wept with relief. But she could feel the tension in Uncle Jack. His grip on her was vice-like and he was muttering under his breath. Slowly, he began to back down the beach, dragging her with him, one arm wrapped around her waist so tightly she could hardly breathe, the other still holding the gun to her temple. She could sense the sheer panic in him. He was using her as a shield, and there was nothing she could do about it. If he managed to get her around the headland again, she was done for. Desperate now, she tried to think clearly. The men up on the road were powerless to help her. They would not shoot in case they hit her. They were probably too far away to see properly in the failing light. But she noticed a movement up to her left on the headland. A man with a rifle had just dropped down behind some bushes. She hoped her uncle had not seen him.

All of a sudden she could hear someone coming through the water behind them. "Jack, Jack! There are police everywhere!" It was O'Connor and he sounded frantic.

Uncle Jack turned his head but kept a firm grip on her. "You idiot, I can see them for myself. Our only chance is the row boats. Are they on their way back yet?"

A pause. "No," O'Connor answered, the panic clear in his voice. "They are still out at the trawler."

"God damn it!" Uncle Jack exclaimed. "They must have seen the police; they will not come back for us."

"We're done for, Jack!" O'Connor shrieked at him, hysterical now. Suddenly there was a bang, a flash and a whirring sound. O'Connor cried out in pain. She heard the splash as he collapsed into the water.

"Liam!" Uncle Jack cried, releasing her. She fell forwards on to the sand and rolled over. He waded into the water to where O'Connor was lying face down.

Uncle Jack spun round. "You bastard!" he shouted up towards the headland, where the sniper had just fired from and was busy reloading. Quickly he came back towards Louisa, who was still down on the sand. He aimed the gun at her, the veins on his neck and forehead standing out. His eyes were wild with anger; flicking continuously up to the headland where the sniper now had him in his sights.

"Is this how you want to be remembered? The man who murdered both his nieces," she said in a trembling voice.

"I did *not* murder Eleanor. I frightened her, that's all. But you have caused me enough harm with your meddling, like your father and grandfather before you. Your life is worthless to me. I've only kept you alive to guarantee my escape."

"How noble!" she scoffed. "You sneer at my father, but he did not kill innocent people."

"Oh really?" Jack mocked. "He was a model husband and father, wasn't he? A hard-working man who provided so well for his little family. Ha! He was weak and pathetic. Money slipped through his fingers so easily it was laughable. Yes, I knew of his progress. It gave me great pleasure to witness his downfall over the years."

"Aunt Milly," she said with disgust.

"Yes, Milly. She has been my eyes and ears in Dublin all these years."

"You knew how precarious our existence was, but you never helped us. You and my aunt – watching from the shadows, enjoying our distress. Why did you hate us so much?"

Jack's eyes narrowed. "Because, my dear niece, your beloved father stole my birth-right and then squandered it. I was the eldest. The estate should have come to me."

Louisa could not fail to see the irony in that. "But then you would have been a landlord, one of the class you despise so much. Those guns are destined to be used against them."

"I would have been different. I proved it here at Bowes. My tenants were fiercely loyal to me because I treated them fairly."

Louisa could not argue with that. She had seen it herself first-hand. "It's a pity you were not content with that. Your activities have blotted out any good you may have achieved here."

"At least I won't be forgotten." He laughed coldly and took a step closer. "Now get up."

She scrambled to her feet, shaking with fear, sure she was

about to be shot in cold blood. But instead he grabbed her, threw her over his shoulder, turned sharply and began wading out into the water. Frantically, she tried to wriggle free. He needed both hands to hold on to her, so he put the gun back in his pocket. It took considerable effort for him to make any progress, and while he was distracted she swung her arm down; she could just reach his pocket. Carefully, she slid her hand inside. She felt the cold hard metal of the gun. If only she had learnt how to fire one, but how hard could it be? She wasn't sure what she needed to do to fire it but she had to stop him. She felt for the trigger, pointed the gun downwards, squeezed her eyes shut, and pulled it before she could change her mind. He jerked, yelled and convulsed in pain and she was dropped unceremoniously into the water, where she was submerged under an incoming wave and then another. She surfaced spluttering, having swallowed several mouthfuls of salt water, and with her eyes stinging. Within seconds there was an outbreak of shouting and she was aware of people running down the beach.

All she could do was sit there in the water, her eyes fixed on her uncle thrashing about mere feet away. She had actually shot him. Abruptly, someone yanked her upright from behind, and half dragged, half carried her out of the water and up the beach. She did not resist – could not. When she looked around she discovered, to her relief, that it was George. They dropped down on to the sand. George was talking to her, asking her questions, but she could not respond. She was soaking wet and started to shiver.

Men were running past them down to the shore. She continued to watch as her uncle was grabbed by two of the policemen and lugged out of the water. They dropped him like a stone once they reached the shore. He continued to roll around in agony, clutching his foot while the men stood over him, unsympathetic to his distress. She recognised Sergeant Cox as he joined the group now gathering around her uncle. Her eyes strayed out towards the water. The lights from the trawler were moving away. Why wasn't anyone trying to stop them, she wanted to ask.

Then Nicholas appeared and knelt down before her and she was overwhelmed with relief. He cradled her face gently, unable to speak. She returned his gaze steadily and tried to smile. After a few moments, he helped her to her feet, took off his coat and wrapped it around her, hugging her close and kissing her cheek. She flinched; it was still sore.

Anger flared in his eyes. "Are you hurt?" She shook her head, but still could not speak. "Take her back to the house. Anna will look after her. She's cold and exhausted," he told George. "I have business to finish here." He embraced her again, before striding away towards the policemen.

"Come along, Miss Campbell. Let's get you out of here," George said, gently putting his arm around her shoulders and turning her away. He helped her up the path that wound through the dunes to a waiting carriage up on the roadway. As she sat waiting for the horses to move off, she took one last look down to the beach. Even from the road she could hear the shouting. Nicholas was being held back by the officers, Uncle Jack cowering before his rage. Sergeant Cox managed to drag Nicholas off and was speaking urgently to him as if trying to calm him down. He still loved her, that was obvious. Why else would he be so outraged? She wanted to cry with relief. But the stark reality of her uncle being alive and what he had done and planned to do soon replaced the comfort she took in Nicholas's continued regard.

Finally, they hauled Uncle Jack up, handcuffed him, still wailing in pain, and shuffled him up the beach. Singlehandedly, he had brought her family to ruin. She would have to bear that disgrace for the rest of her life. Yes, Uncle, a great legacy to leave me, she thought despondently as the carriage moved forward, leaving the scene of her family's disgrace behind.

Anna was shocked to see the condition of her friend. But what disturbed her more was Louisa's inability to communicate other than in monosyllables. She had seen how Eleanor's death had affected her, but this was different; more profound. Unsure what to do about it, Anna concentrated on getting her cleaned up and put to bed as quickly as possible. Louisa's vacant expression as she had tucked her in prompted her to ask if she was all right. Louisa looked at her for a moment before finally answering her.

"I shot my uncle," she said, a deep frown between her brows. "I had to do it, but I will suffer for it."

Anna wasn't sure what she meant. "He would not have thought twice about shooting you. I, for one, am proud of you."

"You don't understand," Louisa muttered, before turning over and shutting her eyes.

Later that evening Anna discussed her concerns with her husband and brothers over dinner.

"Most likely she is in a state of shock. It's hardly surprising after what she went through," John said, trying to reassure her. "When she is rested, I will talk to her and give her what reassurance I can, but she is of strong character – she will be fine."

"I don't know, John, it was odd to hear her speak that way."

"Anna, you must consider what she has been through," Nicholas said. "Her world has been turned upside down. A dead uncle comes back to life, she is abducted in the middle of the night and then there was that awful confrontation on the beach. Now she has to deal with all of this on top of her grief for Eleanor. She will need time to come to terms with it."

"Yes, I suppose when you put it like that … everything has been taken away from her. It is awful."

"Exactly. We will have to work extra hard to make her feel at home here," he answered gently. "To that end, I was hoping you would stay for a few days."

"Of course I'll stay," she said. "Don't forget we have Robert to look after as well."

Robert pulled a face. "I don't need cossetting, as I've told you before. I'm twenty-seven, for heaven's sake." He had already vetoed the nurse that Nicholas had tried to organise.

"Oh pooh, you love it."

"No, I do *not*."

"All right, you two, that's enough," Nicholas intervened,

laughing. "A little decorum, please. What will John think of us?"

"Nicholas, after today, I can assure you, nothing will faze me ever again," John replied, before turning to her. "Unfortunately, I have services tomorrow. I will have to return to Newton this evening. But I will come back tomorrow." She squeezed his hand and smiled at him affectionately.

Robert rolled his eyes at his brother and changed the subject. "What will happen to Campbell, Nicholas?"

"He is in the cells at Newton as we speak, but Inspector Fletcher will arrive tomorrow. I imagine he will have him moved to London where he will be formally charged and stand trial. He will be made an example of. The only danger is that he will become some kind of martyr for the cause."

"Will they hang him?"

"Undoubtedly."

"And the guns?"

"The caves were full of them. They only managed to load some on to that fishing boat. It was intercepted by the navy and boarded a few miles out," Nicholas said. "Fletcher's men also made a grisly discovery. Three sets of remains were found in a chamber at the back of the caves. Do you recall those blacklegs that disappeared during the strike all those years ago? We think it was them."

"Good Lord!" Robert exclaimed. "Campbell was a ruthless son of a ...." He stopped himself in time and smiled apologetically at Anna. "I shudder to think what other mischief he may have been behind. It's a relief they found the guns. It won't be much consolation to the families of those who have died or been injured, though."

"No, but it is progress in the right direction. The Fenian organisation in the north of England has been annihilated once and for all."

Louisa woke early on Monday morning. It felt good to be clean again. The cool feel of the linen, and the fresh smell of flowers in the room were like a balm to her soul, but it could not stop her thinking about what had happened. Her body ached and her mind was filled with images she did not wish to remember. For some time she lay there, trying to pull her scattered thoughts together. Relief to be alive and safe should have been the overriding emotion, but there was no comfort in it. Instead, all she could think of was how everyone would react to her uncle's resurrection and exposed criminal past. Could the friendships she had formed since coming to Cumberland survive? She very much doubted it. Most importantly, how would the Maxwells view her now? Would Nicholas be able to see past Uncle Jack's crimes? She was undoubtedly tainted by association, and although he might try to ignore that fact, deep down he would resent it. Newton society would shun her and she could not bear the thought that he would have to share that fate with her. A crushing sense of defeat and despair almost overwhelmed her. There was really only one course of action left and that was to return to Dublin to pick up the pieces of her life.

She got out of bed and pulled back the curtains, surveying the manicured grounds of Thorncroft. A light mist hung just above the lawn, drifting eerily in a light breeze; the sun a pink glow in the sky to the east. The combined effect gave the landscape a surreal quality. She turned away sadly and looked around the room. She spotted her suitcase beside the wardrobe. Someone had thoughtfully retrieved it from Bowes. That made her wince: she didn't want to think about Bowes at all. On investigation, she discovered that her clothes had been hung up in the wardrobe.

She washed and dressed quickly, completely focussed on her goal. Toilet complete, she put a few items of clothing into the suitcase and scribbled a quick note of explanation to Anna. Without a backward glance, she closed the door and headed down the stairs.

Chapter Thirty

"Are you leaving without saying goodbye?" Nicholas asked. Louisa turned around from the front door with a look of dismay, a guilty blush creeping into her cheeks. He had been up since dawn and had just come out of his study, on hearing footsteps in the marbled-floored hallway. Afraid that she would run back to Ireland, he had kept watch: he knew her well enough to know how her mind worked.

"I ... I have to go," she said as he slowly walked towards her. Panic flickered in her eyes. "Please, you must understand." He did, only too well, but he was determined not to lose her.

"You could at least have some breakfast. I don't believe there is a train for another few hours." He reached forward and gently took the suitcase from her hand and put it down on the floor. "Come," he said. He took her elbow and steered her across the hall to the dining room.

When she was seated at the table, he dismissed the footman and poured out some tea for her. She accepted it in silence. Despite keeping to her room for so long, the dark circles under her eyes proclaimed a lack of sleep or an agitated mind, he couldn't be sure which. He had some idea of her inner turmoil from her unsteady breathing and reluctance to meet his gaze. Her coat was open but still on, as was her hat, and she picked nervously at her gloves where they rested on the table. Escape was still to the forefront of her mind, he realised. He sat down opposite her.

"You know, it is a little disconcerting the way you keep

disappearing or running away. Granted, your uncle had something to do with the former, but if you are going to make a habit of it, you should tell me now. It creates an unfortunate impression, you see. I find myself wondering if it's something I said or did."

"Nicholas, please don't. You know very well why I have to leave," she said in a faltering voice.

It was clear she still didn't trust him enough. He looked at her steadily, trying to hide his hurt and disappointment. "I can guess, but I'd rather you explained it to me."

"All right, I admit it – I'm a coward. I am running away because I can't face people after all Uncle Jack has done. My family shame – dishonour – whatever you want to call it, is now exclusively mine. Are you so eager to share that with me?" Her voice trembled with emotion. "Nicholas, people in Newton will shun me on the street. You know what they are like. The scandal will be impossible to live down and there is still the horror of the trial to be endured and the inevitable outcome of that."

"There will be no trial," he stated flatly. "He's dead, Louisa."

"*What?* No!" What little colour was left in her cheeks vanished.

"I'm sorry, Louisa. He was found hanging in his cell yesterday afternoon. I was informed last night. I asked the authorities not to release the information until you could be told in person."

She sat transfixed.

"I should have guessed he would not be able to resist playing the martyr," he continued. "He knew what his fate would be. His vanity did the rest. He chose what he thought amounted to immortality in the eyes of his fellow Fenians. I can't say I'm sorry he's dead and it angers me that he will not face justice, but you have been spared the distress of the trial. It would have put you in the public eye and ruined you. The press would have hounded you and, be under no illusion, Louisa, they would have followed you, even to Dublin."

"I know that is true: how awful it was going to be. I would have come back for the trial. I was prepared to go through it. I did not fear the truth."

"Anyone who knows you would not doubt that."

"But he's dead. He chose the coward's way out," she said in disgust.

There was a knock on the door and the butler entered. "Mr. Jameson, sir, to see Miss Campbell." Nicholas swore under his breath. George's timing could not have been worse.

George came in, greeted Nicholas and then approached Louisa. "Miss Campbell, I do hope I find you well and recovered from your terrible ordeal?"

"Yes, thank you, Mr. Jameson, I'm … I will be fine. I am glad to have the opportunity to thank you for all you did."

"There is no need to thank me. I was only too happy to help," George replied.

Nicholas went over to the sideboard to refresh his coffee, resigned to the interruption. "Help yourself, Jameson," he said, gesturing to the covered dishes arrayed on the sideboard.

"Thank you, sir, but I have already eaten. Sir, have you told Miss Campbell the news?"

"Yes, just now."

"Good," George said, evidently relieved that he didn't have to do it. "I am sorry; it must be a terrible shock. I am reluctant to add to your distress but I have something for you. This letter was delivered to me first thing."

Nicholas swung around at his words, a heavy feeling in the pit of his stomach. Hadn't she gone through enough? Louisa accepted the letter from George with a frown.

"Come, Jameson, let's leave Miss Campbell in peace to read her letter," he said, barely concealing his annoyance before ushering George out. "We will be in the study if you need us," he said to her as he closed the door.

She placed the letter down on the table. Her name was inscribed on the envelope, in a hand she was only too familiar with; it was from her uncle. She took a deep breath. My life has been punctuated by letters, she thought, without humour. What could this one possibly hold? Trembling with emotions she could not even define, she eventually picked the letter up and broke the seal. It was dated the previous day.

Louisa,

I have just had an enlightening visit from Nicholas Maxwell who claims, rather vigorously, to have your best interests at heart. He has the look and manners of a man deeply in love and I can only hope that you have enough sense to send him packing. Alas, it is probably a vain hope and he was not best pleased when I voiced it to him. No doubt you know the history between us – it is not particularly edifying, but, like your good self, he has always insisted on poking his nose into my business. I have the satisfaction of knowing, however, that I have always managed to stay one step ahead of him and would have continued to do so but for your untimely intervention.

I will not pretend to have any great affection for you, nor can I, in all honesty, say that I regret anything I have done, with the exception of my involvement in Eleanor's death. I was curious about you both when you came to Bowes, and when the opportunity arose that day, I could not help myself. It was only when I was before her that I realised that she recognised me. I can only imagine that the shock was too much for her weak heart. She collapsed almost immediately. I admit I panicked and ran. There is nothing you can say in condemnation that I have not said to myself. It is a heavy burden to carry and I will say no more about it; it will soon be a matter between me and my maker.

However, as your suitor was at pains to point out, I do owe you explanations and I am content to supply them. Firstly, I will digress slightly to tell you something of the family history, as I suspect your father never gave you a true account. Growing up in Galway, we were shielded from the realities of life in a bubble of aristocratic splendour. My father was a weak and indifferent landlord. As I came into manhood, I began to realise just what that meant to his tenants: excessive rent increases and sub-division of land already straining to support far too many people. And all of this was to sustain my parents' lifestyle and in particular, my father's gambling.

I was groomed to take over; as eldest son that was my birthright. I returned from Oxford eager to take on my responsibilities, but my father stubbornly refused to let me be involved. I was rudderless in a society dedicated to pleasure. My companions were spoilt and indulged profligates whose only goal in life was to outdo each other in dissolute endeavours. Totally disillusioned, I gladly joined their ranks and became something of a local legend. When I breached the unspoken limit of what was acceptable, my father denounced me and I was ushered out of the country. Your father stepped very willingly into my shoes. Not long afterwards he completed the picture of the perfect biddable son and married your mother. Her family were not very pleased, as my escapades coloured their view of things considerably, but my father was delighted. The rest you know: my parents died and your father inherited a badly managed and bankrupt estate. He had the dubious honour of completing the downfall of a once noble and esteemed family. All I could do was watch helplessly from the sidelines.

I came to England determined to be a success; to show the world that I was master of my own destiny, but my ambitions were soon checked. I was penniless and those men I had once called friends at Eton and Oxford did not want to know an impoverished Irish immigrant. I soon ended up in the Irish enclaves of London trying to better myself. I fell in with the Catholic Irish who already had my sympathies. They spoke of the injustice they had suffered and I empathised strongly with them. Over time my involvement with the Fenian movement deepened until I was noticed by an eminent member of the Brotherhood in New York, who moulded and schooled me and gave me the resources I needed to fight for the cause.

During those formative years, I was sent back to Dublin several times to gather intelligence and give assistance to my Fenian brothers in their struggles. It was on one of those occasions that I met Milly, quite by accident, on a Dublin street. We had known each other as children in Galway; your mother's family had been near neighbours. She had recently married Nathan Cooper and was very unhappy. He was a cold and indifferent fellow, but vastly wealthy. Our affair lasted many years and when your uncle died, I urged her to join me in England. She always refused, no matter how much I begged her.

So I have had two great loves in my life – Milly and Bowes. The latter I believe you understand. O'Connor told me how you tried so hard to learn about the estate and for that I honour you. Maxwell will have told you how I was so fortunate to win Bowes from his father, but I do not think he understands what a pivotal moment in my life it was. Not only did I relish my role as landlord, a role I was born for, but it gave me a wonderful opportunity to further the cause. I had a ready-made pool of sympathetic tenants and an Irish community in Newton just ripe for tapping. It was the perfect place from which to run my organisation, and by alienating my neighbours, I was able to come and go as I pleased without interference.

I do not know what your plans are and whether they include Maxwell or not. However, there is some property of mine that no one knows of. Over the years I was able to accumulate some wealth and I put it to good use. Five years ago I bought back my father's estate in Galway and this I will bequeath to you. It is rented out, but it would give me great comfort if you were to take it on. I long to see a Campbell back there, even if it has to be you.

So now I will bid you adieu. What I am about to do is not for your benefit, but for the cause of Irish freedom. If I stand trial, they will crucify me. Most likely they would seize all of my assets and leave you destitute, if they found me guilty of treason as well as murder. By the time you read this letter, I will have joined Eleanor in the next world and you will inherit properly this time. If you can understand what my life has been about, then you will appreciate that the cause of Irish freedom has been my life's work, and I will not apologise for it to you or the British government. I do not expect you to grieve or visit my grave. I may not have been the uncle you deserved, but know that everything I have done has been with conviction and for the love of my country. Éire go deo.

Jack Thomas Campbell, Irish Republican Brotherhood.

When Nicholas returned to the dining room, he found her sitting where they had left her. Her hat and coat were off, he noted with relief, but the marks of distress were clearly to be seen on her face.

"Jameson has left," he said when she looked up. "Was it from Campbell?" He looked at the crumpled sheets on the table.

"Yes, but I do not know what he hoped to achieve by writing it."

He walked over to the fireplace, fighting the urge to throw caution to the wind, take her in his arms and speak soothing words to bring her comfort. It would be very easy to overwhelm her with kindness and affection, but he knew it would only be temporary solace. They had to be honest with each other, talk this out, if their relationship was to survive and flourish.

Louisa pointed to the letter. "You visited him?"

"Yes. I went to see him yesterday in Newton police station."

"Why?"

"Someone had to point out to him where his duty lay. He had

already done so much damage to you and Eleanor. I wanted him to take some responsibility."

"And you persuaded him to write to me?"

"It wasn't hard, Louisa. He was only too happy to have an outlet for his insane view of the world."

She looked away, her shoulders hunched and tense. "Thank you, but I know it can't have been easy for you to deal with him. It's hard to believe that one man could cause so much pain."

"That is all in the past; he cannot harm you now."

"Do you really think I can just forget everything that has happened?" she asked incredulously.

"For the sake of your sanity, I strongly suggest you try. Life must go on, Louisa, and you must put this behind you."

"I don't know how to do that, Nicholas. Every instinct is telling me to run and hide."

"Naturally. However, I would advise against it. You have nothing to feel ashamed of and running away will only feed the scandal sheets. Hold your head high and stand your ground. You are a strong woman. You can survive this, and with the Maxwells behind you, no one will dare gainsay you."

"After all of this, after everything he has done, you would support me?" she asked, a quiver in her voice.

Nicholas smiled grimly. "Yes." He watched the play of emotions on her face and felt his own confidence grow. Deep down, he knew that she wanted to stay.

She rose up out of her seat and walked over to the window. Some of the tension seemed to ease from her body as she moved. As she looked out, the sun's rays caught the golden highlights in her hair and when she turned back to him, she had an almost luminous quality that made his heart beat faster.

"I suppose I should be angry with him, but I think I am too exhausted to indulge it. Isn't that bizarre? I don't know what to feel or think. He has single-handedly destroyed my family, my home, and now even my reputation is in tatters. I am completely out of my depth." She shrugged and looked at him with a plea for rescue in her eyes.

But he had to convince her that they were strong enough to survive this. "Yes, you have suffered a great deal at his hands, but he hasn't destroyed you." He closed the distance between them and placed his hands gently on her shoulders. "You are the most resilient woman I know. There is no reason to despair. And you will always have me, no matter what the consequences of the last few days."

"I know," she whispered.

He drew her into his arms and held her close for a few minutes. "Come, you haven't eaten at all. You must not become ill." He guided her back to the table. Then he brought her a plate piled high with food.

"I'll never eat all of that!" she exclaimed with a wobbly smile.

"Try, please," he said, and sat down beside her.

She struggled with a few mouthfuls, then turned to him. "You know, I thought he had adopted the Fenian cause out of boredom or sheer love of mischief, but he genuinely believed in it."

"Most fanatics do. And he was a particularly clever and ambitious one. I can assure you that I left him in no doubt as to my feelings about everything he did."

"Thank you, but I doubt it would have moved him. His hatred for his family was the driving force behind everything he did." Louisa gathered up the pages of the letter. "I think you should read this."

"Are you sure?" he asked. She nodded and he could feel her eyes on him as he read down through it. When he looked up, it was with tears in his eyes. "What a letter to have written. My dear girl, I suggest that you burn it." He held it out to her. When she hesitated, he got up and threw it in the fireplace and struck a match. Together they watched the pages of the letter burn.

He turned towards her. "It was odd. He seemed different somehow to the man I knew before; a victim of his own madness, I suppose. Regardless of defeat, he was strangely pleased with himself, as if he was glad that he had been caught, and could finally boast to me of his achievements." Louisa grimaced. "Yes, I know. It was damn hard to listen to. He went into great detail but would not divulge who his accomplices were, either in England or America. He ranted on along the lines of what you read in the letter. I came away with the conclusion that he was deranged."

"I can confirm it. He really scared me," she said miserably. He flinched as a wave of guilt swept over him. If he had been smarter he might have prevented so much of what had occurred.

"In a way he has won – by cheating the authorities of a trial," she said, as the last embers of the letter glowed and died.

"Perhaps, but he has saved you the pain of it. That is all that matters to me. You are all that matter to me," he said.

"Nicholas – I cannot stay … I'm sorry I just can't," she cried, jumping up. She wrung her hands in her agitation. "You would be giving up too much."

"No. I want to spend the rest of my life with you. Don't you realise how much I love you?"

"I love you too, Nicholas."

"But …?"

"You don't realise what you are giving up. Marriage to me would mean social ruin."

"Nonsense. You were a victim, Louisa. You have nothing to feel ashamed of. I won't hear any more talk of disgrace. He is gone; it's over. With the protection of my name, no one will dare to slight you." He stood breathing hard, looking at her, willing her to listen to him, to trust him. "Now, you had better eat some more. We have a long day ahead of us," he said briskly. When he saw her puzzlement, he took a step closer. "The carriage will be ready in an hour. We are taking a little trip north of the border."

Her eyes widened as the meaning of his words sank in. "To Scotland?" she asked.

"Yes."

Louisa shook her head, but he could tell that her resolve was melting. She took a quivering breath and looked at him keenly. "Are you sure?"

He tried to look offended but smiled foolishly at her instead. "I'm not leaving without you. Robert has even volunteered to give us a head start of two hours before coming in pursuit – just so that it is a fully-fledged elopement with all the trimmings."

"Oh no!" Louisa laughed shakily. "I don't think you should let him."

He took her hand and held it to his heart. "Don't worry. I told him not to be such an insolent pup and to go back to bed."

"And Anna. How does she feel about all of this madness?"

"She is waiting upstairs to help you pack. She begged to accompany us, but I pointed out that John would hardly be pleased with her sudden desertion. Marriage has not improved her one iota. The little minx will probably try to follow us. I'm sorry; we may have to sneak out to the stables when she is distracted. Why my family think I'm incapable of dragging you to the altar unaided, is beyond me." Nicholas sighed, before pulling her into an embrace. She rested her head against his shoulder and he could almost sense the last of the tension in her muscles slip away.

"Are you ever serious? You know I'm not in the humour for any of your jokes," she mumbled into his coat.

With an impatient sigh, he pushed her far enough away so that he could look into her face. "Louisa Campbell, beautiful idiot that you are – will you marry me?"

It is a matter of some debate as to whether she actually ever answered him. Whatever her response was, which was inaudible due to her being kissed rather soundly and repeatedly, Nicholas certainly took it as affirmative.

The End

Acknowledgements

A huge thank you to family and friends for their enduring help and support, especially my daughter Hazel. I am so grateful to Lorna and Terry who managed to stay sane while reading the first draft, a chapter at a time.

Special thanks to my editor, Hilary Johnson, who helped make the dream a reality through her professionalism, patience and generosity.

Finally, I am extremely grateful to Vanessa Fox O'Loughlin at Inkwell, and author Ciara Geraghty, for their invaluable advice.

11938940R00192

Printed in Great Britain
by Amazon.co.uk, Ltd.,
Marston Gate.